Praise for the *Henrietta and I*

For *A Veil Removed*, Book 4

Awards

2019 Readers' Favorite Awards, Honorable Mention in Fiction (Mystery/Historical)

2019 Next Generation Indie Book Awards: Finalist in Romance

2019 Next Generation Indie Book Awards: Finalist in Series

"Entertaining . . . composed of large dollops of romance and a soupçon of mystery, this confection will appeal!"

—*Publishers Weekly*

Praise for *A Promise Given*, Book 3

Awards

2019 Indie Excellence Awards Winner: Cross Genre

2019 IBPA Ben Franklin Awards: Silver in Romance

2019 Independent Press Award in Romantic Suspense

2019 International Book Awards, Finalist, Fiction: Cross Genre

2019 Pulpwood Queens Bonus Selection

2019 Next Generation Indie Book Awards: Finalist in Series

2018 Chanticleer Awards: Finalist in Historical Fiction, 1st place winner in Romance and grand-prize winner in Mystery and Mayhem

2018 Next Generation Indie Book Awards Finalist in Romance

2018 Best Book Awards Finalist in Romance

2018 Best Book Awards Finalist in Cross-Genre

"Cox's eye for historical detail remains sharp. . . . A pleasant, escapist diversion."

—*Kirkus Reviews*

"Series fans will cheer the beginning of Clive and Henrietta's private investigation business in an entry with welcome echoes of *Pride and Prejudice*."

—*Publishers Weekly*

"This is a beautiful story with strong themes of romance, family intrigue, and investigation. The writing is gorgeous and reflects the cultural and historical setting. Michelle Cox's novel is filled with deeply moving passages and emotionally charged scenes. The characters are as sophisticated as they are relatable and the plot is designed to make for the perfect page-turner."

—Readers Favorite

Praise for *A Ring of Truth*, Book 2

Awards
2019 Next Generation Indie Book Awards: Finalist in Series
2018 Chanticleer Book Awards: Finalist: Historical Fiction, Finalist: Romance, Winner: Mystery
2018 Independent Press Award: Winner in Romantic Suspense
2018 National Indie Excellence Awards Finalist in Regional Fiction: Midwest
2017-2018 Reader Views Literary Awards Finalist in Adult Fiction
2017 Chicago Writers Association Awards: Shortlisted for Indie Fiction
2017 Next Gen indies: Romance Finalist, Mystery Finalist
2017 Readers Favorite: Honorable Mention, Mystery
2017 Beverly Hills Book Award Winner in Regional Fiction: Northeast
2017 Beverly Hills Book Award Finalist in Cross-Genre
2017 Beverly Hills Book Award Finalist in Mystery

"There's a lot to love about the bloodhound couple at the center of this cozy mystery."

—*Foreword Reviews*

"Set in the 1930s, this romantic mystery combines the teetering elegance of *Downton Abbey* and the staid traditions of *Pride and Prejudice* with a bit of spunk and determination that suggest Jacqueline Winspear's Maisie Dobbs."

—*Booklist*

"The second book of this mystery series is laced with fiery romance so delicious every reader will struggle to put it down. If you devoured *Pride and Prejudice*, this love story will get your heart beating just as fast."

—*Redbook*

"Henrietta and Inspector Howard make a charming odd couple in *A Ring of Truth*, mixing mystery and romance in a fizzy 1930s cocktail."
—Hallie Ephron, *New York Times* best-selling author of *Night Night, Sleep Tight*

Praise for *A Girl Like You*, Book 1

Awards
2019 Next Generation Indie Book Awards: Finalist in Series
2017 IPPY Awards: Gold Mystery Winner
2016 Readers Favorite: Gold Mystery Winner
2016 Foreword Indies: Gold Mystery Winner
2016 Foreword Indies: Romance, Finalist
2016 Shelf Unbound: Top 100 Notable Indie
2016 Chanticleer Awards: Mystery and Mayhem, Winner
2016 USA Best Book Awards: Fiction Romance Finalist
2016 Beverly Hills Book Awards: Regional Fiction: Midwest, Winner
2016 Next Generation Indies: Romance Finalist
2016 Reader Views: Historical Fiction Winner, Great Lakes
     Regional Winner
2016 Tyler Tichelaar Award: Historical Fiction Winner

"Michelle Cox masterfully recreates 1930s Chicago, bringing to life its diverse neighborhoods and eclectic residents, as well as its seedy side. Henrietta and Inspector Howard are the best pair of sleuths I've come across in ages—Cox makes us care not just about the case, but about her characters. A fantastic start to what is sure to be a long-running series."

—Tasha Alexander, *New York Times* best-selling author of *The Adventuress*

"Flavored with 1930s slang and fashion, this first volume in what one hopes will be a long series is absorbing. Henrietta and Clive are a sexy, endearing, and downright fun pair of sleuths. Readers will not see the final twist coming."

—*Library Journal*, starred review

A Child Lost

A Child Lost

A HENRIETTA AND INSPECTOR HOWARD NOVEL

BOOK 5

MICHELLE COX

SHE WRITES PRESS

Published 2020
Printed in the United States of America
ISBN: 978-1-63152-836-1 pbk
ISBN: 978-1-63152-837-8 ebk
Library of Congress Control Number: 2019916053

For information, address:
She Writes Press
1569 Solano Ave #546
Berkeley, CA 94707

She Writes Press is a division of SparkPoint Studio, LLC.

To Otto Bles Cornejo, the original lost child.
A true poet and visionary whose time has not yet
come, but which may be, in fact, just around the
corner. Let us hope you do not have to wait too much
longer. Thank you for your friendship and for all
you've taught me. I'm grateful to have shared at least
a part of this strange journey with you.

Chapter 1

Elsie sat in theology class listening to Sister Raphael expound on the different types of grace, but she found it hard to pay attention. It wasn't that the material wasn't interesting—it was, actually—but Elsie's mind was unfortunately on other things at the moment. It had been, truth be told, ever since her rather unexpected discovery of a small girl named Anna apparently living in Gunther's hut behind Piper Hall. As she distractedly drew in the margins of her notepaper, she took the time to calculate, concluding that it had been just over a month ago already. She shifted slightly in her chair. They were still no closer to any answers.

She was inextricably caught up in Gunther's story now, whether she wanted to be or not—and probably had been, if she were honest, since she had surreptitiously read his journal while she sat at his bedside in the hospital on New Year's Eve last. That was where she first came across the name Anna, scrawled across the page in his unkempt handwriting, along with various poems and personal notations and ramblings, some of it in English, but most of it in German.

For a long time, Elsie assumed that Anna was a woman, perhaps someone Gunther was romantically attached to from his native Germany. But then Elsie had begun to feel certain stirrings for Gunther herself, perhaps unconsciously, and when he'd tenderly kissed her hand in the hidden greenhouse in the Mundelein Skyscraper, she had fled in terror—not for her personal safety, but for fear of what she might in fact be feeling for him. After a day and a night of avoiding him, however, she had eventually come to the conclusion that she needed to face her fears and confront him, the result being her discovery that the mysterious Anna in his journal was merely a child, which had raised a whole new set of questions and fears, especially when the child had called him "Papa."

Upon discovering the two of them in the hut that day Elsie almost fled in her mortification and her sorrow and probably would have, had it not been for the look of panic on Gunther's face and the broken utterance of her name.

"Elsie . . . "

His whisper had given her sufficient pause—enough to see the silent "please" that followed—his lips forming the word, but no sound escaping. His plea and the desperate longing she saw in his eyes were palpable and hovered in the short space between them, paralyzing and holding her there against her will.

"Elsie, please, come in," he said hoarsely, slowly gesturing toward the interior of the small cottage, as if he suspected she might bolt at any moment and therefore should not employ any sudden movements. She did not bolt, however, though every nerve in her body was taut and ready. She instead took a deep breath and sternly reminded herself that this was why she had come: to hear him out. Hadn't she stood at her bedroom window through most of the night, puzzling out what to do? Near dawn, she had finally come to the decision that she would go to him and listen without interrupting or judging, just as he had done for her, no matter how shocking his explanation turned out to be. And yet there in the frigid morning air, the sun having just crested the horizon, she had already been tempted to run; seeing a little girl standing in front of him addressing him as "Papa" was certainly beyond anything she had heretofore imagined. But as difficult as his explanation promised to be, she knew there was no turning back now. So with just a slight pause, she had stepped across his threshold and thus into his world.

Once inside the small hut, Gunther indicated for her to sit in one of the chairs next to a little wooden table. Anna retreated to a rumpled trundle that sat pulled out from under the main bed, which was also unmade and looked as though it had been recently occupied. Elsie averted her eyes from what was obviously Gunther's bed and instead looked at Anna, who sat cross-legged on her thin mattress, warily watching Elsie with her finger in her mouth, very much reminding Elsie of her little sister, Doris.

Silently, Gunther placed a steaming mug of coffee on the table before Elsie and sat down across from her. Elsie stared at the mug for a moment and then took hold of it, her cold fingers finding comfort in the warmth before she forced herself to look up at him. He in turn was looking at her with such worried, sad eyes that she felt her stomach clench.

"Elsie, please. Do not look at me in such way. I can explain. I tried to explain to you in the greenhouse." He paused. "Many times."

Elsie wasn't sure what to say to that. She looked back at the little girl, if only to avoid his eyes.

"This is Anna Klinkhammer," he said, his eyes following Elsie's, anticipating at least one of her silent questions.

The girl was thin—scrawny even—with very blue eyes and fine blonde hair that looked as though it hadn't been brushed in quite some time, certainly not yet today, at any rate. She had on a plain, brown dress and held what looked like some sort of soft doll, though Elsie couldn't see the face of it. Elsie guessed her to be no more than five. Her face was dirty, smeared at the corners of her mouth with what looked to be jam. At least she hoped it was jam. She glanced over at Gunther, who was still staring at Anna, almost as if he were trying to see her through Elsie's eyes—for the first time, as it were.

"Ach. You have jam, Anna," he said. He stood up and walked the few steps to a small sink.

As he did so, Elsie took the opportunity to quickly glance around.

It was warm and dry in this little hut of a home, clearly intended for one person only. It consisted mainly of one large room, with a bed in one corner and a sink and a stove in the other. Above the sink, various dishes were carefully stacked on a shelf, under which hung a few mugs on hooks. Along the back wall was a chest of drawers, and in the middle of the room stood a table and chairs for two, where Elsie currently sat. Though terribly small, it was clean and cozy and just the sort of room that Elsie liked. In a way, it reminded her of the shabby apartment on Armitage, where they had lived before discovering they were actually part of the wealthy Exley family.

Gunther took up a rag from somewhere in the sink and brought it to where Anna sat. Awkwardly, he attempted to wipe her face despite her squirms. Elsie felt herself wanting to help, but she forced herself to remain seated and instead looked back into her coffee.

"She is not mine," Gunther said quietly, as if reading Elsie's thoughts. "I swear this."

Elsie's eyes darted back up at him.

He stood up tall, and Elsie felt her pulse quicken as he locked his gaze on her. She struggled to gauge the truth of his words, and pulled her eyes away to glance back at Anna, who seemed to have shrunk even smaller, if that were possible, at Gunther's last words. Elsie bit her lip at the little girl's distress.

Gunther followed Elsie's gaze, and when he saw the tears welling in Anna's eyes, his face contorted. "Ach!" he said and reached out and patted her head. His voice softened. "I did not mean that, Anna. *Aber du bist mein Mädchen, genau so, nein?* You are my girl. You will always be my girl, yes?"

The little girl merely gave a slow, methodical nod and put her ragged toy in front of her face. Suddenly, Elsie's heart ached for her—how many times had she herself wanted to hide behind something in her grief and loneliness? She desperately wanted to go to the girl and scoop her into her lap, but she remained seated. Besides the impropriety of it, Elsie felt sure Anna would draw little comfort from a strange lady.

As if he were thinking the same thing, Gunther reached down

and picked up the girl, who wrapped herself around him and rested her head on his shoulder, her eyes watery and a finger in her mouth. "Shhh," he said in a low voice as he rubbed the girl's back. He exhaled loudly, then, and steadied himself, as if wondering how to proceed.

"I do not know where to start," he said with a heavy sigh, his voice low. "But I will try. My father was mathematics professor, as I told you, at University in Heidelberg. He was part of *intelligenz* of German society at this time. When the war broke out, he did not believe in this war, but he was anyway forced to fight in it. He was very patriotic, but he thought the Kaiser had stumbled . . . " Gunther paused here, seeming to search for the right words, " . . . lost his way. Victoria was, you know maybe, the Kaiser's grandmother. The people of England and Germany were very close before the war; my mother was English. How could my father fight them? And yet he was made to. He was killed. He had no idea how to fight," he said sadly, rubbing Anna's back again.

"I'm sorry," Elsie murmured, realizing that it was the first words she had spoken since entering the cottage.

"My mother," Gunther went on, after catching Elsie's eye for just a moment, "especially as English woman, had no way of making money except to take in sewing and rent out rooms in our very old . . . " he made a gesture as if searching for the right word . . . "big? rambling? . . . house that was no good for nothing else. A big house full of books and some said *Geister* . . . ach . . . how do you say? . . . ghosts," he said with a little flourish of triumph. "When I became older, I asked my mother why she did not return to England after war. She said she could not leave my father buried somewhere near border of France in mass grave. Also, that Heidelberg had been her home from time she was little girl. There is nothing and no one for her in England, she said. And so we rented out rooms, mostly to students, who became like older brothers or sisters to me. One or two were not so nice, but mostly they were kind; that or they ignored me. I liked to sit in corner and listen to them debate politics of day or discuss literature—Rilke versus Schiller, as example—before Mother would find me and put me to bed.

"Then about five years ago," he continued methodically, "just as I am finishing my degree at university, a young woman by name of Liesel Klinkhammer came to rent room from us. She was not student, but she had job in one of the cafés in town. How she can afford this room, I do not know. Maybe it was that my mother felt sorry for her. I was not at home most days, either at university studying or working at local school, where I had just found job as a teacher."

Anna murmured, then, and Elsie watched as Gunther began to sway a bit, rocking the child until she quieted.

"When I did see her," he went on more quietly, "Fraulein Klinkhammer rarely speaks to me. She was very quiet and keeps to herself, but little bit by little bits, she begins to trust my mother. She tells her things. She was what my mother would call a *Bauer* . . . peasant? Like poor person. She tells my mother where she comes from. From a farm outside of city. As a young girl, she fell in love with boy from next farm over, she tells my mother. Heinrich is his name. He left countryside to travel to Heidelberg to find work. Fraulein Klinkhammer was . . . how do you say it? *Verrückt in der Liebe?* . . . crazy in love for him? . . . is what my mother said. So the fraulein followed this Heinrich to Heidelberg and found job and room. It is impressive, no?"

Without waiting for Elsie to answer, he went on. "My mother was very glad for the money. But she told Fraulein Klinkhammer to forget this man, to go home. As it was, Fraulein Klinkhammer did not listen to her. And you can take guess what happened," he said, shifting his eyes toward the back of Anna's head, still resting on his shoulder.

The little girl looked to be asleep now, as evidenced by not only her closed eyes, but also by her slack body, her arms drooped loosely around Gunther's shoulders instead of tightly gripping his neck as they had just a few minutes before. Gunther shifted the weight of her and went on in a quieter voice.

"No one knew the fraulein was with child—even my mother, which is impressive. You would know this if you have met her, my mother. It was my mother that delivered the baby—right there in our house. She hears fraulein screaming and runs upstairs to find a big *Unordnun . . .*" Gunther shrugged, searching for the right word. "Mess." He looked at Elsie again as if to gauge her understanding. "Lucky my mother was there," he went on. "Poor Fraulein Klinkhammer was keeping pregnancy a secret, not eating much food, and baby came out little, only four pounds. My mother predicts she will not live, but, yes, she did live." He kissed the side of the sleeping Anna's head, bringing a smile to Elsie's face. "Fraulein Klinkhammer told my mother that she believes baby will bring father around, this Heinrich, but, no, it did not. She discovered that he ran off. To America."

Balancing Anna carefully, Gunther slowly lowered himself into the chair opposite Elsie, shifting carefully to find a comfortable position. Elsie couldn't help but stare at him as he sat across from her. He was not wearing his spectacles, and she could see his fine blond eyelashes. Her eyes observed the smattering of freckles across his nose and cheeks, then travelled lower to his blond mustache and his full lips beneath.

A warmth began to radiate through her as she watched him, and she knew then what she had long suspected; she was indeed falling in love with him despite everything. She couldn't help it. It was inconsequential what else he might say; it simply didn't matter. Anyone this good and this compassionate, this intelligent and caring, who could hold a child as tenderly as he held a poem was to be desired beyond any, no matter what other horrors he had yet to tell. She could probably guess the rest of the story, anyway. Obviously, the young woman fled to America after her lover, and Gunther had then set off on a quest to find her, towing the little girl along. It was admirable to be sure—but as Elsie considered it more closely, did not make a lot of sense. There were several better alternatives that came to her mind in just a few short moments; surely, he must have thought of these, too . . .

"Fraulein Klinkhammer became very *mutlos*," Gunther went on, oblivious to the delicate strands weaving at that moment into a cord of love within Elsie's heart. "Sometimes this happens, my mother says. The woman does not want to know the baby . . . becomes depressed. My mother is thinking that the fraulein should be with her family, but we do not know how to find them, who they are. And Fraulein Klinkhammer will not say. My mother, she tries to help her, but we have other cares to be thinking of. And now baby, too. Many, many nights, baby cries, but Fraulein Klinkhammer does not rise. My mother cannot endure this, and also lodgers complain, so she picks up baby and feeds her each night. Many times in night. Then one day, Fraulein Klinkhammer disappears. She leaves baby and note to say she is going to find this Heinrich. She says she is going to America and that she will be coming back for baby someday when she can."

Gunther stopped to softly rub the sleeping Anna's back again. "That was four years ago. She did not even give her a name," he said sadly, and for the first time he broke his gaze with Elsie and looked down.

"Who named her?" Elsie asked quietly.

"I did," he said, looking up at her again. "My mother insisted I name her, so I gave her the name of Anna. It was my mother's name, too." He gave Elsie a sad smile.

"I'm sorry she died, Gunther."

"Yes, it is very terrible." His voice was soft, his heavy grief still apparent in his eyes. "She should not have come. It was too much for her."

Elsie longed to reach out to him, to touch his arm—something— but she did not. "Why *did* she come?" she instead asked. "Why did all of you come? Why not just you?"

Gunther let out a deep breath. "Ach. I am getting ahead of the story." He paused as if to recount the tale in his mind and then continued. "After the fraulein left, we begin always to argue, me and my mother. We could not agree what to do with Anna." He lowered his voice to just above a whisper. "My mother wanted to put her in a . . .

what do you call it? *Kinderheim?* Orphanage? She is much attached
to Anna, it is true, but she predicts it will only get worse as time
passes. We cannot care for her forever, she says. I argue that is only
for little while, but she does not believe this. She is sure that Fraulein
Klinkhammer will never return. But I insist she will. I try very much
to help my mother to care for Anna, but I admit I find it hard. I am
not so good at this. I am not woman, and I have much demands on
my time at school. Also I am making small fixes on house each day;
always there is problem.

"Finally, after about six months, we receive much welcome letter
from Fraulein Klinkhammer. It says that she is in Chicago, that she
has found job in a school, near place called Mundelein. She has been
ill, the letter says, and that she cannot return for now. She is trying to
save money, but she finds it hard. It was very short letter, written by
friend, she says. She does not say whether or no she found Heinrich,
and she does not ask about baby. That was all. After I read this letter
many times, I understand that she is not going to come back. That
my mother is right. But still we wait, hope.

"My mother becomes, then, very ill. Many weeks pass, and much
of Anna's care falls to me. Some lodgers, too, help me, take pity on
the girl, but I now see how much work it is for my mother to run
house and care for baby. My mother was not young when I was born.
And I see that she will be weak from her illness for maybe long time.
So, I finally agree that we must take Anna to orphanage. My heart
nearly was breaking for this, for I have grown to love her, even then.
She is already turning one year of age. We were very sad, but we
tell ourselves small lie, that it is only for short time." Gunther gave
another shrug. "But we do not believe. My mother packed a bag for
her, and I was preparing things to leave with her when terrible thing
happened . . . "

Gunther trailed off and looked away for a moment, and Elsie was
surprised to see his look of anguish.

"She had a fit," he said quietly, smoothing Anna's hair. "Shaking
on the ground, her eyes going back. It was terrible. We did not know

what to do. We . . . we were very much frightened. One of our old neighbors was there, too, and she says that Anna is possessed by devil. *Schwachsinn!*" Gunther said fiercely. He rubbed his brow as if to calm himself and then went on, steadying his voice.

"We knew we cannot take her to orphanage like that. So we again keep her until we can understand what is happening. I take her to a doctor friend of mine from university. He examined her and tells me that she is probably having something called *Epilepsie* . . . epilepsy? I tell him the whole story and our plan to take her to orphanage. He agrees this would be for the best, but he warned me about the new Nazi laws under Herr Hitler calling for the *Sterilisation* . . . sterilization of the feebleminded. He tells me that in any type of institution, even in orphanage, Anna would probably be early victim. Not only that, he says, but many people have fear that this awfulness might go beyond sterilizing into something of more seriousness . . . maybe killing . . . murdering. I . . . I cannot believe this. It was ridiculous. *Wahnsinn!* How can this be? So I do more asking about this law, and I very soon come to same understanding as my friend. That our country is headed to very dark place."

With his free hand, he reached for his mug and took a drink of his coffee, now cool. "I went to university library and find books about epilepsy," he went on. "I learn more of what it is and how there is no cure. A few scientists predict salts of bromide and say that quiet life, good diet, some little exercise is only known treatment. Either way, me and my mother know then that we can never take Anna to orphanage, even for a short time. The authorities would know of her condition and maybe track her down later? We tried to follow what the books said—to give her a quiet, calm life. We tried these salts of bromide, but they only make her more ill. She fought taking them so much that sometimes it brings on another fit, so we finally stopped trying to give these to her. We tried to keep her fits a secret, but too many of the lodgers knew about them already. We asked them please to be silent about this, but," he said with a shrug, "students cannot always be relied upon. More than them, though, we were having much worry about the neighbor, Frau Mueller, who is now hanging Nazi flag in her front window and is always asking about Anna."

He stopped talking then and stretched his neck, the strain of holding the sleeping girl evident.

"Why . . . why don't you lie her back down," Elsie suggested, nodding toward the trundle.

"Ach, no. She will wake and start screaming. Best to hold her. She did not sleep well again last night."

Elsie looked at him, her heart overwhelmed. Hesitantly, she held out her arms and inclined her head toward Anna. Gunther did not move for several moments, looking at her as if weighing the risk of transferring the girl, his face conflicted. Finally, though, he inched forward and gently placed the sleeping girl in Elsie's arms, watching carefully to see if Anna would settle. Anna did stir, but Elsie carefully cradled her against her body. "Go on with the story," she said softly to Gunther. "Your voice will soothe her."

"There is not much more to say, I am thinking," Gunther said, slowly easing back in his chair and tentatively watching Anna in Elsie's arms. He gazed at her for several moments and then let out another deep breath.

"As time passed, things started to get very much worse. Lodgers started to leave. I suppose people everywhere are ignorant, yes?" he asked grimly. "Some of the lodgers were afraid of either the possessed girl, as she begins to be called, or the Nazis, so they went other places. Then other things not so good begin to happen. In the town." He stopped and pinched the bridge of his nose. "Another war is coming, I am afraid, Elsie. Hitler is not the Kaiser. This is different. Much evil is already happening."

He stood abruptly.

"Like this," he whispered fiercely, gesturing at the sleeping girl. "Only a monster would . . . would *sterilise* her—or worse—because of her illness. Something she cannot control . . . " He gripped the back of the chair and bowed his head down between his arms. "Forgive me," he said after a moment. "This is not the point."

He stood up straight and began pacing back and forth, occasionally looking over at Elsie. "Each week we had less and less money, and we lived more in fear," he said. "It was my mother's idea to come to America. To get Anna out of the country and maybe back to her mother if possible. We had the fraulein's one letter, so we were thinking that maybe we could find her. Idiocy, I know," he said, glancing at Elsie. "Also, I read that this epilepsy can be passed down . . . hereditary? Is that the word?"

Elsie quickly nodded.

"So I am thinking that maybe Fraulein Klinkhammer has this, too. Is this her meaning in the letter when she said she was ill?" he asked, thoughtfully scratching his whiskered chin. "At first, I am thinking to make this journey on my own," he went on. "I was not sure how my mother would be on journey, and Anna, too. I predict that both of them are not being strong enough, but I do not want to leave them behind, alone, even though I have friends at university who might help. But I have no choice. My mother insisted that we all go together. I suggest that maybe I should just take Anna to reunite her with Fraulein Klinkhammer, but she predicts I am not able to take care of Anna alone. But look at me now," he said with a sad grin. Elsie tried her best to give him an encouraging smile in return.

"No, the truth, I am thinking," he said with a heavy sigh, "is that she had no wish to stay anymore. She was afraid. My father, she said, would understand. And so I got tickets and visas, which took some time, and finally we left." He stopped pacing and looked down at Elsie. "Maybe we exaggerated the threat," he shrugged, his voice tired. "Maybe we should have stayed. I do not know. Nothing has turned out as I predict it would."

He slumped down into the chair opposite her again. "As you know, she died on the way over, my mother. I very much grieved her, as did Anna. Very much," he said hoarsely. "Ach, Elsie. What is worse is that it has been for nothing. Look at us. No closer to finding Fraulein Klinkhammer than the day we first arrived."

Elsie was at a loss for what to say to this poor man in front of her. "It must have been terrible, Gunther. What did you do? When you landed, that is. How did you come to be here?"

Gunther let out another sigh. "We docked in New York and made our way, me and little Anna, on the train to Chicago. I . . . I must say I did not understand how big America is, how big the cities are. I was . . . how do you say it? Overwhelmed? I felt despair of ever finding the fraulein, but I have no choice but try. At train station, I asked someone to direct me to Mundelein, and so we arrive here. It is what Fraulein Klinkhammer said in letter, no? That she had found work at a school? I asked many people . . . many of the girls as they walk by . . . if they know of a Fraulein . . . Miss . . . Liesel Klinkhammer. No one has heard this name, they say. I grow more and more upset. Finally, someone had pity on us and took us to see Sister Bernard. This sister welcomed us in, even though we were very dirty and shabby. I did not realize this until we were standing outside her office, how dirty we are.

"I tried to explain that I am seeking Anna's mother. She tells me that this name of 'Liesel Klinkhammer' she has not heard before. She is not student and not worker at this school. I am made very low by this, as I am thinking that my searching is to be nearing an end. Sister Bernard asks me then if maybe this woman is using different name? Or if maybe she moved on to different place? I have no answer to this. Then Sister asked where we are to stay, and I say that I do not know. I was no longer thinking so clear. We had just come from train station. We have nothing and nowhere to go. She has pity on me, I am thinking, and says that we can stay for time in small house behind dormitories. It is small like a hut. It is where old *Hausmeister*? . . . caretaker? . . . once lived. In exchange, she says, maybe I can do odd jobs for them. I agreed, and Anna and I moved in right away, that day. I cleaned the place," he said, looking around the room, "and unpacked our things, which was not much. We have little to bring. Thankfully, I know English because of my mother. She taught me this as child. It is not perfect, I know, but it is enough for me to get by," he said with a small shrug.

"It is very good," Elsie encouraged with a smile. She looked down at Anna and gently brushed her fine hair back from her eyes. "Then what?" Elsie prodded, looking back up at him.

"I . . . I work very hard at new job," he said, pulling his mutual gaze away. "Though I admit I am not skilled at jobs mechanical, but most of work is not hard. Most of it is cleaning. I think constantly about Fraulein Klinkhammer—how I can find her. But I have not much time free and no . . . no help. On evenings off, I take Anna by hand, and we explore neighborhood. I go into shop after shop, asking if anyone has heard of woman with Fraulein Klinkhammer's description. But there is nothing. No one.

"As time goes on, Sister Bernard offered me a permanent job as caretaker if I want. I was happy with this; I have nothing else," he said with a shrug. "But she has condition, she says. Anna, she says, cannot stay. I am shocked by this—angered, too. I say I will refuse, but Sister explained. She says that living in a hut in back of school with man who claims not to be her father is not good life for a child. There is a place, she tells me, called the Bohemian Home for the Aged and Orphans. Not too far away, on Foster Avenue. I can visit often, she says. Many children in orphanages have parents still alive who cannot care for them, she tells me. For reasons many. So they put children there until they can. Or until someone else wants them," he added, looking at Elsie again.

"Sister Bernard is very convincing," Gunther went on, with an odd trace of defensiveness in his voice now. "She tells me that Anna will have good food, some school, a place to run and play, learn better English. It is a good place, she promised. 'Do what is best for Anna,' she says. In my mind, I am thinking she is right. I have to admit that Anna was not doing so good. Constantly she cries for my mother. I tell her to stay in this hut while I work, but two times already I find her wandering by lake and then by road," he said with a nod toward the front of the college, where the busy, twisting Sheridan Road lay.

"I . . . I did not know what else to do," Gunther explained, his eyes pleading. "I did not have much of choice. Not one that I could see. So I . . . I went to this place. This Bohemian Home. And in the end, I . . . I put her there." He looked at Elsie with deep shame in his eyes.

Elsie was just about to reassure him when he suddenly broke down, putting his hand over his eyes to hide his tears.

"After everything. All that we went through in Germany. My mother dying. The terrible trip. All so that Anna could end up in orphanage anyway. Ach, Elsie. I have failed," he groaned, and his shoulders actually shook as he cried.

Elsie's heart went out to him, and she wished she could think of something to say that would comfort him.

"It was all for nothing," he said before she could offer anything. He angrily wiped his eyes with the back of his hand. "I am no closer to finding Fraulein Klinkhammer than I was before. She could be anywhere. Even far away from here. Who knows?"

"Gunther," Elsie began in a low, soothing voice. "You haven't failed. You might not have found her mother . . . yet. But you saved Anna from a potentially horrible fate in Germany. That alone demands credit and praise. Your mother's death was not for naught. She helped save this little girl. As did you." Privately Elsie considered the loss of his studies and his life as a teacher as worthy of sorrow and regret as well, but she did not say so. "All is not yet lost," she said softly, though, in actuality, she did think it to be nearly a hopeless situation. "What about her . . . her epilepsy? Has she . . . has she had any more fits?" Elsie asked tentatively.

Gunther sighed. "As if by miracle, she had none on the ship or during time with me here. I . . . I thought maybe they were over. That this condition has somehow gone away. That she is cured. Something like that. I know it was idiocy to think this." He exhaled loudly again, pausing to think. "I did not tell Sister Bernard or people at orphanage about . . . about Anna's illness because I have fear. Maybe this is wrong, but I decided to . . . what is the word? Zocken? Gamble? I prayed that all would be okay, but no. It was not to be. Since she has been at orphanage these fits have come back. She has had two.

The people at the orphanage—a couple, a man and wife—have much understanding and kindness. They wish to help, they say, but they tell me they cannot keep a child who has fits. They say she should be sent to special institution for feebleminded children in different part of state." Gunther put his hand over his eyes again. "Ach, Elsie," he mumbled. "What am I to do? I must find Fraulein Klinkhammer."

Elsie did not see how finding the fraulein at this point would solve anything, but she didn't want to add to his distress. What difference would it make if they found her? She was a perfect stranger to Anna. And even if Fraulein Klinkhammer really *had* been acting on some sort of maternal feeling by trying to find a better life for her and eventually her child, which was unlikely—even the usually generous Elsie allowed herself to admit—she was probably not any closer to being able to provide for Anna than she had been when she originally fled Germany after Heinrich.

"Is that why she's here with you now? Because she can't go back to the orphanage?"

"No, it is because . . . because sometimes I bring her back. For a visit. I thought maybe it would help her, but all it does is confuse her more, I am thinking."

"Why does she call you 'Papa'?" Elsie asked tentatively.

Gunther sighed. "I do not know. When she was very little, just learning to talk, I called myself *Onkle* to her, but it did not stick. It was probably one of the lodgers who thought it is amusing to teach her to call me 'Papa.' Anyway, she just does. And now I do not have heart to tell her. Constantly, she asks for my mother, her *Oma*. She does not understand she is dead," he said hoarsely, so much so that Elsie thought her own heart might break.

Carefully, she pulled out one of her hands, nearly numb, from under Anna and reached out across the table to take Gunther's hand in hers.

He looked up at her, surprised.

"Gunther, I will help you," she said steadily. "We'll find a way."

"No," he said, sitting up straight and pulling his hand free. "It is not for you to worry about. And I would not take you from your studies. You have much worries of your own. I know this, Elsie." He paused. "But I thank you."

"I would like to help you," Elsie insisted, her face warm from the fact that he had pulled away his hand. "I have very few to . . . to care for. I can study *and* help you to find this Fraulein Klinkhammer."

"But how? You have not much time between your class and your family. Aunt Agatha and all of these. Lloyd Aston," he said with a sad grin.

"I'll think of something. I'm . . . I'm very resourceful, you know."

"I do know."

They stared at each other for several moments, during which time Elsie was tempted to say aloud the words she believed he already knew—but she just couldn't. She opened her mouth to speak, but the words died in her throat. It was not the time for it, or to be thinking of herself, she reasoned.

"Besides this habitual or sanctifying grace there is also actual grace," Sr. Raphael was reading aloud. "Actual grace is that grace which empowers us to perform actions and operations proportionate to our ultimate end, the vision of God in his proper essence. By its means we build up within us the theological virtues of faith, hope, and charity, the cardinal virtues of prudence— justice, fortitude, and temperance—and the moral virtues. Since all of these are the fruit of grace, they are called infused virtues."

Sr. Raphael stopped reading from the book she held in front of her, her spectacles nearly at the end of her nose, and perused the class. "I think that's all the time we have, girls," she said, glancing at the brown wall clock. "You'll have to read the rest of Reverend Lapierre's chapter on Aquinas's interpretation of grace on your own. I had hoped to have time to discuss, but never mind. Instead, I want you to write a paper for Thursday on one of the cardinal virtues."

Elsie gave a small internal groan. She hadn't been listening. Again. Since visiting Gunther in his hut, she had become nearly obsessed with helping him. At one point, she ventured to ask her roommate,

Melody, if she had ever heard of a Liesel Klinkhammer. Disappointedly, she had not—which was significant considering Melody claimed to know almost everyone at Mundelein and "loads" of girls, not to mention boys, at the neighboring Loyola as well. Melody had of course begged to know who this Liesel was, but Elsie put her off by telling her it was "the daughter of a friend of her mother's who had maybe worked here at one point."

"Criminy! Why didn't you say!" Melody had laughed. "I don't know all the *staff*! Pops would not approve of me fraternizing with 'the help,' as he calls them. He's terribly bourgeois, you know, though he doesn't even realize it. For God's sake, his father was a miner! It's perfectly obnoxious. Anyway, why don't you ask Gunther? He's German, too, I think. Maybe he's heard of her."

At this suggestion, Elsie had merely bit back a smile and said that she would.

Since their conversation, Gunther, she knew, had taken Anna back to the orphanage, where the girl so far had not experienced any more fits, at least that Elsie knew of. But it was only a matter of time, Elsie felt sure, as did Gunther, before another one might occur. Elsie also ventured over to Loyola's library, something she had not previously worked up the courage to do, and unearthed several books on the subject of mental diseases, just as Gunther had done back at the university in Heidelberg. It made for slow, painful reading in the evenings, but she had been rewarded with a couple of nuggets of information—the saddest being that there really was apparently no known cure for epilepsy, corroborating what Gunther's colleague in Germany had told him. She had hoped that maybe American doctors had perhaps devised some sort of new, innovative treatment, but no.

Despite her initial opinion that finding Liesel Klinkhammer would not help much with the bigger problem of what to do about Anna, Elsie had since given in to Gunther's insistence that they continue the search for her, perhaps because there seemed precious few other options. Maybe *something* could be resolved by finding her, Elsie convinced herself. If nothing else, it was at least a place to start.

More than once though, she had wondered if Anna should at least be taken to a doctor in town and examined. She had suggested this to Gunther, but he had no money to pay for a doctor, he said, and refused—no, was *offended*—when she had offered even to loan him the money, much less give it to him. So they resorted to finding the fraulein. Sr. Bernard had not been of any help, and it did not seem a matter for the police. But how to find a missing person? Or worse yet, a person who maybe did not *want* to be found? Elsie wondered.

As she gathered up her things from Sr. Raphael's class, Elsie, again thinking about how they could find Fraulein Klinkhammer, bemoaned the fact that her mental abilities were not of a more practical, common-sense nature. Like Henrietta's, she thought glumly. As she pondered this, a stray thought suddenly occurred to her—one which she couldn't believe she hadn't thought of before! It was obvious what they should do.

She was interrupted in this new exciting thought, however, by the tap of a pencil on her arm. Startled, she looked over to see Melody, happily in this same theology class, pointing with her pencil in a very superior type of way, with raised eyebrows, at the hearts Elsie had unconsciously drawn in the margin of her paper.

Melody gave her an exaggerated wink and whispered loudly, "I knew it! I knew you had a secret love! Oh, do tell!" she urged. "Honestly, Elsie, it's horribly unfair if you don't. Haven't I waited long enough? Surely I've earned your trust by now!"

Elsie tried not to audibly sigh. Melody was forever trying to get a confession of love out of her and was relentless in her attempts to "set her up" with various promising Loyola boys, each of whom, Melody declared, was more "perfect" for her than the next, which in and of itself was astonishing, really. Who would have imagined that there were apparently so many "perfect" men out there for her?

Elsie had thus far been successful in thwarting both the confession and most of the attempted dates, not wanting to explain that she was already the subject of the very same attempts by her scheming Grandfather Oldrich Exley and his somewhat unwilling accomplice, Aunt Agatha. Nor did she wish to reveal any of her other "secrets," for that matter, such as her recent desire to become a nun or her sordid past with Stanley and Lieutenant Barnes-Smith. And she most *definitely* did not want to confess, nor discuss, the real object of her tender feelings, which were something very different than any of the fleeting, immature ones that had come before. She had no wish to explain, nor was she really able to, even to herself. All she knew was that Gunther and his woes were all that mattered to her now. And her studies, of course. Where everything else was gray and shallow, this was real and alive and filled with color. It was almost blinding, actually. Gunther needed her, and that alone was intoxicating—not to mention his mutual love of literature, his tenderness with Anna, and dare she admit? . . . his handsome face and his very blue eyes.

"Well, it's a very long story," Elsie said, moving hurriedly toward the door.

"Even better!" Melody gushed, following closely behind her. "Oh, I do so love long stories. Especially long love stories!"

"Later then," Elsie suggested. She was eager to find a place alone so that she could think about her new idea; the one that had just come to her a few minutes ago, which was, of course, that she, or, well, *they*—she and Gunther, that is—should ask Henrietta and Clive to help them find Liesel Klinkhammer! After all, isn't that what Henrietta had told her at Christmas? That she and Clive were hoping to open a detective agency? Perhaps this could be their first case!

The wheels in Elsie's mind were turning furiously, and she made an excuse to Melody that she had to meet with Sr. Sylvester, her math tutor. If she had merely said that she was going to the library, Melody would have found a way to talk her out of it; Elsie had used that excuse already too many times.

"Well, all right, then, Els. I'll let you off for now," Melody said sternly, "but don't forget! You promised!" she added gaily as she set off in the direction of Philomena Hall. Elsie, in turn, made her way toward Gunther's hut, hoping he was there so that she could lay out her idea. She felt sure Clive could find Liesel; after all, hadn't he once been a brilliant detective? And it might be good, Elsie speculated, for Henrietta, too, as she hadn't been herself since she had lost the baby.

Chapter 2

Clive shifted the Alpha Romeo into gear and turned it back toward Highbury. He had just left a private meeting, loosely termed, with Detective Frank Davis, the Winnetka police officer who had valiantly helped Clive—and Henrietta—to kill their nemesis, one Lawrence Susan, a.k.a. Neptune. Davis had been shot and wounded in the altercation, and for a while it had seemed touch and go. Only a few days ago, Clive learned that Davis had finally been discharged from the hospital and had since returned to work at the station—unfortunately, however, still under the direction of the incompetent Captain Callahan.

Davis had agreed to meet at his usual haunt in town, the Trophy Room, at Clive's request. Obviously, it was not up to his usual standard, but Clive needed to do something. Henrietta had not been herself since she had lost the baby, and he was desperate to distract her. He had been disappointed, too, by the loss of the child, and he grieved for it in his own way, but his true despair, his true distress, was regarding Henrietta's pervasive sorrow.

He had never seen her cry—sob—the way she had the morning it all happened. It was terrible to witness, and his heart ached for her, even now. She had since put on a brave face, but overall, she was still listless and dull. She positively moped about the house and seemed uninterested in anyone or anything around her. She would go with Antonia to the club if asked, but Clive could see she didn't care about it. Not that she ever had, really, but up until this current melancholy juncture in time, she had at least put her best foot forward—especially when it came to impressing his mother and trying to fit in.

He didn't understand this need in women, he thought, as he pulled into Highbury's long lane—this desire to bring forth life. Of course, he enjoyed children, to a certain extent, and he guiltily knew he was supposed to produce an heir, lest his vile brother-in-law, Randolph Cunningham, inherit the Howard fortune. But as Clive saw it, perhaps this wouldn't be such a bad thing. The fortune would consequently trickle down eventually to Randolph's sons—Clive's nephews, Howard and Randolph, Jr.—who, though only little still, did not seem to be so far taking after Randolph in his cruel boorishness. But then he would inevitably hear his father's voice in his head, saying, "Ah, but it's not the same as your own flesh and blood, is it, my boy?"

Clive sighed. He supposed not. Another errant thought occurred to him from time to time, an almost laughable one, really, that perhaps he could alter his will to leave the whole of the estate to his cousin, Wallace, in Derbyshire, England. But Wallace already had Linley Castle to contend with, which he wanted to turn into some sort of boys' school or home for shell-shocked soldiers, or some such thing, once his father, Clive's Uncle Montague, finally died. Lord Linley had recently been brought very low, not only by the news of his brother, Alcott's, sudden death, but by the discovery that Wallace, his only remaining son after the decimation of the Great War, had secretly married a penniless French nurse and had not one, but now two sons by her. Wallace's failure to marry into money spelled certain ruin for the Linley estate, and Montague Howard had not ever quite recovered from the blow. He was mostly an invalid at this point, Wallace wrote in his occasional letters to Clive, for which Wallace claimed he felt immense guilt and responsibility. But what could he do? he had written more than once; he had to follow his principles and his heart.

—

But there was more to it for women, Clive knew, than merely producing a legacy. It was some biological yearning to reproduce and nurture that wasn't the same as it was for men, he surmised, though he admitted that he barely understood it. He had sought his mother's advice after Henrietta's unfortunate womanly trouble—a miscarriage, they were calling it in hushed tones. But could it even be called a miscarriage? he had asked his mother, for which he was promptly scolded.

"But she couldn't have been more than a month along, Mother," he argued quietly. "Could she have been mistaken that she was even pregnant at all?"

"Don't be ridiculous, Clive! Of course, she would know if she were pregnant or not," Antonia hissed over tea one morning not long after it had happened. "If you take my advice, which you probably won't," she sniffed, "you'll proceed with caution. Be tender and understanding. Henrietta is made of sterner stuff than first appearances; she'll come round, I should imagine. Provided you're not a brute," she added.

Not a brute? Clive had said to himself, hoping that she didn't mean what he thought she meant. "No, Mother, I haven't been 'a brute,' of course," he said testily. "What do you take me for?"

"Well, in my experience, darling, all men are the same."

In truth, he *had* been very tender with Henrietta, trying his best to comfort and console her. But he kept discovering her crying in the darkest part of the night, lying balled up beside him in their massive four-poster bed. Cut to the quick by this, he would quietly say her name or rub her shoulder, which only served to produce a tearful apology from her, as if the whole thing had been her fault. The first time this had happened, he merely held her, hushing and soothing her as best he could. The next time, however, he had tried levity, saying, "Don't be ridiculous, darling, of course it's not your fault," the result of which was shockingly a fresh crop of tears. Frankly, any attempt at consoling her usually resulted in such. He had tried telling her that it didn't matter, that there would be more chances, that he was sure they would have *tons* of children—too many, more than likely, he had tried to say with a grin—but none of these comments seemed to bring her any comfort. In fact, it seemed to make things worse.

Naturally, in due time he had tried to make love to her, thinking that she would respond, if not out of the sheer pleasure they both derived from their previous nights of passion but as a way to potentially create another baby. He had always been able to please her before, to skillfully bring her to a climax, with her always crying out or even groaning with pleasure as he loved her. And my God, it wasn't difficult to do; she never failed to arouse him. But she would have none of it now, which confused him. Never had she rejected his advances, except once on their honeymoon when they had argued. Now, he wasn't sure how to proceed. He had told her on their wedding night that he would never force himself on her, but it had been more than a month and still she held herself from him. He was beginning to worry about what the future might hold. What was he to do?

Real advice had finally come to him in the form of a suggestion from Bennett, his father's right-hand man, and indeed, Alcott's confidant and friend, at the firm, Linley Standard. Since his father's death and the discovery of his killers, Clive and Bennett had come to an arrangement of sorts regarding the running of the firm, which, though not secret, strictly speaking, was, on the other hand, not one they bandied about, even to Antonia. The agreement was simply that Clive would fulfill the role of Chairman of the Board in name only, as had been the case with his father. Like Alcott, Clive would be merely a figurehead, which would allow for the brilliant Sidney Bennett to employ his astute business acumen in running the company, as he had done for all these years, leaving Clive free to pursue private detective work.

With this agreement satisfactorily negotiated between them, their business relationship now seemed to hover on the brink of being something more, just as it had been something more of a friendship between Alcott and Bennett as the years had gone on. On more than one occasion since his father's death, Clive found himself turning to the calm, steady Bennett for advice. He reminded Clive of his father at times, but Bennett was more grounded, more practical than his father—the son of an English lord—had ever been. Many times, Clive had to shake himself a bit to remember that Bennett was indeed *not* his father, such as when he occasionally stopped at the house for a late-night drink, usually under the guise of needing Clive to sign some documents or other. They would sit across from each other in his father's—now Clive's—study in the leather armchairs in front of the fireplace, just as Clive and his father had so often done. Bennett could easily have sent whatever documents he needed signed via courier, or request that Clive stop in at the office, if nothing else but to keep up appearances with the staff. So Clive felt it very keenly that Bennett made an effort to come in person, as if Bennett somehow knew he might need to privately talk.

It was during one such evening, about a month after Henrietta's . . . mishap . . . that Bennett casually asked if Clive had any detective cases yet come his way. When Clive responded that he had not, Bennett suggested that perhaps he try to unearth one—and that he should make sure it was one in which he could involve Henrietta.

"I don't think she's quite up to something like that at the moment," Clive responded, peering intently at the fire.

"Oh, I don't know," Bennett answered. "Seems to me that's exactly what she needs. Take her mind off things." He glanced sideways at Clive.

"Ah," Clive said, turning it over slowly in his mind. It wasn't a bad idea, really. Why hadn't he thought of it before? "Yes," he said, sitting up in his chair. "I see what you mean." He looked over at Bennett, feeling very grateful all of a sudden.

"Merely a thought," Bennett said quietly.

Clive packed some tobacco into his pipe, wondering how he could find a case, a real case. He couldn't just rustle one up out of thin air. Nor was he going to sniff around the Winnetka Police

Station looking for crumbs, not with that idiot Callahan in charge. Clive had more than once suspected that there was something fishy there. No one could be as unaware and naïve as Callahan claimed to be and still sit as the chief of police, even if it *was* a sleepy little village twenty miles north of Chicago. And there had been a brief moment during the investigation of his father's murder when Clive thought he saw something telling, something more knowing beneath Callahan's bumbling exterior, a chink in his armor, as it were. But it was only a feeling, nothing he could prove. It was enough to cause a certain suspicion on Clive's part, however, though he had no wish to deal with him at present. Well, he thought, taking a deep puff of his pipe as Bennett poured himself another brandy, at least he now had an idea of how he might help Henrietta.

Weeks had gone by, however, and nothing had surfaced, causing Clive to wonder if he really should formally advertise his services in the local paper. It was a thought he loathed for various reasons, one of them being the chance that his mother might see it, when he had inadvertently heard that Frank Davis was back at the station. After the Neptune affair, Clive was sure an understanding of sorts existed now between them. Indeed, he and Henrietta had visited him in the hospital on more than one occasion, Henrietta noticing that no other family or friends ever seemed to be there, an observation that Clive duly stored away for later use. Surely Davis, Clive had thought with more excitement than he knew he should feel, would have a lead, something he—or rather, *they*, he should say—could sink their teeth into.

The Trophy Room, where Davis had suggested they meet, was filthy and had an overpowering smell of mold (or was it sewer?) to it. Why the hell this was Davis's preferred drinking establishment, Clive didn't know, but it didn't matter. It occurred to him as he walked in and looked around for Davis that perhaps Davis had chosen this place on purpose to rattle him, as the Howards' wealth was frequently the butt of his rather dry, sarcastic humor. Well, Clive thought, it would take more than this to throw him. He had been in his share of seedy, rotten, sweaty establishments in the city, and before that it had been the horror of the trenches in the war.

He spotted Davis at a low table in the back. As he approached, he noted that Davis looked as scruffy and disheveled as usual, his near-death experience apparently having done little to change his habits, at least outwardly. Davis was slouched forward over his pint of beer but held out his hand to Clive, who took it. Clive tossed his hat on the table and rested his hands on his hips. "So how are you?" he asked gruffly.

"Been better."

"What are you drinking?" Clive asked, nodding at Davis's nearly empty pint.

"Pabst."

Clive looked around for a waitress but could see none.

"Butler's off duty," Davis said as he leaned back slowly and lit a cigarette. "'fraid you'll have to get your own."

"Piss off, Davis." Clive retreated toward the thick, grimy bar stained with water marks and deep gouges. His choice of drink was single malt, but after a quick perusal of the paltry stock lined up behind the bar, he ordered a Pabst, too.

"Charming place," Clive muttered as he placed two glasses of beer on the table in front of Davis and pulled out a chair. He slid one of the glasses toward Davis and took up the other. "Cheers," he said and took a long drink.

"Not quite the Drake, but it serves its purpose," Davis said wryly, exhaling a large cloud of smoke.

"So do you have anything for me, or not?" Clive asked, having already spoken to Davis on the telephone earlier in the week, saying that he was eager for a case, but not mentioning exactly why.

"Not much," Davis shrugged. "You know the chief. 'There isn't any crime in Winnetka.'"

"Well, you must have something, or you wouldn't have called me out here."

"It's pretty flimsy," Davis said, finishing his first beer and shoving the empty glass aside. "You won't like it."

"Try me."

"Suit yourself." A grin crept across Davis's face. "Got a case of some psychic. A spiritualist, she calls herself," Davis said as he inhaled deeply and looked at Clive as if to gauge his reaction.

Clive sighed. "Go on," he said wearily.

"Not much to tell. Two days ago, a man shows up at the station, a Mr. Tobin, I think he said. Claims his wife's been 'hypnotized' by this spiritualist and wants us to investigate."

"This is hardly a matter for the police."

"But you're not the police, are you?" Davis said, slouching over his beer again, one eye involuntarily squinting shut, perhaps from the pain of leaning over.

"Come on, Davis. Give me something better than this."

"I don't have anything better than this, *Howard*," he exhaled. "Look, there aren't that many real cases to begin with, and I can't go giving them all to you under the table, can I? I'd be helping myself right out of a job."

"All right, all right," Clive said, waving his hand at him, as if to stop the sob story. He rubbed his brow and tried to think. A spiritualist case? This smelled rotten. He had been hoping for something open and shut, like a stolen car or something. Was it really wise to involve Henrietta in such a . . . what would you call it . . . vaporous type of case? Something told him it wasn't a good idea, but what choice did he have? If he and Henrietta were to really operate a detective agency, it naturally followed that it was going to be fraught with danger and nastiness, which is why he had always been less than enthused about the whole thing in the first place. It was never going to be some sort of gay scavenger hunt that Henrietta always seemed to think it would be. Detective work, by its nature, involved the uglier sides of humanity: theft, murder, rape, kidnapping, blackmail, and every other kind of vice.

Why couldn't Henrietta be happy strolling about the grounds of

Highbury and entertaining his mother's bridge club? he groaned to himself, but he made himself stop before he got too far down that line of thought. He could have had any number of women who would have been content to sit at home and knit, but it had been Henrietta's spunk, he reminded himself, that had originally attracted him. Her sense of adventure coupled with her naiveté had been irresistible. They still were, actually, though she was sadly lacking in both at the moment.

"Okay," he sighed again. "What do you got on it?"

"Not much," Davis responded with an annoying grin. "This Mr. Tobin says he found his wife packing up all her jewelry—not that it's worth much, he claims. When he questioned her, she says that she's giving it to this quack—as a gift, she says. Tobin says she's been acting all funny lately. Like she's in a trance or somethin', going around the house mumblin', so Tobin's convinced it's this spiritualist that she's been going to see. Claims she must have hypnotized her. Too scared to go see this charlatan himself, he claims, lest he get hypnotized, too, he says, so he wants us to check it out."

"What was the chief's response?" Clive asked, fingering his glass.

Davis just raised an eyebrow, suggesting Clive should already know the answer to that.

"Okay, so the basic shell game type of thing. Only with a bit more song and dance to it. Got it. Give me the address to this Tobin," he grumbled. "And where do I find this 'spiritualist'?"

"Apparently, she's set up shop in that one-room schoolhouse out on Willow Road. You know the one?"

"Yeah," Clive said, fishing for a piece of paper in his inside jacket pocket. "Out by Crow Island? She got a name?"

"Calls herself Madame Pavlovsky."

Clive rolled his eyes and reluctantly wrote down this information and Tobin's address. Quickly he downed his beer and stood up, the chair scraping behind him on the sticky floor. "How's your wound?" he asked, nodding at Davis's abdomen.

"Coming along."

"Good to hear," Clive said, putting his hat on firmly.

"Don't forget—you owe me a whiskey," Davis said, referencing Clive's offer to him in the hospital as a debt of thanks.

"Yes, yes, of course," Clive said absently. "You'll have to come over some time to Highbury so we can thank you properly." He winced at the thought of how irritating that would be to arrange with his mother.

"Should I use the servants' entrance?" Davis asked, gingerly leaning back.

"Fuck off, Davis. I'll get back to you when I know something," Clive said and walked out, leaving Davis sitting at the low table, a sly grin on his face.

Chapter 3

Henrietta folded up the letters, slipping them back in their envelopes. She set them to the side and looked into the mirror of her vanity, patting her hair one more time. She needed to snap out of it.

She chose a lipstick in a faint shade of peach to match her salmon-colored Zimmerman crinkled crepe and gingerly applied it. Turning her head from side to side to observe herself, she decided she was satisfied and stood up.

She had no desire to go and pay a visit to Ma in Palmer Square, but Elsie had been very insistent on the telephone. Saying she had something very important to discuss with her. Henrietta couldn't imagine what it could possibly be, except something to do with their grandfather's bullying efforts at marrying Elsie off. She hoped this wasn't it; she was not up for a fight at the moment.

Henrietta knew she was being ridiculous and cowardly, but she couldn't seem to help it. She couldn't shake the dreary malaise that had come upon her since . . . since, well, since she had lost the baby. It's not that she was a stranger to grief. She had naturally been sad and cried for weeks when her father killed himself, but somehow that grief had been different. This was more acute and aching, as if a part of her had died as well. In both instances, however, she felt the need to hide her grief, to push it down inside of her. The shameful nature of her father's death, the taking of his own life, had prevented them from mourning publicly. And Ma's bitter rage prevented them from mourning privately at home, as she forbade them to ever speak of Pa again.

But this little death was somehow shameful, too, Henrietta felt. She could not shake the deep sense of failure that threatened to swallow her up. The failure she had previously felt at not being able to get pregnant was nothing compared to the feeling of having finally achieved it and then failing to carry it through. Oh, why had she told so many people? Now everyone knew about her failure, and while they were very encouraging and sympathetic, of course, none more so than Clive himself—somehow this made it worse. Everyone either looked at her with pity, she was sure, or patted her on the hand, saying, "Not to worry, dear! There'll be another!" as if that somehow should make her feel better. And the fact that it didn't, made her feel worse yet again.

She had been so happy, so proud when she had realized she was pregnant. But she suspected too many times now, perhaps that had been the key. She had been too proud, and this is what had happened. And surely Ma, of all people, would not hesitate to remind her of this.

She let out a deep sigh. She had no wish to face Ma later this morning, but she would have to get it over at some point. No doubt Ma would have something choice to say, something like, "I told you so" or "That's what you get for marrying outside your place!"

Well, there was nothing for it. She had to face the world again, and not just at Antonia's ludicrous committees at the club. More importantly, though, she had to make herself try to *care* again. She could see that Clive was suffering, too, at her despondency, and if nothing else, she knew she needed to be stronger for him. Many women miscarried, the doctor had told her, and went on to have many children.

Clive had anxiously asked the doctor before he had left that awful day what should be done. What treatment could they give her? The doctor had said that no treatment was necessary; just to have her rest for a good week, not to excite herself.

Mary, the cook, however, had taken it upon herself to concoct various "teas" that she sent up to Henrietta with Edna, saying that these were old remedies that were sure to "put the color back in her cheeks." The gesture had touched Henrietta in a way that sometimes only grief can, so that when she was eventually allowed to leave her room, she made it a point to go down to the kitchens to thank Mary personally. It meant even more when Mary related to her that many of the "teas" had been old Helen's recipes from the days when she had been the head cook at Highbury. It was yet another connection to Helen, the old servant who had died on the grounds last summer, and whose photograph of herself and her little family Henrietta kept on her little desk in her and Clive's private sitting room.

Gathering up her gloves, Henrietta decided at the last moment to place the letters she had just received this morning in her handbag, too. There was one from Herbie, of course, who wrote faithfully each week from New Hampshire where he, Eddie, and Jimmy were at boarding school at Philips Exeter, and one from Mrs. Hennessey. She knew that Herbie wrote to Ma, too, but if the conversation later became too labored or sparse, as she predicted it would, then perhaps she could offer to read them aloud to pass the time. No doubt Elsie's little "trouble," whatever it was, would take little time to clear up.

Henrietta had tried on the telephone to persuade Elsie to come and visit her at Highbury to impart her news, but Elsie had said she couldn't spare the extra time it would take to get to Highbury and back, nor did she wish to make poor Karl drive her all that way. Henrietta had been wont to retort that this was in fact his job, but she had refrained. She had then graciously offered to visit her at Mundelein instead, but Elsie had declined that option as well, saying that there wasn't really any truly private place in which for them to talk. The front parlor of Philomena Hall was open to anybody to use, she said, so there was no real assurance of privacy, and her dormitory room, she added, was also not a likely option, as who knew if her roommate, Melody, would be in or not. If she was, she would most probably have a whole gaggle of friends surrounding her. *And,* Elsie went on, her voice crackling over the telephone line, if she were to politely ask Melody to vacate the room for even a short time, Elsie was sure to be mercilessly subjected to a whole torrent of questions from a delighted Melody, always eager for any kind of news or gossip, which, Elsie said, she did not think she could face just at the moment—a feeling Henrietta could certainly understand.

So, in the end, Henrietta had sighed and agreed to meet Elsie at the Palmer Square house, disappointed not only because it meant having to interact with Ma but also because Henrietta rather liked Mundelein, truth be told, and enjoyed being there. Like Elsie, she found it to be a peaceful, interesting sort of place and more than once had thought that she wouldn't have minded being a student there herself.

"Good morning, madame," said Karl upon opening the thick front doors of the Palmer Square house to her. He was the man servant her grandfather had hired to act as both butler and chauffer for the Von Harmons. To Henrietta's eyes, he appeared older and sleepier than even two months ago when the boys had still been at home. Now with just Ma and little Doris and Donny to serve, as it were, Henrietta thought he might have regained some energy, but instead he seemed to have lost some, as if lack of use was positively rusting him.

"This way, madame," Karl said after he had taken her hat and coat, and he obediently led her to the front parlor. As they walked the short distance, Henrietta smoothed her dress and was surprised to hear what she thought was a man's voice coming from the parlor, as well as that of Ma and Elsie. Could Eugene be home? she wondered nervously, her stomach sinking. Was that what Elsie had wished to tell her? And what new disaster did that spell? But before she could follow that line of thought to some predictably dismal conclusion, they arrived at the parlor.

According to proper etiquette, Karl should have announced her as

"Mrs. Howard" to the already assembled personages in the room, but instead he merely gave a sort of awkward wave of his hand, made a slight bow, and then disappeared.

Henrietta sighed. She had spoken to Elsie before about holding the servants more accountable—Antonia would have been shocked by such behavior!—but it wasn't really Elsie's concern anymore. Not that it ever had been, really, and especially now that she had moved out to attend Mundelein College. Henrietta considered whether she should bring it up to Ma, but before she could decide, her attention was instead caught by the sight of a man seated rather close to Elsie on the horsehair sofa. They were seated at a right angle to Ma, who was perched in her usual spot in one of the velvet armchairs by the fire. The man politely stood upon Henrietta's entering the room and gave her a slight bow. Puzzled, Henrietta looked from Ma to Elsie, who stood up hurriedly now, too.

"Oh, Henrietta!" Elsie said in a rush. "You've finally come! This is my . . . my friend, Mr. Stockel," she said, and Henrietta did not fail to notice how Elsie ever so briefly touched his arm as she did so.

"Mr. Stockel, this is my sister, Mrs. Howard," she said, gesturing toward Henrietta.

The man before her was, if not dirty, then slightly disheveled. His clothes were relatively clean but ill-fitting—a bit too big for him— and worn thin. They looked to have been well-made and of quality material once upon a time, but now were quite old and faded. He had a shock of blond hair, a trim blond moustache and beard, and the bluest eyes that Henrietta thought she had ever seen. He stood look-ing at her, his eyes inquisitive behind his gold-rimmed spectacles. Henrietta thought she saw kindness there, but perhaps a trace of fear, too. She held out her hand to him.

"Good afternoon, Mr. Stockel. You must call me Henrietta, of course. Since you're a friend of Elsie's," she said, smiling stiffly.

The man took her hand and kissed it. "Please, I am Gunther. I am honored to meet you. Elsie speaks very much highly of you," he said sincerely in a thick German accent.

Henrietta moved to the armchair on the other side of the fireplace from Ma and shot Elsie an inquisitive look, as she and Gunther moved to sit back down as well. Elsie twisted her hands together and glanced surreptitiously at Ma, inclining her head just a little, suggesting to Henrietta that perhaps she did not wish to speak openly in front of Ma, which slightly irritated Henrietta. Why had Elsie arranged for them to meet here, then? And—if the callouses Henrietta felt on his hands were any indication—why had she brought this German laborer with her? Perhaps he was in trouble? Or in need of a job? Elsie was forever picking up strays as a child, only to have to release them in the end because the family had barely enough to feed themselves, much less mangy animals. Elsie wanting to help this man in a similar capacity would be infinitely superior than any other uncomfortable explanation that had come to mind since she had entered the room, especially after she had witnessed Elsie gently placing her hand on his arm.

"Tea, Henrietta?" Ma asked, nodding toward the pot on the elaborate service set on the small table between them.

"Yes, thank you," Henrietta said.

"You pour it, would you?" Ma asked, settling herself back in her chair. Henrietta could not help but smile to herself, even in her current state of mind. Despite the fact that she was now the wife of Clive Howard, heir to the fabulous Howard fortune and nephew to Lord and Lady Linley, and as such possessed a veritable army of servants to do her bidding, luxury cars, jewels, and houses across the country—none of that meant anything here amongst her family. Here, she was still just Henrietta.

With a weak smile, she silently poured herself some tea and then looked across at Elsie, whose eyes, she saw, were on Gunther and that she was looking at him, Henrietta could not fail to observe, in a more intimate way than should reasonably exist. Surely Elsie didn't care for him, did she? Henrietta worried. My God, was Elsie so love-sick that she fell in love with every man that even remotely came into her life? Henrietta had known plenty of women like that, but she never dreamt that her sister would be one of them!

Henrietta looked around the room at each of them as she took a sip of her tea. Why didn't anyone say anything?

"Well," Henrietta said, clearing her throat. "How nice of you to join us, Mr. Stockel. Gunther," she added when he looked about to correct her.

"I'm sorry not to have told you, Henrietta," Elsie said, clenching her hands together and stuffing them into her lap. "Gunther thought it best if he came along, too, but it was too late to telephone and tell you. So . . . I . . . I hope you don't mind," she said anxiously.

"Of course, I don't mind," Henrietta said placidly. "How kind of Gunther to escort you."

Gunther looked as if he were about to say something, but Henrietta again noticed Elsie lay her finger on his hand, this time as if to caution him. Gunther responded by twisting his cap in his hands. Henrietta looked over at Ma, who remained oddly quiet. She was nibbling on a biscuit and looked as contented as a cat. Henrietta thought it best to turn her attention there, since Elsie was apparently not yet ready to impart her pressing news.

"So how are you, Mother?" Henrietta asked, assuming a formal address in the presence of a third party, and sitting up straight as if to brace herself for whatever mood Ma might be in. "Have you heard from the boys? I've a letter here from Herbie," she said, patting her handbag. "Would you like me to read it?" Henrietta was glad she had had the foresight after all to bring it, as the current conversation was indeed lacking.

"Not right now," Ma answered. "I've one from him, too. Not many from Eddie, of course. Takes after Eugene, that one does. Jimmy writes from time to time but can't make anything out of it usually. Haven't seen *you* in an age," Ma sniffed.

Henrietta sighed. Well, here it was, at last, she thought. Ma's bitter callousness finally surfacing. At least she knew now how to proceed.

"I've been a bit under the weather, you could say, Ma," Henrietta said bitingly. Had Ma not one sympathetic bone in her body? She had come expecting a certain level of blame or . . . or something, but to completely refuse to acknowledge what she had just been through was infinitely worse. Henrietta knew she was being unfair, however, in wanting it both ways. On the one hand, she was sick of everyone at Highbury walking on eggshells around her and insisting she rest as though she had some sort of terminal illness, but on the other hand, she couldn't help but to feel hurt now, too, that not only was she not receiving any sympathy regarding her loss, but that it wasn't even acknowledged at all. But how very typical of Ma, Henrietta fumed. Even in the face of death, all she could think of was herself. Why had she expected anything more?

"Least *these* two have been to see me since Christmastime," she said, nodding at Elsie and Gunther. "Has a look of Stanley about him, doesn't he?"

Henrietta was more than a little thrown off at the revelation that Gunther had already been to the Palmer Square house and had already met Ma! Whatever could that mean? And why was Ma comparing him to Stanley? Surely that was not a good sign. *Oh, Elsie!* Why was she forever getting herself into these scrapes? If Elsie was indeed involved with this . . . this man, it would be Henrietta who would have to ultimately answer to Grandfather. Hadn't she assured him that by Elsie attending an all-women's college run by nuns, she would not have even the slightest chance of romantic attachments? And yet here she was, bringing home men off the streets, apparently. Where else would she have met him? It was too much, really, even for Elsie. Something was clearly wrong with her.

"What's going on, Elsie?" Henrietta finally asked, ignoring Ma's jabs at her and not caring anymore whether or not Elsie wished to speak in front of Ma. This needed to be sorted out quickly.

"Well . . . you see, Gunther here is the caretaker at Mundelein," Elsie began in a pleading tone. "Though he was once a teacher in Germany," she said, Henrietta not failing to catch the pride with which she said it—another indication that alarm might be in order. "I . . . I did try to tell you about him that day you came to say good-bye to the boys . . ." There was a trace of hope in her voice. "Remember?"

Henrietta quickly leafed through her memories of that day and only vaguely recalled something of Elsie's tale about a custodian being injured on New Year's Eve, but, admittedly, she hadn't been paying much attention at the time. It was a bad habit she had—not really listening to Elsie, she realized shamefully. It was a habit she would have to try to break.

"I think so," she said hesitantly.

"Well, you see, he came here from . . . from Germany about eight months ago looking for this little girl's mother. Not *his* little girl," she said, looking from her to him quickly, "but a little girl that was left at his mother's boardinghouse. By one of the lodgers. Her name is Liesel Klinkhammer—the mother, that is. The little girl is Anna."

Henrietta was having a hard time following.

"We need to find her, you see," Elsie rushed on. "This Liesel. So we, well, *I* thought that maybe you and Clive could help?" Elsie's voice was getting higher and more faint as she spoke. "You know, with the new detective agency," she said quietly, shooting a glance at Ma.

"Detective agency?" Ma blurted out. "I thought he gave all that up!"

"Well, sort of, but—" Henrietta began before Elsie interrupted her.

"Forget that for now, Ma! It's not important. Remember? I told you all of this before," Elsie pleaded.

Ma gave a sniff, but she fell miraculously silent, Elsie's firm handling of Ma surprising Henrietta.

"Anyway, this little Anna needs help, Henrietta. We need to find her mother."

"What sort of help?" Henrietta asked, intrigued, looking around. "Is she here as well?"

"No, she's at an orphanage on Foster Avenue."

"The Bohemian Home?" Ma broke in unexpectedly, looking up from her plate of cookies.

"That's right, Ma; it is. But she's epileptic, apparently," Elsie said, turning her attention back to Henrietta. "And they won't keep her much longer if her fits continue. They want to send her to some sort of place for the feebleminded. Like an asylum."

"It would probably be Dunning they would send her to," Ma said matter-of-factly. "That's an awful place. For anyone, much less a child."

Henrietta looked from one to the other, baffled by what was unfolding. None of this made sense. "I'm afraid I don't quite understand, Elsie. Why don't you start from the beginning?" she suggested.

"Yes, I suppose you're right," Elsie said, clasping her hands together nervously and taking a deep breath, collecting her thoughts. She then proceeded to tell Henrietta, and Ma by default, the whole of Anna's story, just as Gunther had told her, including how, based on a letter he had received from Fraulein Klinkhammer, he followed her here to Chicago. They felt it important, Elsie explained, to find this Fraulein Klinkhammer, perhaps if not to immediately reunite mother and child then to at least discover if she might be able to shed some light on Anna's epilepsy, and to likewise inquire if she herself was subject to similar episodes.

"If you could help, Mrs. Howard, in any way, I would be very much grateful. I . . . I cannot pay you just at the moment, but I will find a way," Gunther said when Elsie was finished. It was the first he had spoken since they had been introduced. "If not for me then maybe for Anna. The Bohemian Home is not so bad, though they say she cries for my mother, even still—but she cannot go to asylum. Please," he begged, looking so morose that Henrietta felt she might suddenly cry, as tears were never far from the surface these days.

"Yes, of course I'll help you," she said softly. "If I can." She paused, thinking. Could she and Clive really find this woman? It seemed an impossible task, and yet isn't this what detective work was? It might be good for Clive to have a challenge, she reasoned hopefully. Surely, he would know how to go about it. "It might be best to ask Clive," Henrietta said to Elsie.

"But don't *you* have any ideas?" Elsie asked. "Maybe just to get us started?"

Henrietta touched her finger to her lips, thinking. "Well. You say that you received one letter from Liesel while you were still in Germany, correct?" she asked Gunther.

He nodded.

"And in the letter, she says she is working at a school near Mundelein?"

Gunther nodded again. "Yes, this is why I go to Mundelein."

"Maybe she meant Loyola?" Henrietta mused. "Do you happen to have the letter with you?" she asked him.

"I did, yes, bring it," he said, reaching inside his jacket pocket and pulling out a creased envelope. He handed it carefully to Henrietta. It looked like it had been handled and read many times, its original crispness having melted now into a buttery softness. She looked it over. She could not read the address in German, which she presumed was his mother's boarding house. The stamp was American, as was the postmark.

The return address caught her eye, however.

"Look here," she said, pointing at the return. "She sent this from Mundelein, Illinois. Not Mundelein College. If she were writing from Mundelein College, the return city would be Chicago." Henrietta held out the envelope for them to see, and Gunther looked at Elsie for confirmation of Henrietta's explanation.

"Yes, you're right, of course," Elsie said excitedly. "I didn't even think to look at the envelope. Well done, Henrietta!"

Henrietta gave a little laugh, her first in a long time. "Well, I haven't found her yet, but this is a good clue, I think."

"Where is Mundelein, Illinois?" Gunther asked. "Is it close by? It is different from university?"

"Yes," answered Henrietta. "It's also the name of a town. Outside of the city. North, maybe?" she said, looking at Ma.

"Yes, it's north and west," Ma responded. "Maybe forty or fifty miles or so."

"I wonder how she got there," Henrietta contemplated as she opened the letter and quickly perused it. The ink was faint. "Why is it written in English?" she asked.

"She does not know how to read or write, I am thinking. She says in letter that she had a friend write it for her. So maybe this is problem, too, with the information. Fraulein Klinkhammer does not know English. At least she did not in Germany. She must know some little bit now, but maybe wrong thing got written down?" he suggested.

"So this isn't her handwriting, then?"

Gunther shook his head.

Henrietta gazed back at the letter and began to read.

May 10, 1933

Greetings, Mrs. Stockel,

I make it safe to America. I find job at school in Mundelein. It is school for priests. I am cleaner here. My friend Teresa Wolanski writes this for me. She is cleaner, too. I am trying to learn English, but it is hard and I am very much sick many times. I do not find Heinrich, and I do not think I will be going to. I think I have no hope to find him. I have no money to send, but I keep working to save money. I am being sorry that I go with no saying good-bye. You understand, I hope.

Liesel Klinkhammer

Henrietta looked up from the letter. Not much to go on.

"Well," she said. "I can see how the mistake was made. Although, this was written almost four years ago," she said, looking at Gunther. "You're sure no other letters came?"

Gunther shook his head. "None that I know," he said nervously.

"Well, maybe she did send more but they somehow didn't make it, or perhaps you crossed them on the voyage over."

"Maybe yes," Gunther said, but Henrietta could tell he was not convinced. He had been a teacher, Elsie had just said, and Henrietta could imagine him as such. He seemed intelligent, and the kindness she thought she had first perceived about him seemed genuine. It made her want to help him even more. She perused the letter once more.

"Let's see," she murmured. "She mentions a school for priests. That must mean a seminary. Do you know of a seminary out in Mundelein, Ma?" Henrietta asked, turning to her.

Ma shrugged. "There might be; I wouldn't know."

"Well, if she's still there, it shouldn't be too hard to find her," Henrietta said encouragingly. "Seems all we need to do is telephone this place. That or drive out there. Shouldn't be so hard," she said, though privately she confessed that not hearing from this woman in almost four years was not a good sign.

"I don't know why you're all so eager to find this woman," Ma said. "I don't think it matters all that much. Your real problem is this Anna. If she's one that has fits, it's only a matter of time before she has another, and they boot her out. That's what you should be thinking about."

"Ach. Yes, I know. You are right," Gunther said forlornly.

"Ma!" Elsie chastised her.

"Me saying it out loud doesn't change the truth," Ma retorted.

"Listen." Henrietta's tone was calm. "I'll speak to Clive tonight, and we'll either place a telephone call or drive out to Mundelein as soon as we can to investigate. Hopefully we'll uncover at least *some* information, or maybe even Liesel herself," she said, trying to give Elsie an encouraging look. "In the meantime, I'll try to think about what to do about Anna. Don't worry," she added, giving Gunther a smile. "We'll think of something. It sounds to me like she should have a full medical examination. But first thing's first."

"Oh, Henrietta! Thank you so much!" Elsie exclaimed. "That's what I thought, too."

"You're welcome," Henrietta said. "It's the least I could do." She stood up now. "I should be going. I'd like to talk to Clive about all of this and get started, and it's a long drive back."

Gunther hurriedly stood up as well. "How can I thank you, Mrs. Howard? Henrietta," he corrected himself. "I am in your debt."

Henrietta smiled and again held out her hand to him, which he again took and kissed.

"There's no need to thank me, Gunther. I'd like to help. Can I drive you back?" she asked them both, withdrawing her hand.

Gunther looked to Elsie.

"No," said Elsie, returning his glance and then looking up at Henrietta. "We . . . we want to take the bus and walk a ways."

"Do you really want to take the bus? You sure this doesn't have something to do with inconveniencing Karl?" Henrietta asked, her eyebrow arched.

"Well . . . his hip is bothering him . . ."

"Elsie! Fritz can easily take you."

"Well, we wanted to sit a while with Ma, anyway."

Henrietta sighed. "Suit yourself," she said, pulling on her gloves.

"Maybe we could have another game of rummy," Ma said eagerly, looking at Elsie and Gunther.

Henrietta swiftly looked to Elsie, who blushed profusely.

"It turns out he knows how to play rummy," she said with an embarrassed shrug. "And another game called euchre that he's teaching us."

"Can I have a word, Elsie?" Henrietta asked. "Perhaps in the foyer?"

"Yes, of course," Elsie said weakly.

"Good-bye, Ma," Henrietta said. "I'll see you soon, I'm sure. Mr. Stockel," she said inclining her head toward him. "Good day. Nice to have met you."

"Good day, Mrs. Howard. Thank you," Gunther said, still standing, and twisting his cap again. "I should go and find driver and tell him to bring the car?"

"Yes, please. That would be kind," Henrietta answered him.

Once in the hall, Henrietta turned toward Elsie, trailing along behind her.

"What is going on, Elsie?" Henrietta demanded.

"What do you mean? I . . . I just told you everything," Elsie stammered, not able to hold eye contact with Henrietta for more than a few seconds.

"You know what I mean! Do you . . . do you *care* for Gunther?" Henrietta whispered urgently.

There was silence for several moments as the two girls stared at each other.

"You do, don't you?" Henrietta said, incredulously.

Elsie bit her lip. "I . . . I think I might, Henrietta. I'm sorry," she whispered. "I can't help it."

A hundred thoughts went through Henrietta's mind as she tried to absorb this. This would never do. No one, much less Grandfather, would accept this. But she would have to tread carefully. Hadn't she resolved to help Elsie more? To listen?

"Are you sure you can't help it, dearest?" Henrietta tried to say calmly. "Because not so very long ago you were in love with Stanley and then Harrison—enough to want to throw everything away and elope with him, let's not forget. Surely you must see how this looks? And fickle is not the only word that comes to mind."

Elsie's face turned crimson, and she sighed. "I know it looks bad, Henrietta, but this is different. Truly, it is. I've . . . I've never felt this about anyone ever before," she tried to explain hurriedly. "If you only knew him, as I do, you'd see—"

"Your current feelings aside, Elsie," Henrietta interrupted, "do you know how much work I went through to get you into Mundelein?"

Elsie surprisingly shot her a look of incredulousness. "You?" she retorted hoarsely. "Yes, you stood up to Grandfather, I'll give you that—but I'm the one who did the work to get in!"

Stunned by this rare show of defiance, Henrietta had to admit that Elsie had a point. "Fair enough. But so you're just going to give all that up? Run off and marry Gunther, like Ma did with Pa? And then what? You'll be cut off, you know! Is that what you want?"

Henrietta didn't know why she was so upset, but she felt almost betrayed by Elsie, as if Elsie were her child and she was going astray. She knew she had no right to say such things to Elsie—she was practically a grown woman, and wasn't she always going on about how

Elsie should make her own choices? But yet . . . how could she just stand by and watch her throw her life away?

"No one said anything about marriage, Henrietta," Elsie said quietly. "You asked if I cared for him, and I do. Why is that such a crime?"

"Oh, Elsie," Henrietta sighed. "It's not, of course. But usually that leads to other things; of all people, you should know that. I thought you wanted an education, that you wanted a life of teaching children and being independent."

"I never said I wanted to be independent. That was you," Elsie retorted, though her voice was controlled, or perhaps just sad. "You don't have a monopoly on love, you know. Some of us get to have it, too, sometimes."

"Oh, Elsie!" Henrietta exclaimed, again feeling in danger of crying. "I—"

She was interrupted by Ma shuffling into the foyer. "You still here?" she said to Henrietta, looking out the side window panel. "Car's out there," she nodded.

"Very well," Henrietta said briskly and looked pointedly at Elsie. "I'll telephone you." Karl shuffled in then with her fur coat and hat.

"Here you are, madame," he said holding the coat for her while she slipped into it.

"Good-bye, then," Henrietta said, hastily wiping a tear from her eye. Why was she so upset?

Ma stunned her, then, by coming forward and wrapping her arms loosely around her, which was the closest Ma had ever come to a real embrace. "I'm sorry about the baby," she whispered into Henrietta's ear. "I know what it feels like to lose a child." She gave Henrietta a squeeze before she pulled back.

Fresh tears formed in Henrietta's eyes, momentarily blurring her vision. So touched was she by her mother's rare words of sympathy that a whole torrent of tears threatened to burst from her. Fiercely, she kept them at bay, however, though her throat ached from the effort.

"You'll be all right," said Ma in rare, kind voice. "You always are."

Henrietta managed a faint smile. "Thanks, Ma," she said and, not knowing what else to do, hurried out the door.

Chapter 4

Rose banged on the door, waiting. She was unfortunately wearing high heels, and the freezing slush she had waded through on her way to Lucy's and Gwen's had leaked into every crevice, rubbing her feet raw and numbing them. In fact, she could barely feel them at this point. She chastised herself for not grabbing her boots when she had fled the house, Billy with her, but she hadn't been thinking clearly.

"Lucy!" Rose called, as she banged again. She felt she might cry at any minute, but she knew it would set Billy off, so she closed her eyes and tried to remain calm. Her father was at it again. Drinking. There was rarely a night these days that he wasn't drinking.

His drunken rages had been bad enough to endure when they only happened a couple of times a week—usually Wednesdays because it was poker night at Lou's, the bar just down the street, and Fridays because it was the day he got his paycheck. But now it was almost every night. Invariably on those nights, he would stumble home and in a slurred voice, demand his dinner, though Rose and Billy had already meagerly eaten theirs hours earlier. Rose would obey, however, and hurry to set down before him the plate she had kept warm in the oven. But it was always a crap shoot as to how he would respond. Usually he would devour it, some of it inevitably spilling down the front of him. But sometimes he would find some small thing to object to on the plate, such as there being too much gravy, or not enough gravy, or that the beef was too dry, or that he didn't like peas (even though he did). It could be anything, in fact—any small minutia had the potential to cause him to suddenly pick up the plate and hurl the whole thing at the wall.

Rose wanted to cry each time this happened, not because of the shock of it (not anymore, anyway) or the mess she would have to clean up, but because of the awful waste of food. After he eventually passed out, she and Billy would sometimes pick through the broken shards of smashed pottery for any salvageable chunks of food, especially the meat. Rose had become rather adept at brushing off small shards of glass or crockery and had only a couple of times cut the inside of her mouth as a result of their salvaging. Sometimes, though, it was hopeless, and nothing could be saved.

Rose had learned early on, when she had taken over the role of cooking after her mother died when she was just seven, not to serve him anything besides meat, potato, and a vegetable, if she had enough money to get some. A couple of times, however, when the groceries and the money were running low, she had attempted to serve him eggs or even tuna salad, but the result had been fury and rage, with her father screaming that it wasn't a fit dinner for a working man.

These dinner rants were usually followed by an Act Two of sorts, which consisted of a volley of obscenities, aimed sometimes at her but more often than not at Billy, his backward son, whom he especially seemed to despise. Billy did not ever appear affected by his father's verbal abuse, however, and would dumbly take it, after which he would go upstairs to his room and whittle, emitting a sort of droning, humming noise as he did so and rocking back and forth. It drove Rose crazy, his constant humming, but she never tried to stop him, as she suspected it was his only way of coping.

When they were little, when their mother was still alive, her father never hit Billy, though he had shoved him up against the wall plenty of times, usually because of some mistake Billy inevitably made, either in what he said or didn't say, or what he accidentally did, like knock something over, or didn't do, like forgetting to fill the coal bucket. Recently, however, perhaps due to the increased drinking, something seemed to have worsened in her father's deranged mind, and he had taken to beating Billy on a regular basis.

Billy was a large, beefy twenty year old, with thick arms and matching thick lips. And while her father was not a small man by any means, perhaps he had never initially hit Billy out of some unconscious fear, as Billy was easily twice the size of him and had been since he was fourteen. But something lately had made him lash out at Billy for the first time, to actually strike him across his thick cheeks, and Billy had not fought back. He had just stood there like a dumb animal, like a cow, Rose had thought in the moment, taking the abuse without a word, which seemed to have fueled their father's rage all the more. And now it had become part of the routine. First a torrent of verbal abuse, then the violence, often involving him taking off his belt to whip Billy, not satisfied until some sort of blood was drawn.

Tonight had been particularly bad. It was the usual scene unfolding, Rose watching from the corner, unable to say anything to stop it. She had tried that before, but it only made it worse for Billy. Tonight, however, after he had hit Billy a number of times about the head, Billy had sunk to his knees and tried for the first time to block the blows with one of his arms, emitting a simple "please," as if he were still a little boy, his face scrunched up as if he were going to cry. This desperate begging had touched something off in Rose, and she felt her own fury erupt. Without really thinking about it, she had grabbed a frying pan and hit her father on the back of the head with it as hard as she could and watched, with equal parts satisfaction and horror, as he slid to the floor.

With shaking hands, she stumbled across the room and put the pan back in the oven, hoping that he wouldn't remember what had hit him when he woke up in the morning. She helped Billy to his feet, then, bundled him in his coat and dragged him out into the freezing late February air, though he protested loudly. She had barely put anything on herself, but she did not feel the cold; she was sweating and panicked. Even Billy's hand felt hot in hers as she pulled him along Damen Avenue. She didn't really have a plan—all she knew was that she had to get Billy out of that house. She would not stand for it one more minute.

Two blocks into the escape, however, it occurred to her that now that her father was knocked out, they could have remained in the house in relative safety for the night. She paused at the corner of Damen and Waveland, wondering if they should go back. After all, how could Lucy and Gwen really help her at this point? But she had imagined an escape so many times, and now that she had dared to begin it, she didn't want to retreat, though she realized regretfully, their breath crystalizing around them as she hesitated, that she hadn't really planned it out all that well, after all. Well, it was too late now, she decided, and trudged on, still pulling Billy—who had begun the awful droning—along behind her down the remaining streets until she reached Lucy and Gwen's apartment building on Evergreen, just off Damen.

"Gwen!" she tried shouting, and just as she was about to bang again, a bleary-eyed Lucy opened the door, pulling her robe tighter around her upon feeling the blast of cold air.

"Rose? What are you doing here? What happened?" she asked, her eyes looking over the hulking Billy, his nose and part of his forehead caked with frozen blood. "Get in here; come on," she said, opening the door.

The two of them shuffled inside.

Gwen appeared from down the hallway dressed in men's pajamas. "What's going on, Luce? Jesus, Rose, what happened?"

"Let me guess," Lucy said bitterly, helping Billy out of his coat. "Here, Bill, sit down on the sofa there," she said, pointing to it, though he instead hunkered down into the armchair next to it, as if he hadn't heard her.

"It's a shame we don't have a fireplace, just those stupid things," Lucy said, nodding at the radiator under the front window.

"And our ass landlord controls the heat, so that's why it's fucking freezing in here," Gwen added.

"It doesn't matter," Rose said morosely. "Do you have a wet towel maybe?"

"Sure, Rose. Just a minute."

Lucy headed off to the kitchen, which lay behind a thick, battered swinging door.

"He at it again, poor kid?" Gwen asked, pulling Rose over to the couch.

"I'm sorry to bother you," Rose said, her voice unsteady as she collapsed in a heap on the sofa and tried to hold back her tears. "I didn't know what else to do."

"Hey, kid, it's okay," Gwen said, rubbing her back. "We don't mind, do we, Luce?" she said to Lucy, who had just come in with a tray of mismatched mugs.

"Course we don't," Lucy said, setting the tray down in front of them. "I put some coffee on. Here," she said, handing Rose a wet rag. "For him," she said, nodding toward Billy. "I'd do it, but I don't think he'll let me."

"No, he won't. Thanks, Lucy," Rose said, wiping her eyes with the back of her hand and getting to her feet. She stood in front of Billy and tapped her knuckle under his chin so that he tipped his head, the back of which she cradled with one hand while she began to gingerly dab his nose and then the gash above his right eye.

"No!" he roared, pulling back.

"Bill!" she said in a firm voice. "Sit still now. This'll just take a minute. Be a good boy." Her voice quieted as she dabbed. "Shhh . . . that's it. Hold still. Good boy. Jesus," she said, wincing. "Gwen—do you think this needs a stitch?"

Gwen got up and peered at the wound. "Probably. But he'll live without it. It'll be a bad scar, but it don't matter on a man."

Lucy disappeared and reappeared with some cotton and tape. "Sorry we don't have anything else," she said, holding it out to Rose.

"This'll do fine, Luce, thanks. I should have grabbed something on the way out, but I didn't think. Here, Billy, you hold this," she said, handing him the wet rag. "Sit still. Don't move." Gingerly, she placed the cotton squares on his wound while Lucy ripped off strips of brown tape and handed them to her. "Billy! Don't suck it!" Rose said, referring to the wet rag, the corner of which Billy had just put in his mouth. Billy ignored her, however, and went on sucking while Rose applied the tape.

"Give me that," Rose said, pulling the rag from his mouth and using it to wipe the dried blood from his nose, though he tried to pull back. "Billy! Sit still. Almost done." She dabbed quickly. "There now," she said softly, when she had removed most of it. "Good as new. Just sit there." She took a step back from him, observing him, as if to detect any other wounds she should bind. She was sure there were plenty of wounds and old scars in his simple mind, but she couldn't do anything about those. "I said don't suck it!" she chastised him, but he kept the end of the rag in his mouth anyway, making him resemble a large, overgrown dog.

"Oh, I don't care what you do," she sighed and sank back onto the sofa next to Gwen.

"I'll get him a drink," Lucy said, hurrying off toward the kitchen. "The coffee should be ready by now anyway."

Lucy came back in carrying a coffee pot and a glass of water, which she handed to Billy. Eagerly, he drank down the whole thing at once. She poured the coffee into the three waiting mugs on the table and handed one each to Rose and Gwen, and then balanced herself on the arm of the sofa beside Gwen, as there were no other chairs. "Sorry we don't have any cream. All out until we get paid next."

"That's okay. Black's fine," Rose said, staring at hers instead of drinking it. The three of them sat in silence for a few moments until Rose finally spoke. "I didn't know what else to do," Rose said, looking at both of them. "He was . . . he was terrible tonight. Like he was possessed or something."

"And he's not usually terrible?" Gwen asked, piqued.

"Tonight was different," Rose said, glancing over at Billy.

"How'd you get away?" Lucy asked, her long blonde hair tied up in a simple ribbon behind her head.

"I hit him with a frying pan," Rose said solemnly.

"Thatta girl!" Gwen said fervently. "You should have killed him and said that it was an accident. That he slipped and fell and hit his head."

"Gwen!" exclaimed Rose, though it was unsettling to hear the thing she herself had thought of a hundred times said out loud—and by someone other than herself.

"Good riddance to the bastard. You'd be doing humanity a favor, the way I see it. The sooner he's off the earth the better."

"Gwen!" Rose admonished again, nodding her head toward Billy, who was rocking now, staring forward and sucking on the wet rag covered in dark-brown bloodstains.

"One of these days," Gwen said in a low voice, "he's going to cross my path, and I really will fucking kill the fucking bastard. Just like that."

"How?" Rose said, actually a little curious.

"Gwen, come on," Lucy interjected. "Knock it off. What are you going to do, Rose?"

"Can Billy stay here?" she asked hesitantly. "Just for a little bit?"

Lucy looked over at Gwen.

"Well, sure, sweets," Lucy said with just a trace of hesitation as she looked back at Rose. "But not permanent, right? Not that we mind, but . . . you know . . . we all work crazy hours, and Bill, while being a fine man," she said in his direction, "isn't exactly self-sufficient, is he?" she whispered, this last bit at Rose. "Know what I mean?"

"That, and, like I said before, our landlord is a real jerk, and if he found out we had a guy living here with us, he'll charge us extra. That or kick us out. He's an ass like that."

"No, not permanent! Of course not," Rose said hurriedly. "But . . . just until I can figure something out . . . "

"Like what?"

"I don't know," Rose sighed. "Something."

Out of the corner of her eye, she saw Lucy look over at Gwen, and she felt a corresponding knot in her stomach. They were obviously uncomfortable keeping Billy, but what could she do? "I'll come over early in the mornings and get him off to work," she said quickly. "He knows the way to work from our place, but he might be confused from here, at least at first. He won't be any trouble, will you, Billy?" she said to him. "You want to stay here tonight, Billy? Have a visit with Aunty Gwen and Aunty Lucy?"

Billy snapped out of whatever daydream he appeared to have been in and looked at Rose, fear and distrust writ large across his face. He was so like a lost child most of the time that her heart skipped a beat every time he looked at her like that, with that pleading sort of panic.

"You're staying, too, right, Rosie?" he said thickly.

"No, I've got to go back and look after Dad. But I'll come back in the morning."

"I don't want to stay without you, Rosie," he whined.

"Hey, Bill, I'll make apple fritters in the morning," Lucy said temptingly. "You'd like that, right? Nice and warm and gooey . . . "

Billy's face cracked a smile as he nodded at her.

"And Aunty Gwen will tell you a story, won't you, Aunty Gwen?"

Gwen shot Lucy a quick, annoyed look before she turned toward Billy and gave him a big, false smile. "Sure I will, kid," she said. "It's the one about Little Red Riding Hood and the wolf that gets boiled in a pot of water at the end."

"You're mixing up your fairy tales, Gwen," Lucy commented.

"So?"

"See, Billy?" Rose broke in, ignoring them. "This won't be so bad, right?"

"Okay," he said dully, sucking the rag again.

"Maybe you should stay, too, Rose," Lucy said quietly. "Sure you'll be all right?"

"Yeah, I think so. I've got to go back and clean everything up, so he hopefully won't know what happened. Somehow get him up to bed."

"Sure he won't take a swing at you? Billy won't be there, you know, to deflect it . . . "

"Nah, I'll be okay."

In truth, she *was* a little bit apprehensive to go back, but she knew it would be worse if he woke up that way. Normally, he didn't hit her, though he had taken off his belt to her many times in her room for a different reason, even as a girl, and she had learned early a different meaning of misery and despair.

As she grew older, she finally grew bold enough to lock her door and burrow deeper under her thin quilt each time she heard him try the handle of her door. He would bang on it, then, which would sometimes cause Billy to shuffle from his room and stand in the hallway, looking at him with his usual dumb expression on his face.

"Go back to bed, Billy," their father would snarl. "This don't concern you."

"No," Billy would say, resolutely.

"You don't say 'no' to me, you fuck," her father would say, or something similar, and then usually shoved him up against the wall. But it was enough to distract him from Rose, and once he stumbled off to bed, Billy would disappear back into his room. She had tried sometimes to whisper *thanks* to Billy before he retreated, nervously poking her head out from behind the door, but he always refused to look at her, as if he felt ashamed for her.

This had worked for a while, but in a mad fury one night he ended up kicking her door in—despite Billy's attempts to stop him—and shattered the wood holding the lock, rendering it useless from that point on. She had no choice but to submit to him that night, but after that, she had gotten the gun. It was just a little thing; a Baby Browning that she had bought at a hardware store, but it shot real bullets just the same. She had pulled it out from under her pillow one night, her hands shaking as she pulled the hammer back, and he had just laughed. His smirk turned to rage, however, when she actually fired it and a bullet whizzed past him, and even now was lodged in the plaster of her bedroom wall. He had stood there, stunned, and in his fury took another step closer to her. But when she fired a second time, this one barely missing him, he finally left, calling her a "stupid bitch." He hadn't ever tried to come into her room again, but she still found it hard to sleep deeply most nights.

"Still got the gun?" Gwen oddly asked her, as if reading her thoughts.

"No, I lent it to Henrietta, remember?" Rose answered.

"Shit, you can't go back there then!"

"It'll be all right. He doesn't know I don't have it. He won't try anything more tonight."

"You need to get that thing back."

"Yes, I know. But I don't have a telephone, remember? And in case you haven't noticed, we don't exactly run in the same circles. Our butler just quit," she said, attempting a weak joke.

"I'll telephone her tomorrow for you," Lucy said anxiously.

"Thanks, Lucy. But that's the least of my worries these days."

Gwen took a big drink of her coffee. "Yeah, what about the dope? Can't he do somethin' to help?"

"Don't call him that, Gwen," she said, giving a warning nod of her head toward Billy, who, though sitting straight up, had his eyes closed. "Stan's all right, you know. For a guy."

"Still gonna marry him?"

"Of course, I'm still going to marry him. What choice do I have?"

Gwen seemed about to retort but stopped when Lucy gave her a quick shake of her head.

"Like turning tricks?" Rose asked bitterly. "No—I can't do that anymore. I think that's when he started beating Billy. Like he knew somehow. It's too risky; it's like playing roulette."

"You could live with us," Lucy offered.

"Yeah? With Billy?" she asked wryly.

Neither Lucy nor Gwen said anything to that.

"Nah, it's better to marry Stan," Rose went on, their silence adding to a sadness she barely knew she felt. "He's a good enough guy."

"Does he . . . does he know everything?" Lucy asked quietly.

"Not everything, but enough. He's not exactly prince charming; he's more the woodsman that comes along and saves Red Riding Hood, kind of by accident, if we're talking fairy tales. It's not really what he set out to do, but something he stumbled upon. He's trying to do the right thing."

"But are you?" Gwen asked.

"Oh, just lay off, Gwen. I'm doin' the best I can."

"Well, sor-ry. I gotta ask, though. What kind of friend would I be if I didn't?"

Rose chose not to answer.

"Come on, don't be sore," Gwen urged. "What are you going to do about Billy? Is he going to move in with you two once you're hitched?"

"Of course, he is. That's the whole point."

"Does the dope know that?"

Rose hesitated. "I think so."

"When you gonna inform him?"

"I'll get to it eventually, Gwen," Rose said, standing up now. "Anyway, I'd better go."

"Still aiming for a June wedding?" Lucy asked.

"I guess so. His parents approve of me, apparently. Just . . . " She gave a small curtsey. "I'm supposed to convert so we can get married at his church." She shrugged as she buttoned up her coat. "It don't matter to me. Whatever I need to do, I'll do."

She walked over and kissed Billy on the cheek. "Bye, Billy," she said as he sleepily opened his eyes. "See you in the morning, okay?" She rubbed his short stubble of hair, another thing their father insisted on—that Billy have a shaved head at all times. Billy hated it, though, and screamed every time Rose brought out the scissors or the razor, making Rose wonder if her father insisted on it just to torture him. Billy reached up and put his arms around her neck as she bent toward him and held on tight.

"Bye, Rosie," he said sadly, not letting go. Finally Rose had to unhook his arms from around her neck, giving him a quick kiss on the head as she did so. She picked up her wet coat she had dropped on the floor when they came in and shrugged back into it.

"Thanks, girls," she said as she buttoned it. "Be back in a few hours."

"Be careful," Lucy said as Rose tugged open the door and stepped out into the freezing air.

Chapter 5

"Ah, darling, there you are," Clive said as he entered their small sitting room in the east wing of Highbury, the whole of which had been converted for their private use upon their marriage. "I wasn't sure you'd be back in time for dinner."

"Yes, I wasn't sure, either," Henrietta said, unpinning her hat. "I've only just arrived. I'm glad I did, however, as Edna informs me that Bennett will be dining tonight. I would hate to leave your mother outnumbered," she added with a smile.

"Bennett?"

"Yes, I assumed you had asked him."

"No, I didn't. That's odd. Maybe he's stopped by with some documents for me," Clive said, letting out a sigh and running a hand through his hair. "Well, whatever it is, it can wait. I'll investigate later. How about a drink before we dress?" he asked tentatively.

"Yes, all right. Maybe a small sherry."

"I've had rather an interesting day," he continued, leading the way to their small sitting room, which already had a low fire burning in the grate. Clive strode toward the fireplace and, taking a poker from the stand, jostled some life into the flames. He turned to look at Henrietta staring out the garret window at the darkness beyond. He was unsure of how to proceed, how to bring up the case.

"It's getting darker later each day, isn't it?" Henrietta said, turning toward him now. "I simply can't wait for spring." A small smile crept across her face as she stepped forward to take the glass of sherry he had poured for her. She seemed in a better mood than she had been in a long time.

"Did you enjoy your trip into the city?" he asked, encouraged, taking a sip of brandy from his thick, crystal glass.

When she proposed a visit to her mother and Elsie following a telephone call she had gotten not two days ago from Elsie, he wasn't sure it was what she needed at the moment. Usually trips to see her mother left her disquieted or depressed. But Henrietta had been insistent that Elsie needed her help with something, and he didn't want to thwart her, as it was the first thing she had shown any interest in since before the mishap. However, he had foreseen the possibility that it could go rather badly, as it usually did.

"I did in fact," she said with a mysterious smile. "But you first. You said you had an interesting day."

"Well," he said, turning toward the radio set and absently rubbing the top of it. "As it turns out, I've been to see Davis this afternoon."

"Oh, you should have told me! I would have liked to come, too."

"He's out of the hospital now and back to work."

"Oh, I see. How is he?" she asked, concerned.

"Seems all right. Usual scruffy self. Turns out he has a case he'd like us to look into," he said, taking care to use the word "us."

"He does?" She seemed skeptical.

"Well, yes." Clive tried to sound convincing, hoping she couldn't already see through this ruse. "He's asked for our help."

"Why doesn't he just investigate it? Or the chief, for that matter?"

"Well," Clive scrambled. "You know what the chief's like. And Davis claims it's not really a case for the police, so he naturally thought of us."

"Well, it must not be all that serious, then," Henrietta said with a shrug.

"Well, I wouldn't say that. Just a bit . . . unconventional perhaps."

This was certainly not the reaction he had been expecting from her. He had thought she would be thrilled to have a case before them. Maybe she had changed her mind about detective work . . .

"Such as?" Henrietta asked, raising an eyebrow at him.

"It has to do with some sort of spiritualist, apparently," Clive responded, deciding just to plunge straight into it.

"A spiritualist?"

"Yes, a man by the name of Tobin came into the station the other day. Spoke to Davis, thank God, and not the chief, claiming that some spiritualist his wife's been seeing has 'hypnotized her'— I think his words were—into packing up her jewelry and carting it off to her."

"Is that a crime, though?"

"Well, not enough for the police to get involved," said Clive, taking another drink. "But Davis suspects a fraud. A charlatan, obviously, taking advantage of people's gullibility. Might be underhanded. These things usually are."

"I see," Henrietta mused.

"As he's just getting back to work, Davis says he's got several things to look into and is still not fully recovered. The doctors have advised him to take it slowly, not take on a full load right at the beginning . . . but it seems the chief wants him back in action." Clive hoped she would believe him. "So he thought maybe we could help. I suppose we owe him, don't we?" he managed to say in a rueful tone. "It'll probably turn out to be nothing, but we should check it out, don't you think? Maybe drive out there tomorrow?" He watched her carefully out of the corner of his eye.

"Yes, of course we should help Frank," she said, biting her lip and looking into the fire.

Why did she always call him Frank? Clive wondered. Ever since the Neptune incident when the two of them had paired together to rescue Clive from Neptune's grasp, she had become very familiar with Davis in a way he wasn't always comfortable with. He understood why, of course, but it had irritated him when she had insisted on going to see him so many times in the hospital, bringing him flowers and chocolates. As if a man liked those things, anyway.

But now was not the time to bring up all of that.

"I'm not sure we'll have time, though," she answered, looking up at him.

"What do you mean, darling?" he said, his brow furrowed. "We have plenty of time."

"Well, as it turns out, I've found a case as well. It's a missing person's case. And it's very interesting, Clive."

Clive groaned internally. This must be what Elsie had called about for help. It explained Henrietta's chipper mood upon returning from the visit. He so badly wanted to make a sarcastic comment about it being a "missing" college student who would undoubtedly turn up in a couple of days, having successfully slept off a particularly bad bout of drunkenness, but he managed to resist the temptation. "Oh?" he said, with passing sincerity.

"Yes," Henrietta went on enthusiastically. "It seems Elsie has gotten involved with the custodian at Mundelein, who finds himself in a bit of trouble."

"What do you mean *involved*? Please tell me you don't mean romantically?" he said with a sigh.

What was it about Elsie that seemed to attract these rather precarious predicaments? he wondered. Granted she appeared to have lost quite a bit of weight from the time he had first met her, but she still had a large build, so unlike Henrietta's. They looked nothing alike. And since Agatha Exley had gotten ahold of Elsie, she had certainly smartened up. Her clothes were stylish now, and with the way she did her hair these days, she could almost pass for pretty in a certain way. So why did she seem to always be a target for men who wished her harm? He supposed it was either the lure of the Exley money or the prospect of an easy conquest, as Elsie practically oozed naiveté and gullibility. It made sense that she was constantly being taken advantage of. Though he hated to admit it, Clive, like Oldrich Exley, had hoped that by Elsie attending Mundelein, there would be an end to such affairs. But apparently not. He was learning that nothing about Henrietta's family was predictable—except that they were unpredictable.

"Well, it may have strayed in that direction," Henrietta answered, "but that's not the trouble, at least not yet, if I can help it."

"I beg to differ, but go on; enlighten me."

Henrietta then proceeded to share the whole long story regarding Gunther and Liesel and Anna, though she was not as clear on how Elsie had gotten mixed up in it all. "It's obvious, though, that there's been some sort of miscommunication. The poor man has been working at Mundelein College, looking for this Liesel woman, who all the while has been somewhere in Mundelein, Illinois."

"Hmm. Most likely the seminary out there."

"You know it?" Henrietta asked eagerly.

"Know *of* it. Never actually been there," he said with a tilt of his head, "not ever having the 'calling,' shall we say, to become a priest."

"Well, perhaps we could go and check it out. See if we can find her. What do you think?"

Clive paused, thinking. Four years was a long time not to have heard any news, and he unfortunately did not share Henrietta's optimism that this woman might still be there. More than anything else, this had the flavor of someone who didn't want to be found. Yet, he hated to dampen her spirits. "I suppose we could," he said slowly, rubbing his chin. "But I'm not sure finding this Liesel is going to help matters. Seems to me, this Gunther has more of a problem of what to do with the child."

"Oddly, that's what my mother said. And Gunther agreed, poor man."

"You've met him?" Clive asked, intrigued.

"Yes, he was at the Palmer Square house when I went today. Elsie brought him along."

"What's he like? Seem on the level?"

"Yes, actually. He's rather nice. He speaks English very well. He was a teacher or a professor or something in Germany."

Clive let out a deep breath. A German. Of course, it had to be a German just to make things more unpleasant, Clive thought disgustedly. He took another drink of his brandy. He knew it was wrong to continue to have a prejudice against Germans as a whole—but it was difficult after everything he had been through in the war, all the atrocities he had witnessed. As a detective on the force in Chicago, however, he had many times had to look past many things he hadn't agreed with, and this was no different. He forced himself to put it in the background.

"Well," he said, clearing his throat, "it seems we have our day planned out for us."

"So, we're going to do it?" Henrietta asked excitedly. "We're actually going to go looking for her?"

"Why not?" Clive said, unable to deny her and hopeful that she might finally be on the mend.

"But what about this other case, this spiritualist case?" Henrietta asked. "Are you going to take that one as well?"

"That's up to you."

"It's *your* agency," Henrietta said, looking up at him.

"No, it's *our* agency," Clive corrected her.

A smile crossed Henrietta's face. "Well, I suppose we shouldn't let Frank down," she said thoughtfully, "should we?"

"No," he replied, wondering if she were teasing him. "Indeed not."

"I'm not sure it will really lead to anything, but I think he really needs us, don't you?" she asked innocently.

As much as he had been trying to hold back from touching her with any degree of intimacy these past weeks, Clive could not help but reach out and stroke her cheek with the back of his finger. "Must we talk of Davis?" he said, his voice thick. He was finding it hard to control his rising desire for her.

Henrietta's brow furrowed. "Are you jealous?" she asked, her tone incredulous, but he thought he saw her old mirth hovering about her eyes. Clive pulled his attention from them to her very pink lips. He so badly wanted to taste them, to hold her, to cup her breasts in his hands, but she had rebuffed his advances a number of times now and he had no wish to be a brute—as his mother had so grossly put it—nor to break the fragile camaraderie that had sprouted between them just now. But she was seeming so much like her old self . . . even to the point, he could swear, of giving him that look of longing that she so often used when she wanted him to take her in his arms. But he didn't want to be wrong . . .

Before he could decide how to proceed, however, she placed the tips of her fingers on his chest, sending an electric shock through him. She further surprised him by leaning forward and brushing her lips against his.

"Make love to me, Inspector," she whispered, and he thought he might explode right then and there. Instantly, he wrapped his arms around her and kissed her tenderly, then gradually with more pressure, the taste of her lips exciting him and making him want more.

"Oh God, Henrietta, I've wanted you so badly," he said between kisses, his fingers eventually making their way to the buttons on her blouse.

"Yes, it's been too long," she said intoxicatingly. "Oh Clive," she groaned, as his hands found their way under her brassiere while she undid his tie and opened his shirt, kissing his chest. He pulled back and, shaking a bit, shrugged out of his shirt and unfastened his belt as she slipped out of her skirt.

"Shall we go into the bedroom?" she whispered.

"No," he said, pulling her toward the large couch perched in front of the fire. "I can't wait that long."

"This is quite risqué, Inspector," Henrietta said with a delicious smile, as he pulled her down on top of him. Her auburn hair was splayed out against the pale skin of her bare shoulders. She looked like a heavenly vision to him. An angel. He took her face in his hands and kissed her.

"What if the servants come in?" she asked, breathlessly, through his kisses.

"I don't care," Clive said, moving to her neck.

"Oh Clive, I've missed this." She arched her body toward him.

"The feeling's mutual." He grunted and shifted his body, rather skillfully, he thought, if he did say so, so that she'd be under him, a position he much preferred. He felt his heart speed up when he felt her arms roam his back now. *God, he couldn't get enough of her.* He ran his hand down her thigh and back up again, stopping at the top of her stockings to insert his finger inside the lace at the top. He looked down into her eyes and kissed her again, softly, trying to slow this down. But when she bit his bottom lip, he felt a tremor roar through him. He instinctively moved his hand to her underthings, tugging at them until they were around her knees.

"Clive, don't rip them; they're new," she panted.

"I'll buy you some new ones," he mumbled as his fingers slipped into the soft place between her legs, feeling the delicious warmth of her. She groaned, and he felt himself stiffen even more. He didn't know how much longer he could stand it. Accordingly, he abandoned her lower regions and shifted his attention to her breasts instead, cupping them and kissing her stiff nipples.

"Oh, Clive, don't stop," she moaned. She moved her hands from his hair, where they had been delightfully entwined, down to his chest, and then lower still, taking him in hand so that he was in imminent danger of losing control completely. He kissed her hard, his hand returning to her warm spot until she was squirming under him and moaning. "Clive, please," she begged.

She opened herself to him, and he eased himself in. She felt so deliciously good that he almost erupted right then, but he controlled himself by breathing deeply and pulling himself away from her lips. Once he had regained a small measure of control, he cupped her breasts, determined to please her. He began to slowly thrust, rubbing her nipples and kissing her neck until quickly and almost effortlessly, he brought her to a moaning climax, which was quickly followed by his own shuddering explosion.

Breathing heavily, he lay on top of her for a few glorious moments before he raised himself up and showered her face and neck and shoulders with tiny kisses.

"God, I love you, Henrietta," he said through his kisses. "You mean everything to me, you know." He looked into her eyes.

"I love you, too, Clive," she said, panting slightly, a lazy smile crossing her face as she traced his jaw with her finger. "I've missed you."

"That's an understatement," he mumbled.

Unexpectedly, she laughed, and he joined in. He felt light and almost giddy at the fact that they seemed back at the place they had been at the very beginning, only closer somehow, if that were possible.

He shifted his weight to squeeze beside her. "I was just thinking that—" he began, but broke off and became suddenly still. He could swear he heard something outside in the hallway. He froze, listening.

"What is it, Clive?" Henrietta stiffened and looked at him with concern.

"Go away, Billings," Clive said loudly toward the door, while Henrietta quickly reached for something to cover herself. He nearly laughed again when he saw that what she held was one of the embroidered pillows that had been earlier tossed to the floor in their haste.

"Very good, sir," came Billings's nasal drone from the other side of the door.

"How could you hear him?" Henrietta whispered.

"Years of growing up in this house, listening to Billings creep around," he muttered. "Tell my mother we won't be dining tonight," he said, raising his voice to a shout again. "We're indisposed!" He looked down at Henrietta and kissed one of her breasts. Henrietta stifled a laugh.

"Very good, sir." There was a short pause. "Shall I have a tray sent up, sir?"

"Yes," Clive shouted back. "With lots of champagne!"

"Very good, sir."

Clive heard him move away, and he relaxed, rubbing his fingers along her arm.

"This is very wicked of us, Clive. What about Bennett? Now your poor mother is going to have to entertain him on her own. Perhaps we really should go down."

"Oh, she can handle him. Anyway, it was probably she who asked him to stay to dinner in the first place. Serves her right."

"Well, make sure it's not me who gets the blame," she said, running her finger over his lips as he kissed the tips of them.

"Of course not, darling," he said flippantly. "And anyway, we're still newlyweds, after all. We're allowed a bit of 'indisposition,' I should think."

"Naughty!" she said, pinching him.

"Minx!" he shot back, kissing her again, his hand running down her leg. "I'll just have to teach you a lesson . . . " he said, joy filling his heart that she was back.

"All right, then," she responded with a sly smile. "Do."

Chapter 6

Early the next morning, Clive and Henrietta bundled up into Clive's Alfa Romeo and headed up Highway 41 toward St. Mary of the Lake Seminary in Mundelein, Illinois. It was fortunate that Antonia had at least a periodic need to be driven about, thus thankfully requiring the services of poor Fritz, who might otherwise be left with precious little to do but to wash and polish the many cars of Alcott's collection—all of which stood in mint condition in the garage, Antonia insisting that not one be sold, even after his untimely death.

Clive still steadfastly refused to be driven around by a chauffeur, unless he was going to a board meeting at Linley Standard, having reluctantly acknowledged that it would never do for the chairman of the board to arrive downtown in something so crass as a sports car, and that certain appearances must be maintained. Plus, being driven by Fritz in the Rolls to the few meetings at which his attendance was unavoidably required gave him time to read through the various reports he was supposed to have studied ahead of time in preparation. Bennett always briefed him, of course, but Clive liked to have his own sense of things if he could.

Clive and Henrietta had decided to tackle the German case first (as they were calling the Elsie-Gunther affair), it seeming the more urgent of the two, as the fate of a little girl was potentially hanging on its resolution. Henrietta, assuming it was a simple case of crossed wires, half expected to find Fraulein Klinkhammer this very morning, though Clive was annoyingly persistent, in Henrietta's opinion, anyway, in taking a more pessimistic view, repeatedly saying that four years was a long time. Henrietta managed to ignore this, however, and was looking forward to telling Fraulein Klinkhammer that her child was indeed on these shores and in fact very near to her. Many times, she imagined the joy that would fill this poor woman's face, and she felt an unexplained eagerness to give her this gift, to reunite the lost mother with her child. There was something noble, she couldn't help but feel, in giving someone else the very thing she herself had been denied.

The drive started out quietly, Henrietta taking an unexpected pleasure in watching the scenery pass by as Clive expertly drove, his pipe gripped between his teeth. She had never been this far north before and wondered, as the many villages and tiny towns slipped past, what it would be like to live in such a rural setting. She didn't think she would like it, she decided; she was too much of a city girl. This had more the flavor of Elsie to it. Winnetka was as far north as she wanted to go, though Highbury, she admitted, was growing on her. As was the eccentric, privileged life she had taken up with Clive, despite her early misgivings and their early trials.

"Shouldn't be too much farther," Clive said, breaking in on her thoughts, as they finally turned off the highway onto Route 176. "According to Fritz, the seminary's on this road, a little ways past Libertyville. So keep your eyes open."

"Are you sure?" Henrietta asked, looking out the window at the farms passing by. "It looks like we're in the middle of nowhere."

"Well, why don't you check the map, then," Clive suggested archly, nodding at the map that lay on the seat between them.

Henrietta did not have much experience reading maps, but she decided she would try. She picked it up and began to unfold it—gingerly, when it became apparent that its pages were brittle. "This looks a little old," she said, attempting to further open the map without tearing it.

"It *is* unfortunately. It's Fritz's, of course. Hopelessly ancient. Most of his maps are from before the bloody war, I imagine," he said, removing his pipe momentarily. "I would have purchased a new one if I'd had time. Still, I'm sure it will do the trick. The seminary isn't marked, but it's supposed to be somewhere between Libertyville and Mundelein by a big lake—hence the name—so look for that."

"You know, it's no wonder that Gunther and Fraulein Klinkhammer couldn't find each other," Henrietta said as she worked.

"What do you mean?"

"Well, there's Mundelein the town, Mundelein the seminary, and Mundelein College in Chicago. It really lacks imagination, don't you think?"

Clive let out a little chuckle. "Yes, I suppose you could say that."

Henrietta studied the map, now finally unfolded, in front of her. "Actually," she said after a moment, "I don't see Mundelein at all." She traced the road that was 176 west across the page with her finger. "After Libertyville is a town called AREA, it looks like. Written in capital letters."

"Ah, yes. I forgot about that," Clive said, slowing down now that they had entered Libertyville proper. Henrietta looked out the windows and thought it looked rather quaint. She wished they had time to stop and maybe walk through some of the shops.

"According to Fritz, there was some sort of business school out here," Clive went on. "The founder was a quack who persuaded the town to change its name to match the school's motto, which was AREA."

"Area?"

"Apparently, it stands for ability, reliability, endurance, and action."

"Are you teasing me?"

"No!" Clive said with a grin. "Unless Fritz was teasing *me*. Anyway, the school folded, and Cardinal Mundelein arranged for the church to buy it and all the surrounding land to expand their seminary. So the town changed its name again."

"Well, I suppose they knew what side *their* bread was buttered on," Henrietta said practically.

Clive laughed out loud. "Darling, wherever do you come up with these rustic turns of phrase? Someone might easily confuse you with a peasant. You really should make up your mind which you're to be."

Henrietta wanted to laugh herself, but she managed to contain it. "I'll let you know," she instead answered with an easy smile, looking out the window again. "Whatever the case," she said, turning back to him, "this Cardinal Mundelein is obviously very popular."

"Well, I don't think *popular* is quite the right word, but he's certainly influential. He's a decent enough chap, I'll give him that."

"You've met him?" Henrietta asked, intrigued.

"At a dinner party or two. Never really had a conversation beyond the usual niceties, however. Someone else always wanted his ear more than me."

Henrietta's stomach churned just a little. It still stunned her sometimes to think about the prominence the Howards had in Chicago and beyond. She looked out the window again. They had already passed through Libertyville and were headed into what looked like a forest. The trees on either side of the road were quite dense.

"Wait a minute!" she said, a stray thought creeping into her mind. "You knew Cardinal Mundelein all this time? You could have perhaps used that connection to get Elsie into Mundelein . . . "

"Ha!" Clive said with a short laugh. "It seems to me," he said looking over at her, his eyebrow raised, "that Elsie did rather well on her own. Getting in, that is," he added.

"But you didn't even think to ask!"

"Well, I did have a few other things on my mind, darling. Such as my father's murder," he said wryly. "And how quick you are to use the family connections. To think how innocent you were just a short time ago. Shame, really. And here I was—sure you weren't a gold digger," he teased.

"Well, here I was—sure you weren't a cradle robber."

"Henrietta!" he exclaimed, laughing. "How could you suggest such a thing?" He shifted the car into a lower gear.

"Why are we slowing down?" she asked, looking around.

"According to this thing," he said, jabbing his pipe at the map she still held, "it should be right around here, in the woods itself."

Henrietta looked back at the map. "Yes, you're right."

Clive rolled the car to a stop. "As a matter of fact, I think we've found it."

To the right of the road stood a tall wrought-iron archway, presiding over a narrow lane that stretched as far back into the woods as they could see. "St. Mary of the Lake Seminary" was woven into the metal arch, the letters painted gold, with elaborately curved black metal vines winding their way through the black iron bars. There was no gate at all, as if anyone were free to enter or leave at any time.

"Well spotted, Inspector."

Clive eased the car into the lane and slowly proceeded down it. It seemed to stretch on and on, with no buildings or signage in sight. Eventually, they came to a fork in the road, but there were no signs there, either, to indicate what lay down each path. After pausing for a moment, Clive chose the road to the right. It began as the main road had, surrounded by trees, but as they continued along, the trees began to thin somewhat, and they saw glimpses of what looked to be a rather large lake to their left. It reminded Henrietta of the massive estates she had seen in England on their honeymoon; Linley Castle in particular.

They eventually left the woods completely, the vista further opening up to reveal a set of buildings neatly laid out, facing the lake and centered on a large column, around which the drive circled and then continued on. The building in the center looked to be a sort of chapel or a church, with several buildings symmetrically flanking it. In front of the chapel was the column and beyond that a shrub-lined mall, which ran all the way down to the lake itself, ending in a stone balustrade.

Clive pulled the car into a tiny lot where a smattering of other cars were parked and came around to open the door for Henrietta. "Ready?" he asked.

"Yes, and I know what you're going to say," she said, taking his arm. "Let you do the talking."

"Not necessarily. I've changed, you see," he said solemnly.

Surprised by this, she was about to comment, but he spoke before she could.

"Well, how about I do most of it?" he said, adjusting his hat as he grinned down at her.

"I knew it!" she said and couldn't help but laugh.

As they stepped onto a stone pathway that led to the main buildings, the sun broke through the rather dense cloud cover, and Henrietta was obliged to shield her eyes as she took her first look around. She gazed at the placid lake, so smooth that it looked to be made of glass. From this angle, she could see that beyond the stone balustrade at the end of the mall were stone stairs on either side which led down to a terrace and then another below. From there, a bricked overlook emerged, at the end of which sat a sort of stone gazebo, supported by stone columns. Two piers curved out into the lake from either side of it, giving the appearance that this central gazebo, or boat house, as it appeared to be, was attempting to throw its stone arms around the lake.

Looking at it, Henrietta felt as if they had magically been transported into some foreign place, or maybe a fairy tale, and she half expected a prince or some other royal person to step out and greet them at any moment. The sun was oddly almost blinding now, so much so that she kept having to look down and, for the effort, was delighted to notice several daffodil buds poking up through the few clumps of snow that remained. In some spots farther along, where the snow had melted completely, she could see crocuses, and they cheered her immensely in a way she didn't expect.

"This place is so big," she said, pulling her gaze from them and looking around again. "How are we ever going to find Fraulein Klinkhammer?"

"First thing's first," Clive said confidently. "That looks like an administrative type of building." He nodded toward a columned building to the right of the chapel. "Shall we?"

Henrietta nodded and again held her hand up to her eyes to study the buildings in front of them as they walked, trying to guess if their columns and domes were of a Renaissance style, or maybe Georgian. She wasn't sure—but she was trying to learn these things. It was something Clive had said he wanted to educate her on as they traveled through Europe, but having to rush home for Alcott's funeral put that particular bit of her education on hold for now.

They hurried up the shallow steps, and as they stepped inside what they hoped was the administration building, Henrietta was surprised at how opulent it was, again reminding her of the estates she had seen in England. This was certainly not what she imagined a seminary would be like.

They had stepped into an open courtyard of sorts in the center of a two-story building, though above them was, of course, not open air, but instead a beautiful ceiling of leaded stained glass. Doric columns lined the room, which served to support the Ionic colonnade above.

"It's beautiful," Henrietta whispered, her head back, observing the intricate, geometric patterns in the ceiling.

"May I help you?" snapped a young priest sitting behind a desk off to the right, catching their attention. Henrietta hadn't even noticed him when they first came in, so mesmerized had she been with the interior.

"Yes, as a matter of fact," Clive answered as they made their way over to him.

"Yes?" The young priest eyed them carefully and seeming not overly pleased with what he saw. He had very short, dark-brown hair that looked as though it wanted to curl and very green eyes that continued to look at them disapprovingly. His face was angular and severe, making the rounded dimple in his chin look almost out of place. "Are you selling something?" he asked sharply. "Or are you here to see someone? Visiting hours are on Sundays only, from two until four. They should have told you that," he chirped, rapidly tapping his pencil on the paper in front of him. Henrietta winced at how much the feminine inflection of his voice reminded her of Eugene.

"We're not selling anything, and we're not here to visit anyone," Clive explained stiffly. "We're looking for one of your cleaning women, I believe. A Miss Liesel Klinkhammer? Where would we find her?"

The priest's brow furrowed. "You can't just barge in here and talk to the staff," he said incredulously.

"Why not?"

"Because . . . because it's against the rules," the priest blustered.

"Look, Father . . . ?" Henrietta said.

"Moran."

"Father Moran, is there someone else we could talk to?" she asked politely.

"Yes, who's in charge?" Clive demanded.

"The most Reverend Monsignor Gaspari is our rector," Fr. Moran said irritably, as if this was information they should have known. "And he would be very annoyed to be bothered with something this trivial. Why do you want to talk to this woman, anyway? Are you family?"

"No, I'm a private detective. Clive Howard. And this is my wife, Mrs. Howard. No one's in trouble," he said, reaching inside his suit coat to produce one of the business cards Henrietta had surprised him with at Christmas, the sight of which now thrilled her. He handed the card to the priest. "We just have some information. Of a personal nature, shall we say. Now, we'd like to talk to her." His eyes darted to the hallways beyond before returning his gaze to the young priest before him.

Fr. Moran examined the card in his hand. "I'd better go ask about this. Monsignor is very busy, however."

"Well, maybe someone else could help us," Henrietta suggested.

"No, no, no," Fr. Moran said impatiently, still studying the card. "The monsignor will want to know about *this*." He stood up, revealing his long, black cassock. "I'll see if he can find a moment to see you. Wait here," he said crisply and then disappeared down a hallway.

"Find a moment?" Henrietta whispered to Clive once Fr. Moran was out of earshot. "What does he possibly have to do all day? It's not as if there's a crowd out here." She gestured at the palatial interior.

Clive shrugged. "It's the usual runaround. He'll see us," he said confidently.

"Runaround?" Henrietta asked with a smile. "Now who's using plebian phrases?"

Clive laughed. "Plebian? I think the word I used was 'peasant,' or are you trying to one-up me? I—"

"Right this way," called Fr. Moran from somewhere down the hall, gesturing with two fingers to follow him.

"See?" Clive said under his breath, and Henrietta felt obliged to pinch his arm.

"Ow!" he mouthed, silently.

They caught up to Fr. Moran, who led them down a marble hallway with dark walnut wainscoting.

"This is highly unusual, by the way. The monsignor is a very busy man," he repeated without looking back at them. "I do hope this won't take up too much of his time. We have ordinations just after Easter, and we're all exceedingly busy. Especially the monsignor. So be quick," he warned, pausing outside the last door in the hallway. He gave the beveled, chicken-wire glass panel on the door a quick knock and, without waiting for an answer from within, opened the door and gestured them inside. "Mrs. Middleton will see to you."

"Mrs. Middleton?" Henrietta asked, as they stepped into a small antechamber.

"Monsignor Gaspari's secretary," he said, nodding at the woman cramped behind a small desk. "She'll see to you. Good day." He gave a quick bow and left them standing in front of Mrs. Middleton, who looked up at them from the stack of envelopes she was addressing with what could only be called apathy, or perhaps extreme boredom.

She was a frail-looking woman, her shoulders rounded forward as if her thin, wispy body were not strong enough to hold them up entirely. Her eyes had a sort of haunted, miserable look to them, and her graying brown hair was tied neatly in a bun, with only a few errant tendrils having escaped to hang about her face, creased already with wrinkles. She wore a brown checked housedress and brown oxfords. Indeed, everything about Mrs. Middleton seemed dull and brown.

"You can sit down if you'd like," she said, nodding toward two wooden chairs against the far wall, which reminded Henrietta of the principal's office back when she had attended school. "The monsignor will be with you in a moment," she said without any facial expression and continued to write.

Before they could even move toward the chairs, however, the door opened behind her to reveal a small man with greased, black hair lined with streaks of gray and silver spectacles.

"Mr. and Mrs. Howard, I believe?" he asked in a clipped, professional tone that reminded Henrietta of a businessman, or maybe a doctor. In fact, he only resembled a priest but for the long black robes he was dressed in. "This way, please," he said, stepping aside for them to pass through to his inner sanctum.

"Hold my calls, Mrs. Middleton."

"Yes, Monsignor," she said, without looking up from her task.

Henrietta followed Clive into the office and was again surprised by what she saw. While the antechamber was cramped and small, the monsignor's office was quite spacious. It was a round corner office with large leaded glass windows taking up almost half of the circular room, a narrow band of stained glass running above them. On one wall was a beautiful fireplace with columns carved into it in a sort of bas-relief, topped with a marble mantel. Above it hung an old oil painting of Jesus and Mary . . . or was it Jesus and Mary Magdalene? Henrietta wondered.

On the other side of the room was a very large desk, ornately carved, as well, in front of which were two tufted leather chairs. On the wall above the desk hung a large crucifix, which depicted Christ with such lifelike wounds that Henrietta became unusually unsettled by it. She tried to avert her eyes, but they kept morbidly straying back to it. She supposed that the viewer was meant to be drawn to the gruesomeness of Christ's suffering, but she had experienced her fair share of blood and suffering for now.

"Please, sit down," Msgr. Gaspari said with a gesture, closing the door behind them and gingerly taking a seat behind the desk. "Now, what's this all about? Father Moran informs me that you are a private detective," he said carefully, glancing down at Clive's card, which had somehow found its way to a spot on the desk in front of him. "Is something wrong?" he asked, his eyes piercing each of them in turn. He had an air of shrewdness about him that reminded Henrietta of her grandfather.

"No, no one's in trouble," Clive answered. "It's a very simple matter. I'm sure someone else could have answered it for us, but your Father Moran was quite insistent that we speak directly with you."

"Yes, Father Moran is very exacting in his duty. And he was quite right to bring this to me," he said dismissively. "Now, perhaps you'd tell me what this is all about?" he repeated with what seemed to Henrietta to be a rather insincere smile.

"We're looking for a young woman," Clive said, sitting back in his chair and crossing his legs smoothly. "We believe she is employed here as a cleaner of some descript. Her name is Miss Klinkhammer. Liesel Klinkhammer. Ring a bell?"

Henrietta noticed the priest's right shoulder stiffen slightly. "Hmmm," he said calmly as he pressed his hands together, the tips of his two index fingers forming a steeple that rested against his pursed lips. A large ruby ring adorned one of his fingers, but Henrietta was instead mesmerized by his eyes, as if he could see through people and any lies they might be telling. She forced herself finally to look over at Clive, who, on the other hand, seemed amazingly unruffled by the priest's scrutiny. Indeed, he was returning it in kind.

"There are a great many staff members, you know," Msgr. Gaspari went on. "I'm afraid I don't know all of their names." He gave a small shrug. "Cigarette?" he offered Clive, as he reached for a silver cigarette case on top of his desk. He smoothly flipped it open and held it out.

Clive declined the offer with a wave of his hand, and Henrietta watched as the priest took one himself, lit it, and then inhaled deeply.

"You might recall her," Clive said. "German immigrant? Not much English, apparently."

Msgr. Gaspari let out a big stream of smoke through his nostrils. "Oh, her?" he said slowly. "Yes, I do recall her, as a matter of fact. Unfortunate case," he tried to say with a smile.

"Why is that?" Clive asked.

"She's no longer with us, I'm afraid."

"But she *was* employed here?"

"Yes, if we're talking about the same person."

Clive gave him a wry look. "What happened?"

Msgr. Gaspari inhaled again and sat back in his chair. "She was working here for quite some time, I believe, and then she suddenly became ill. Quite seriously, as I remember. Fits or some such thing. Obviously not something we are particularly adept at unraveling here, so after one particularly bad episode, we called an ambulance to take her to the hospital."

"Which one?" Clive asked, his eyes narrowed.

"Probably Victory Memorial," he said blankly. "I'm not really sure, to be perfectly honest."

"And then?"

"I don't know," he said, inhaling. "She didn't come back."

"She didn't come back? Didn't you find that odd?"

"Not really," Msgr. Gaspari said, flicking some ash into an ashtray perched off to the side on his desk. "Happens all the time. It's quite commonplace, actually."

"For a staff member to go to the hospital and never come back?"

Msgr. Gaspari looked intently at Clive with his piercing gaze. "For the staff to quit. Especially the cleaners."

"Why is that?"

Msgr. Gaspari gave another shrug. "You know immigrants. Always scrambling for something better."

Clive let out a sigh. "So no one followed up? No one went to see her?"

"Not that I know of. Not in an official capacity. It wouldn't have been seemly."

"For a priest to visit a sick woman in the hospital?"

"For the administrator of a college to go to the bedside of one of the cleaning women," he said, his eyes narrowing as he inhaled deeply. "I'm a very busy man, detective."

"So I've been told. A number of times now." Clive stared at him coolly, but Msgr. Gaspari did not flinch.

"She had a friend, I believe," Henrietta said quietly, deciding finally to speak.

Msgr. Gaspari's eyes traveled to her as if he had forgotten she was there.

"By the name of Teresa Wolanski," Henrietta said tentatively, her heart already sinking at the realization that they would most probably not find Leisel Klinkhammer today. "She wrote a letter for Miss Klinkhammer and mailed it to Germany for her. Perhaps *she* went to see her in the hospital and might be able to tell us something. Might we speak with her? If she still works here . . . that is?"

"Like I said, Mrs. Howard," Msgr. Gaspari said, looking at her with a touch of derision, "There're a great many staff members. I'm not familiar with each one. However, Mrs. Middleton can find that information for you. Now, if that's all, I'll wish you good day. I have an appointment coming up. You were fortunate that I was able to give you even this much time."

Henrietta judged his smile to be genuinely false now as he stood up, signaling them to do the same. He inclined his head slightly at Henrietta and held out his hand to Clive, which Clive gripped tightly.

"We may have more questions," Clive said thinly.

"Then I'm sure you'll be kind enough to make an appointment next time."

"Yes, thank you for seeing us on such short notice."

"And who did you say you were hired by?" Msgr. Gaspari asked, looking down at the ashtray as he snuffed out his cigarette.

"I didn't say. And it isn't pertinent, actually."

"Ah, I see. So you're not operating in any *official* police capacity?" he said slowly. "Just so I understand the whole picture."

"Oh, I think you understand well enough, Monsignor. And I'm well connected, you should know."

"Is that a threat?"

"Not at all. Just so you understand."

The two stared at each other.

"You haven't said why you're looking for her," Msgr. Gaspari finally said guardedly.

"No, I did not."

"It's a reasonable question."

Clive held the Monsignor's gaze for several moments before he finally spoke. "She left behind a child."

"Ah. Typical." Msgr. Gaspari shifted then, relaxing slightly. "Mrs. Middleton!" he shouted.

"Yes, Monsignor?" came the woman's warbly voice from beyond the door.

"Mr. and Mrs. Howard are needing some information on one of our employees. Please help them with that if you would."

"Yes, Monsignor."

"Isn't it unusual for a seminary to hire a woman?" Clive asked coolly as he walked toward the door. He put his hand on the doorknob and glanced back at the monsignor, waiting for an answer.

Msgr. Gaspari cleared his throat. "It is unusual, yes, but not unheard of."

"Surely you have many young men who could easily fill the role of personal secretary," Clive suggested.

"Mrs. Middleton's son was a priest here, if you must know, but he died of polio. It was the least we could do to offer her a form of employment. She would be destitute otherwise. A case of

Christian charity, you might say," Msgr. Gaspari said in a patronizing tone.

"I see," Clive said, still observing him carefully before opening the
door and passing through.

"Your next appointment is here, Monsignor," Mrs. Middleton said
without looking back, as Clive and Henrietta made their way into the
windowless chamber. It seemed very dully lit compared to the pleasant morning light that flooded Msgr. Gaspari's office.

"Send him in, please," called the monsignor, again now seated
behind his desk.

Mrs. Middleton gave a nod to a young, nervous-looking priest
sitting on one of the wooden chairs along the opposite wall, who
stood up, then, and hurried into the office, shutting the door quietly
behind him.

"So, which are you looking for? Liesel Klinkhammer or Teresa
Wolanski?" Mrs. Middleton asked, finally looking up at Clive and
Henrietta with her sad brown eyes. For a brief moment Henrietta felt
a flutter of hope, thinking she saw Mrs. Middleton give her a wink,
but she realized after watching her carefully, that it was merely a tick,
her right eye involuntarily winking every few seconds.

"How did you know—?" Henrietta began to say.

"I can hear everything he says," Mrs. Middleton sniffed.

"We are looking for a Miss Liesel Klinkhammer," Clive said. "We
believe she was a cleaner here."

"Yes, she was a cleaner here," Mrs. Middleton answered simply,
rubbing the red, raw patch under her nose with a small handkerchief.

"And I understand she was taken to the hospital some time ago,
is that correct? Some sort of fit?" Clive asked.

"Yes, that's right," she said slowly.

"Well, what happened to her? Did she come back? Or perhaps she's
still there? Do you know anything of her?" Clive asked impatiently.

"I couldn't say what happened to her," she said, picking up one of
the envelopes in front of her. "She didn't come back, as far as I know."

"How long have you worked here, Mrs. Middleton?" Clive asked.

The woman seemed surprised by the change in questioning. "About five years, I suppose," she said, her right eye twitching. "Why?"

"And have you always worked under Monsignor Gaspari?" he asked.

"Yes," she answered hesitantly. "Why?"

"I understand your son was a priest here. And that he died of . . . polio? Was that it?"

A wave of something rippled across Mrs. Middleton's face, the first sign of emotion they had seen yet. "Yes, that's right," she said absently. "Excuse me, Mr. Howard, but if that's all, I need to finish these."

"What about Teresa Wolanski?" Henrietta asked softly, shooting Clive a private scowl.

"What about her?"

"Might we talk with her instead, since Liesel isn't here? It seems she wrote at least one letter for Liesel, so she must have known her."

"Yes, I'd say they knew each other. They shared a room in the staff residence."

"Where's the staff residence?" Clive asked.

Mrs. Middleton looked up at the black institutional clock on the wall. "It wouldn't do any good to go over there now. Teresa's on duty at the moment, working, just like I should be," Mrs. Middleton said, picking up the whole stack of envelopes and tapping them crisply on the desk. "Please, that's all I know, and I have to get on here."

"Of course, Mrs. Middleton," Henrietta put in. "We'll be going now. But could you perhaps tell us where on the campus Teresa might be cleaning, so we can try to find her ourselves? It would really help us."

Mrs. Middleton sighed. "This time of day," she said, looking at the clock again, "she's probably in the refectory."

"Refectory?" Henrietta asked, looking at Clive curiously.

"Dining room," he answered.

"Thank you, Mrs. Middleton," Clive said, moving toward the door. "You've been very helpful."

"Yes, thank you, Mrs. Middleton," Henrietta said, following him. "And I'm sorry about your son," she added quietly.

Mrs. Middleton did not respond to this nor did she look up, but Henrietta could see, under the desk, that her leg was shaking.

Having ascertained directions to the refectory from the still sulking Fr. Moran behind the front desk, Clive and Henrietta decided it would be faster to walk across the sprawling campus than to drive, and accordingly made their way there via a maze of pathways. At the entrance they happened upon several young students who paused to hold the door for them, and Clive took the opportunity to ask one of them if he could direct him to one of the cleaners, a Miss Teresa Wolanski. The young man shook his head, almost in an embarrassed way, saying that he didn't know any of the cleaners by name.

It was then that Henrietta spotted an older woman with her head down, mopping the floor in the far corner of the room. She tapped Clive's arm and inclined her head toward the woman. She felt an unexpected thrill when Clive's face lit up and he shot her a sly smile. Taking that as encouragement, she led him across the room.

The refectory was a large, vaulted room with long tables where only students appeared to be sitting. On the other side of the room, separated by a short screen, were more elegant tables with white tablecloths at which sat a smattering of priests. Lively discussions seemed to be unfolding on both sides of the room, allowing Henrietta and Clive to pass through relatively unnoticed—but perhaps the sight of visitors and guests was a common enough occurrence to not attract attention.

The woman they approached was plump, her gray uniform dress stretched tight across her broad shoulders and her brown stockings pulled thin over her massive calves. Somehow she seemed to sense them as they neared and turned to look at them, a worried frown forming on her face.

"Miss Wolanski?" Henrietta asked tentatively.

"Mrs."

"Mrs.," Henrietta corrected, trying not to look at the large birthmark that covered the woman's neck and part of her face.

Mrs. Wolanski stood up a little straighter, her mop still in hand. "What is wrong?" she asked nervously, her Polish accent thick.

"Nothing's wrong, Mrs. Wolanski. We . . . we're looking for a woman I believe you know. Liesel Klinkhammer?"

Mrs. Wolanski remained silent for a few moments and peered at Henrietta. "Yes?" she finally asked. "What of her?"

"She was in the hospital recently," Henrietta began.

Mrs. Wolanski nodded.

"We were told she had some sort of fit. Was she ill? What can you tell us?"

Mrs. Wolanski hurriedly made the sign of the cross. "Yes, she had spell. Like possessed," she said just above a whisper, her eyes darting toward the rows of priests that were filing in to find places at the long tables.

Henrietta glanced at Clive, who was standing slightly behind her with his arms crossed. He seemed willing to let her take the lead, so she went on.

"Did she often have these spells?" Henrietta asked.

"No. Never. Then one day, terrible. On floor, rolling. Like devil. I get Father. I say 'she has devil.' He say 'no. Not devil. Sick.' Send to hospital," she said, gesturing helplessly.

"Do you know how long she was there? Did you go to see her?"

Mrs. Wolanski shrugged. "Week? Maybe two? I not go. Devil jump," she said, gesturing from the imaginary Liesel toward herself. "I very worried."

"Did you write a letter for her? You speak German?"

"Yes, some. Yes, I write. Not too good, but . . . " she said with a shrug.

"Do you know where she is now? Did she come back here?"

"No," Mrs. Wolanski said worriedly. "They send to crazy house."

"Crazy house?"

"Yes, for *wariatkowo* . . . crazies. In city."

Henrietta paused to consider this. Surely it couldn't be . . . "Do you mean an insane asylum?"

Mrs. Wolanski nodded enthusiastically. "*Tak. Dom dla psychicznie chorych.* Crazy house."

"Do . . . do you know where? Which one?"

Mrs. Wolanski slowly shook her head as if trying to remember.

"How do you know this?" Clive asked sternly, causing her to look up at him in alarm. He softened his voice and then asked again. "How do you know she was sent to an asylum?"

"I finally go. To hospital. I very worried about Liesel. I bring crucifix for devil. But she gone. Nurse tell me where she go. I forget," she said, rubbing her forehead. "Starts with *D* . . ."

"Dunning?" Henrietta offered, her heart racing a little at the thought of it.

"*Tak!*" Mrs. Wolanski said, looking up at her. "That is one. Dunning."

"Jesus Christ. They sent her to an insane asylum?" Clive muttered.

Henrietta looked at him briefly before turning back to face Mrs. Wolanski. "I'm sorry about your friend, Mrs. Wolanski. We'll try to find her and let you know somehow."

Mrs. Wolanski's face looked troubled. "Excuse, but what is name?" she asked, nodding toward Henrietta. "You know Liesel, too?"

"Oh, I'm sorry," Henrietta said. "My name is Henrietta Howard, and this is my husband, Clive. We're . . . well, actually, my sister and her friend, Gunther Stockel, are looking for Liesel—"

"Gunther from Germany?" she asked, incredulously. "Is here?"

"Yes, he got your letter . . . well, the letter addressed to his mother . . . and came looking for Liesel. He brought Anna with him. Her child," Henrietta added upon seeing Teresa's confused look. "He got mixed up, though, and is living in the city. He didn't realize that she was out here," Henrietta said with a wide gesture.

"Baby is here, too?" Mrs. Wolanski exclaimed, tears forming in her eyes. "Liesel will be so happy. Have joy."

"I hope so," Henrietta said. She considered telling Mrs. Wolanski about Anna's similar fits, but then thought better of it. "You were good friends with her, Mrs. Wolanski?"

The woman nodded. "Yes, good friends," she reiterated. "I miss her. She very sad always."

"She came here looking for a man, I believe. By the name of Heinrich?"

Mrs. Wolanski's eyes narrowed. "Yes. This is so."

"Did she ever find him, do you know?" Henrietta asked, wondering why Mrs. Wolanski suddenly seemed apprehensive again.

"*Tak*. He find her, and then she have spell," she said fearfully and crossed herself again.

Chapter 7

"But you simply have to go!" Melody begged. "Please, Elsie! It's all arranged. The boys are coming in half an hour! You can't back out now!"

"Why ever not? Clarence Frazier doesn't give a hoot for me, Melody."

"But he does! Or he might, anyway, if you'd give him the time of day."

"Get Vivian to stand in for me. He probably wouldn't even notice. And if he does, he'd probably be pleased, actually."

"Oh, for heaven's sake!" Melody said loudly, sitting up on her bed and crossing her arms. "What am I to do with you?"

"Must you do anything with me?" Elsie asked with a sigh, remembering a very similar conversation she once had, in fact, with Aunt Agatha. Why was everyone so determined to plot out her future? Why couldn't she be left to her own devices? Was she so boring and nondescript that people saw her as putty—something they couldn't resist playing with? This was exactly why becoming a nun had been so attractive. It was the only way she could think of that would allow her to chart her own path . . .

"Well, of course I have to do something with you! You're my very best friend!" Melody exclaimed.

Given the large number of friends Melody possessed, Elsie very much doubted she was her *best* friend, but she let the comment go.

"Essentially we're here to find husbands, Els; let's face it."

"Well, I'm not!" Elsie retorted, tossing her pencil onto the open history textbook in front of her.

"Oh, yes, this again. Wanting to be a teacher and all that. Well, you're more than likely wasting your time. You won't be able to work once you're married, so why bother? Have fun, like the rest of us! You're much too serious, Elsie. Has anyone ever told you that?" she asked, her bright eyes flashing.

Almost everyone, in fact, Elsie thought, biting her lip, including Lloyd Aston who, unbeknown to Melody, had actually proposed to her downstairs in the parlor just over a month ago, if *proposed* was even the right word. More like *demanded* she marry him, due to some apparent backroom arrangement between his father and her scheming grandfather. She had disappointed everyone, she knew, in rejecting him, most especially her Aunt Agatha, who, in a rare fit of emotion, had nearly despaired, when she'd heard the news, of ever helping her again. But like herself, Elsie guessed that Aunt Agatha's life was likewise not her own, and she had more than once wondered what claim her grandfather must have on his daughter-in-law to convince her to be his puppet.

"Of course, Charlie and Douglas and even poor Clarence, I'm sad to say, are ridiculous dolts," Melody continued, interrupting Elsie's thoughts. "They're virtually harmless, which makes them the perfect suspects to practice on. You know, for your *real* lover," Melody whispered excitedly.

"For the last time, Melody—I don't have a lover!" Elsie insisted, but the hint of a blush on her cheeks was not lost to one such as Melody. "And I know for a fact that you don't think Douglas Novak is a 'ridiculous dolt.'"

"Perhaps not," Melody replied with a dimpled smile. "But you can't fool me! I saw the hearts you drew on your paper in theology!"

"That was just . . . just something to draw!" Elsie flustered. "Not everything means something, you know," she said with an effort at nonchalance, but she was shocked at how close Melody was coming to the truth. Elsie knew she couldn't put her off forever.

"Come on, Elsie, aren't you ever going to tell me? You promised, remember? Aren't we pals by now?" Melody pleaded in a much more somber tone.

Elsie stared at her new friend, and as much as she wanted to confide in her, she just couldn't. She was feeling increasingly cornered and trapped where Melody and the girls were concerned, who seemed to think of nothing else but boys and weddings. It was a type of anxiety that she suspected Ma perhaps suffered from as well, which explained why Ma sometimes acted as she did. It wasn't as hard for her to understand Ma as it was for others, especially Henrietta.

"I . . . " she began, but then fell silent.

Melody gave her a look of disappointment and sighed. "Well, if you don't have a lover, then you have no excuse to not go out with Clarence and the rest of us," she said matter-of-factly, brushing the palms of her hands back and forth against each other. "And anyway, it'll be terrifically fun!" she continued, her enthusiasm already rising again. "Charlie's borrowing his dad's motor and—"

"I'm thinking about becoming a nun," Elsie suddenly blurted out in a panic, and then instantly regretted it.

Melody stared at her.

"A nun?" she said finally after several moments awkwardly ticked by. "No, you're not!"

"I am. Actually."

"You can't really be serious . . . " Melody said with a nervous laugh.

"Why not? Don't you . . . don't you think I'm good enough to become a nun?" Elsie asked, her face well and truly flushed now, doubts about her self-worth creeping forward again.

"Of course, you're *good* enough, no one could question that," Melody exclaimed. "It's just that . . . gee whiz, Els, a nun?"

At the sight of Melody's distressed face, Elsie suddenly felt a wave of guilt at so meanly deceiving her new friend, but it had just come out, as it seemed the only way to steer clear of Melody's many schemes of love for her. Last month it had been Bernie Talbot; this month the chosen victim was Clarence Frazier. She could have just told her, she supposed, that she was in truth in love with Gunther— but she wasn't ready to tell anyone that just yet. That was something private . . . almost holy, she felt . . . and she wasn't ready to share it. Besides, with so many unanswered questions regarding Fraulein Klinkhammer and Anna, she didn't know what she could realistically expect from Gunther.

Just last night, she had received a late telephone call from Henrietta, relating what she and Clive had so far discovered regarding Fraulein Klinkhammer's whereabouts. Elsie had been stunned that they had tracked her down so quickly, and she was now desperate to tell Gunther the awful news—that poor Liesel was in an insane asylum! Doing so last night after the call from Henrietta was out of the question, and this morning she tried seeking him out early at his hut, before her classes began, but he was not there. No one answered when she knocked at his door, even Anna, whom he had said he was going to extract from the orphanage this weekend for a visit. But perhaps Gunther had instructed her not to answer the door? For a moment, she considered calling out, but upon second thought, she decided it would not be a good idea. Clearly Gunther wasn't in.

She asked various persons throughout the day if they had seen him to no avail. She had therefore been obliged to finally consult Sr. Bernard herself, who had told her, after peering over her spectacles at Elsie in a most uncomfortable way, that she had sent Gunther out on a variety of errands. She then asked for what purpose Elsie would need to address the custodian in the first place. "Oh, it's nothing, Sister," Elsie flustered. "I . . . I . . . my door handle is loose."

Sr. Bernard did not answer but merely continued to stare, convincing Elsie that she could see right through the fib.

—

"Have you told anyone? Besides me, that is?" Melody asked incredulously, calling Elsie back to the here and now. "I knew you had a secret!"

Elsie fingered the corner of a page in the open book before her, thinking about how to proceed. She hated lying, but it seemed the best option at the present moment. She couldn't go prancing about on silly dates with Melody and Cynthia and Douglas and Charlie and whomever else they dragged along. "As a matter of fact, I have," she said, clearing her throat, and looking up at Melody. "I've spoken to Sister Bernard."

"Gosh! No! What did she say?" Melody asked, grabbing up a nearby pillow and hugging it.

"That I needed to pray about it for a year, and then, if I'm still sure, she'll let me enter the novitiate," she said quietly, hoping that in so doing, it would soften the blow.

"Gosh, Elsie," Melody said, letting out a sigh. "I knew you were a dark horse, but . . . gee whiz. A nun? I mean, good for you, I guess, but I . . . I was hoping we could have some fun times . . . " She released the pillow, tossing it on the end of the bed.

"Well, we still can," Elsie said eagerly, wishing now that she hadn't gone down this path, but it was too late to change course. "Just maybe not dates and the like . . . "

"Yes, I suppose that's out of the question now, isn't it?"

"Well, yes, it's probably for the best."

Melody's face contorted to one of utter dejection, and Elsie's stomach churned at how terribly she was disappointing her new friend.

"Listen, I . . . I can still go tonight," she said cheerfully. "I still want to be part of the gang," she continued hesitantly. "No one . . . no one has to know my plan. And who knows . . . maybe I'll end up changing my mind in the long run. . . "

Melody's face brightened instantly.

"Gosh, really, Elsie? That'd be swell. Are you sure, though?"

Before Elsie could answer, however, Melody stood up and looped her arm through hers. "It's just that they'll be here any minute, and

I hate to let the boys down. Clarence is so terribly shy. That's why I
thought you'd get on. But no matter! No one need know. I won't tell!"

"Thanks, Melody," she said, giving her a smile.

Melody tilted her head back as if to more carefully observe her.
"I'm happy for you, I guess," she said, "but, gee, Elsie, are you really
sure?"

As it turned out, it was a pleasant enough afternoon. Elsie was
glad when Melody explained that the excursion was to be a trip
to the pictures. Apparently, the original plan had been to go ice
skating, but as Cynthia had sprained her ankle just a few days ago,
they proposed going to see *Love Before Breakfast* at the Granada
instead. Elsie was secretly relieved; she knew it was probably the
only activity that could successfully distract her from her current
worries. And, besides that, she secretly adored the movies, though
she had in actuality seen precious few—a fact she didn't want to
reveal to the gang, especially Melody, whom she suspected would
never let her hear the end of it. Elsie had been stunned when
Melody once told her that she and her kid sister, Bunny, had seen
every single picture ever released at the little theater back in her
hometown of Merriweather.

Likewise, the gang's afternoon plan afforded her a reason not to
have to talk all that much, though, as Melody had explained, Clarence
was indeed a rather shy boy, even more so than Elsie, if that were possible. They sat next to each other in the theater, of course, and though
he had bought her a bag of popcorn beforehand, he kept his hands to
himself and acted a perfect gentleman. She could feel the vibration
of his leg jittering up and down, however, and heard him periodically
clear his throat, but that was all. She felt a little sorry for him, actually,
and spoke kindly to him all the way home, asking about his mother
and father and siblings back in Benton Harbor, Michigan, where he
said he was from. It was too bad, really, that she . . . that her heart lay
elsewhere . . . because she might have once upon a time taken a shine
to Clarence. She hoped they could be friends, as she suspected they

would often be thrown together if Charlie and Douglas had anything to do with it. Although, maybe Melody would stop inviting her now that she had told her that she wanted to become a nun. Already Elsie was concerned that perhaps Melody was treating her differently. She couldn't help but notice, for example, that Melody glanced over at her in the dark when Cesar Romero had kissed Carole Lombard on the big screen in front of them.

When they finally returned to Philomena, Elsie awkwardly made an excuse and extracted herself from the gang, stiffly shaking Clarence's hand in good-bye before she ascended the stairs, trying not to run. It wasn't that she was desperate to get away from the gang—in fact she might have liked to join in the game of charades that someone had suggested, but she simply *had* to find Gunther. It had been almost a whole day since Henrietta had rung her on the telephone, and Elsie didn't think she could wait one more minute.

Once upstairs in her room, she hurriedly changed out of her polka-dot shirtwaist dress with the broad white collar and white cuffs—which Melody had selected for her, saying she looked simply adorable in it—and into a plain, blue-and-cream houndstooth Hooverette and sensible shoes. Thankfully, Melody was otherwise occupied, as she would have accused Elsie of dressing like a house-wife if she saw her in this current ensemble, or lack of ensemble, that is. But it was comfortable and plain, which Elsie liked, and she had no desire to appear in stylish, expensive clothes in front of Gunther. As she gathered up her things, her thoughts again turned to her current woes, all thoughts of Cesar Romero and Carole Lombard trickling out of her mind as quickly as they had entered.

How had Liesel ended up in Dunning, poor woman? Elsie wondered, looking for her gloves. Did she perhaps suffer from the same fits as Anna, and therefore been taken to an asylum? Gunther's explanation of why he had fled with Anna from the rising Nazi sentiment in Germany seemed a bit extreme to Elsie when he had originally explained his fears, but perhaps he had not been exaggerating. If nothing else, it made her all the more worried about little Anna. If

Fraulein Klinkhammer had ended up at Dunning, what did that mean for Anna?

Quickly, Elsie bent down and pulled a brown-paper package out from under her bed where she had hidden it. Last week she had walked to Ferguson's Bookshop on Sheridan Road and purchased an illustrated copy of Robert Louis Stevenson's *A Child's Garden of Verses*, to give to Anna when next she saw her, which, she hoped, would be tonight. Though the staff at the orphanage advised against taking Anna in and out to avoid confusion and disruption to her routine—an opinion Elsie happened to share, and one which Gunther did not—she welcomed a chance to see Anna again. There had been such little contact between her and Anna since the day she had discovered her in Gunther's hut. She seemed like a sweet, shy child, and she reminded Elsie a bit of herself.

Taking a deep breath, she slipped on her coat then, the package tucked neatly under her arm, and crept down the back stairwell of the mansion so as to avoid the front parlor, where Melody and any number of people might still be gathered. She tiptoed through the kitchen, where she had sat for many nights with Gunther while the rest of the school had been on Christmas break, and out the back door, cutting across the back lawn.

The temperature had dropped since even an hour ago, the sun already beginning to set, when she knocked at the hut's wooden door. She was relieved when Gunther answered it, and even more so to see the genuinely pleased expression on his face as he gestured her in.

"This is nice surprise," he said with a warm smile. "See who is here, Anna." He turned to a little bundle hiding behind and clinging to his leg.

Elsie stepped inside and felt instantly excited but nervous, too, to be so close to him again. She wanted to blurt out her news, but she schooled herself to wait for the right moment, preferably when Anna was out of earshot.

"Here, let me take your coat," Gunther said, and Elsie shrugged out of her sturdy wool coat, having put her fur, which Melody *insisted* she wear to the movies (she was just like Henrietta and Julia!) hurriedly back in the closet of her dorm room when she had returned from the pictures. She managed to hold onto the brown package as she did so, however, and held it up for Gunther to see. Hesitantly, she tilted her head toward Anna, who was still hiding behind him.

Gunther understood immediately. "What is this, Miss Von Harmon? You have brought us something, no?"

"Yes, it's a present for Anna. Is she here?" Elsie asked, breaking into a smile.

Anna slowly poked her head out, then, from behind Gunther's leg and gazed up at Elsie. At the sight of the brown-paper package, she smiled a tiny smile and looked up at Gunther. Gunther nodded, and Anna took a little step forward.

"Here you are," Elsie said softly and handed her the package, which looked so big in the little girl's arms.

Anna's eyes grew large, and she nervously looked up at Gunther again.

"Open it," he encouraged. "Go on. Let us see what the good lady brings us."

The little girl gently tore off the paper and looked back up at Elsie, the book in her hand.

"Oh, my!" said Gunther. "It is a fine book," he said, clearly surprised and impressed. "What do you say, Anna?"

"*Danke schön,*" she said softly.

"You're welcome," Elsie said with a smile. "It's a favorite of my little brother and sister. And they're not too much older than you, so I thought you might like it, too."

"We thank you, Miss Von Harmon," Gunther said uneasily, "but you should not have spent so much money. We could have gotten it at library."

"It's only a small thing," Elsie replied. "And we all need something of our own, don't we?" she said to Anna.

The girl looked at Gunther, puzzled, and he quietly translated Elsie's last words: *Wir alle brauchen etwas Eigenes, nicht wahr?*

The girl nodded shyly and then held the book up to her.

"You want me to read some?" Elsie asked, delighted the girl seemed to like her.

Anna nodded, and Elsie smiled.

"Is that all right . . . Uncle Gunther?" Elsie asked awkwardly.

"*Nein.* Papa," the girl said.

"*Onkle,*" Gunther corrected her gently. "Yes, it is fine."

Elsie held her hand out to the girl, and Anna took hold of one of her fingers and, gripping it, pulled her toward one of the only two chairs. Elsie saw no choice but to take the girl on her lap and was surprised at how light she was compared to Doris or Donny. She weighed barely more than a feather!

Gently, Elsie cracked open the book, and the two of them spent several moments just looking at the beautiful illustrations, Elsie enjoying them as much as Anna seemed to. Elsie pointed to a cat and said "cat," and looked expectantly at Anna who answered "*Katze.*" When Elsie repeated "*Katze,*" the little girl gave her first true smile to Elsie. Elsie then pointed to a tree and looked at Anna. "*Baum,*" said the little girl, and Elsie repeated it, causing Anna to let out an infectious little giggle.

They kept at this little game while Gunther made some coffee and placed a steaming mug on the table in front of Elsie. He sat down in the other chair and watched them, his head propped on his fist. Finally, after many minutes, he said, "Perhaps we should let Miss Von Harmon read now, no?" Anna nodded and looked up expectantly at Elsie.

"Let's start back at the beginning, shall we?" Elsie said and could not help but look across at Gunther, wondering if he caught a deeper meaning there, as she herself did. Steadily he returned her look, though she couldn't tell what he was thinking, but she felt her stomach clench anyway. She cleared her throat and turned her attention back to the book. "To Alison Cunningham, from her boy," she read, beginning with the introductory poem.

For the long nights you lay awake
And watched for my unworthy sake:
For your most comfortable hand
That led me through the uneven land:
For all the story-books you read:
For all the pains you comforted:
For all you pitied, all you bore,
In sad and happy days of yore:—
My second Mother, my first Wife,
The angel of my infant life—
From the sick child, now well and old,
Take, nurse, the little book you hold!
And grant it, Heaven, that all who read
May find as dear a nurse at need,
And every child who lists my rhyme,
In the bright, fireside, nursery clime,
May hear it in as kind a voice
As made my childish days rejoice!

Elsie dared not look at Gunther when she was finished—her emotion hovered too near the surface. Already she was afraid she might cry, and to look into Gunther's eyes right now would certainly push her over the edge, she was sure. Instead, she looked down at Anna. She probably hadn't understood much of the poem, Elsie guessed, but still she turned the page and pointed to the next one.

"You want me to go on?" Elsie asked, a giddy little laugh rising up for some reason and then escaping, which was answered with an eager nod from Anna. They went through the entire book this way, Elsie convinced that Anna wasn't grasping even half of the poems' meanings—but she seemed to enjoy it just the same. Perhaps it was just being held in someone's lap that the girl was enjoying, Elsie speculated, remembering vividly what it felt like to be small and insignificant. Elsie gave the girl a little kiss on the head.

"*Es ist Zeit fürs Bett, jetzt, Kleines,*" Gunther said softly to Anna.

At these words, Anna nestled into Elsie tighter, clearly not want-ing to let go. Elsie gave her a squeeze and another kiss.

"I know you do not wish to sleep, but it is late," Gunther said to Anna.

Elsie felt the girl dig herself in deeper.

"Is it bedtime already?" Elsie asked the small bundle in her arms, guessing the meaning of Gunther's words. "I do hope so! Isn't it nice to snuggle under the covers?" she asked into Anna's hair. "And . . . oh . . . " Elsie said, shifting her now to reach into her dress pocket. "I almost forgot," she said and pulled out a toffee wrapped in shiny pink paper and held it out to Anna. It was a trick Stanley had often used to win over Doris and the boys whenever he had come around to visit them at their shabby apartment on Armitage, and Elsie had decided to copy it.

"First book and then sweet!" Gunther exclaimed. "What do you say?"

"*Danke schön*," Anna said as she took it and slid off of Elsie's lap.

"And what else?"

"Good-night, fraulein," she said in English as she gave her a wobbly curtsey.

"My mother taught her this," Gunther said to Elsie as he watched Anna, obviously pleased. "Go lie down now." He nodded Anna toward the little trundle at the back of the room.

"Wait," Elsie said to her, extending the book in her hand. "You forgot this."

Anna looked at her and then at Gunther. When he nodded, a big smile erupted across her face. "*Danke*," she said softly, and took the book from Elsie's hands.

"Yes, thank you," Gunther said, standing up to refill their mugs, as Anna slipped into her nightgown at the back of the room and curled up on the trundle, her tiny head barely making a dent on her thin pillow. She lay with her arm around the book, her fingers in her mouth, watching them with her large, blue eyes.

"Thank you for tonight," Gunther repeated, setting down a fresh cup of coffee. "You spoil us," he said softly. "I wish I have something more than coffee."

"Oh, I don't mind at all," Elsie said, thinking of how much she preferred this to the endless glasses of wine and champagne that were handed to her at the many gala events of the gilded set that she was required, even now, to attend. "And I think Anna could use some spoiling, don't you?"

Gunther gave her a grateful look and sat back down across from her.

"There's been some news," Elsie said quietly. "About Liesel."

"Already?" Gunther asked, incredulous, his previously relaxed attitude vanishing. "What is it?" he asked eagerly. "Have they found her?"

"Apparently, yes," Elsie said, looking over her shoulder at Anna, whom, she could see, was still watching them, albeit with very heavy eyes. "Well, they haven't found her just yet, but they know where she is. It's . . . it's not good news, Gunther."

Elsie saw his jaw tighten. "Go on."

"She's in an asylum," she whispered. "For the . . . for the mentally unstable. A place called Dunning. It's west of here, on Irving Park."

Gunther let out a deep breath. "An asylum?" he asked, his brow furrowed. "*Ach. Guter Gott . . .* " He cradled his head in his hands. "This is much worse than I imagined." He paused, thinking. "How did this come to be?" he asked, looking up at her. "Though now I understand why we have had no word."

"Henrietta telephoned me late last night to tell me that they went to the seminary in Mundelein and were able to confirm that Liesel had been living there and that she had indeed been employed as a cleaner. Apparently, though, she had some sort of fit," she said quietly, her eyes darting to Anna, "and she was taken to the county hospital. Henrietta said they followed up at the hospital, which confirmed that one Liesel Klinkhammer had been admitted there, treated, and then transferred to Dunning. Apparently, it's the closest institution to them."

"But why?" Gunther asked.

Elsie bit her lip, dreading to tell him the next part of the story, which was certainly the worst. "She was diagnosed with schizophrenia," she said in a low voice. "I'm sorry, Gunther."

"Schizophrenia?" Gunther asked in a hiss.

"Papa?" Anna asked nervously from her corner, alarmed by his outburst.

"Shhh, Anna. *Schlaf ein, Kleiner*—Go to sleep, little one," he managed to say in a soothing voice. "How long has she been there?" he asked Elsie quietly, anxiously rubbing his forehead.

"I'm not sure . . . a couple of months maybe?"

"A couple of months!" he groaned. "I must go there. I must find way to go there."

"As it happens, Clive is suggesting that we meet them there tomorrow morning. Can you make it? Surely, Sister Bernard will let you off, won't she?"

"Yes . . . yes . . . I suppose yes, but what am I to do with Anna? I went to get her just today. But I cannot take her to such place to meet her mother, can I? It has been years—"

"No, Gunther. We mustn't take Anna there," Elsie whispered. "I've heard it's a . . . it's a terrible place." She could not resist putting her hand on his.

"But Liesel will want to see her. I am sure of it. I cannot take Anna back to orphanage already tomorrow," he said, absently rubbing Elsie's forefinger with his thumb.

"It . . . it might be for the best, Gunther," Elsie said softly, thrilling at his touch. "Until you find out what's happened to poor Liesel. It will be a shock for her to see even you . . . and who knows what the state of her mind is, especially after she has been sent to such a place."

"You are right," Gunther said sadly as he looked over at Anna, who seemed to have finally drifted off. "I pray she does not blame me." Gunther slowly pulled his hand from Elsie's, as if suddenly aware that it was there.

"Liesel, or Anna?" Elsie asked softly, acutely feeling the withdrawal of his hand.

"Both."

Worriedly, Elsie tried to think of an alternative. "I suppose we could . . . we could take Anna to my mother's house in Palmer Square," she suggested finally. "She could spend the day in the nursery with Doris and Donny. I'm sure Nanny Kuntz wouldn't mind. With a name like Kuntz, maybe she even speaks German," Elsie urged, though she scolded herself for not knowing this about a woman she had been living with for months and months.

Gunther looked at her for such an extended time that Elsie began to wonder if she had somehow offended him.

Finally he spoke. "You would do this for me?" he asked quietly.

"Yes," she said, a smile of relief breaking out across her face. "Yes— of course I would."

"Elsie," he said, taking her hand back and squeezing it. "I do not deserve this kindness. Thank you, but no. You and your sister are already doing enough for me. But I feel your offer. Very deeply. It will be better anyway for Anna. Better not to risk a new place and new people. Who knows what brings on these fits," he added, letting go of her hand again.

"Then . . . then why don't I stay with her? I'll sit here with her while you go and meet them. That seems the best, doesn't it?" she suggested. She desperately wanted to go and meet this Liesel and be part of what was seeming to be an adventure, but more so, she wanted to be of service to him. "You don't really need me there. I'm sure you can find the way."

"But I . . . I do need you there. I want you there. I . . . no, I will have to take Anna back tomorrow, very early."

Though she was sad for Anna, of course, Elsie could not help her heart from fluttering a little, and a smile inched across her face. "Are you sure?" she asked, looking into his eyes.

"Yes, yes, I am sure."

They looked at each other for several moments, the air between them charged with something warm and static.

"I should go," she said, standing up awkwardly.

Gunther stood as well and after hesitating a moment, went to get her coat.

"Henrietta suggested we meet them at Dunning at nine, but that doesn't give you much time to get Anna back," she mused, putting on the coat he held out to her. "I'll telephone her from Philomena and ask them to meet us at eleven instead. Is that enough time, do you think?" She buttoned up her coat and wrapped her scarf around her neck.

"Yes, that is fine." He stood before her with his hands in his pockets. "Would you like me to walk you back?" he asked quietly.

"Oh, no! Don't leave her," she whispered with a nod toward Anna. "It's just across the way, anyway."

There was silence between them as she pulled on her gloves.

"Thank you, Elsie," he said finally.

He was standing very close to her now, looking at her so longingly that he seemed almost in pain. Why would he not kiss her? she wondered, sensing this to be his desire. It was her desire, too, she knew, her heart pounding. Why did he never do so? What held him back?

He surprised her then by taking a step closer so that they were just inches apart, so close that she could see his chest rising and falling. Tentatively, she reached out and put the tips of her fingers on his chest and felt his trembling beneath the linen of his shirt. He leaned forward, and she closed her eyes, waiting . . . wanting to feel his lips on hers . . . but instead she felt him take her fingers from his chest and hold them gently in his.

"Ach, Elsie," he said, his breath catching, as he turned his head.

Without thinking it through, she leaned forward and kissed him lightly on the cheek, feeling the stubble there and inhaling his scent as she lingered there for a few seconds.

"Good-night, Gunther," she whispered and then turned and opened the door. She hurried out, bending low against the wind as she stepped onto the wet path, her pulse positively racing at what she had done. She had kissed *him!* Only once did she look back. He was leaning against the doorway, his hands returned to his pockets, watching her go as the wind tousled his hair. He looked sad and forlorn, like a man lost; but perhaps she was only imagining it. She waved to him, but he did not respond. She turned and hurried on.

Chapter 8

The Chicago State Hospital, or Dunning, as it was more popularly called, lay on a sprawling 320 acres on Chicago's northwest side. When it was built in 1854, it was designed to be an almshouse for the city's poor and destitute, but it had gradually, over the years, evolved into a place to primarily house the insane or the mentally disturbed. It was believed that the open space and the country air would be calming and restful for the inmates—but ironically, it was anything but a serene or peaceful place for these lost souls.

Dunning, almost from the beginning, was shockingly over-crowded and rife with abuse. In fact, most people began to refer to it as a veritable "tomb for the living." And while it had come under the scrutiny of the state at the turn of the century, which had resulted in many reforms being instituted, the mention of the word "Dunning" still sent shivers up people's spines. Indeed, many parents throughout the city still used it as an effective threat for naughty children by telling them that they would get "sent to Dunning" if they didn't behave.

Clive himself was not immune to a decided feeling of unease as he and Henrietta drove up to the front gates the day after their initial inquiries at the seminary and then at Victory Memorial. He had been hoping, when they had driven over to the hospital immediately following their visit to the seminary, that perhaps Teresa Wolanski had somehow been mistaken. As it turned out, unfortunately, she had not, and this was becoming a more complicated case than Clive had first imagined.

Having first inquired at the front desk at Victory Memorial, Clive and Henrietta had eventually been escorted to Medical Records, which was housed, depressingly, in a gloomy subterranean part of the building. There, they were greeted by an older woman with glasses so thick that her eyes were difficult to even see, swimming behind the glass in a foggy blur. She stood behind a counter of sorts with a lone light hanging above her, which gave the woman an odd glow and simultaneously cast the rest of the long, low cavernous room in shadow. No other staff seemed about to help her, which may have explained why she did not seem overly pleased to assist them when they had asked to see Liesel Klinkhammer's chart, saying that she had stacks of filing to do, and it wasn't really her job to pull individual charts for general members of the public.

"You have a written release?" she asked in a gravelly voice, pausing in her work long enough to study the two of them. The woman's large, distorted eyes shifted from one to the other, as if looking at them from inside a fishbowl.

"No, not exactly."

"You relatives?"

"I'm her cousin," Clive said with a false smile.

The woman merely grunted.

"Look," Clive said, reaching inside his jacket for his wallet and smoothly pulling out a five-dollar bill, which he carefully placed under the corner of her desk blotter. "I understand your time is valuable, Mrs. . . . ?

"Nicholson," she said, looking at them uneasily before finally reaching out and taking the money, which she held up in front of her glasses, examining it closely before slipping it quickly into her dress pocket. She stared at them for a few more moments before asking, "Who'd you say you're looking for?"

"Klinkhammer. Liesel."

Mrs. Nicolson shuffled away and disappeared down one of the many rows of metal filing cabinets lined up behind her, which almost resembled tunnels. Clive and Henrietta stood in the feeble light, peering after her. Henrietta looked about to whisper something to him, but she stopped when they heard a drawer scrape open. After just a few moments, they heard it scrape again and close with a click. Mrs. Nicolson reappeared then from the depths of the tunnel, holding the open file very close to her face and reading aloud as she walked.

"Name: Liesel Klinkhammer," she said tremulously. "Address: Mundelein Seminary, Date of Admission: September 28, 1935, Date of Discharge: October 12, 1935, Place: Chicago State Hospital." Having reached the counter, she looked up at them questioningly as if to see if this was the information they sought.

Clive groaned internally. So it was true—Liesel *had* been sent to Dunning.

"What was her diagnosis?" he asked, arching his neck in an attempt to see the contents of the file himself. He wasn't able to make anything out, but he did observe that there was precious little written at all.

"Says here 'schizophrenia,'" Mrs. Nicholson mumbled.

"Schizophrenia? What's that?" Henrietta asked, looking at Clive.

"That means crazy," Mrs. Nicholson answered for him. "You know—hearing voices and all that."

"We understood she was here due to an epileptic fit," Clive said, ignoring her explanation.

"Doesn't say anything about epilepsy here," Mrs. Nicholson said with a shrug. "Says schizophrenia."

"Are you sure? The light is quite dim in here and, forgive me for saying, but your vision seems to perhaps be somewhat impaired," Clive suggested tentatively.

"What do you mean by that?" the woman said indignantly, her eyes enlarged and blurry behind her glasses.

"Listen, can I take a look at that?" Clive asked, holding out his hand.

"What'd you say your name was, again?" she asked suspiciously.

"I didn't. My name is Clive Howard. This is my wife, Henrietta," he added, noticing that she was looking at Henrietta now.

"You aren't really her cousin, are you?"

"Does it matter?" Clive asked. When she didn't respond, he let out a deep breath. "Look, Mrs. Nicholson, I'm a detective. We're trying to locate Miss Klinkhammer."

"Well, I've already told you where she is," Mrs. Nicholson said, straightening up and taking a small step back. "Or where she was discharged to, anyway."

"Indeed. But you see, that's what's puzzling us. To our knowledge, she wasn't mentally unstable. What were her symptoms? Does it say?"

"No," she said, pressing the file to her chest. "That's confidential information."

"But isn't what you've already told us confidential?"

"Not exactly. Oh, fiddlesticks! Listen, young man, I've told you all there is to tell. Now . . . good day," she said curtly.

"I see," Clive said, rubbing his chin. The woman's shoulders relaxed a little at his apparent acceptance of her dismissal, but immediately stiffened again when he slyly threw in another question. "Does it say that she was hearing voices? That's one of the more obvious symptoms, as you've said."

"I really couldn't say," she faltered.

"Tell me, Mrs. Nicholson, do you have a German interpreter on staff?"

Mrs. Nicholson stared at him blankly, her big eyes swimming in panic.

"Because she was German. Does it say that there?" he asked, pointing to the file, which she pressed even tighter to her bosom. "Miss Klinkhammer doesn't speak any English, so I'm sure it was quite difficult to diagnose her, is all I'm saying."

"What police force did you say you're from?" Mrs. Nicholson asked nervously.

"None, as a matter of fact. I'm acting in a private capacity."

Mrs. Nicholson pulled herself up as straight as her sagging shoulders allowed. "Well, you can be certain, Mr. . . . what'd you say your name was?"

"Howard."

"Mr. Howard, that the hospital did not do nothing wrong. Now, I've told you that Liesel Klinkhammer was a patient here, and I told you where she was released to. That's all I can say." She paused for a moment. "I've told you more than I'm s'posed to, now that'll have to be good enough. Best be on your way, or I'll have to call one of the security guards," she said, her eyes darting reassuringly toward the big, black telephone on her desk.

"We're just leaving," Henrietta said, speaking for the first time. "Weren't we, Clive? Thank you very much, Mrs. Nicholson. You've been very helpful." She looped her arm through his.

"Yes, thank you," Clive said gruffly, and after giving her a nod, thrust his hat on his head and led Henrietta up the stairs and out into the fresh air.

It occurred to Clive as he nervously put the Daimler in park in front of the vast expanse of Dunning before them, that, from a distance, anyway, it almost resembled the heavily wooded campus of the seminary with its collection of beautifully designed buildings, set back from the road and built, one imagined, to offer troubled souls a place of respite and peace. But looks could be deceiving, Clive knew, having accompanied the chief here years ago in pursuit of a murder suspect and being summarily shocked by what he had witnessed. And, unlike the seminary, which was bordered only by woods and pasture, Dunning was surrounded by a tall, spiked fence on all sides, culminating in the massive, locked gates of iron bars before which Clive and Henrietta now sat, giving the whole place the decided feel of a prison rather than a place of healing and compassion.

Clive looked over to the left of the gates at the brick guard building, one corner of which appeared to be sinking into the muddy ground around it, making it look slightly lopsided and precarious, as if it might eventually topple over at some point. He could see two guards standing inside, but when neither of them seemed in any hurry to come out and open the gates for them, Clive gave the horn of the car an impatient toot.

One of the guards looked out the tall, rectangular window of the booth. "Hold yer horses! Most people is dying to get out, not in!" he shouted with a gruff laugh. A moment later, however, he sauntered out, scratching his whiskers, clipboard in hand. He was a heavily formed man with a thick, bushy moustache that curled up at the ends.

Clive rolled down the window as far as it would go, which was only about halfway, and the guard bent down and asked their business.

"Just visiting," Clive said as he drummed his fingers on the steering wheel.

"Name?" asked the guard.

"Clive Howard."

"And the little lady?" he asked, looking up briefly from his clipboard where he was scratching down their names.

"Mrs. Howard."

"Christian name?"

"I daresay that's not necessary, officer."

"Eh?" he said, looking up.

"It's Henrietta, officer," Henrietta said, leaning over Clive to answer for herself.

"Thank you, miss," the guard said, scratching it down, and then waved to his associate, who had meanwhile made his way over to the big wrought iron gate and was in the process of unlocking it.

"It's *madam* to you," Clive said in a clipped tone as he put the car back into gear and began to ease it forward through the now-open gate.

"Don't get all high and mighty with me, bub," the guard shouted after them, but Clive did not respond.

"You sounded surprisingly like your mother there, you know,"

Henrietta said to him with a grin as they drove slowly down the main lane.

"That's not amusing, Henrietta," Clive said clearly annoyed.

"Clive! I was only joking!" she said, and he could feel her looking at him closely.

He pulled at his tie with one hand.

"You're very cross today," she said more seriously now. "Are you nervous?"

"Of course, I'm nervous," Clive said shortly, as he followed the drive around the main building to a sort of parking lot. It was filled with potholes and stray bits of garbage, which had presumably escaped from the large trash barrels lined up at the far end of the lot. Some kind soul at some point in time must have attempted to beautify the grounds with small planted patches of daffodils here and there, a few of which had already managed to bloom despite their mean surroundings. Clive absently stared at them through the car window as he put the car in park, and felt a sudden odd sadness that their beauty was marred by bits of trash that had blown up against them and gotten entangled. "You should be, too," Clive said sternly.

"Well, I *am*, actually, but there's no need to bark at me. Or the guard, for that matter. He was only doing his duty."

"Henrietta, I'm sorry," he sighed. "But you have no idea what this place is like. I wish you would have stayed home as I asked you to. This is no place for a lady."

"I wasn't always a lady. Remember, Clive? I know what poverty looks like."

"Yes, you were so a lady," Clive said irritably, looking over at her. "Despite your circumstance."

"Until I met *you*, that is," she said, playfully putting her finger under his chin.

He had to fight down the conflicting turmoil and desire rising up in him even now. How could she always have this effect on him?

"Henrietta," he said taking her hand in his. "Be serious. This is an awful place. I was here once on a case with the chief. Expect to see anything—filth, nudity, swearing, screaming. All manner of abuse, though I daresay they won't parade it out in front of visitors."

"As a matter of fact, I *have* seen all of those things before, darling. But I thank you for the warning," she said lightly.

Clive did not respond. *God, this was a mistake.* Again, how had he gotten Henrietta into such a jeopardous situation? It had seemed like an innocent case, just something to do, really. Something to distract Henrietta. Drive out to Mundelein and find an errant cleaning woman. But somehow it had gotten more complicated, as usual, and now he was about to take her into fucking Dunning, of all places. He put his hand on his brow. And Elsie would be in tow, to make things worse. He hoped this Gunther had his wits about him, at least. It had been Henrietta's idea to ask them to accompany them. When she had proposed it, saying that it would be less of a shock for Liesel, less frightening if Gunther were present when they finally found her, to explain and maybe translate, he had thought it a good idea. Now, however, with the foreboding brick building looming ahead of them, he was having second thoughts.

"Where the hell are they?" Clive asked, looking impatiently at his wristwatch and then out the car window back toward Irving Park Road. An old-fashioned truck with a smashed headlight rumbled past them from somewhere deeper into the grounds, carrying what looked like a load of dirty laundry.

Henrietta laid a hand on his arm. "Come on. Maybe they're already inside, or maybe they're delayed. At any rate, it's no use sitting out here. Let's go in. The sooner we find this woman, the sooner we can leave."

The entrance of the asylum sat behind a set of triple brick archways, accessed by a short flight of steps to the main doors, which looked to have been painted white once upon a time. Now, however, large patches of the dull, gray concrete beneath could be seen where the paint had worn away. As they ascended the steps, Clive felt the unmistakable beginning of a fit and nearly panicked. He could feel another one of his attacks brewing, and he fought desperately to control it, though a part of him knew it was hopeless. He hesitated at the door, trembling, causing Henrietta to glance over at him.

"Are you all right, darling?" she asked, her voice one of concern. "You look white as a ghost!"

"I'm fine," he managed to answer and made himself reach for the door handle. He pulled on it and held it open for her, though the smell that escaped almost crippled him. The miasma of urine, feces, mold, and vomit took him immediately back to the war. Henrietta gently put a hand on his arm, and he struggled not to grab and crush it to his nose. Instead, he gave her what he hoped was a smile, though he suspected it came out as more a grimace. She turned her gaze from him, then, and stepped inside. Taking several deep breaths, he followed her.

The room they found themselves in was a sort of shabby main lobby, which looked as though it may have once upon a time been the foyer of a grand estate, with its thick crown molding and large, wooden pocket doors. Like the steps outside, however, the walls had been painted white, though it appeared to be a job done long ago, as everywhere the paint was peeling and flaking, the broken bits and flakes of paint forming a trail which lay collecting along the baseboards and gathering in the corners. Likewise, to add to the room's current state of negligence, several of the windows, which were barred, were cracked and dirty.

Clive removed his hat and gripped it, trying to steady his shaking hands. The door had closed behind them, and a horrible, claustrophobic feeling began to creep over him, further setting off the wheels of panic. He could feel the sweat dripping down the back of his neck. It wasn't just the smell that set him off—it was the noise. Not the sound of gunfire or shells, but the sound of low moans coming from one of the lobby corridors that paralyzed him completely. He tried to focus his gaze on the large wooden desk that sat in the center of the room, behind which stood two apparently frazzled nurses engaged in a heated discussion, but his vision was blurry.

Mercifully, Henrietta glanced over at him again and seemed to immediately sense what was happening to him. Quickly, she threaded her arm through his and gripped his hand. "Take a deep breath," she said quietly, leaning into him as she said it so no one could hear; not that anyone was listening anyway. He was tempted to bury his head in her chest, but he fought it. "You're all right," she whispered. "I'm here. You're all right, darling. Here. Sit down, here," she said, leading him to a couple of thick, scuffed chairs pushed forlornly up against the wall just inside the door.

Clive slumped into a chair and closed his eyes.

"Droppin' off?" asked a voice from behind Henrietta. Clive opened his eyes to see a young man swimming before him. He was wearing a white, tunic-style top with white uniform pants and loosely brandished a clipboard and pencil, apparently ready to write down their information.

"No, of course we're not dropping off," Henrietta said crisply as she turned to face him.

"I just need a minute," Clive said hoarsely.

"Yes, of course, darling," she said, not looking at him, but moving her body further so that Clive was completely blocked from the man's view. "As a matter of fact," she said stiffly, in her own splendid rendition of Antonia, "we're here to visit one of your patients. Never mind him," she commanded the orderly, who was still eyeing Clive carefully. "We are looking for a young woman by the name of Liesel Klinkhammer. How would we find her?"

God, she's marvelous, Clive thought.

"Patient?" he asked.

"Yes, a patient."

The young man did not say anything, but merely pointed his pencil toward the desk across the room. "Suit yourself, lady. But he don't look too good," he said, nodding at Clive.

"He's just getting over a particularly virulent flu and tires easily," she said stiffly, which caused Clive to smile despite his condition. He tried to watch her as she marched across the room, but a wave of nausea overcame him and he had to close his eyes to try to stop the room from spinning. With shaking hands, he took out his handkerchief and placed it over his nose, inhaling deeply and closing his eyes again.

Get a hold of the situation, he scolded himself; he had seen and heard much worse during his years on the force. Why was he having an attack now? It must be the combination of effects, he thought miserably, and continued to breathe deeply into his handkerchief. Not only did doing so block out the vile smell around him, but the cloth's faint traces of tobacco and linen and the woodsy smell of his cologne calmed him. He kept his eyes closed and tried to imagine the trees around Highbury and the deeply calming Lake Michigan that butted up to Highbury. He tried to envision the waves gently lapping, tried to concentrate on the rhythmic sound he remembered from all of the years of his boyhood.

"I'm looking for a Miss Liesel Klinkhammer," Henrietta said to the frazzled nurse seated behind the big front desk. The other one seemed to have disappeared. "She's a patient here, I believe," Henrietta added.

The nurse let out a sigh of impatience. "Recent?" she asked.

"A couple of months ago. October maybe?"

"That's recent," the nurse said, pulling out one of the thinner volumes of the massive ledgers stacked up behind the desk. Henrietta assumed that they had once been orderly, some of them still neatly tucked into the spot apparently assigned to them, but many had escaped and were stacked haphazardly on the desk and even the floor.

The nurse opened the ledger and ran her finger down the columns for what seemed to be several minutes. Suddenly a loud screech came from the depths of the open corridor to the right, and Henrietta jumped at the sound of it. The nurse did not react at all, however, and continued running her finger down the columns. When the screech was heard again, the nurse looked over her shoulder for a brief moment and then slowly stood up, as if she thought perhaps she should go investigate, but her finger and her eyes remained on the book in front of her.

"Ah, here it is. Ward 3C. Upstairs. Joe can take you if you want," she said without giving Henrietta a second look, instead turning quickly toward the corridor. She was in such a hurry that she nearly collided with another harried nurse coming from inside.

"It's Lichter again," this one said. "Can you give me a hand?" Without responding, the desk nurse followed her back into the corridor, pulling the big wooden pocket doors shut behind her.

Henrietta turned from the desk, then, and herself nearly collided with the same orderly who had addressed them moments before, and whom she assumed was the Joe the nurse had just mentioned.

"Ward 3C yer wantin'?" he said, an annoying toothpick dangling from the corner of his mouth now. He had short, flaming orange hair with a face full of freckles.

"Well, yes, thank you," Henrietta said, "but we're just waiting for some people to join us. My sister," she added.

"Ah! A regular tea party," he grinned. "Or is it a search party?" he asked with a short laugh and strode off. "All right, sister. You let me know when yous want to go up," he said, throwing himself into an abandoned chair by the desk and crossing his legs.

Before Henrietta could respond to this, another of the doors across the room opened. An elderly man, unshaven and oddly dressed in what looked to be a thin hospital gown, cut off somehow to form a sort of top and dirty black trousers, slipped out. He had no shoes or socks, and Henrietta shivered at the thought of how cold he must be. Having quietly emerged, the man did not look at anyone in the room. His eyes were focused on the entrance doors, the obvious object of his current mission, and he slowly shuffled toward them. It took Joe only a minute to spot him. He had tipped the chair back on two legs so that it was leaning against the dirty wall behind him, but now he snapped it forward and jumped up, lunging toward the elderly, creeping man.

"Hey, Bugsy!" Joe shouted. "Wheredya think yer goin'?" He

grabbed him by the sleeve. "Get back in here, you old coot," he said impatiently, pulling him back toward the doors from which he came. The man did not say anything or even react, but defeatedly allowed himself to be led. "How many damned times?" Joe said under his breath, holding the man with one hand and pulling open one of the doors with the other. "How do ya manage it?" he asked, pushing him through and following behind.

Henrietta watched as the door swung shut behind them and took advantage of the moment alone afforded them to turn and look at Clive, who smiled up at her weakly.

"Darling, are you okay?" she asked, trying to keep calm herself.

Clive nodded. "Forgive me, Henrietta," he said. "I shouldn't be so weak. I know I should be stronger, but sometimes I . . . these attacks just come upon me, and I . . . "

"Shhh," she said, putting her gloved fingertip to his lips. "There's no need."

Clive formed his lips into a kiss on her finger until she lowered her hand.

"I don't know how much longer I can just sit here, though," he said. "I need to be doing something or I'm going to go crazy myself. Maybe Elsie isn't coming," he said, glancing over at the main doors. "Perhaps we should go up without them, at least initially, locate this Liesel and get on with it. The sooner we find her, the sooner we can sort this out and leave."

Henrietta considered this for a moment. Perhaps he was right, though she dreaded the thought of Elsie walking into this nightmare on her own. Gunther would be with her, though, she reasoned, and for Clive's sake, she quickly decided it would be best to go on ahead. "Yes, I think you're right," Henrietta said, holding out her hand to help him up. "But are you sure, Clive?"

"Yes, I'm quite recovered," he said stiffly. "Now where did that orderly run off to?'"

Henrietta contemplated whether she should go look for Joe beyond the doors he had disappeared behind, just as he conveniently

burst forth from them alone, apparently having deposited the wandering Bugsy back where he belonged. Joe pulled down his tunic as
he walked, as if he had just been in some sort of struggle. Brushing
his hands against each other, he approached the two of them now.

"Had enough of sittin' there?" he said, grinning. "Thought ya
would. What about yer sister?"

"We'll go on ahead. If they do arrive, please escort them. It's a Mr.
Gunther Stockel and a Miss Elsie Von Harmon."

"Got it. But I think I could probably figure out who they were
without the names," he said with a roll of his eyes. "Don't get all
that many visitors. Anyway, Ward 3C? Come on; this way," he said,
walking toward the set of double doors directly behind the desk. He
pushed on one of the doors with his shoulder, and it easily swung
open, revealing a long, low corridor beyond. Clive and Henrietta followed him through.

"Infirmary," Joe said casually, as they walked along. Henrietta
could not help but peer into the various bedchambers that opened up
every hundred feet or so, but there was nothing unusual about them.
It resembled an ordinary hospital. She could see patients lying in bed
or propped up in a chair. An occasional moan could be heard from
time to time as they strode past, along with one shout for "nurse!"—
but it was otherwise unremarkable, except for the overwhelming
smell of urine mingled with a trace of excrement.

"I say, man, do you always lead visitors through the infirmary?"
Clive asked. "This is highly unsanitary."

"Not always, but this is the fastest way, and I'm in a bit of a hurry,
if ya don't mind."

Finally, they came to the end of the seemingly endless hallway,
where sat a pale green metal door, which possessed several dents
and scuffs and which likewise had its own share of peeling paint. Joe
paused in front of it and fished into his pocket for a large ring of keys.
Rifling through them with amazing speed and agility, he found the
one he wanted and bent down to unlock the door before him.

"This is a locked ward?" Clive asked.

"At this end, yeah."

They stepped through the doorway into a small antechamber, not more than six feet square, which seemed to serve as a connection between one section of the asylum and another. There was a spiral staircase of rusty metal to the right, and straight ahead seemed to be another wing. As Joe bent to relock the door they had just come through, Henrietta tentatively peered into the next room through a small circular window that was cut into the door. She could see various patients, mingling about, slumped in chairs along the wall or lying on mattresses that lined the room's corridor as far as she could see.

"Their beds are in the hallway?" she asked Joe incredulously, turning to look back at him.

Joe shrugged. "Ain't no more room. Better a bed on that floor than under a bridge somewhere in the city where it's freezin'. Head count always goes up here in winter. Peculiar, ain't it?" he grinned. "Come on." He started up the stairs. "Up we go." He walked up a few steps before turning to look at them more closely. "Just why are yous here, anyways? Come to see the freaks? Or are you reporters?"

"Of course, we're not reporters!" Henrietta said. "We're here to visit one of your patients, as I've said. Why would you think we're reporters?"

"'Cause ya look the type. And if yer not, then it don't add up. You look like you've got money, and people who end up here don't got no friends with money."

"What do you mean?" Henrietta said, a little breathless now that they had reached the third floor.

"People with money don't end up here, do they? If yer rich and crazy, people call you eccentric or something like that and yer relatives stick you away somewhere in yer big ol' house and get some biddy to look after ya. But if yer *poor* and crazy, well, yer not so lucky then, are ya?" He bent to unlock the door at the top of the stairs, and Henrietta momentarily thought of Ma in light of Joe's explanation. Could she be considered eccentric, or worse, crazy?

"You can save us your speech," Clive said crisply.

"Well, sorry to have offended, *sir*. Where's me manners? You'd think we were in the loony bin, wouldn't ya?"

"Are all of these hallways locked?" Clive asked, ignoring him.

"In this wing, yeah. But not in all of 'em. Like the small buildings out back—those is fer melancholias. Depressives. Mostly women. Hysteria. Those ain't locked."

"Are the patients in this ward really such a danger?" Henrietta said, nodding toward the door in front of them, wondering how and why Liesel would have been consigned here.

"Nah. The really dangerous ones is down below. Basement level. These ones here," he said, inclining his head. "Dangerous to themselves maybe. They're the schizos. Loons. They try to shock ' em every so often. Usually does no good. But whadda I know?" he said, pulling the door open now. "This ward's only women. Male schizos is on a different floor."

Clive went through first, with Henrietta gingerly stepping behind him. This ward was arranged differently from the other ones they had passed. It appeared to be set up to at least partially resemble a normal home. There was a common area in the center, delineated by a frayed rug, upon which sat a few ratty armchairs and two rocking chairs. A table stood in the center of these with a jigsaw puzzle on top of it, only partially completed. The unused pieces were strewn haphazardly about the tabletop, though Henrietta could see that several had fallen to the floor, and she had to resist the urge to go pick them up.

The bulk of the furniture in the room, however, consisted of wooden, straight-backed chairs, which lined the walls beyond the "parlor" area and which were all occupied by patients, most of them staring blankly into space like so many worthless paint flakes, crushed and collecting along the walls in the lobby down below. The ones who hadn't been lucky enough to get a chair this day leaned listlessly against the wall, some of them with their eyes closed, but some of them muttering to themselves or to an un-listening neighbor. At least it didn't smell as bad up here.

Henrietta could not help staring at them, though she tried not to make it obvious. Many were rocking slowly back and forth, as if they were in some sort of trance or meditation. One woman tapped the windowsill nervously with her fingers, and one was picking the skin on her arm, so much so that blood had been drawn. Overall, she noticed that most of them were not donned in hospital gowns but were dressed in normal clothing, though many of their ensembles were mismatched and either too big, or in other cases, too tight-fitting. Some had oddly shaved heads, so that they did not look like women at all save for their clothing.

Henrietta turned her attention to the patients in the chairs in the center of the room atop the rug and observed that one woman, uneasily perched in one of the rocking chairs, shockingly appeared to be holding what looked to be a baby. Henrietta was stunned. Surely they wouldn't allow children in this awful place! She wondered if the woman had given birth in the infirmary below, and her heart went out to her and this poor baby, born into such a place. It reminded her of one of Charles Dickens's novels that Elsie had once read to her. Which one was it? *Little Dorrit*?

The woman looked up and caught Henrietta's gaze. Henrietta offered her a pitying smile, but the woman did not return it. Instead she shifted herself so that her back was toward Henrietta, and she appeared to grip the baby tighter.

Henrietta felt tears well up in her eyes, though she could hardly explain why, but her attention was pulled away by Clive's address of the apparent nurse in charge, a large tank-like woman standing behind a desk that stood to the far left of the room. It seemed less a nursing station, and more an observation station in the wild or a triage unit in a battlefield. There was nothing on it—no pens or sharp instruments of any kind that Henrietta could see, just more ledgers and a hulking black typewriter. It seemed as if it would serve no purpose except to be a seat of command for the head nurse. Several patients sat on chairs in front of the desk or to the side, as if they needed the extra reassurance of proximity to the nurses, like needy dogs. Behind the hulking nurse, who appeared to be the one in charge, crouched another nurse, this one thinner and presumably younger, if the tendrils of jet-black hair that poked out from under her trim cap were any indication. It was hard to get a good look at her, however, as her back was to them as she bent to talk to one of the patients.

"Excuse me, nurse . . . ?" Clive asked the tank-like nurse.

"Nurse Harding," the woman growled in the lowest, deepest voice Henrietta had ever heard in a woman. In fact, she looked very much like a bulldog or at least a man, with a faint black moustache on her upper lip and several long, wiry hairs growing out of a large mole on the side of her face.

"Nurse Harding," Clive said obligingly. "We're looking to visit one of your patients, I believe. A Miss Liesel Klinkhammer."

"German lady?" Nurse Harding asked, her eyes slightly squinting as she pursed her lips.

"Yes, that's the one," Clive said eagerly.

"She's dead," the tank said matter-of-factly.

Henrietta felt an immediate blow to her stomach. "Dead?" she exclaimed, stunned. "Are you sure?"

"I think I know if one of my patients dies, missy. Yeah, she's dead. A few weeks now. Ain't that right, Caroline?" she said, attempting to turn her head toward the young nurse behind her, but the large roll of fat around her neck prevented her from doing so completely. Instead, her tiny eyeballs shifted to the extreme corners of their sockets to make up for the lack of dexterity in her neck, making her resemble, God forgive her, Henrietta thought, a pig.

"Yes," said the young nurse, standing up straight now and turning toward them. "I'm so sorry," she said kindly. She had warm brown eyes and a pretty smile accompanied by a slight dimple in her right cheek. "Liesel was a lovely woman. We'll miss her."

"Look—I'd like to talk to whoever's in charge," Clive said, slowly rubbing his forehead.

"And what makes you think that ain't me?" asked the tank.

Clive stared at her for several moments before he answered calmly, though Henrietta could see he was irritated. "All right, then. I'd like a word. In private."

"What about?"

"About Miss Klinkhammer, of course. I'd like to know what happened, read her chart."

"Who are you, anyway? Relative of hers? Left your visit a little late, didn't you?"

"As it is, I'm a private detective," Clive answered, just as a scrape of keys was heard and the door to the ward creaked open once again, Joe stepping quickly through.

"Knew it. Knew you was somethin'," he said with a grin. "I can always tell. Would have put money on you being from the *Trib*. Didn't think of detective. Anyways, here's yer pals."

Gunther and Elsie stepped through then, looking utterly disquieted. Elsie looked as though she might cry, and upon seeing Henrietta, she nearly ran to her. "Henrietta!" she said with relief as she embraced her. "I . . . I'm sorry we're late, we . . . we had some problems with Anna at the home," she said, releasing her sister and looking back at Gunther, who had taken a few steps into the room and was looking around nervously.

Henrietta took a deep breath, dreading the thought of having to tell them the horrible news. "We've just heard some bad news, I'm afraid," she said softly, looking at each of them in turn. "I . . . I'm afraid Liesel is dead, Gunther. I'm so sorry."

Henrietta saw him grip the hat in his hands as he bowed his head, his eyes shut tight.

"Dead? Oh, no!" Elsie cried out. "She can't be!"

"Are you sure?" Gunther asked hoarsely. "Sure it is her and . . . and not another maybe?"

Before Henrietta could answer him, Elsie spoke again.

"Henrietta, what happened?" she asked, her eyes darting to the nurses for the first time.

"We don't know any of the details," Henrietta tried to say calmly.

"We just found out ourselves." She looked over at Clive and then back at Gunther.

"I knew it," Gunther said quietly, putting his hand over his eyes. "I think always I have known this."

"Oh, Gunther," Elsie said, going to him and putting a hand on his arm. "I'm so sorry."

Gunther put his hand on top of hers and gripped it tightly, his face contorted as he sought to control his emotion.

Clive approached them and held out his hand to Gunther. "Mr. Stockel? Clive Howard," he said. "Sorry to meet under such sad circumstances. You've my sincere condolences. My wife tells me she was a friend."

"A friend of sorts. Yes." Gunther removed his hand from Elsie's to shake Clive's. "What am I going to do now?" he asked Elsie as he turned back toward her.

"Not to worry," Clive said to him. "We'll get to the bottom of this. I understand there's a child, is this correct? And I understand that she might be afflicted with the same condition which Liesel suffered from?"

Gunther looked up at him and seemed grateful that Clive had clearly grasped the situation and nodded. "Yes, that is so," he said.

"Nurse Harding, I really must insist that we speak to someone about this woman's condition," Clive demanded. "She's left behind a child, and any records would be of great help to us."

"You her husband?" the tank asked Gunther.

"No," Gunther answered.

"The father, then? Of the child?"

"No," Gunther answered again. Henrietta could tell by the way Clive was looking at Gunther during this exchange that he was attempting to assess the truthfulness of his words.

"Don't know how much I can say," the tank said with a shrug. "Confidential, you see." She moved her heavy arm to rest on top of one of the ledgers.

"Well, you can at least tell us the cause of death," Clive said, irritably.

"I think it was heart failure, wasn't it, Nurse Harding?" the thin nurse said faintly from behind her.

"I think you might be right, there, Nurse Collins. I believe it was, now that I think about it."

"Look, I demand we speak to the physician in charge—that or I'll have to seek out the administrator," Clive said sternly.

"All right, all right," the tank said with a harrumph and stood up heavily. "Follow me." She picked up the ledger and held it to her chest as she came from around the desk.

"Perhaps you'd like to stay and collect her things?" Nurse Collins suggested kindly, looking at Henrietta and Elsie. "Not that there were very many."

Henrietta looked to Clive for direction, who in turn gave her a slight nod and ever so slightly inclined his head toward Nurse Collins. Understanding, she hoped, his meaning, and thrilled that he was giving her an assignment, she nodded her answer to the young nurse. "Yes, that's a good idea, thank you."

"Mr. Stockel, why don't you come with me?" Clive suggested, and the two of them followed the tank toward the door.

"Nurse Collins, you have the floor," the tank growled without looking back.

"Want me to stay and help mind them?" Joe asked Nurse Collins with a tiny wink.

"No, I should be okay, Joe, but thanks," she answered. "She won't be long."

"Suit yerself," Joe said with a shrug and sauntered toward the still-open door. He stepped through and shut it without another word, and they could hear the key grinding the metal gears closed. It seemed uneasily loud to Henrietta, and she fought down her own sense of panic at being locked in, reminding herself that surely Nurse Collins had her own keys.

Nurse Collins turned to Henrietta and Elsie then and spoke. "Her bed's already been taken by another patient, I'm afraid, but I'll go and get her things. They're just in here," she called out as she walked away. "Won't be a moment."

Henrietta watched her disappear into what looked like a storage or a stock room, situated behind the desk, slightly to the left of it. From where she stood, Henrietta could see wooden shelves with various linens stacked upon them, but she could see nothing beyond, as the door was only slightly ajar.

"Henrietta, what's happening?" Elsie whined quietly now that they were alone. "How could Liesel be dead?" Small tears formed in the corners of her eyes. "This is terrible for poor Gunther."

"I know, Elsie. I don't understand it either. We'll try to get to the bottom of it, though," she said, protectively wrapping her arms around her. It felt good to hug her sister, and they stood this way for several moments until they heard a loud cough behind them. Henrietta released Elsie and turned. The woman with the baby sat calmly, looking at them, gently rocking. Suddenly, an urge came upon Henrietta to look at this baby, to face something inside of her that had been welling up all afternoon. She let go of Elsie's hand and took a step toward the woman.

"May I see your baby?" Henrietta asked gently, bending toward her.

Up close, the woman looked older than Henrietta had first surmised. She peered back at Henrietta, as if she hadn't heard or understood her, but then gave a tiny nod and held up her bundle. Henrietta bent closer and pulled back a part of the blanket and gasped. It wasn't a baby at all, but a doll!—the face of which was smeared with dirt and whose lifeless eyes stared blankly at the ceiling.

Elsie, who had crept up behind Henrietta and now peered over her shoulder, let out a scream.

Nurse Collins burst forth immediately from the depths of the storage room. "What is it?" she asked worriedly, rushing toward them. But as she observed the scene, she slowed her pace. "Oh, you've met Mrs. Wojcik," she said calmly.

"I'm sorry!" Elsie stammered. "I . . . I didn't mean to scream. I just . . . "

Mrs. Wojcik's face held a look of deep disgust as she pressed the doll close to her chest and quickly turned her body away from them as if to protect her "baby."

"It's all right, Mrs. Wojcik," Nurse Collins said soothingly as she gave the woman a soft pat on the back. "They didn't mean to scare you."

She looked disapprovingly at Henrietta and Elsie and nodded toward the desk. "This way," she said, then in a lowered voice. "It disturbs them if we talk in front of them."

"I'm sorry," Elsie mumbled again.

"Why is that woman holding a doll?" Henrietta asked in a low voice once they reached the desk.

"Her baby died in childbirth three years ago, and she apparently became deranged in her grief. Now she's here. She came in with the doll. We've tried to get it from her, but it makes things worse. She screams and becomes violent, so we let her have it. There's no harm in it, and it calms her."

"But surely that's not helping her to get well, to . . . to . . . well, to face it? To get better?" Henrietta asked uneasily.

"I think she's beyond curing," Nurse Collins smiled sadly. "Anyway, here are Liesel's things." She gave the thin stack of clothes on the desk in front of them a little pat, thereby changing the subject. "I'm very sorry. She wasn't with us long, I'm afraid. A sad case."

"Forgive me, but how . . . how did she end up here? We believe she may have suffered from epilepsy, but this . . . " she said gesturing around the room. "I think there might have been some mistake."

"Yes, she was severely epileptic; she was having at least one fit a day. We were treating her, but nothing was working."

"But isn't this ward for schizophrenics?" Henrietta asked. "She wasn't schizophrenic, was she?"

"I don't know that. But she did seem to have visions, see things that weren't there."

"How do you know that? I'm fairly certain she only spoke German," said Henrietta, following Clive's ingenious lead at the hospital.

"Nurse Harding speaks German."

"She does?" Henrietta asked, surprised.

"She served in the war. Picked it up there, I understand. Well, enough to get by, so she says." Nurse Collins gave them a small smile.

"So she was able to speak to Liesel? What did she say?"

"I'm not really sure . . . gibberish, mostly."

"Did she ever say the name Anna?" Elsie asked timidly.

Nurse Collins paused to think. "She may have," she said, nodding slowly. "It was very sad. She only ever had the one visitor."

"A visitor? Who was it?" Henrietta asked eagerly.

"I can't say," Nurse Collins said with a slow shake of her head.

"Was it a man or a woman?"

"A man, I think."

"Can you remember his name?" pressed Henrietta. "Was it Heinrich?"

Nurse Collins paused to think again. "It may have been. I'm not sure. I'm sorry. There are so many patients," she said wearily, and Henrietta noticed the deep grooves at the corners of her eyes and the purple patches under them. "We can't save them all, I'm afraid," Nurse Collins went on. "And sometimes it's better if they go. For them that is. Your friend is in a better place now, don't you think?"

"Yes, but—" Henrietta began but was interrupted by a loud crash that came from somewhere down the corridor, which caused even the staid Nurse Collins to jump.

"You'll have to excuse me," she said distractedly and before either Henrietta or Elsie could say anything, she hurried off.

Henrietta watched her go, trying to take in all of this new information. What were any of them to do now? And what was to be done with Anna? Remembering, then, what Elsie had said about she and Gunther having trouble with Anna just this morning, she turned to ask her about it—but then nearly screamed when she felt a cold hand grasp hers. She spun to her right to see a patient standing very close to her. She was just a wisp of a woman and was clothed in a dull, gray housedress that practically hung on her skeletal frame. Henrietta wasn't sure if the fabric of it was originally gray or if it was instead the victim of too many launderings, or perhaps not enough. The woman was much shorter than even Henrietta and had glasses that were so smudged, it was hard to tell how the woman could properly see out of them. They were much too big for her face, making her resemble a type of owl. Her face was deeply wrinkled, and her skin was as loose and baggy as her dress and deeply veined. The woman swayed slightly as she stood there peering at her, giving Henrietta the impression that she might collapse at any moment.

"That one is an angel," she said, mysteriously, nodding toward the hallway where Nurse Collins had just disappeared down. "Not like the big one. She's a mean devil, she is."

"Is she?" Henrietta said as gently as she could, not wanting to disturb yet another patient.

"I've been here almost twenty years, I have. Seen lots of things."

"Yes, I'm sure you have," Henrietta said. She wanted to pull her hand away, but the woman gripped it tightly as she swayed. She said nothing further, but merely stared absently at the wall beyond. Desperately, Henrietta tried to think of something to say.

"Do you . . . do you like it here?" she finally managed.

"No, I don't," the woman said, looking at her now. "But I can't get out, you see. I tried, but they always catch me."

"Oh . . . "

Henrietta did not like the sound of this and wondered if it were true. "What happens then?" she asked tentatively, her curiosity getting the better of her.

"Bread and water, water and bread for one half of a full moon," the woman answered in a raspy voice. "That's what happens. The bread has creepy crawlies in it, though. Weevils and other creatures. You have to eat it fast so's you don't feel them squirming."

At this image, Henrietta felt her breakfast rise to her throat and fought down an urge to retch. Likewise, she heard Elsie gasp behind her.

"Did you . . . did you know a Miss Klinkhammer?" Henrietta

managed to ask after a moment. "Liesel was her name. She was a patient here a few weeks ago. She was a German lady."

"Oh, yes, I knew her. Frightened she was. And sad."

"What was she frightened of?" Henrietta asked.

"She was possessed by an evil spirit."

Henrietta let out a deep breath, her hopes of any useful information dashed. Not this again, she thought, but the way the woman was staring at her now caused a shiver to run up her spine.

"I tried to show her how to escape, but the demon blocked her ears from understanding. She died then."

"What can you tell me about her death?" Henrietta decided to ask, though it seemed hopeless to try to get any real information.

"I can tell *you* how to escape, I can," the woman whispered cryptically, shifting her eyes from side to side. "The rats come out of the walls at night and whisper it to me," she went on hurriedly, without waiting for Henrietta to answer. "There's a golden city, underground. You must dig to the center of the earth where the other humans live," she said eagerly. "They are the kind ones. Not like these," she hissed. "The tunnels are already dug, but they are very secret. Only the rats know. But they are very greedy. Very greedy."

At this, Henrietta tried to pull her hand away, but the woman held it fast and squeezed it to the point of hurting. "Their civilization is very ancient, but very advanced," she whispered. "You must find your way there and come back for me. You must promise!"

She was looking desperately at Henrietta, pleading with her eyes, when suddenly Nurse Collins's footsteps could be heard approaching, and the woman quickly released her grip on Henrietta's hand and took a step back. Nurse Collins appeared in the room, then, and shot them a glance.

"Mrs. Goodman," she called out, not unkindly, "you're not bothering our guests with your tales are you?" She paused in her approach to adjust a patient who had slumped over onto the shoulder of the woman sitting next to her.

Mrs. Goodman took the opportunity to nod at Nurse Collins and whisper, "But that one's an angel. Floats through the halls she does, at night. Bringing good things to those who wait."

Henrietta gave her an uneasy smile. "Well, good-bye," she said awkwardly. She took Elsie firmly by the arm and walked back toward the desk, leaving Mrs. Goodman to sway on her own. The whole morning's experience was beginning to wear on Henrietta, but she told herself that she had to be strong.

"So, there's nothing more you can tell us?" she asked Nurse Collins, who finally now handed them Liesel's small bundle. "About Liesel, I mean. She died of heart failure?"

"As far as we know, yes," Nurse Collins said gently. "She died in her sleep."

"That poor woman," Elsie said, finally speaking. "I can't imagine what she went through." She wiped a tear from her eye, and then paused to mutter, "And poor Anna. What's to become of her, Henrietta?"

"I don't know, Els," Henrietta answered, shaking her head. It was a good question, but one Henrietta couldn't focus on at the moment. At this point, she just wanted to get out.

Chapter 9

"I'm coming, already!" Stan shouted as he shuffled toward the front door of his parents' modest bungalow on Mozart, but the furious knocking continued. "Gee whillikers, hold on!" he said, opening the front door to see none other than Rose standing there, shivering like crazy. She had a scarf wrapped over her head and tied under her chin, which oddly concealed much of her face—usually Rose was a bit flashier—and she was nervously smoking a cigarette.

"Gee whiz, Rose! What are you doing here?" Stan asked, bewildered. "Shouldn't you be at work now?"

"Who is it, Stanley?" came the sound of Stanley's mother's voice from somewhere deeper in the house.

"It's Rose, Ma!" Stanley shouted back, only slightly turning his head toward the inside of the house as he did so, his eyes glued on Rose. There was something wrong; he could tell.

"Well, ask her to come in!" came the cheery voice.

"Oh, yeah, sorry," he said with a lopsided grin, opening the door wider and gesturing for her to come in. "Come in." But Rose merely shook her head no, as she took another drag of her cigarette.

"I need to talk to you," she said in a low voice. "In private?"

"Right now?" Stan asked, looking over his shoulder back into the house.

Rose bit the side of her cheek in what looked like annoyance. He didn't like it when she did that; he knew it meant she was upset.

"Yeah, now. Can we go somewhere?"

"Well, I guess so," Stan said hesitantly and just stood looking at her.

"Get your coat, then, Stan!" she hissed.

"Oh, yeah. You want to step in, while I get it?" he gestured again, but she merely shook her head and tossed her cigarette butt on the cement steps, grinding it out.

"All right, just a minute." He reached into the closet by the front door and grabbed his hat and coat.

"Hurry, Stan!"

"I'm just going out for a minute, Ma!" he called, thrusting his arms into his coat.

"I thought Rose was coming in," Mrs. Dubowski shouted. "Ask her to stay to dinner. It's meatloaf."

"Okay, but I don't know if she can."

"Where are you going, anyway?"

Stan looked out at Rose for the answer, but she merely shrugged, inclining her head toward the sidewalk.

"Just for a walk," Stan shouted.

"It's freezing!" said his mother in a normal tone of voice now as she came out of the kitchen and approached the front door where Stanley stood. "Where's your muffler?"

"Ma! I don't need that. We won't be gone long," he said and looked toward Rose for confirmation, but she had already retreated down the steps and was standing on the sidewalk.

"Hi, Rose!" Mrs. Dubowski called down to Rose, as she wiped her hands on a dish towel. "Won't you come in?"

"I just felt like a walk, Mrs. Dubowski," Rose called up thinly. "Thanks, though."

"Well, suit yourselves. In my day, courting couples always sat in the front room and had conversation with the parents—"

"Ma!"

"Go on, then. Be back by five. Sharp," she called as Stanley plopped on his hat and rushed out the door. "You'll stay for dinner, won't you, Rose?" she called.

"I . . . I have to work, Mrs. Dubowski. But thank you."

"Well, how about Sunday?" she shouted as they began to walk away.

"Maybe."

Stan joined Rose, his hands stuffed in his pockets, and they began walking briskly down the street, though Stan had no idea where they were headed.

"Want to get a cup of coffee?" she asked without looking at him. They turned onto Armitage, into the wind, causing them to bend slightly forward.

Stan wanted to point out that they could have had free coffee if they'd stayed at his parents', but he didn't say so. Clearly, Rose had something important on her mind. "Sure," he said and then added, "so what's this all about, Rose? Something wrong?"

"I'll explain in a minute," she said loudly over the wind, still bent slightly and looking down at the sidewalk as they walked.

They continued in silence until they reached Kaufmann's and went inside, the shop bell tinkling as they entered. Rose led them to a back booth, and Stan slid onto the thick, leather seat. Rose sat opposite him. Stan looked at the small chalkboard hanging beside a Coca-Cola sign to peruse the specials before remembering that they weren't actually here to eat. He pulled his eyes away from the menu to look at Rose now, but as he did so, he nearly cried out loud. She had removed her coat and slightly pulled back her scarf to fully reveal her face, the right side of which was swollen and purple.

"Jesus, Rose!" Stan bellowed, his stomach churning at the sight of her bruised face. "What happened? Did you fall?" Then it suddenly dawned on him. He could see tiny tears in the corners of her eyes. Jesus Christ. "Was it . . . it wasn't your dad, was it?" he asked, his breath labored.

Rose gave the tiniest of nods and looked away.

Stan felt as though he had been punched himself, fury shooting through him. How dare her old man! He would kill him! he resolved wildly. His urge was to go right then and there. Why were they sitting calmly in a diner? How could . . . how could anyone hit a woman, and *your daughter* at that? He knew Rose's father was a drunk, but it didn't excuse it.

"I'm going to kill him, Rose!" Stan huffed, grabbing his hat just as the thick waitress appeared beside the table.

"What'll it be, kids?" she asked dully.

"Stanley, just calm down," Rose said firmly. "We'll have two black coffees," she said to the waitress.

"That it?" the waitress asked, clearly annoyed.

"For now," Rose said, staring her down.

"Nice shiner," the waitress said, looking over at Stanley as if he were a piece of dirt.

"Hey!" Stanley said, realizing the meaning behind her withering look, but she had already moved away.

"Jeez, Rose. I said if he ever touched you, I'd kill him! So, now I'm going to kill him." He threw his hat back onto the seat.

"Come on, Stanley, be serious."

"I *am* being serious!" He was filled with rage and . . . and what? Mortification? Humiliation? Rose was his! No one had the right to touch her but him, and even then . . . Suddenly, he felt he might vomit. He couldn't look at her face for more than a few seconds at a time.

"Stanley, I don't know what I'm going to do!" she said suddenly, cradling her forehead on the tips of her fingers and beginning to cry.

Stanley felt a flood of something else release within him now, a desperate sort of pity mixed with panic. "Rose . . . hey, Rose!" he said gently. "Hey, it's going to be all right. We'll think of something."

"He's getting worse, Stan. He beat Billy again. And I can't keep taking him to Lucy and Gwen's. They were nice enough to keep him for a while. I thought things had calmed down, so I brought him back a few nights ago. It was a mistake, I guess. The ol' man had a go at him the very first night. I tried to stop it, and this is what I got," she said pointing to her damaged face. "I took Billy back to Lucy and Gwen's, but I could tell they weren't too happy. I mean, I guess I wouldn't be, either. He can't just stay there forever."

The waitress appeared with two coffees. Seeing Rose's tears, she gave Stanley another snide look and walked away, mumbling "men" under her breath.

Stanley wrapped his hands around one of the thick white mugs and tried to calm himself. What the hell was he going to do? So far he had been elusive in describing Rose's familial situation to his parents, particularly his mother, only giving the barest of facts that Rose's mother was dead and that she lived with her father and younger brother. Rose had been elusive, too, during the few times she managed to come to dinner at the Dubowski's, and Stanley had taken his cues from her—not only on this subject but regarding many topics, actually. He was impressed, truth be told, by how smoothly she outfoxed his mother—a difficult feat by any stretch, one which he and his father had given up trying to achieve long ago. His first thought was that they should explain the situation—partially, maybe?—to his parents. But to what end? He could maybe talk them into letting Rose move into the spare bedroom, but where did that leave Billy? That seemed to be the real problem here. Billy. He hadn't yet mentioned to his parents that his fiancé's brother was backward. He wasn't sure what they would say to that. Well, he could guess . . .

"I . . . I'm desperate, Stan," Rose was saying. "I don't have enough money to move out on my own, and we can't stay there anymore. I can't take it. I don't mind for myself, but I can't take Billy being punched and kicked and . . . " She broke down into sobs, covering her face with her hands.

"You all right, doll?" the waitress called from where she poured coffee at the counter for other customers.

"Yeah, she's fine," Stan called out weakly, turning slightly toward the counter. The waitress, holding the coffee pot midair, continued to stare at Rose, waiting for some kind of confirmation from her.

As if sensing the waitress's eyes on her, Rose looked up and nodded sadly.

"Jeez," Stan mumbled. "A guy can't win."

"I . . . I have an aunt. A great-aunt, actually," Rose said faintly, blowing her nose into the handkerchief she had fished out of her pocket. "My mom's aunt, Millie. She lives in Indiana. It's the only family I know of that's left on her side. I'm . . . I'm thinking about writing to her. Asking her if Billy and I can move in."

"What!?" Stan exclaimed. "Move in? What . . . what about our wedding?" A new level of panic coursing through him.

"Well, I don't know," Rose said, twisting her lips into a grimace.

"What do you mean, 'you don't know'?" he hissed, dread filling him that yet another woman was going to slip through his grasp. First Henrietta, then Elsie. Well, he wasn't going to let that happen with Rose. He had made his choice, once and for all, and that was that. And, anyway, he loved Rose; he was sure of it this time. She was so very pretty with her blonde hair and green eyes, and especially her long legs. Stan longed to run his hand up them, but so far he hadn't dared. They had kissed plenty of times now, and each time he had been left breathless and almost panting. Somehow, she knew all the right places to put her hands until he was positively on fire. Many times, after an evening with her, he had had to . . . well, let's just say, he had done things in his room at night that required him to go to confession the following Saturday. Only once had a stray thought come into his mind while they were kissing that had disturbed him. He had pulled back, his lips wet, and he dared to ask her if she was . . . well . . . if she was still a virgin. Not that it mattered, he had mumbled—but in truth, it *did* matter to him. He wanted to be the first. And he wanted her to be his first, too. "Of course," she had whispered as she kissed his neck and then sucked his earlobe, causing him not to care at that moment. "What did he take her for?" she had asked. He had chosen to believe her then, and still did, he told himself, but every once in a while, she seemed . . . well, very experienced. Put it that way. But it was more than her looks and her sexual prowess that attracted him, he had told himself many times. He just liked being with her. She usually went along with whatever he said, which always caused his chest to swell, but on the other hand, she had a way of helping him to know just what to do in every situation. He felt comfortable with her. And she was even converting for him. That said something, for sure. So the thought now of not being with her, of not marrying her, caused a fresh burst of anxiety to wash over him.

"You can't leave, Rose. I . . . I love you; you know that, don't you?" he whined.

"Well, I love you, too, Stanley, but . . . but things are just too terrible at home. We . . . we might have to give each other up."

Stanley could swear she was batting her eyelashes at him, and he found himself staring at her lips. "No, we're not!" he almost shouted. "We're getting married. I gave you a ring!" he squeaked.

She let out a small sigh. "Stanley, we've never really talked in detail about what will happen when—if—we do get married. About where we'll live. I need to know," she said quietly.

Stanley fidgeted and twisted his feet under the table. He hadn't fully thought this through. His parents were suggesting that Rose move in until the young couple had saved enough to get their own place. That's what they had done, they had told him a hundred times. Lived with Grandma and Grandpa for nearly five years before they got their own apartment. In fact, Stanley had been born at Grandma and Grandpa's. He would be happy enough with the proposed arrangement, he knew, but he had hesitated bringing it up to Rose, as somehow he sensed she would not be all that enthused. "Well," he said tentatively. "I was thinking you could move in with us . . . you know, till we have enough money to get our own place . . . "

He saw her bite the side of her cheek again and therefore knew she didn't like the idea. She was silent for a moment, gripping her own mug. "That's a swell idea, Stan," she said stiffly, "but what am I going to do with Billy? I can't leave him."

Damn it! Stan thought to himself. He hadn't entered Billy into the equation at all. He had assumed he would keep living with the father. But he saw now that that plan wasn't going to work. This was a two-for-one type of situation, he realized with a sinking feeling. "You mean Billy would have to live with us?" Stan said slowly.

"I know it's not ideal, Stan, but I can't just leave him there," she repeated. "I know it's not what you signed up for, though. You've been a real sport. But we . . . we don't have to go through with this. Billy and I can go live with my aunt—if she'll have us, that is—and we can go our separate ways." She moved one of her hands to his and rubbed his thumb with one of her fingers. Even that small gesture madly elicited a response in his lower regions, but he managed to ignore it.

Slowly, she pulled her hand away then and tugged at the tiny ring he had given her, setting it on the table between them. "It's all right," she said, smiling weakly. "I understand. I guess it just wasn't meant to be."

She looked up at him with her big green eyes that somehow, even in their sadness, mesmerized him. An errant thought zipped through his mind, suggesting that she was perhaps testing him, but he pushed this thought away. It was replaced almost immediately by a similar thought, however, that perhaps he should be cautious here. He picked up the ring and rolled it between his thumb and forefinger. A part of him knew that if he proceeded now, there was only one path forward. But he didn't want to think about the alternative, about losing her, which meant there was nothing to do but plow ahead.

"Whaddya mean?" he tried to ask lightly. "I asked you to marry me, and I meant it! We can't let the first obstacle derail us, can we, Rose?" he asked resolutely. "For better or worse, don't they say?"

"Are you sure, Stan?" she asked hesitantly. It almost seemed like she was having second thoughts . . . why wasn't she happier?

"Course I'm sure! Aren't you?"

She looked at the table and let out a deep breath, and for a few awful moments, he thought she was going to actually back out after all. When she finally looked up at him, she gave him a smile, though it seemed false, and said, "Course I am. But I'll . . . we'll have to take care of Billy . . . You understand that, right? You're okay with that?"

Stan gripped the ring tighter, knowing this was his moment. It was now or never . . . he gave it one last consideration . . .

Well, dang it, what did it matter if Billy did live with them? he resolved. He seemed decent enough, hard-working, quiet. He'd have his own room, and they would have theirs. It could even be a good thing, actually . . . yeah, this could be a good thing, he convinced himself. What had he been thinking? What did it matter?

"Yeah, I don't mind having Bill around," Stan finally said with his lopsided grin. "He's okay in my book."

"Oh, Stan! Do you mean it?" Rose gushed, and the sight of her happy face, despite the discoloration and swelling, was enough to melt Stanley's heart. It would be worth having Billy around just to be able to come home every night to Rose's smile and what he hoped was her good cooking and to lie next to her each night. It sounded like heaven! Even with Billy in the next room.

"Give me your hand," he said, holding out his. She put her hand in his, and with trembling fingers, he thrust the ring on her finger. "No more takin' that off!" he said with mock sternness.

"But, Stan, this is nice and all—but it doesn't really solve anything," she said, pulling her hand free and touching her bruised face.

"Goddamn it," Stan fumed again. It certainly didn't. "I don't know, Rose. Got any ideas?" He loved that both Rose and his mother always seemed to know what to do in any situation. He was sure they would get on fabulously as the years went on . . . Maybe they could even name a daughter after his mother, Stan thought dreamily . . . Constance Dubowski . . . little Connie they would call her . . .

"Stan!" Rose was saying. "Did you hear me? I said maybe we could get married right away—"

"Married right away?" Stan cried.

"How much money do you have saved?"

"Three hundred and seventy-five bucks," he said proudly.

"I have a little, too," Rose added. "And Billy has some, though Dad takes most of it off him. But that would be enough to get a little place."

"Get a little place?" Stan asked. "I thought we were living with my parents . . . "

"With Billy?" she asked, giving him a sort of irritated look. "We need to get an apartment right away, so that Billy and I can get away from Dad. Maybe even this week?"

"This week?! But we can't move the wedding up *that* fast! They're still reading the bans at church . . . and you're not even done with your catechism . . . " Stanly fumbled.

"Well, we can still get an apartment—"

"We can't live in sin, Rose! I'm drawing the line there. And what would I tell my parents?"

"Listen . . . maybe we don't need to tell them."

"Don't need to tell them? I think they might notice if I moved out next Tuesday."

"You kids need a refill?" the waitress said, suddenly appearing by the table with a stained coffeepot in hand. Both Rose and Stan moved their mugs to the edge so that she could refill them.

"Thanks," Rose said. "And we'll have a piece of apple pie, too."

"Got it. One pie," the waitress said, writing it on her little pad, and went back toward the counter.

"I haven't had dinner yet, Rose!" Stanley grumbled. "*And* we need to save money, it seems."

"Well, this *is* my dinner, Stan. I've got to go soon, or I'll be late for work."

Stan stared gloomily at his coffee.

"Look," Rose said encouragingly, "why don't we get married by the justice of the peace? No one has to know. We get an apartment, spend our wedding night there," she said, giving him a delicious wink, "and no one's the wiser. You still live with your parents until the church wedding, and then you move into the apartment. See? Easy." The waitress reappeared and set down the pie.

"We have two weddings?" Stan asked, confused.

"People do it all the time," Rose said, picking up the fork straddling the plate and taking a bite of the pie. "Usually if there's a kid on the way so that it's not born a bastard. Then they have a church wedding. You know, you have to have the marriage blessed, right?" she said, looking suddenly pious, though as she said it, she slowly slid the fork from her mouth, her lips pressed tightly on it, which Stan could not help staring at. "And we have a different kind of kid we have to think about, so it makes sense." She offered him the fork to share the pie.

He shook his head. How could she eat right now? This was a serious thing she was proposing. When she explained it, it seemed to make so much sense—but did it? Wasn't this wrong somehow?

"Look, Stanley, I know this is a bit rushed," she implored, "but there's no other way. I can't stay much longer in that house, and I can't keep taking Billy to Gwen and Lucy's. It's either this, or I'm going to have to move to Indiana. I don't have many choices." More tears began to well up in her eyes, and he felt slightly panicked again. He shifted in the booth.

"Aw, gee, Rose, I don't know," Stan mumbled. "But why do we have to get married? Can't I just give you the money for the apartment, and we wait till June like we planned?"

Rose was silent for an agonizing moment. "I suppose we don't *have* to get married," she said slowly with a lopsided sort of a shrug and a pout. "I just thought you would want to. But men set their mistresses up all the time in an apartment, so I guess it would sort of be like that—"

"You're not my mistress!" Stan exclaimed furiously, looking from her to the dirty fan on the ceiling slowly swirling even though it was winter and freezing out, as if the diner owner had forgot that it wasn't summer anymore. It sure was warm in here, though, Stan thought, as he pulled at his collar. "I just . . . " he began. "I don't know, Rose, I just . . . " He wished he could talk this over with his mother. Without her trusted guidance, he wasn't sure what to do . . .

"I thought you would like to be married . . . make it all official and have a special wedding night in our own place . . . " she trailed off. "No more waiting." One of her hands was somehow on his knee now, causing parts of him to stiffen. "I just thought it was the more honorable thing."

Yes, Stan thought, though he was having trouble thinking clearly at this particular moment. It did make sense, he supposed. It was the more honorable way. And what choice did he have, really? It was either she stay with her father and be beaten by him, which still made his blood boil—not that he needed any help in that department—or have her move away, or set her up in an apartment. And she was right, it would either be as his . . . well, his mistress, he supposed—though he didn't plan on consummating their relationship unless they were well and truly married—or marry her and make it proper. None of these were particularly comfortable choices, but he supposed that getting married sooner than later made the most sense. He would simply have to do the honorable thing and hope that his mother would never find out.

"Well . . . when would we do it?" he asked hesitantly.

Chapter 10

"I still can't believe they gave her electric shock treatments," Henrietta said sadly. She and Clive were sitting in the morning room at Highbury, having breakfast and the pleasant benefit of being able to speak freely, as Antonia had not yet come down from her wing.

"Yes, it's terrible, isn't it?" Clive said over his newspaper.

They had already discussed many times now what they discovered at Dunning about poor Liesel Klinkhammer's demise, or rather, what Clive and Gunther had discovered. Henrietta had little to share from her meager conversation with Nurse Collins, nor did she see the point in telling him about her strange conversation with Mrs. Goodman, nor the woman with the baby—Mrs. Wojcik, was it?—either.

Clive, for his part, had finally forced Nurse Harding, albeit amid loud protests and several harrumphs, to grant them an interview with the day's attending physician, one Dr. Ingesson. Dr. Ingesson, however, didn't even give Clive and Gunther the courtesy of sitting down with them somewhere private, but instead allowed them all of about five minutes in the midst of the infirmary as he did his rounds. He had been very curt, Clive later told Henrietta, not to mention condescending, demanding to know who he was exactly and what relation he was, if any, to the deceased. Accordingly, Clive had introduced himself and Gunther, explaining that Gunther was sort of a relation to the departed woman in question.

"Don't let him fool you, doctor. This one's a detective," said the tank, who still accompanied them, with a nod toward Clive.

"Yes, that is true," Clive responded, shooting a dagger at Nurse Harding. "I've been helping Mr. Stockel to find this woman. I'm a friend of his."

Dr. Ingesson seemed to be considering something as he looked them over and then let his eyes drop to the chart the tank had handed him when they first approached. After only a few moments of examining it, he confirmed what Nurse Collins had already told them; that heart failure had brought about Liesel Klinkhammer's sudden death.

"This happens sometimes in cases of electric shocktreatment," Dr. Ingesson said dismissively. "It is rare, but it does occur occasionally. Unfortunately, there's no way to know," he added with a shrug. "I'm very sorry. Now, if you'll excuse me."

"Electric shock?" Clive had exclaimed. "Of the brain? That seems rather extreme. Is that your usual course of treatment for epileptics?"

Dr. Ingesson had already begun to turn away, but looked back at Clive now. He studied him coolly before opening the chart again.

"Ah, yes," he said. "She came in with classic epileptic symptoms, which looks to have unfortunately progressed into schizophrenia. Not uncommon, really. We tried a healthy dose of electric shock, but it seems it did no good. Sorry," he said looking up at Clive again. "We did our best."

"But that's madness!" Clive burst out. "Barbaric, even."

Again Dr. Ingesson turned back, only now with an air of defensive irritation. "Not really," he said stiffly. "Electric shock therapy is a new treatment for any number of mental maladies—epilepsy and schizophrenia included. Another is hosing."

"Hosing?" Gunther asked cautiously, finally breaking his silence. "I do not know this word."

"Yes, it is a new theory from Switzerland. A quite prominent researcher there found that hosing down depressives with a fire hose has had excellent results in some cases. Occasionally we try that here as well, but our preferred treatment, based on the latest theories, is electric shock. So you see, we are not so barbaric as you might think." He snapped the chart shut and handed it back to the tank.

"Be that as it may," Clive went on, "I find it difficult to understand her diagnosis. Schizophrenia? What were her symptoms?"

"Really, Mr. . . . ?"

"Howard."

"Mr. Howard. I don't see how this matters much. She would have been given the same treatment whatever her diagnosis was, and which I don't really have to discuss with you. Now, if you'll excuse me; I'm very busy."

"Do you have a German interpreter on staff?" Clive asked.

Dr. Ingesson gave him a puzzled look.

"I didn't think so," he said disgustedly. "I demand to see this woman's records." He glanced over to where the tank tightly pressed the chart against her massive bosom.

"For what purpose? What more do you want to know?" Dr. Ingesson asked, his eyes narrowing. "Surely, you don't suspect some sort of foul play?"

Clive merely raised an eyebrow.

"Mr. Howard," Dr. Ingesson said sternly, "I can assure you. There was absolutely *nothing* suspicious about this woman's death. People die here every day. The cemetery's proof of that." He inclined his head in the apparent direction of the patients' final resting place. "This is an asylum. People don't get better here. They just eventually die. Now, again, if you'll excuse me, I have sick people to attend to. If you persist in wanting to read this poor woman's chart, then you'll have to produce some sort of legal document. But you won't find anything. We tried our best, for which we of course get no thanks. She died. Case closed."

He turned abruptly and picked up the chart of the patient whose bed was closest to them, making a point of studiously reading it and thereby dismissing them. Nurse Harding then chased them out, complaining and uttering many "I told you so's" on the way.

Henrietta stirred some cream into her coffee and watched the swirling pattern dissolve into a dull brown. She took a sip and looked across at Clive, who was still intently reading the paper.

"So, what do we do now?" she asked.

"Well, I thought we'd drive over to investigate this spiritualist Davis is on about. Madame Pavlovsky is what she calls herself, I believe. Shouldn't be too difficult to sort out," he said, casually turning the page. "He telephoned yesterday to check our progress, so I suppose we should get on with it."

"No, I meant, what are we going to do about the Liesel case?" she asked.

"Well, as I've said before, darling, I don't think there's anything more we *can* do."

"So you really don't suspect foul play?" she asked, reaching for another piece of toast.

"Not really," he said, folding his paper. "Darling, we've been through all of this before." He sighed. "There were perhaps dubious medical practices, maybe even wrongful death, but not foul play. For one thing, there's no motive."

"But you admitted that Nurse Harding and even Dr. Ingesson's responses were quite suspicious. Like they're hiding something. Why else would they not let you read the ledger or the chart, or whatever it was?" she said, taking a bite.

"Guilt maybe? That their prescribed method of treatment didn't work?"

"Exactly!" Henrietta said.

"Yes, so her death may have been a result of the treatment, but I don't think they *meant* for her to die. I do believe it was accidental."

"But maybe it wasn't!"

"But why would they want to kill a poor immigrant woman?"

Henrietta thought for a few moments. "Overcrowding?"

"Henrietta," he said, his voice oddly one of patient concern. "I believe we can safely say that the Liesel Klinkhammer case, if you want to call it that, is closed."

Henrietta knew he was right, logically, but she just couldn't seem to let it go. She looked away from him.

"Listen, darling," Clive went on. "It was our first case together, you might say—unofficial, that is—but we can record it as a success, surely that means something to—"

"A success?" she interrupted.

"We were charged with finding this woman," he said matter-of-factly. "And we did."

Henrietta could feel her irritation rising. The room felt stuffy suddenly and her breathing deepened. How could Clive possibly be so dismissive of the situation? His laissez-faire attitude about the whole thing aggravated her. Surely, he wasn't this unfeeling? How could he not see that something wasn't adding up?

"But what about her mysterious visitor?" she exclaimed. "The man? Maybe it was Heinrich, Anna's father. Shouldn't we try to find *him*? And what about this 'gibberish' that she was supposedly telling Nurse Harding? Don't you find that odd?" She was growing more agitated by the moment. "Maybe Nurse Harding doesn't really speak German, and this poor woman wasn't really insane! You don't know that she was!" she cried and suddenly burst into tears, much to her own surprise and also vexation.

She wasn't sure what was bothering her about this case and why she was reluctant to let it go. Deep down she knew that Clive was probably right. There was nothing they could really do at this point, and, anyway, it didn't matter. Liesel was dead, one way or the other. Oh, she thought, as she covered her eyes with her hands, trying to stop her tears, they should never have gone to Dunning. Hadn't Clive almost been brought to his knees by one of his attacks because of it? He had since dismissed it, refusing to discuss it, even when Henrietta tentatively asked him later that night if he was recovered. He was back to his usual strong, steady self, as if nothing "weak" whatsoever had happened. Oddly though, within the safe confines of Highbury the tables seemed to have turned—and Henrietta now appeared to be the one afflicted. Whereas she had been strong at Dunning all through the investigation, her sadness and depression seemed to have now returned.

She supposed that the whole experience at Dunning in actuality disturbed her more than she initially thought, and even distanced a bit from it as she was now, she continued to feel its effects. For one thing, she was haunted by the lifeless eyes of the doll that Mrs. Wojcik had held in her arms. She knew it was illogical, but last night she laid awake, imagining somehow that the baby Mrs. Wojcik held was *her* child, the child that had died within her. Her heart ached, not just for herself, but for her cold, dead baby and even for Mrs. Wojcik, reduced to carrying around a dirty doll, having gone insane in her grief. How many other women at Dunning suffered from the same thing? Joe the orderly had mentioned other buildings, mostly for women—"depressives" he had called them—"melancholias."

How did one end up at Dunning? Henrietta wondered nervously. What constituted a label of "mental instability" or "lunacy" or "imbecility," or even "insanity" itself? She thought about Mrs. Goodman, the woman who had grasped her hand and told her about the race of humans living in the center of the earth and the rats that whispered to her in the night. Had she gone into Dunning that way, or had years in Dunning done that to her? Had *she* been given electric shock or been subjected to the hosing that Clive had told her about? And what of someone like Ma, whom Henrietta would certainly quantify as a "depressive?" Was it only money, as Joe had alluded, that kept her from such a place?

And what about herself? That was the *real* question, the one that terrified her. Couldn't she be labeled as such now? A depressive? She was still at times given to fits of melancholia and secret tears. At least she hoped they were secret. If she did give in to them, she tried her best to cover the evidence with powder, hoping Clive wouldn't notice.

Surprisingly, she felt Clive's hands on hers as he lowered them from her eyes. He had swiftly come from around the table and was kneeling before her.

"Oh, my dearest love," he said gently, handing her his handkerchief. "This has been too much for you. I see that now. I was wrong to involve you."

"No, Clive," she sniffed, taking the proffered handkerchief and quickly dabbing her eyes with it. "I'm better now. Honestly." She gave him a sad smile.

He squeezed her hand still in his and looked at her with such pitiful concern, that she thought she might not be able to breathe.

"Clive, please don't look at me that way," she whispered.

"Henrietta, don't leave me," he pleaded. "Promise. Promise me," he said hoarsely.

She stared into his hazel eyes, level with hers, the first thing she had noticed about him the night they met at the Promenade, when he had bought a ticket to dance with her.

A memory came into her mind then, of how he had almost cried once on the terrace when he had spoken of all the deaths he felt responsible for in the war, his own men slaughtered at the hands of the Germans because of a command he was forced to give. Somehow that night, in the warm July air, she had realized that she was perhaps the stronger of the two in this particular regard—as far as their emotions went, that is. That for all of his strength and desire to protect her, there was a part of him that was the more fragile of the two. This understanding had given her a certain sense of courage and responsibility that night, and she felt it again now, having very nearly forgotten it after she lost the baby. She needed to be strong for him, to take care of him. She needed to put this "silliness" behind her, she thought for the hundredth time. After all, she had already been through much, she reminded herself; she could get through this, too.

Especially considering what she saw now as the alternative to getting better on one's own—ending up at a place like Dunning—and she resolved to not succumb to further bouts of melancholy.

Gently, she pulled her hand from his and laid it against his cheek, causing his eyes to close at her touch. "I promise," she said and leaned forward to brush her lips against his. She rested her forehead against his, and she heard him exhale deeply. "But don't leave me out," she whispered. "Let me . . . let me still help you. I need to, Clive. You must understand that. Please."

He pulled back and took both of her hands in his again, looking at her as though his heart might break. "Are you quite sure, dearest?" he asked quietly.

"Very sure," she said and gave him what she hoped was a believable smile.

He let out a deep sigh and wearily stood up. He walked to the window and pulled back the curtain to reveal the massive Lake Michigan that butted up to their property. For a moment, Henrietta thought he was working up his courage to dismiss her, but instead he turned and gave her a tired sort of smile. "All right, then, I suppose you'd better go get your hat, if we're still going to investigate this Madame Pavlovsky."

A wave of gratefulness flooded through Henrietta as she returned the look of love he gave her now. She knew he was pushing himself to include her, and so she determined that she would push herself, too. If not for herself, then for him. "I'll just be a moment," she said, stuffing his handkerchief in her pocket as she stood up from the table. She went over to him, planted another kiss on his cheek, and ran up the stairs to get her things.

The drive to Crow Island on Willow Road was much shorter than Henrietta had anticipated—or wanted, actually, as the whole prospect of interrogating a spiritualist or a psychic, or whoever she portended to be, was just a bit unsettling.

Henrietta had little knowledge of such persons beyond the

mechanical fortune-telling machine that was set up each year at the St. Sylvester carnival, the presence of which she had always considered somewhat hypocritical, seeing as "fortune-telling" of any kind was touted as a most definite sin by the church. Cynically, she had long before now come to the conclusion that perhaps Fr. Finnegan overlooked this small detail of church canon in the case of the carnival machine, perhaps for the monetary contribution its presence afforded the church coffers. That, or perhaps he wasn't even aware of its existence at all on church grounds, as he was rarely seen to attend the annual carnival anyway, a fact which was, indeed, a constant cause of critical grumbling among the older ladies of the parish. If they had to endure the heat and the crowd, why shouldn't he? they often crowed.

Henrietta herself had never given money to the fortune-telling machine, not because she didn't have any money, though she actually did have very little, but because she had no wish to know the future, even an obviously phony one such as the machine produced on a little white card. Eugene, Herbie, and Eddie had done it often enough, but Henrietta, and Elsie, too, always refused, saying what a waste of money it was and a load of rubbish to boot.

"Have you ever heard of people who inhabit the center of the Earth?" Henrietta asked Clive abruptly as they drove.

Clive laughed, and Henrietta looked over and smiled at him, realizing how silly her question sounded when spoken out loud. But it felt good to hear him laugh. There seemed to be something about the two of them when they were out and about on their own—outside the confines of Highbury—that made them more relaxed, more themselves.

"No," he said. "Have you?"

"Not really. It's just something that one of the women at Dunning was talking about."

"A patient?"

"Yes, of course a patient," she said, rolling her eyes.

"Well, I think that explains it, then, doesn't it?" he said, slowly turning the car now onto an unmarked road that led into a sort of woods.

As it turned out, Crow Island wasn't really an island at all, but rather what seemed to be a clump of land surrounded by swampy wetlands. It was heavily forested and at some point in history, anyway, had apparently been inhabited by a large number of crows and other birds, hence its name. For some reason, it was deemed an appropriate place for a schoolhouse, which was then erected by the town's forefathers and largely funded by one of the more successful entrepreneurs of the group, Cy McPherson.

The McPherson schoolhouse, as it came to be called, faithfully served its purpose without issue until a larger school was eventually required, which was logically built more toward the center of town. But for a traveling group of artists who had taken up residence there for a time and the occasional passing hobo, it primarily sat abandoned. That is until now, Clive explained, when this Madame Pavlovsky had moved in and set up shop.

"Yes, it's just that it . . . it sounds familiar," Henrietta commented, still referring to what Mrs. Goodman had told her at Dunning. "I don't know why. It's probably some sort of myth," she mused.

Clive stopped the car now, the road having abruptly ended. From here, they would have to walk across a grassy stretch to where the old schoolhouse lay. It wasn't exactly a cheery place, Henrietta observed, as she studied the dull, gray structure in front of them. There were only traces of white paint left on it, and the cupola on top of the roof stood empty, its bell having long ago fallen off or perhaps even been stolen. Only the small plume of smoke from a chimney pipe thrust through the roof gave any indication that the building was inhabited at all.

"Explain why we're starting the investigation with her," Henrietta said, nodding toward the structure as she gathered up her handbag. "Don't you think we should have gone to see this Mr. Tobin first?"

"As a matter of fact, I did indeed telephone Mr. Tobin just after Davis gave me the information."

"You did? Why didn't you tell me?"

"It was the day you went into the city to visit your mother and found Elsie and Gunther there, and then we got caught up in finding Liesel Klinkhammer. I suppose it slipped my mind until now," he said as he exited the car and came around to her side.

"Well?" she asked eagerly, once he opened the door for her. "What did he say?"

"No answer," he said with a little shrug.

"Odd."

"I did try to telephone him again last night when we got home, but, again, no answer. So we might as well start here." He nodded toward the schoolhouse as they proceeded down the worn gravel path.

"I suppose you're right," she said, pulling her coat tighter around her neck. She had forgotten her scarf and the March wind was bitter today. She observed, however, that weeds, bright green in their newness, were already sprouting alongside the path. Why did weeds always grow first? she wondered. The things that no one wanted . . .

"You ready for this?" Clive asked, pausing on the little porch at the top of the three wooden steps they had tentatively climbed. "I can't say for certain what we'll find, but I have a pretty good idea. Something along the lines of theater, I should imagine."

"I'm ready," she said with a stiff nod that she hoped was convincing. A part of her was undoubtedly curious, but she was nervous, too. What if it turned out this woman really could read minds or predict the future? Henrietta worried. Why would anyone want their future predicted? Who would want to know if bad things were going to happen? Knowing these things would certainly doom one to a life of fear and dread, ticking off the days until the predicted bad thing did indeed occur. And if good things were seen in the future, she would also rather those be pleasant surprises.

Well, she told herself, raising her head in her best Antonia imitation, she must remember that this woman was merely a charlatan, as Clive called her. An imposter. There was absolutely nothing to worry about!

Still, she was startled, despite her resolve, when they heard a gravelly voice shout "Enter!" just as Clive had raised his hand to knock. Without meaning to, Henrietta gripped Clive's arm a little tighter. He gave her a tiny wink then, and they stepped through the door that had somehow opened before them.

The interior of the schoolhouse—not that Henrietta had ever been in a one-room schoolhouse—was unlike anything she had ever seen, though the first thing to hit her was not something in her line of vision, but the smell. It was a woodsy, sweet, burning smell that she couldn't quite identify. It was sort of like the incense at church, but nicer. Nervously, she peered around. A floor-to-ceiling black curtain was haphazardly strung across the room, apparently cutting the room in two and creating what seemed like a front and a back portion, the back presumably being the woman's living quarters. Thick, purple velvet curtains hung in front of each window, blocking out all outside light. Even the light coming through a small round transom window up high was blocked by a circular shade of sorts that had been hung in front of it and which depicted a crescent moon and several stars.

In the middle of the room was a table, covered by a shimmering gold cloth, on top of which sat what Henrietta guessed to be a crystal ball, just like in the mechanical fortune-teller's booth. She dared to look at it only briefly before pulling her eyes away from its murky interior. There were odd chairs here and there, a sagging sofa and large pillows strewn upon the floor, which was itself covered by oriental rugs, threadbare in some places. On the walls hung what looked to be star charts, placards with the zodiac, and maps of places Henrietta did not recognize, as well as strange symbols. Also along the walls stood small tables, each of which held a peculiar assortment of items. Upon one sat a bizarre sort of lamp that looked to be made out of animal bones. Similarly, a skull of some type of animal sat upon another table alongside various gems and other stones. And on a third table sat a celestial type of globe surrounded by tiny little figures, possibly made of clay. Henrietta felt a desire to go over and pick one of them up, but instead shifted her eyes to a hulking book-case next to the table. It had glass doors, inside of which were several thick tomes with fraying bindings. On top of the bookcase, Henrietta spied the presumed source of the lingering fragrance. A long, thin stick in a type of dish was smoldering, though it looked too thin to be a cigarette or a candle. Her eye went from that to the corner behind it where she saw a cage on a tall stand, holding what Henrietta at first thought was a raven. When it didn't move for several moments, she drew the impression that it must be stuffed. Why was it in a cage, then? she wondered. And where was the woman who had entreated them to enter? The whole place gave her the jitters, and she remained close to Clive's side.

She jumped when a woman slid from behind the black curtain and said in a deep, throaty voice, "I have been expecting you."

Henrietta gripped Clive's arm a little tighter and hoped her fear didn't show as she beheld the woman in front of them now. She was perhaps of middle age, which was younger than Henrietta had expected, and certainly more attractive. She was a buxom woman, very curvaceous. Not fat, exactly, but certainly not thin. She wore her weight attractively and her turquoise dress clung to her curves nicely. Behind her flowed a turquoise sort of cape that seemed part of the dress itself, and a silver turban sat on top of her long, frizzy black hair. Her eyes were big and blue, almost purple, and she easily filled the room with her magnetic presence. Henrietta could not help but stare at her; she was not what she had been expecting at all. She thought they would encounter some sort of wizened witch, not a buxom, attractive woman.

"Yes, I'm sure you were," Clive responded matter-of-factly. "Look, we'd like to ask you a few questions."

"Many do," she said with a slight Slavic sort of accent. "You seek something, no?"

"Listen, we're not here for all this mumbo jumbo," Clive said frankly, waving his hat around the room. "We're here to ask some serious questions."

Madame Pavlovsky let out a guttural sort of laugh. "Is that what you call it? 'Mum-bo jum-bo,'" she pronounced deliberately. "Come," she said, waving her hand at the cushions on the floor. "Sit. And we will hear these serious questions. All questions are serious."

Clive looked skeptically at the pillows on the floor, and instead led Henrietta to the sagging sofa while Madame Pavlovsky made a show of elegantly positioning herself on a chair in the center of the room, facing them. It was an old-fashioned sort of winged chair, the upholstery of which was oddly covered in a type of purple velvet fabric. The chair itself sat on a little wooden riser, which gave it the distinct flavor of being a sort of throne.

"Now, what is it you wish to know?" Madame Pavolovsky asked in a grave tone, her hands forming a triangle with her fingertips lightly touching each other.

"Shouldn't you already know that?" Clive asked flippantly.

"I do. But it helps most people to say it aloud," she said mysteriously.

"Oh, for Christ's sake," Clive said with a sigh. "Listen. We're here to investigate you. There have been some complaints lodged with the police about potential thefts, fraud, that sort of thing."

Madame Pavlovsky stared at him for a few seconds, and Henrietta saw her left eye quiver just slightly before she answered. "But you are not the police, are you?" she asked calmly.

"No, I'm a private detective. Clive Howard. "And this is—"

"Your wife," Madame Pavlovsky said mysteriously.

"Obviously, this is my wife."

"Not obvious. No."

"I'm Henrietta Howard," Henrietta said, trying to smile.

"So you are," Madame Pavlovsky said, looking her over carefully.

Henrietta wasn't sure what she was supposed to say to that, so she remained silent.

"And you are working for . . . ?" Madame Pavlovsky asked, looking from one to the other.

"That isn't important at this juncture," Clive said stiffly.

"It is Mr. Tobin, is it not? Yes, I see this."

A little chill went through Henrietta. How could she have known that?

Clive sighed. "Look, let's drop all this nonsense, shall we? Some serious allegations have been made, and this whole operation could be shut down at any moment."

"I have broken no law," Madame Pavlovsky said, nonplussed.

"Robbing Mrs. Tobin of all her jewelry?" Clive asked bluntly.

"It is not robbery if she wishes to give these things to me. I did not steal them."

"Do you deny you asked her for it?"

"That depends on what you mean."

"Damn it! Did you, or did you not, ask Mrs. Tobin to bring her jewelry to you?"

"No, I did not, not in so many words. But what if I did? There is no crime in that."

"But you coerced her."

"Coerced her?" Madame Pavlovsky said loudly and let out a shrill screech of what Henrietta assumed was a laugh. "No, not coerce. It is different thing what I ask."

Clive exhaled deeply. "Do you understand that I could have this whole thing shut down?"

"What do you mean 'this whole thing?' This is my home. I bought it. Legally," she said, her eyes narrowing.

"Do you have a permit to operate a business on this property?"

"Business? This is no business!"

"Do you deny that you accept payment for whatever you dispense here?"

"I do accept a type of payment, but not this kind you mean, I think. There is no money exchanged for what I give, if that is being your meaning."

"Just jewelry or any other expensive trinkets, am I right?" he said, looking around the room as if to spot any.

"If people *choose* to give me something—a gift—that is their choice," she said smoothly.

"Sounds awfully like a business to me," Clive said skeptically. "Bartering is a form of payment, as I'm sure you're aware. Where did you say you were from? Originally?"

"I did *not* say," she answered stiffly. "But if you must know, I am from Russia." She drew herself up, staring Clive in the eye. "Near Siberia. And yes, I know of bartering. But I have no need of money or these material goods of which you speak."

"I'll bet," Clive scoffed. "Let me guess. You don't take anything per se, but you get them to tell you things. Like maybe where the safe in their house is located? Then you have some lout who works with you go in and do the dirty. Am I close?"

"This is your fear speaking."

"Just what are you dispensing? *For free*," he added sarcastically. "Let me guess—fortune's read, the future explained, that sort of thing."

Madame Pavlovsky did not answer but just gazed at him. "There is much hurt in you," she said quietly.

If Clive was ruffled by this, he did not show it. "There's hurt in everyone," he said wryly. "Try again."

"What *do* you give?" Henrietta asked softly before she could stop herself.

Madame Pavlovsky's eyes flashed to Henrietta and studied her. "So you do allow her to speak," she said now to Clive.

"Of course, I allow her to speak!" he exclaimed angrily. "I mean, it's not up to me, of course."

"Is it not? Of this I am glad," she said with an arched eyebrow.

Madame Pavlovsky turned her gaze back to Henrietta again. "I speak to the spirits," she said gently, oddly without her previous air of mystery. "To those who have gone on from this world to the next dimension. I am able to reach through the veil that separates us and hear what they would tell us from beyond."

"You speak to those in the grave?" Henrietta asked, suddenly feeling goose bumps on her arms and up her neck.

"In grave? No. They are not in grave. They are in different world, and yet they are here with us, too. Never far are the loved ones," she said, looking from Henrietta to Clive, who merely crossed his legs and rolled his eyes.

"How . . . how can they be in another world and yet here, too?" Henrietta questioned.

"Henrietta, don't encourage her," Clive chided.

"Ah. So she does not speak for herself," Madame Pavlovsky said, pursing her lips.

"You're good, you know that?" Clive said, nonchalantly scratching his chin. "I've seen them all, and you're pretty slippery. Go on, then, enlighten us," he said, with a wave of his hand, leaning back into the worn sofa.

Madame Pavlovsky merely gave him a withering glance before looking back at Henrietta. "It is hard to explain. They are able to be in both places at once. There are more—how you say? Dimensions? than we know. More than this," she said, waving her hand around.

Henrietta just stared at her, aware that her heart was beating a little faster. She longed to ask her more, but she didn't dare.

"You wish to ask me more," Madame Pavlovsky said, surprising her.

"That's obvious," Clive said disparagingly.

"There are children . . . " Madame Pavlovsky said, closing her eyes as if to concentrate.

"A baby?" Henrietta said, her voice catching with a gasp.

"A baby? No." Madame Pavlovsky paused, her eyes still closed.

Henrietta's heart sank, but she supposed it made sense. She had barely been two months along. Of course, Madame Pavlovsky wouldn't be able to commune with something that had only been a bloody mess. But what did Madame Pavlovsky mean by children? she wondered. Could she possibly mean her brother and sister that had died years ago in the flu epidemic?

"Are they siblings?" Henrietta asked tentatively. "A boy and a girl?"

"Yes! Yes, that is it. They are here. Never far from you. They wish to say they love you."

"Oh, my," Henrietta said, tears suddenly coming to the corners of her eyes as she put her hand up to her mouth.

"That's enough!" Clive barked. "She's been through a bit of shock lately. She's been ill, and I won't have her upset."

"Losing a child isn't being ill," Madame Pavlovsky said to him with a frown.

"Oh, my!" Henrietta said again, wiping away a tear that had spilled down her cheek. "How did you know?"

Madame Pavlovsky didn't say anything, but merely stared at her.

"Oh, Clive," Henrietta said, putting her hands over her face and leaning forward into her lap to cry. Clive put his hand protectively on her back.

"There is man—"

"I insist that you stop this instant!" Clive nearly shouted. "We're leaving."

"No! Clive, please!" Henrietta said, sitting up with a start, her face wet with tears and flushed. "No. Tell me more! More about the children," she begged the woman, apparently not having registered Madame Pavlovsky's mention of a man, and Clive wasn't about to point it out. "Their names were Lester and Dorothy," Henrietta said unevenly.

"Yes, Lester and Dorothy," Madame Pavlovsky repeated. "I see this. They are happy. At peace. No pain, no sadness. They are free. Free to fly where they wish."

"Oh, Clive! Isn't it wonderful? Wait till I tell Ma!" she said, but he did not seem to share her enthusiasm. Instead he was looking at her with concern and perhaps pity? Why was he not more affected?

Gently he took her hand. "We must go, darling. It's time."

"Yes, I suppose so," Henrietta said, pulling her handkerchief from her handbag and dabbing her eyes. She desperately wanted to ask more, but she didn't know what to ask and Clive seemed not only impatient to leave, but also clearly annoyed.

They stood up. "Thank you, Madame Pavlovsky," Henrietta said shakily. "Thank you ever so much."

"You are welcome, my dearest sparrow. There is more I see, though. It is hard to understand. There is hospital. How you say? Infirmary? Someone is speaking, but I cannot understand it all. She says your work there is not done."

"All right, all right," Clive said irritably, ushering Henrietta toward the door. "You've cleverly managed to thwart the investigation for today, but don't think I won't be back."

"There is a man near you, too," Madame Pavlovsky said calmly, even as they walked away from her. "Your father, I believe. He stands by a large house. 'Linley' is engraved in cornerstone."

Her arm through his, Henrietta felt Clive bristle, but he did not turn.

"He sends his love to you," Madame Pavlovsky called out.

"I'll be back," Clive said without turning around, opening up the door to get out.

Chapter 11

Elsie was weary by the time she and Gunther returned to Mundelein, though it was only three in the afternoon. Clive and Henrietta had kindly driven them back, but that meant she and Gunther hadn't been able to discuss between them the awful news, especially as Gunther sat up front with Clive, and she and Henrietta were tucked into the back seat. Indeed, the whole ride to Mundelein had a funerary air to it, and they mostly rode in silence, all of them seeming to dwell on their own thoughts.

Just before they pulled up in front of Philomena, however, Gunther had turned to Clive and offered his most sincere thanks for his assistance, saying in his broken English that he was indebted to him and that he hoped to be able to do him some kindness someday. Elsie also thanked the two of them and leaned over to give Henrietta a quick kiss and a hug before she climbed out of the Daimler, Clive having the forethought to select a bigger car than the Alfa this morning. Sadly, Elsie realized that he must have been expecting to leave Dunning with Liesel in tow.

Gunther and Elsie stood awkwardly on the icy sidewalk, watching as Henrietta slipped back into the front of the car, saying as she did so that they must come very soon to visit them at Highbury. Henrietta gave Elsie a sad little wave as Clive drove around the circle, and Elsie felt unusually sad to see her sister go. She watched as Clive pulled out onto Sheridan and disappeared into the traffic before slowly turning toward Gunther. She was about to suggest that they go back to his hut to discuss what to do next, but before she could utter any words, he spoke first.

"I must go, Elsie," he said, his face grim. "I have work to do, and Sister Bernard has already been very generous to give me time off."

"Oh," Elsie said, disappointedly. "I . . . well, what are you going to do? About Anna, I mean? Don't you want to talk about it?"

"Later maybe. Not now. I need to think." He twisted his face into a failed sort of smile. "I must go. Later, yes?"

"Yes, all right." She tried to smile in return. "But what about—" she began, but he was already striding off, either not hearing her or perhaps simply choosing not to respond. She watched him hurry off down the sidewalk toward Piper and waited to see if he would turn and perhaps wave before he rounded the corner, but he did not.

She sighed, then, and turned to mount the stone steps of Philomena. Naturally, he was upset, she reasoned uncomfortably; it had been such a long day. They had both known it was bound to be an emotional one, but neither of them could have predicted how it had eventually turned out.

The first shock of the day had actually occurred when she appeared at his hut earlier this morning with the idea of offering to go with him to the orphanage to drop off Anna. Timidly she had knocked and was rather taken aback when he answered the door without his beard! He had shaved! Why? she wondered, trying not to stare as he warmly gestured her inside. She admitted that she liked this new look very much; it suited him and made him look younger—almost like a boy—but it gnawed at her that it was obviously done for Fraulein Klinkhammer's benefit, assuming that the two of them were to be reunited this day. Regardless, it definitely threw poor Elsie out of sorts, and she almost lost courage to ask him if he wanted her to accompany him. But she persevered and was glad that he accepted her help (after asking her several times if she was really sure) with what seemed to be, if not overwhelming delight, then at least relief.

"Yes, of course, I'm sure," Elsie insisted, trying not to stare at his barren jaw, almost as if it was somehow inappropriate like seeing a part of him naked.

The three of them rode the bus together to Pulaski and Foster, Anna sitting wedged between Elsie and Gunther. Elsie was delighted that Anna allowed her to hold her hand for a little bit while they again read from the Robert Louis Stevenson book. Gunther had thought it best not to tell Anna where they were headed, an opinion Elsie did not share, but she did not say so. Instead, she suggested they bring along Anna's new book, thinking it might come in handy as a needed distraction. It indeed provided a pleasant occupation on the ride over, but once they alighted and began walking up Pulaski, it failed to further capture Anna's attention, as she seemed to know almost immediately where they were and promptly began to whine. The whining quickly progressed to crying, which was eventually followed by Anna refusing to walk and pulling back on Gunther's hand, which churned Elsie's stomach into a knot. Gunther very smoothly, however, simply scooped the girl up in his strong arms and carried her. His patience was amazing, Elsie thought amid her own distress.

Luckily, the orphanage was not far, and they soon came upon the large three-story brick building set back off the road. *Bohemian Home for the Aged and Orphans* was carved into the lintel above the wooden, scuffed front doors. There were some evergreen bushes hugging the foundation and a smattering of oak trees off to the left, but it still looked cold and barren to Elsie's eyes. No wonder Anna didn't want to return here, Elsie thought, as she hurried up the steps ahead of Gunther to knock on the door with the heavy brass ring that hung there. She looked back at Gunther with an uneasy smile, and again wished he would have taken her suggestion to bring Anna to Palmer Square for the day.

She was about to offer this option once again when the door suddenly opened. Elsie spun around, dropping her hands that were twisting themselves together, and was surprised to see only a small boy. His eyes lit up at the sight of Anna, though her arms were wrapped tightly around Gunther's neck and her face was buried in his neck.

"Oh, it's you, Anna!" said the little boy who, to Elsie's eyes, looked to be about seven. "You're back early. Mama!" he shouted down the hallway. He opened the door widely, and Gunther awkwardly shuffled inside, followed by a nervous Elsie. Before the little boy could even get the door closed behind them, a young woman who looked not much older than Elsie emerged and walked briskly forward. They were roughly the same height, though the young woman was thinner. Her chestnut hair was tied up in a pretty bun, and she wore a black dress, which seemed fitting if she were indeed the matron of the home. Elsie was surprised that someone so young would already be in such a position of responsibility. She had a determined air to her, however, Elsie assessed, but she seemed kind, too. Elsie diverted her eyes from the woman for a moment and quickly looked around, further surprised by how warm and cozy the home seemed, at least from where they stood, and she thought she could smell cinnamon. Based on Anna's whining and crying, she had been expecting something terrible inside, but, indeed, it seemed quite pleasant.

"Pavel, there's no need to shout," the woman said gently. "Ah, Mr. Stockel," she said, observing him. "We did not expect you today. Is something wrong?"

"I am sorry, Mrs. Lasik," Gunther said uneasily, shifting Anna in his arms. "I need to bring Anna back early . . . I . . . there has been a discovery . . . "

"I see," she said, her eyes darting briefly to Elsie before she turned her attention back to Gunther. He was attempting to put Anna down, unsuccessfully, as she whined and tried to cling to his coat sleeves.

"Anna!" he said. "*Sei jetzt ein gutes Mädchen.*"

His words had little effect on the girl, however, and she continued to cry.

"I did warn you, Mr. Stockel," Mrs. Lasik said over Anna's howls, "not to bring her in and out. You break her routine, and she doesn't settle. And considering her condition—"

"Anna," Elsie suddenly broke in, desperate to help and unable to keep silent any longer. "Don't you want your book?" she asked, holding it out awkwardly. Anna's face, however, remained pressed against Gunther's knees.

"Anna," Mrs. Lasik said gently, squatting down near the girl and fluidly putting her arm around Pavel as she did so, pulling him close. "Come now. We've all missed you. And see who's here? It's your friend, Pavel." Her eyes glanced up briefly at the book Elsie still held. "And what is this?" she asked expertly. "A new book? Your very own? My, it's quite lovely. Full of beautiful pictures, I'm sure."

Anna lifted her head slightly from Gunther's knees and out of the corner of her eye, glanced at Mrs. Lasik and Pavel.

"Wouldn't you like to show Pavel your treasure?" Mrs. Lasik asked. "You'd like that, wouldn't you, Pavel?"

"Oh, yes, Mama!" he said, his blue eyes very bright. "Come on, Anna, show me your book. Please," he begged. "I won't mess it. I promise."

Elsie watched, almost holding her breath, as Anna turned slowly to look at Pavel. She wanted to encourage Anna, but she didn't dare break the fragile tension of the moment.

"Come on, Anna," Pavel went on. "I'll let you hold my marbles," he tempted, pulling a lumpy brown suede bag tied with a leather cord from his pocket and holding them up.

Anna hesitated and looked back up at Gunther then. "*Papa?*" she asked, her voice quivering.

"Go now, Anna," Gunther answered softly. "I will come back soon. I have to work. But I will come back for you soon. Stay here with kind Mr. and Mrs. Lasik."

For a brief moment, Elsie was afraid that Anna was going to cry again, but Mrs. Lasik smoothly intervened before that could happen. She held out her hand for the book, which Elsie hastily gave her. "Papa will be back soon," Mrs. Lasik said, handing the book to Anna now. "Go to the dayroom with Pavel and show him. I'll bring you each a cookie, later, if you're good," she promised.

Pavel's face lit up. "Race you!" he said to Anna encouragingly. He looked barely older than Anna, and yet there was something very knowing about him. He was a curious little thing.

Elsie watched as Anna's face finally broke into a small smile, and with just one final look at Gunther, she ran off after Pavel as best she could with the big book in her arms.

Elsie breathed a sigh of relief and tried to ignore the little stab of disappointment that Anna had not said good-bye to her. Well, that was to be expected, wasn't it? She barely knew Elsie. But there was something else that was needling Elsie, which she also fought to push away. Why had Mrs. Lasik referred to Gunther as "Papa?" Surely she knew the truth, didn't she? Or maybe not?

"Thank you," Gunther said now to Mrs. Lasik. "I am sorry to have caused this trouble."

"Well, like I said, Mr. Stockel, this is most upsetting. You need to let her be, let her settle here. You think you are doing a kindness, but it is really making things so much worse. Surely you can see this?"

"Yes, I am sorry, Mrs. Lasik. I will try to remember in future," Gunther said, rubbing his forehead.

"You spoke of a discovery," Mrs. Lasik finally said, looking briefly at Elsie again. "I'm Josephine Lasik, by the way." She held out her hand to Elsie.

"Ach. I am sorry," Gunther said. "I am not myself today. Mrs. Lasik, this is Miss Elsie Von Harmon. She is a friend who is helping me to find Anna's mother. Elsie's sister is married to a detective, which is good fortune for me, and he believes he maybe has found her. We go now to see."

"Oh, that's wonderful news, Mr. Stockel," Mrs. Lasik said happily.

"Well, maybe yes, but maybe no," he said, looking over at Elsie uneasily. "She is in place called Dunning," he said quietly. "It is for the feebleminded, no?" He gave her a pleading sort of look, as if begging her to correct him.

"Oh," she said instead, her face blanching a little. "I'm very sorry to hear that."

"Maybe it is mistake, or not same woman. I do not know," Gunther said sadly. "Or maybe she has already left there. We will see."

"Ah, Mr. Stockel," came a deep, smooth voice from down the hallway, and a tall, wide-shouldered man approached them. "Good to see you. I thought I heard your voice. Or rather, Anna's," he said with a grin, as he peeled off his wire-rim spectacles. He was dressed in shirtsleeves only, and his yellow-and-blue-striped tie hung loosely about his neck as though he were just finishing the day, not beginning it. He was a very handsome man with deep-blue eyes and dark-brown hair that was thick and wavy.

"I'm Petr Lasik," he said, holding out his hand to Elsie, which she shyly grasped.

They make a terrific couple, thought Elsie, despite the fact that they were not at all whom she had expected to be running an old folks' home and an orphanage. She wondered how they had come to be installed here, what had led them to this position.

"I couldn't help but overhear what you've told Jo," he said to Gunther. "It's wonderful that you might have located Anna's mother."

Gunther nodded.

"Don't worry too much about her being in Dunning," Mr. Lasik went on kindly. "People are sent there all the time that don't belong. Perhaps she suffers from the same fits as Anna and found herself there because of them."

"Yes, but this is not such a good thing, is it?" Gunther asked anxiously.

"Better that than being there for some other reason," Mr. Lasik said encouragingly. "But we will hope for the best, won't we, my dear?" He looked over at Mrs. Lasik.

"Yes, of course," she said with a smile. "Anything's better than not knowing, though, isn't it? At least then you know where you stand," she added, looking back at Mr. Lasik in such a knowing way that Elsie could not help but think there was a story there.

Gunther merely nodded.

"You know," Mr. Lasik said gently, "if you do find her, there's an epileptic colony downstate in Dixon. It might be a good place for her. And for Anna. They would get the care they need."

"A colony?" Gunther asked.

"Yes, the Dixon State Hospital. But it's more of a farm, really, than a hospital. Good clean air. Might be just the thing."

Gunther stared at him as if he were trying to absorb this information. "Yes," he finally said absently.

"We'd better go, Gunther," Elsie had said quietly, not wanting to interrupt them, but she knew they were in danger of being late. "Henrietta and Clive will be waiting."

They took another bus to Dunning, then, riding along in silent hope, only to have eventually discovered the awful truth that Liesel Klinkhammer was, in fact, dead, and had been for some time, rendering all of their private and collective thoughts regarding what to do next as essentially useless.

All the way back to Mundelein in Clive and Henrietta's car, Elsie tried to process the limited information they had been given. How could Anna's mother be dead? Every so often, Elsie had glanced at the back of Gunther's head, wishing they were sitting beside each other in the back seat of the Daimler or that he would at least look back at her from time to time, but he did not. She couldn't imagine what he must be feeling, his long quest to find Liesel Klinkhammer now suddenly at an end, and certainly not in the way he had expected. He and his mother had been burdened with this little girl for nearly five years, and what was he to do with her now? That was the real question that Elsie (and Ma, for that matter) had thought the most relevant from the very beginning. She had never thought that finding Liesel Klinkhammer would solve much, but it had seemed the obvious first step. Now they needed to face what had always been there, staring them in the face: the fact that Anna was still a sick child and apparently needed some sort of specialized care. The poor thing, Elsie thought, her mind shifting gears and her heart nearly breaking for this motherless girl. But then again, she tried to remind herself, Anna had never even known Liesel and therefore surely wouldn't mourn her. As Gunther had rightly pointed out, the girl was instead mourning the death of his own mother.

Elsie desperately wanted to talk to Gunther about it all, how he was feeling, what his next action would be—but he had abruptly left her standing at the foot of Philomena. Well, she didn't really blame him. He had said he needed to think, and she could understand that, not to mention the fact that he needed to get back to work. It wouldn't help matters at all if he lost his job on top of everything else, and, yet, she couldn't really see Sr. Bernard being that cruel.

As she climbed the steps to Philomena, Elsie had a quick thought that maybe they should confide in Sr. Bernard and seek her advice, but, really, what advice was there for her to give? After all, she had already given her advice in pointing Gunther to the orphanage.

As Elsie entered the grand foyer of Philomena Hall with its old, dark wood and cool tiled floor, she felt the usual feeling of peace she got from this place. She was pleased to see that Sr. Joseph, one of her favorites, was on desk duty today.

"Hello, Sister," Elsie said politely as she made her way past the desk toward the beautiful staircase. The Tiffany window on the landing, which Elsie had instantly loved upon her first visit to the school, was currently dark, the sun already beginning its descent.

"Just a moment, Elsie," Sr. Joseph called to her. "You have a visitor waiting for you in the front parlor."

"A visitor?" Elsie asked nervously, suddenly filled with dread that it might be Lloyd Aston, trying again for her hand per his father's and her grandfather's wishes. Would he never give up? How could this day possibly get any worse? She was already exhausted from the extreme emotions of the day—first the scene at the orphanage with Anna and then the appalling state of Dunning and the discovery of

Liesel Klinkhammer's death. She didn't know how much more she could endure. "Who is it?" Elsie whispered.

"She announced herself as your aunt," Sr. Joseph said quietly, accompanied by a sympathetic smile.

Her aunt? Oh, no! It must be Aunt Agatha! Elsie let out a little moan.

Aunt Agatha was the wife of one of Ma's brothers—John, to be exact—and had become the unfortunate pawn in assisting her own father-in-law, Oldrich Exley, in his attempts to see Elsie strategically married, so as to either increase the amount of money in his coffers or to increase their rank on the social ladder—preferably both. Lately, a scheme had formed between himself and one Granville Aston, which consisted of Aston demanding that his son, the playboy Lloyd, propose marriage to the innocent Elsie Von Harmon. Lloyd, for his part, had begrudgingly played his hand as instructed, but only after a threat to cut off his monthly allowance. No one had expected that it would be Elsie herself who foiled the plan, which she did by out-and-out refusing Lloyd, much to Oldrich's wrath and to Agatha's despair.

But why would Agatha Exley have come all this way? It was true that Elsie had been ignoring Aunt Agatha's letters of late—not only because she hoped that in doing so, Aunt Agatha might somehow leave her in peace (which, logically, she knew, was impossible given her grandfather's ruthless determination). But also because, in truth, she had been busy with her new classes, helping Gunther, and even with trying to appease Melody by going out on frivolous outings. A visit seemed an extreme reaction to a couple of unanswered letters. She had thought that Aunt Agatha understood the Lloyd Aston affair, if it could even be termed "an affair," to be well and truly over. So why would she come here? Elsie wondered nervously. Something must be dreadfully wrong!

Elsie smoothed down her skirt and patted her hair into place. She felt dirty and soiled from being in Dunning, and she had been craving a bath since the moment they stepped foot out of the dingy asylum and back into the fresh air—but she supposed she shouldn't keep her aunt waiting any longer.

"Has she been here long?" she whispered to Sr. Joseph, who gave her a slow nod.

Elsie sighed. Well, there was nothing for it but to face her. She knew Aunt Agatha would be horrified by what she was wearing—a simple black skirt and a white, cotton top. It was at least a Lavin skirt, but she wasn't sure Aunt Agatha would be able to tell.

Slowly she slid open the pocket doors to reveal Aunt Agatha, sitting very primly on the divan upon which Melody herself so often sat to hold court. Indeed, it caused Elsie to look twice, as if Melody had been transformed into the plump, oldish woman before her now.

"Elsie! Where have you been?" exclaimed Aunt Agatha in a wounded way. "Do you know how long I've been sitting here? And that Sister What's-Her-Name out there could not even account for your whereabouts! How do you explain that?"

"Well, we're not prisoners, Aunt Agatha," Elsie offered weakly. "We can come and go as we please. After all, we *are* grown women."

"Barely," Aunt Agatha sniffed. "Be that as it may, this is very irregular. And what are you wearing? Oh, Elsie, I despair! I simply despair," she said, as Elsie tentatively sat in the chair across from her.

"Is . . . is there anything wrong, Aunt?" Elsie asked hesitantly.

"Wrong?" Agatha said sharply. "Besides the obvious, you mean?"

"I thought we'd been through this all before, Aunt. The whole business with Lloyd Aston, that is."

"Indeed, we have," Agatha said archly. "I still don't understand it, Elsie. Why you would reject such an eligible young man." She gave a deep sigh. "However, what's done is done."

Elsie felt a deep breath escape her.

"But why you choose to spend your days *here*," Aunt Agatha continued, looking around the room distastefully, "is beyond me. I will say, though, that in the time I have been delayed here, I have carefully observed several of the girls walk through, and they seem well-dressed, I'll give them that. But surely you must see how difficult you make things for me, Elsie. Especially when you don't return my letters."

"I'm sorry, Aunt Agatha, really I am. I . . . I've just been so busy, you see, getting used to my classes, and, well, other things—"

"Well, never mind. What I was so urgently trying to communicate to you is that you are to come with us to Miami. It was Father Exley's idea, actually, and I must say it's not a bad one," she said, leaning toward Elsie with an excited sort of smile. "We're to stay at the Flamingo," she rushed on. "Very posh. John and I haven't been there for years, but it definitely attracts a better crowd. In fact, we've had it on good authority that the Armours, the Fields, and perhaps even the McCormicks will be vacationing there at the same time. So you see, it could very well work to our advantage, which is what Father Exley surely had in mind," she twittered. "It will be ever so much nicer to take up our little quest somewhere sunny and bright, don't you think?" she said cheerfully, her buck teeth poking out only just a little between her large, chipmunk cheeks.

Elsie paled. Miami? She couldn't go to Miami right now! What would she do about Gunther, not to mention her studies? "But . . . Aunt Agatha, I . . . I couldn't possibly go to Miami just at the moment. I can't leave school. I've only just begun . . . " she pleaded.

"Tut, tut, child. I'm speaking of your spring break, of course. I've already ascertained the dates from Sister What's-Her-Name out there. Surely you can spare ten days at least, perhaps more," Aunt Agatha cajoled. "It's not as if this was really all that important anyway, Elsie. You must realize that. Father Exley is indulging you in this folly, I daresay because of your sister's influence, but you can't really be serious about finishing. I understand you wanted to get away, a distraction, as it were, after the scandal with that reprobate, Barnes-Smith, but surely you don't mean to actually come away with a degree, do you?"

Elsie gritted her teeth. Why did no one ever take her seriously? And why did Aunt Agatha insist on calling her grandfather "Father Exley"? It made him sound like some sort of priest—and a corrupted one at that! Elsie let out a deep breath. "As a matter of fact, I do want to come away with a degree, Aunt Agatha."

"Surely not," Aunt Agatha exclaimed, as if chiding a child. "In what, pray tell? Possibly artistic studies? That *may* enhance your conversational skills," she conceded. "I'll give you that. But, Elsie, if you'll only be led by me in these matters, you'll find yourself before too long, hopefully, in a grand house full of servants. Employment is certainly out of the question. All you need to be able to do is to orchestrate amusing parties."

Elsie hesitated, wondering if now was the right time to share her desire to become a teacher, thinking it might be a good first step in breaking free of the larger web she currently found herself in. Perhaps Aunt Agatha, herself a pawn of the very same powers, might in actuality be sympathetic.

"I . . . " Elsie began tentatively. "I thought I might become a teacher, Aunt."

"A teacher? Ridiculous!" Aunt Agatha said with a limp wave of her hand.

Elsie, her sensitivities already strained by the events of the day, felt a little flame of anger well up at her aunt's quick rejection, and before she could completely think it through, Elsie reached for the next available weapon and awkwardly launched it at the unsuspecting Agatha. "Actually, Aunt Agatha, I . . . I've been meaning to tell you something," she said, her hands twisting in her lap. "I suppose that's why I've been putting off writing to you recently. It's just that I . . . I think I . . . well, I think I might want to become a nun," she finally blurted out, somehow managing to look Aunt Agatha directly in the eye as she said it.

Poor Aunt Agatha looked so startled—like she had perhaps seen a ghost—that Elsie squirmed in discomfort and almost regretted the fib. After all, it wasn't Aunt Agatha who was her enemy or even the real source of all of her problems. If only she had written to her grandfather when the idea of taking Holy Orders had first presented itself, back when it was a quite honest desire, she might have avoided all of this. But each time she had tried, her courage failed her, and she crumpled up the start of her letter, tossing it into the little wicker wastebasket that stood beside her desk. And then things progressed so very quickly, and in desperation she found herself using the nun excuse on Lloyd Aston as the ultimate reason for rejecting his proposal when he had pressed past her initial voiced misgivings. She had assumed, perhaps even hoped (just a little) that Lloyd would have repeated this information to the powers that be, therefore putting a stop to any further schemes while also saving her the burden of having to do so herself, but apparently not. Or, if her grandfather *had* been told, it was quite clear by Aunt Agatha's current reaction that he had not related this to his minion.

Elsie almost felt sorry for her aunt now, still sitting there in a state of shock, opening and closing her mouth like a fish. But, Elsie argued with herself, she had had to say something! She couldn't possibly leave for Miami at this critical time!

"So . . . so, you see," Elsie bravely went on, "there's really no point in trying to introduce me to any more young men so that . . . so that I can marry well. I . . . I plan to be a teacher for the poor, you see," she said, deciding to emphasize that particular detail of the plan. "So it *is* rather important that I study. And I do mean to try to come away with a degree—"

"You can't be serious!" Aunt Agatha interrupted, finally finding her voice. "Certainly, you are deluded, poor child. Brainwashed!" she declared, almost quivering. "Yes, that must be it," she said, almost to herself. "I told John that nothing good could possibly come from you being here. That you would be corrupted somehow! And now I've been proved right! This is folly in the extreme. A nun, for God's sake! Elsie, whatever are you thinking?"

"I . . . I'm quite in earnest, Aunt Agatha," Elsie tried to say. "I've . . . I've already spoken to Sister Bernard about it. So, you see—"

"Impossible!" Agatha interrupted. "You'll just have to unspeak whatever it was you said."

"I . . . I can't."

"Of course, you can, you silly girl. No vows have been taken! Have they?" she asked nervously, raising her eyebrows.

"No, of course not. But I *am* in earnest, Aunt Agatha."

"Doubtless you don't know your own mind. Don't misunderstand me—it's a noble calling, but not for the likes of you," she said stiffly. "You've had a trying time with men, I'll grant you that. But we all of us have our little heartaches before we put all of that behind us and settle down. That's the way of things. You didn't like the look of Lloyd Aston. Very well. There are other fish in the sea, my girl."

Elsie felt so tired, so weary from the day that she wasn't sure how much more she could endure. Telling Aunt Agatha that she wished to become a nun had failed to elicit the response she had hoped for, and she couldn't think what else to use in her defense. Perhaps she should have just blurted out that she was in love with a poor German immigrant, she mused, and a small delirious sort of smile formed on her lips as she imagined the hysteria that such an announcement would cause.

"Yes, chin up," Agatha said now with a nod, misunderstanding the cause of her smile. "You'll see. We'll go to Miami and get a change of scenery. It will do you the world of good. You look dreadfully pale. And no wonder, shut up in what one might just as well call a nunnery.

"I say," she said abruptly, looking around, "is there not even a porter or a footman who could at least bring us some tea?"

Chapter 12

"Good afternoon, sir, madame," Billings said crisply as he opened the front doorway of Highbury to Clive and Henrietta. "I trust you've had a pleasant afternoon." He gave a slight bow as he stepped aside to allow them inside.

"Tolerable, Billings. Thank you," Clive answered tersely, handing him his hat and coat.

The short drive home from Crow Island had been fraught with a variety of emotions—first tears on Henrietta's part and then excitement as she began to enthusiastically chatter about Madame Pavlovsky's "extraordinary" clairvoyance. For his part, Clive had said little, allowing Henrietta to ramble on, all the while trying to decide how to proceed in this delicate situation.

He looked over at Henrietta now as she removed her hat and could see that her eyes were still slightly puffy and red. If Billings noticed, as he took her things, he had the discretion not to say anything.

"Any messages, Billings?"

"Yes, sir. Two telephone messages, sir. I've laid them in your study. There is one for you, and one for Madame as well," he said, nodding at Henrietta.

"Very good," Clive answered briskly, rubbing his hands from the cold. "Is my mother at home?"

"Yes, sir. She is upstairs in the long gallery with Mr. Bennett."

"Upstairs with Bennett? Whatever for?"

"I really couldn't say, sir. 'Perusing the art before dinner,' I think is what Mrs. Howard said."

Perusing the art? Since when did his mother care about art? His father had forever been trying to interest her in it, especially as they possessed so many priceless works, but he had failed to ever spark in her any real appreciation for it besides how it might elevate them in the eyes of their peers. "Is Bennett staying for dinner?" he asked Billings.

"It would seem, sir," Billings said emotionlessly.

Clive wondered why Bennett was showing up so regularly these days and dreaded having to later confer on more issues regarding the firm. He had a feeling Bennett was here to implore him to make an appearance downtown; it had been a while. Still, he could have requested his presence via telephone, could he not? Perhaps he had more documents for him to sign, Clive guessed with a sigh, trying not to be irritated.

"I see. Well, we'll be in the study," he informed Billings and, looking over at Henrietta, inclined his head toward the direction of the study.

"Very good, sir."

The study was deliciously warm and inviting as the two made their way in. The fire had been recently tended, Clive noted with approval, and several lamps in the corners had been left on, presumably in anticipation of their arrival. Clive felt himself relax a little and poured two sherries. He handed one to Henrietta, who had eased herself onto the sofa, and then sat down beside her.

"Clive," she began, "you've said so little. Why? Do you . . . do you not believe what Madame Pavlovsky told us?"

Clive did not respond, but merely sat looking at her, one arm stretched across the back of the sofa.

"You don't, do you?" she asked incredulously. "But how can you possibly explain her knowing all of those things? About my brother and sister? About me . . . about me losing the baby?" she asked with what uncomfortably sounded like desperation. "And what about your father?"

Clive sighed and took a drink of his sherry, reflecting that he should have poured himself a brandy. All the way home, he let her go on about their encounter with Madame Pavlovsky, not wanting to reveal his skepticism for fear of how she would take it. He had been trying to think of a way to gently expose this woman to be the fraud that she so obviously was, but he loathed to, as Henrietta seemed to derive so much comfort from her words. He hated the unavoidable task before him of telling her that it was a false comfort. But that was the trick of these charlatans, wasn't it? Clive knew. To play on people's emotions, to get them where they were vulnerable. And what better way to get to people than through their 'dearly departed?' Clive knew a huckster when he saw one. And yet, a tiny part of him *did* wonder how she had known about Linley . . . the rest he could explain away. But that one detail was harder . . . she must have done her homework. But how would she possibly have known they were coming in order to research? That was hard to explain away as well.

Clive sighed. "Darling, we have to look at this rationally. As detectives," he reminded her.

"I am!"

"No, you're not, darling. The truth is that she read you, and she's very good at guessing."

"How could she have possibly guessed all those things, Clive?" Henrietta asked irritably.

He had hoped to avoid this, but he saw there was no other way than to be brutally honest. "Henrietta," he began tentatively. "You fed her the information. Think about it. She tells us that she communicates with the dead and then vaguely says that she sees children . . . "

"Aha!"

"But that's just a good guess. Every family has at least one child who has died. You yourself gave her the information she needed by asking if they were siblings and even suggested they were a boy and girl."

Henrietta took a sip of her sherry, apparently thinking this through. "But how do you explain her knowing that I lost a baby?" she asked finally. "Remember she said, '*Losing a child isn't being ill*'?"

"Another good guess. You distressfully asked her if she saw a baby. So she guessed you had lost a baby."

"That's a bit of a stretch, Clive, admit it."

"Well, like I said, she's good at guessing."

"Well . . . what about mentioning your father?" she asked pertly.

"The Howards are obviously well known," Clive said with what he hoped was a nonchalant shrug. "She could easily know that he had recently died."

"And her mention of Castle Linley?"

"She could have somehow researched that. A book on heraldry and English estates—something like that. Or she could have asked one of the servants."

"Really, Clive," she exclaimed, letting out a deep breath. "What utter nonsense. You can't believe she would go to all that effort. For what? And she couldn't have known who we were—*or* that we were coming."

"A con will go a long way for a sting, Henrietta."

"A sting? For what purpose? What can she possibly gain by telling you that your father loves you?"

"My trust?" he responded, an eyebrow arched.

Henrietta shot him an icy look, and he knew he had upset her. He rubbed his forehead. It *was* hard to explain this woman's knowledge of Linley, but he refused to give in to such nonsense. It could still have somehow been a guess, he tried to convince himself, remembering that these types of charlatans relied on fear and superstition to ply their trade. There must be a rational explanation, he knew, and he was determined to figure it out.

"And what about her telling us that our work at the hospital or the infirmary isn't done?" Henrietta went on. "Could she be referring to Anna, seeing as she's at an orphanage and apparently the only loose thread? Maybe *the infirmary* is a reference to her illness?" she suggested.

Clive thought of several negative things he wanted to say in response to these questions, but after a moment's consideration, decided to simply remain silent.

"Or could she have meant Dunning?" Henrietta went on. "Something we missed maybe?"

Clive sighed. Not this again. "Darling, I'm sure there are many unrighted wrongs at Dunning, but it is not our job to uncover them all. We've been through this."

"But what's to become of that little girl, Clive?" she asked, momentarily confusing him by the shifting of subjects. "The poor thing's lost her mother, no father to speak of, and apparently epileptic. It's awful, Clive. She needs proper medical care, not to be stuck in . . . in some sort of orphanage or asylum because of it . . . somewhere like Dunning. That's cruel." Her voice caught a bit.

Clive let out a deep breath. Of course, he felt sorry for this girl, but there were thousands more out there, just like her. In some ways, he knew she was lucky to be in some sort of institution; he had seen too many children living on the street. He had been like Henrietta when he first began police work after returning from the war. He had wanted to right all the wrongs, stop the suffering and the poverty and the pain he saw in the streets. But the emotional toll had been great, and the chief finally had to have a word with him. They couldn't save them all, he told Clive kindly over a whiskey. Their job was to catch the criminals, stop them from hurting more innocent people. They weren't running a charity, he told Clive sternly, and ended their session by suggesting that Clive choose between being a detective and a social worker. Both of them were needed, he pointed out, but not at his station.

So Clive had chosen detective work and learned to harden his heart a little. The chief was right. He needed to see things objectively and not let pity get in the way. But then he had met Henrietta, and his cold heart, nearly frozen from both the war and his subsequent detective work, began to thaw until it had melted completely, making him feel more alive than he ever had—as well as uncomfortably vulnerable. Again, he wondered how running a detective agency was really going to work. They were already stumbling, and this was an easy case. Well, the Madame Pavlovsky case was anyway. In his mind, Liesel Klinkhammer's death was not a case at all, though there was something niggling there, he had to privately admit. He just didn't know what, and he dared not tell Henrietta. She needed no encouragement to see things where there were none. It was better to treat this poor woman's death as a charity case—as his chief would have called it—and let it lie.

"Surely *we* can help her somehow," Henrietta was saying. "It can't be left up to Gunther. I feel sorry for him, too. He was trying to do the right thing, and now he's caught up in this mess, with no one or nothing to help him, besides Elsie, I suppose, which isn't saying much. She's already overwhelmed. Surely we could at least pay for the girl to be examined by a reputable doctor?"

Clive rubbed his chin. "Yes, I suppose we could do that," he said. Upon meeting Gunther the other day, Clive found that he liked him more than he thought he would, though it was a trifle hard to get past the fact that he was German. He wondered how old he was . . . he seemed too young to have fought in the war. His initial impression of him, however, had been good despite the circumstances; he appeared to be an intelligent sort, solid. He wondered about Elsie's interest and hoped that she wasn't forming an attachment. Gunther didn't seem the lecherous type, but still . . . there would be no end of problems if Elsie developed feelings for him. "We have to be careful, darling," he said now to Henrietta.

"Careful? Of what?"

"Careful of getting too emotionally attached to our cases," he said gently. "It's wise advice the chief once gave me. Our job is to catch criminals, not to help the victims. That's a different sort of thing altogether."

"Honestly, Clive! I don't see why not. What a curmudgeon you're being. And this isn't a case, so you keep reminding me. Please."

She looked up at him with her big blue eyes, and he felt a rush of love for her. How could he deny her anything, especially something so easily in his power to grant?

"All right. You win," he said with a small wink. He drained his sherry and moved toward the desk to refill his glass. "I'll make some inquiries. But no guarantees," he added, noticing the phone messages Billings had mentioned, lying neatly on the right-hand side of the blotter. He picked up the one addressed to him and opened it. "I'm not sure there's much we can do for the girl," he said absently as he began to read and then tossed it back onto the desk. "Doubtless, Gunther has some plan of his own," Clive went on, looking at Henrietta now. "Maybe he'll go back to Germany."

"Go back to Germany! That's ridiculous."

"Here, this is yours I believe," he said, handing her the folded message with "Mrs. Clive Howard" scrawled across the front in Billings's tiny, neat handwriting. He watched as she opened it and quickly read it.

"Anything of interest?" he asked, taking another drink.

"It's from Lucy. She wants me to telephone her back as soon as I can," Henrietta said with a frown.

"Ah."

"And yours?"

"Our missing Mr. Tobin rang," he said. "I'll telephone him back after dinner. Perhaps he will agree to meet with us. Hopefully, Mrs. Tobin will also be on hand and we can get to the bottom of this whole mess."

Henrietta did not respond but merely took a drink as she looked at him. She was thinking something, he could tell.

"I think you're afraid, Clive," she said, finally. "Afraid that Madame Pavlovsky is not really a fraud. That she's real."

Clive tried not to audibly sigh. "Hardly, darling," he said, trying instead to force out a chuckle. "There are much scarier adversaries out there than the likes of Madame Pavlovsky."

"Scarier than someone who can talk to the dead?" she countered.

"We can all 'talk to the dead,' Henrietta. It doesn't take much effort. I myself talk to my father every day."

"You know what I mean, Clive."

Now he really did sigh. How had they gotten back to square one?

"There's something about her . . . " Henrietta went on as she rose, presumably to dress for dinner; it was getting late. "Something I just can't explain."

The next morning found Henrietta seated in the back of the Rolls with Fritz at the wheel. She and Clive had breakfasted early, as they were to be separated for the rest of the day. Clive, as he had guessed, had been asked last night by Bennett if he might possibly attend a shareholders' meeting the following day at 9:00 a.m. sharp. Clive had reluctantly agreed, of course, but not without commenting that it was damned little notice. Bennett had apologized for that, saying that it was indeed a last-minute announcement and that he would be happy to make his excuses for him if he were otherwise engaged. But Clive had given in, then, telling Henrietta that he felt too guilty to deny Bennett, as he had spent so little time there of late and that Bennett was indeed shouldering much of the burden of running the firm.

"It's just as well," she had replied and then told him of the call she returned to Lucy, in which Lucy asked if she might be able to meet up with Rose to return her little pistol to her, sooner than later, she had added, which worried Henrietta. She asked Lucy for more details, but Lucy said that she didn't want to say more in case people were listening in on the party line.

So Clive had assigned Fritz and the Rolls to Henrietta, while he himself dusted off his father's Mercedes-Benz Roadster, surprised that it still started after all these months lying dormant in the stables. He was quite happy, he said, to drive himself for a change to the Linley Standard headquarters on LaSalle, and judged that the Roadster fit the part more than the Alfa.

—

Having given Clive a very long kiss in the foyer despite Billings standing at attention, Henrietta had slipped into the Rolls and instructed Fritz to drive her to Poor Pete's on Mozart and Wabansia. This is where the Hennessey's corner bar was located, the place she began working at thirteen, just after her father had killed himself. She had started cleaning floors there and gradually worked her way up to being a waitress and then to a 26 girl, the Hennesseys becoming almost like another set of parents to her over the years. It was, in fact, Mr. Hennessey who had walked her down the aisle at her wedding, much to Oldrich Exley's fury.

On the telephone call last night to Lucy, Henrietta had first suggested that she drive directly to the Melody Mill, where the girls all worked, to deliver the gun to Rose, but Lucy had informed her that Rose was no longer working there. Surprised, Henrietta asked why, but Lucy didn't answer and instead mysteriously suggested that Rose herself might explain it all. Not knowing where else to meet, Henrietta had offered Poor Pete's as an alternate, especially as she was long overdue for a visit to the Hennesseys anyway. She had been putting it off for too long, she knew, for purely selfish reasons.

While Henrietta was still on her honeymoon, Elsie had written to her to say that she heard word that the Hennessey's daughter, Winifred, was pregnant with her first child—who promised to be the Hennessey's first grandchild—as far as they knew, anyway. The Hennessey's son Tommy had moved out west somewhere years ago and was estranged from them now, and who knew what he had been up to? Mrs. Hennessey had often joked. Maybe he was married with children as well, she had once or twice suggested hopefully, but Mr. Hennessy always knocked this notion back, saying that Tommy had always been on the wild side and frequently in trouble with the law. "He isn't the marryin' kind, my dear," Mr. Hennessey would say, and all seemed to agree that an image of peaceful domesticity did not seem to fit their middle son. More than likely, Mr. Hennessey had more than once suggested, if any child *had* been issued from Tommy's loins, it was probably unknown to him and a bastard at that. The Hennessey's oldest child, Billy, whom Henrietta knew had secretly been their favorite, had been killed in the war, before he even had a chance to catch the eye of a girl, much less walk down the aisle with her.

That left only Winifred, a teacher out east who was reputed, by Mr. and Mrs. Hennessey themselves, to have a somewhat chilly disposition, as the only possible source of a grandchild. She and her husband, Roger, had been married these fifteen years, but no child had thus far been forthcoming from their union, and the Hennesseys had all but given up hope. So it was with much surprise—and almost glee—when Mr. and Mrs. Hennessey received the news of Winifred's expectant state.

Mrs. Hennessey herself had then written to Henrietta to tell the good news, though Henrietta had already read about it in one of Elsie's letters. Of course, Henrietta was happy for the Hennesseys and for Winifred, whom she had never met, but it had been more than a little bit trying to hear about while she had been doubting her own ability to get pregnant. And now . . . now that she had lost the baby it was harder still, and she knew it was the reason she was avoiding visiting the Hennesseys or communicating with them much at all of late. She expected it to be just too painful to have to listen to Mrs. Hennessey go on and on about prams and diapers and little fingers and toes. On the other hand, Henrietta knew that she was being a little unfair, as she had of course told no one outside of her immediate family about her loss, so it was not Mrs. Hennessey's fault that she was so ebullient and public about sharing her daughter's news.

But now Henrietta was determined to put all of that grief and self-pity behind her as well as any selfishness she felt toward the Hennesseys in particular, so that when she was on the telephone with Lucy, it had occurred to her that Poor Pete's might be the perfect place to meet, thereby killing two birds with one stone. She would meet with Rose and return her gun, as well as visit with Mrs. Hennessey and allow the good woman to talk as much as she liked about the baby who had been born just a month ago, a little girl Winifred had apparently named Prudence Fern, or so Mrs. Hennessey's letter had announced.

When Fritz accordingly pulled up in front of Poor Pete's, Henrietta was surprised to see that Rose was already standing outside, a scarf wrapped up tightly around her head and face. Why hadn't she gone in? Henrietta wondered. Surely the door wasn't locked? She had telephoned Mrs. Hennessey and told them they were coming, which had pleased the older woman immensely, especially when Henrietta suggested they come at 9:30 a.m., a half hour before opening time, as they both knew that once the clock struck ten, a couple of regulars would drift in to take their seats at the bar for the day.

Fritz opened the car door for her, and she knew that Rose was watching as she climbed out. If she had known that Rose would be waiting outside, she would have instructed Fritz to drop her off a block down the street to avoid such a showy arrival. Evidence of her new wealth always made her uneasy around the girls, not that she saw them that much. Fritz quietly informed her that he would wait around the corner, ready to retrieve her at her convenience. She thanked him in an equally low voice, grateful for his discretion. Besides Edna, of course, Fritz, with his trim, gray mustache and beard, was becoming one of her favorite servants. Unlike Billings, she didn't sense that he judged her, and he had proven he could be trusted when she had asked him to take her to various locales, even ones of a more seedy nature like the Melody Mill, which is where she had gone to get the gun in the first place, without reporting these destinations back to Clive.

"Rose!" Henrietta exclaimed, embracing her now. "Why didn't you go in? Is the door locked?"

"Did you bring it?" Rose asked, oddly looking at the pavement instead of her. "I can't really stay."

"Of course, I brought it. But can't you come in and visit for a little bit? Mrs. Hennessey says she remembers you from the wedding,"

Henrietta said, referring of course to her own wedding, which is where Stan and Rose had first met.

Indeed, Mrs. Hennessey *did* remember seeing Rose and Stanley together, she had intimated when Henrietta telephoned her to ask if she and Rose could stop by. Oh, yes, she would be tickled to meet the girl who had "caught Stanley's fancy," Mrs. Hennessey had said. "Thought it was odd, him dancing with a tart, beg your pardon, like," Mrs. Hennessey had added, delighted to be gnawing on a tidbit of gossip. "I reckon she must not really be a tart, though, not if Stan's taken up with her. Reckon his mother had a thing or two to say. But I did think so at the time, that she was a tart, that is," Mrs. Hennessey had gone on to confide. "Gettin' married, are they? Well, I never. We'll just have to hear all about it, won't we?" she said eagerly before Henrietta had finally found a chance to say good-bye and ring off.

"I don't think I should," Rose said, finally looking up at Henrietta.

"Oh, Rose!" Henrietta murmured, noticing the heavy purple-and-yellow bruising covering the whole right side of Rose's face. "Oh my God, Rose, what happened?" Her first thought went to Stanley, but she instantly dismissed the idea of him as the perpetrator as being ridiculous.

"I fell?" Rose said.

Henrietta instantly dismissed this, of course, her mind racing, and eventually came to the obvious: Rose's father, the very person she needed the gun for, Lucy had once hinted. Henrietta's stomach roiled with guilt, knowing it had just been lying for months in her closet at Highbury, almost forgotten, actually. This was all her fault!

"Oh, Rose! It was your dad, wasn't it?" she asked.

Rose did not answer but merely looked at her.

"Oh, Rose, I'm so sorry! This is all my fault! I should have gotten the gun to you before now. I'm so sorry."

"Hey, don't worry about it, sweets. It ain't your fault."

"Of course, it is! I . . . I just didn't realize that . . . that you really needed it. I guess I thought . . . oh, I don't know what I thought . . . "

Henrietta trailed off. How could a person live with someone whom they needed a gun to protect themselves against? Henrietta had seen abject poverty, but this was definitely an extreme.

"Don't go blamin' yourself, kid. Even if I had it the night I got this," she said gesturing toward her face, "it wouldn't have mattered. I always keep it under my pillow, and I wouldn't have had time to run and get it. Smacked me in the kitchen. I was tryin' to stop him from beatin' Billy. Forget about it," she said with a shrug. "I'll get over it. It's better than it was."

Henrietta shivered and could only guess why Rose kept a loaded gun in her bedroom. What other evils did her father commit in the dead of night? Henrietta had heard of that sort of thing, too, in the shabby apartment building where they had been forced to live after her father's suicide, but she didn't want to think about it.

Henrietta looped her arm around Rose's. "Come on. Let's go in. At least have a cup of coffee." Rose offered no resistance this time and allowed herself to be led into Poor Pete's.

"Mrs. Hennessey?" Henrietta called out as they stepped into the dim interior that smelled of stale cigarettes and spilled beer, which no amount of scrubbing was ever able to eradicate.

"Oh! There you are!" came a cheerful voice attached to a plump woman who appeared from the back room and hurried out around the bar. She was a middle-aged woman with gray hair, which was braided and tied up neatly behind her head in an old-fashioned style. She wore a simple housedress with an apron—Henrietta could count on one hand the number of times she had seen Mrs. Hennessey without an apron, her own engagement party and wedding being two of them—and thick, old-fashioned black boots. She had fleshy cheeks that wobbled slightly as she almost ran toward them and bright dark eyes that lit up at the very sight of Henrietta, a reaction that caused Henrietta to instantly feel more than a little guilt that she had waited so long to visit.

"Hello, Mrs. Hennessey," Henrietta said weakly as the older woman hugged her tightly to her massive bosom, as if she were a lost doll.

"Here you are, girl! Finally!" Mrs. Hennessey exclaimed, using their old nickname for Henrietta as she clutched her. "Ain't you a sight for sore eyes? Bless you, you poor thing!"

Henrietta smiled at Mrs. Hennessey's familiar phrase—everyone was always referred to as a "poor thing" by Mrs. Hennessey. She eventually released Henrietta, but not before grabbing hold of one of her hands and holding her at arm's length as if to better survey her. Proudly, she looked her up and down as if Henrietta were her own creation.

"Just look at you, girl. All fancy now. You're beautiful, you are. But then you always were. Me an' William could see that early on. An' now you've got all the clothes an' the jewels, too, just like a princess," she said eagerly and paused for just a split second before charging on. "But we've been so worried, we have. Elsie's told us bits here an' there, about how you went to a castle an' all over in England on your honeymoon, an' weren't we impressed! 'That's our Henrietta,' I says to William. 'She's made us proud,' I says to him. But then we was so sorry to hear the inspector's dad passed so sudden. Awful, wasn't it? Had to read it in the paper. Woulda been nice to hear it from you yourself, like, but I suppose you've been busy. But, never mind. Least you're here now, ain'tcha? An' this must be Rose!" she exclaimed, finally breaking her stream of words to take a quick breath. She turned to observe Rose, standing forlornly off to the side. "I recognize you," she said knowingly and wagging a finger at her. "Stan sure does go for the beauts, don't he?" She put her hands on her hips. "My, my. Look at those legs! Always did think you two was gonna get married," she said to Henrietta, obviously referring to Stanley. "But William didn't think so. Not that he woulda minded, like, but he thought you should catch someone better. No offense to Stanley," she said, glancing quickly in Rose's direction. "In fact, I says, 'What's wrong with Stanley?' 'Nothing,' says William. 'Stanley's a first-rate lad. Kind a boy I'd be proud to call me son,' he says. 'Just don't see him with our Hen. An' he were right, weren't he? Never mind that you broke Stan's heart, the poor thing. S'pose that's all water under the bridge, ain't it? Now that he's found you, a course," she nodded at Rose. "Saw you two dancin' at the wedding. Thought it was odd he weren't dancin' with Elsie, but then, Elsie was busy with the lieutenant an' hurt her ankle, an', well, everything happens for a reason is what I always say. Ain't that right? 'Cause look at you now. Engaged!" Mrs. Hennessey paused to take a deep breath. "What did you say your family name was? Rose what? Jesus, Mary, an' Joseph!" she said suddenly in a low voice, noticing Rose's bruised face. Without asking, she gently tugged the scarf back to reveal the full extent of Rose's injuries in the dim light. "This ain't Stanley's doin', is it?" she asked, shocked. "Can't believe it of that lad!" She looked worriedly from Rose to Henrietta.

"No, it wasn't Stan," Rose said, taking a step back from Mrs. Hennessey's reach. "I fell."

"Tsk, tsk. Like that, is it? Well, you don't need to tell me the whole story, but not much gets past me, working in a place like this," she said, looking over her shoulder at the bar. "Seen it all in here, an' not much of it nice; is it, girls?"

"Maybe we could have some coffee?" Henrietta suggested, taking advantage of the fortuitous break in Mrs. Hennessey's torrent.

"Lord, yes! I forgot the coffee. Here's me standing here yacking. Come on, take off your coats an' sit down," she said, gesturing at the tables. "Or do you want to come upstairs?"

Henrietta was about to say yes, knowing that the Hennessey's upstairs apartment was much nicer than the sticky bar, but Rose spoke first. "No, I can only stay for a few minutes," she said, unbuttoning her coat and pulling out a chair, its metal legs scraping loudly across the black- and-white tiled floor, which Henrietta had scrubbed, on her hands and knees, about a thousand times in her youth.

"Suit yourselves," Mrs. Hennessey called, hurrying to the back room. "I'll just be a minute."

"Sorry about that, Rose," Henrietta whispered to her, as the two of them sat down. "She's a little bit . . . well, odd. But she means well."

Rose waved her hand, "Oh, I know that. Don't worry; I don't care."

"Here," Henrietta said, opening her purse and pulling out the gun.

Rose clutched it quickly and stuffed it into her own bag in a matter of seconds.

"Thanks," she said quietly.

"Well, like I said, I'm sorry."

"Forget about it."

Henrietta paused, thinking. "Lucy said you aren't working at the Melody Mill anymore. Why's that? Did you quit?" she asked hurriedly, sensing Mrs. Hennessey would reappear any moment.

"I got fired," she said bitterly.

"Fired? Why?"

Rose gestured at her face again. "Turns out the owner don't like dames with bruised faces. Says it's bad for business. 'People come here to have a good time, dance,'" Rose said in a pseudo deep voice in an apparent attempt at imitating her boss. "'They don't want to see no dame with a smashed-in face who can't keep her man happy. Puts 'em off.' So I'm out of a job on top of it all," Rose said sourly.

"Will he take you back?"

Rose shrugged. "Who knows?"

Henrietta sighed. "What does Stan say?"

"About my face or the job?"

"Either."

"He doesn't know about me getting fired. Not yet. Says he wants to kill my dad, which is a laugh." Rose opened her handbag again and pulled out a pack of cigarettes. She offered one to Henrietta, who shook her head. Rose shakily put one to her own lips and then fumbled in her purse for a pack of matches. She finally unearthed some and after striking one into a flame, unsteadily lit the cigarette that dangled now from her mouth.

"What are you going to do?" Henrietta asked, watching her.

Rose inhaled deeply, her good eye momentarily squeezing shut to match the bruised one. "I convinced Stan to move up the wedding," she said, exhaling a large cloud of smoke as she leaned back in her chair.

Mrs. Hennessey bustled in then carrying a carafe in one hand and grasping three mugs in the other, which she set down roughly on the table in front of Rose and Henrietta. "Now just a minute while I find some milk an' sugar. Don't have no cream," she said, hurrying back toward the room Henrietta knew served as the kitchen, though it was really more a large pantry. Not much food was ever produced back there. Poor Pete's was mostly just a drinking man's type of establishment. "What's this you're saying about the wedding?" Mrs. Hennessey called out from inside the pantry. "Wait for me! I want to hear it all!"

After a few moments, she bustled back in with a small pot of sugar that already had a spoon in it and a small, cracked pitcher of milk, which she also set down in front of them. "There you are!" she said, plopping heavily into a chair, gesturing at the carafe and mugs. "Help yourselves."

Henrietta took the initiative and began to pour out three mugs of coffee.

"What didya say about the wedding? When is it?" Mrs. Hennessey said, nodding her thanks to Henrietta as she took the steaming mug she offered her and blew on it.

Henrietta saw Rose bite the side of her cheek before she answered. "Well, it was supposed to be in June at St. Sylvester's, but we're thinking of moving it up. As in maybe next week," she said, glancing out of the corner of her eye at Henrietta, who had paused mid-stir of her coffee.

"Next week?" Henrietta exclaimed.

Mrs. Hennessey chuckled. "Well, you know what they say. Babies take nine months to come, except the first one, which can come *any* time!" she said mischievously.

"I'm not pregnant," Rose said with a roll of her eyes. "No chance of that with ol' Stan. He's a regular saint."

"It's to get away from your dad, isn't it?" Henrietta asked quietly.

Rose looked up at her, surprised, and then sadly nodded. She looked like she was about to cry.

"So that's who gave you the shiner," Mrs. Hennessey said. "Bastard."

Rose gave a tiny false smile. "Yeah. It's a secret, though, so . . . the wedding, I mean."

"Why a secret?" Henrietta asked, though she thought she could guess.

"Stan's parents want a big church wedding. I'm converting," she said wryly, as if this amused her. "So we're going to get married by the justice of the peace next week, if Stan can figure out all the papers, that is, and find an apartment so that Billy and I can get the hell out of there. Stan's gonna stay at his parents until we go through with the church wedding. No one's the wiser, see?"

"And Stan agreed to this?" Henrietta asked incredulously. "What about Lucy and Gwen? Can't you stay with them?" she suggested and felt immediately guilty that she was not offering them a place at the palatial Highbury. And yet, how could she? She could only imagine what Antonia would say, especially with her annual Spring Garden party coming up. It was times like this when it bothered her that she didn't have her own home. While it was true that Antonia had basically given her and Clive a whole wing of the mansion for their private use, it's not as if Henrietta could really ask people to come and stay. Like Rose, now, and Billy, or even little Anna, an idea that had occurred to her, actually, on the drive here. And she knew that it was pointless to bring this up to Clive, predicting that he would merely say something like, "Of course, you can invite whom you like, darling," or some such thing, but she knew that it wasn't that easy, especially where Antonia and even the servants, some of whom had their own prejudiced standards, were concerned.

"Yes, they've helped out," Rose answered. "In fact, Billy's back with them now, but we can't live with them all the way until June. Their landlord is apparently already complaining. It's either a quick wedding or I'm off to Indiana to live with my great-aunt. Last I knew she was in Fort Wayne; I'm hoping she's still there. Maybe Billy and I could go live with her. Anyway, I sent her a letter just in case."

"But what about Stan?"

"What about him?" Rose challenged. "Look, sweets, I can't take my ol' man beating Billy one more time. He can do what he likes with me," she said, looking away as she took another drag of her cigarette. "I can take it, but not Billy." She looked at Henrietta steadily until her face suddenly crumpled and she broke down, covering her face with her hands as she sobbed. "I don't know what else to do."

Henrietta, surprised by Rose's rare show of emotion, reached over and gently put her hand on her back. "Oh, Rose. Don't cry. We'll figure it out," she said softly.

"It don't take no figurin'," Mrs. Hennessey said calmly. "It's easy. You move in here with us!"

"No!" Rose looked up suddenly and hurriedly tried to wipe her tears. "It's all right. I've said too much. I'll be fine," she said in almost an irritated tone.

"It's not charity, you know," Mrs. Hennessey said matter-of-factly as Henrietta handed Rose her handkerchief. "Did I hear you say you was fired? Well, that's perfect. You can work here till you get back on your feet. You can be the house 26 girl. Turns out we didn't have the heart to replace Henrietta here when she married Prince Charmin', an' I'm terrible at it. William's always goin' on about me. Says I talk too much an' don't push the drinks enough. You'll be a welcome change, you will," Mrs. Hennessey said, looking pleased with herself.

"It's very kind of you, Mrs. Hennessey," Rose said genuinely, "but I really couldn't."

"Sure you can. Now, who's this Billy? Let me guess—kid brother? You wouldn't mind sharing a room with him, would you? We've got three bedrooms above this place, if you can believe it. Two whole rooms sittin' empty, just goin' to waste, they are. That's practically a sin! So you an' Bill move on in. In exchange, you can work some for me, or pay me, let's say, five dollars a month if you find some other job. Stay as long as you like. I'd give you both rooms, but turns out Winifred an' Roger are comin' soon for a visit with little Prudence—the first time Winifred's visited us since her wedding, can you believe it? So I'm havin' a little party for them, an' both of you two are invited, of course. Or, Rose, maybe you could help me with it? This way," she barreled on, "you an' Stan can take your time decidin' when to get married, no need to rush if you don't want to. Stan's like a son to us; he really is, ain't he, Henrietta? An' so we'd like to do this for the two of you. An' it turns out good for me, don't it? I get some help around here an' help with the party. An' isn't it strange that your brother's name is Billy? Just like our Billy. Everything happens for a reason, as I say, an' what more proof of that is there than this? It was meant to be, I say. It would be a real treat to have a Billy around again an' have you around, too, Rose. I get lonely at nights, not that I'd expect you to stay in with me, but still, William's always down here. So it might be nice." Mrs. Hennessey stopped abruptly here and took a short breath.

Henrietta looked at Rose and could tell that she was hesitating.

"It's not a bad idea, Rose," Henrietta said gently, Mrs. Hennessey's words about so much wasted space being a sin secretly stinging her.

"But Billy's not normal," Rose said finally with a frown.

"Not normal?" Mrs. Hennessey asked. "Whaddya mean?"

"He's . . . he's backward," Rose replied. "You know, he's slow. He . . . he works at the electrics, but he doesn't say much. He's simple, if you know what I mean."

"Oh! That all? Well, that don't matter. Had a cousin like that. Don't bother me none. Maybe he could even do some of the liftin' for William, the poor thing. It's getting harder for him to lift the kegs into place. Breweries are supposed to do it, but these days they just drop the kegs an' go. Swine," she muttered. "So. It's all settled, is it?" She folded her hands, resting them on top of her plump stomach.

"I . . . I don't know," Rose said tentatively. "It's very generous, Mrs. Hennessey, but I . . . Can I think about it?"

"Course you can! But why don't you move in tonight?"

Rose broke into a small smile. "I'll think about it," she repeated, standing up abruptly. "But I should get going. Thank you. For the coffee and . . . and for the offer."

"You sure you have to go? All right, then. But hope you come back tonight. Bring Billy. I'll make a stew. How's that sound?"

Rose didn't say anything but seemed deep in thought as she buttoned her thin coat.

"It's just as much for Stan, you know," Mrs. Hennessey reminded her. "We love him, we do; an' this way you can have a nice wedding an' do things the right way. You don't want your married life to start out with a lie, do you?"

Rose mustered up a sad smile and looked over at Henrietta as if she might cry again. "See ya round, sweets," she said, huskily. "Say hi to the inspector," she added before hurrying out.

"I suppose I should go, too," Henrietta said slowly.

"Oh, you can't go yet! You haven't told me anything!" Mrs. Hennessey pleaded. "You have to tell me all about the honeymoon and how all the family's doin'. Is it true the boys is all out east at some fancy school?"

Henrietta took a deep breath and resigned herself to being there awhile and hoped Fritz wouldn't mind. Quickly she tried to remember if Antonia had any committee meetings later today that might require one of the cars and Fritz's services. Well, she reasoned, Albert, the new footman hired to replace the errant James, could always drive her in the Daimler if necessary.

Henrietta then proceeded to catch Mrs. Hennessey up on all that had happened with each member of the family since the wedding, ending with Elsie's going to college and meeting Gunther and even the recent search for the epileptic Liesel Klinkhammer in Dunning. Henrietta wisely decided not to go into the Madame Pavlovsky story or Mrs. Hennessey would no doubt ask so many questions, she would never escape. As it was, Dunning was more than subject enough to prompt a whole string of questions.

"Ooh, Dunning," said Mrs. Hennessey, taking her turn at pouring them more coffee. "Now that's a terrible place, that is. Wouldn't step foot in there if you paid me. Can't believe the inspector took you along. That ain't no place for a rat, much less a lady like you are now."

"Yes, it was pretty shocking," Henrietta said, deciding not to respond any further.

"Had a niece that worked there for a time, as a nurse," Mrs. Hennessey said with a proud little dip of her chin. "But she quit after a while. Couldn't take it, she said. Got a job eventually right over here at the Jefferson Park."

"I can't imagine working at a place like Dunning. No wonder she quit," Henrietta mused.

"Not that she's a quitter is our Ida, the poor thing. Don't want you to think that of her. Tried to warn her before she started there, but she went ahead an' did it anyway. Worked there almost a year, afore she quit. Didn't want to say 'I told you so,' but I did tell her so. She didn't want to talk that much about it. Only thing she would say is that something spooked her."

"Like what?" Henrietta asked, goose bumps suddenly rippling up her arms.

"She never would elaborate, would Ida. Drove me crazy at the time. But something happened. Something that scared her, she said, something she wanted no part of. So she up an' quit, just like that. Takin' a risk, I told her. Jobs bein' scarce an' havin' to take care of her ma, me brother bein' dead these last ten years. But you can ask her yourself," Mrs. Hennessey said, smiling placidly. "Perhaps she'll be chattier with someone like yourself. Course that was over a year ago now—"

"Ask her myself?" Henrietta interrupted.

"Well, she's going to be at our little gatherin' for Winifred an' Roger, ain't she? An' you an' Clive will come, right? An' Elsie, too, if she wants, like. Have to show off our grandchild to the family. Or what's left of it anyway. Might be our only grandchild we ever get, that is unless you an' Clive ever get busy. We might call ourselves the honorary grandparents, like, though between your ma an' all those rich folks, we probably won't even get a look in. No, we're determined to show off little Prudence, though Winifred's already told us not to make a fuss. An' wouldn't you know, Winifred claims that the baby looks *exactly*, that's how she wrote it in her letter—*exactly*—like Roger's mother. But there must be some of William there, don't you think?" she asked, reminding Henrietta that Mrs. Hennessey was in fact merely the stepmother of the three Hennessey children, a fact that Mrs. Hennessey herself never seemed to remember, to her credit, having come into their lives when they were all still very small.

Many times, Mrs. Hennessey had told her the story of how the three of them had looked when Mr. Hennessey brought her home to meet them all. "Like lost kittens, they were. Like wild strays. Just needed a little love is all," she had said more than once, though Henrietta had privately reflected many times since, that the three Hennessey children, based on Mrs. Hennessey's own tales, never seemed very grateful for having been rescued by the likes of Mrs. Hennessey, an observation which had always negatively colored Henrietta's perception of the three of them. She was more than intrigued to meet this Winifred, of which she had heard so much over the years, and wondered if she could convince Clive to come.

"When is it?" Henrietta asked, gathering up her things.

"It's to be Monday next," she said. "'Cause that's our slow night, as you know. Even closin' the tap for the occasion! But you're not goin', are you?" Mrs. Hennessey asked, sadly. "William will be sorry to have missed you. I think he's still asleep up there," she said, frowning. "He sleeps later an' later these days. I'll just run up an' get him, should I?"

"I really have to be getting back, Mrs. Hennessey. Fritz has been out there waiting all this time," she said, standing up.

"No! He should've come in with you! Oh, my," she said, distressed. "Out there in the cold all this time?"

Henrietta could not help but let out a laugh at the thought of Fritz pulling up a chair next to Antonia and Victoria Braithewaite at the club. "He's used to it. Even if you had asked, he would never have agreed, anyway. It's his job to wait," Henrietta tried to explain, though she was instantly conscious of how bad that sounded.

"Well, I suppose you know best," Mrs. Hennessey said doubtfully. "Before long, you won't want to even know *us*!"

Henrietta laughed again. "That's not true," she said, kissing the older woman on the cheek. "I'll speak to Clive about the party. We'll try our best. Tell Mr. Hennessey I said hello."

Mrs. Hennessey embraced her and finally let her go, but not before telling her one more story about a neighbor down the street and then, just when Henrietta was finally about to leave, having grown very warm standing there all bundled up, Mrs. Hennessey again delayed her by insisting she pack up some pound cake for her. "You know, the one you used to enjoy so much?" she called over her shoulder as she hurried to the back room to get it. "Won't take a minute!" she called. She took so long to return, however, that Henrietta began to wonder if something had happened to her.

"Do you need any help?" Henrietta called out as she glanced at her wristwatch and pulled at her scarf.

"No, no," Mrs. Hennessey said, waddling back into the room carrying a brown-paper package that she handed to Henrietta. "Here you are, case you get hungry on the way, or maybe you can have it with your tea with Clive an' his ma. I'd be glad to give her the recipe if she wants it. Whenever I make it for any doin's at St. Sylvester's, I always get asked at least once for the recipe, but you already know that, don't you?" she said with a proud smile.

Henrietta had to stifle a laugh at the image that leapt to her mind of Antonia unwrapping the pound cake wrapped in creased brown paper and serving it at Highbury. She wanted to laugh, but instead she gave Mrs. Hennessey another hug and kiss. "I will," she promised.

"Don't forget about the party!" she called out, as Henrietta slipped out the door, the pound cake tucked carefully under her arm.

As expected, Fritz had parked the Rolls halfway down the street and upon seeing her walk toward him, quickly got out of the car to open the door for her.

"I trust you had a pleasant time, madame."

"Yes, thank you, Fritz," she said. "I'm sorry it was so long. I didn't expect it to be."

"No trouble at all, madame," he said with a slight bow before walking around to the driver's side and getting in.

Henrietta set the bag of pound cake on the seat beside her and looked out the window at the neighborhood that used to be hers, many thoughts going through her mind as Fritz pulled out onto California. At the forefront of her mind was poor Rose's dilemma. She felt sorry for Rose, of course, but she couldn't help but feel sorry for Stan as well, whom she knew was being used in this situation. She could hardly blame Rose for wanting to escape her miserable situation, but would such a marriage really work? She supposed most marriages ended up being unhappy ones. She didn't want that for Stan and Rose, but how could a marriage built on so flimsy a foundation not end up as such? Especially if Rose didn't really like men in the first place . . .

Henrietta watched a woman walk down the street, holding a child by the hand, until she stepped into Woolworth's with him. Mrs. Hennessey's playful criticism of her and Clive not "getting busy" to produce a child (and thus a pseudo-grandchild for them) had initially stung a bit, but it had dissipated when she reflected that she should have just told Mrs. Hennessey the truth, that she *had* been pregnant but had lost it. Surely Mrs. Hennessey would have been more than sympathetic. And now that the opportunity had passed, Henrietta desperately wished that she'd had the courage to do so, as it would have been nice to be comforted by this woman who had been more of a mother to her than Ma. Why hadn't she? she fretted. But, then again, she reasoned, she had not really had the chance. Not with the discussion so heavily centered on Rose and Stan and also Winifred. Actually, Henrietta mused, she was surprised that talking about Winifred and her new baby was less painful than expected. Did that mean she was finally getting better? She thought she had been, but then the whole encounter with Mrs. Wojcik and Madame Pavlovsky had stirred it all up again.

The windows were beginning to fog up, blurring her vision of the outside world they were passing, so she wiped the one nearest to her with her gloved fist and peered out. It was an uncharacteristically warm day, and the snow was beginning to finally turn slushy. She unwrapped the scarf from around her neck, her mind drifting back to Dunning and the melancholy women that had, through one circumstance or another, ended up there, a fate Henrietta felt would be worse than death. How would being committed to such a place cure anyone suffering from depression? If it wasn't so terrible, it would be laughable in its absurdity. Her mind went to Mrs. Hennessey's niece, then, and she wondered what it was that had scared this Ida so badly that she quit. Was it something that one of the patients had said or done? Henrietta wondered, or, her mind wandering suddenly to Nurse Harding, was it one of the staff?

Chapter 13

"I don't see why the police can't come themselves," Mr. Tobin growled. "This was a legitimate crime. This woman must be stopped!"

Clive bit his lip, trying to swallow his annoyance.

"Don't expect me to pay you," Mr. Tobin went on with a scowl. "I didn't ask for a private detective. I wanted the real police."

"Monetary remuneration won't be necessary, Mr. Tobin," Clive said thinly.

"Eh?"

"It means you don't have to pay us," Henrietta said gently.

Mr. Tobin's eyes darted to where she sat next to Clive on the Tobins' front room sofa in their small brick home in the neighboring village of Northfield. "I don't think I asked you," he snapped.

Clive felt a rush of heat to his face, and he had to fight the sudden desire to grab Tobin and throw him up against a wall. "That's my wife," he said sternly. "And you will show her the respect she deserves."

Mr. Tobin, apparently unaffected by Clive's tone, merely gave him a dismissive, pitying sort of look, which was more irritating than one of anger or provocation would have been. Unfortunately, Clive knew the type sitting before him. The self-important type that craved power and attention but never seemed to get enough. He even had the look. Small, thin, balding head but for a few black strands arranged thinly on top. Thick, black-rimmed glasses with small piercing eyes that lay behind them. Small, thin mustache. This type, unable to bully other men because of their small stature, usually took their frustrations out on women, enjoying being able to laud it over and control at least someone.

They had yet to be introduced to Mrs. Tobin, but Clive guessed she was hovering somewhere near—perhaps in the kitchen—listening and waiting to be called in by her master. She would be a certain type, too, Clive knew. Diminutive and slight, rounded shoulders and little eye contact. In a way, Henrietta's sister, Elsie, sometimes struck him as that type—though she had admittedly seemed a little different this last time when they had seen her at Dunning. Maybe school was indeed good for her. If so, he hoped she would stay there, if nothing else than to avoid falling prey to a cruel, domineering husband, as she had so very nearly done in the form of Lieutenant Harrison-Barnes or even that cad Lloyd Aston. Clive had of course crossed paths several times with Lloyd Aston at various North Shore events, and he had secretly been glad when he heard that Elsie threw him over.

"Let's get one thing crystal clear, shall we?" Clive said. "I'm working in conjunction with the Winnetka police, and my wife is my partner. I'm an acting deputy, and, as it is, I've had the misfortune to be assigned to this case. So you can answer our questions—*both* of our questions—or we can walk out of here right now and stop wasting our time. *Or* I can take Mrs. Tobin to the station and question her privately."

"Fine, fine," Mr. Tobin said, brushing Clive off as if he had commented on the weather. "Let's get on with it, then, shall we? It's my Elks meeting tonight, and I'm the treasurer, so I can't be late."

In point of fact, before going over to question Mr. and Mrs. Tobin, Clive had made a slight detour to the Winnetka Police Station to, in fact, discuss with Davis the problem of his limited powers.

Upon Clive and Henrietta's arrival at the station, they had asked to see Sergeant Davis, and the officer on duty behind the main reception counter went off to find him. Within moments, Davis unexpectedly appeared, the officer trailing behind him. Without greeting them and with uncharacteristic swiftness, Davis quickly ushered them into a small antechamber off to the side of the main foyer, which looked as though it was being used as a sort of coatroom.

"What are you doing here?" Davis asked in a low voice, his hands on his hips. "The chief's in today." He inclined his head toward the back of the station, his gaze traveling from Clive to Henrietta as he did so. He crossed his arms in front of him, then, and flashed a rare smile at Henrietta. "Not that I mind seeing *you*, though."

"Do you mind?" Clive asked, irritated. "You make it so terribly obvious."

"You'd only figure it out anyway," Frank said as he rifled through his pockets for a cigarette. "So why hide the fact that I think your wife is divine."

"Frank!" Henrietta said with a little laugh, her face a deeper shade of pink. "You mustn't say such things."

"Why not? It's the truth," he said, lighting his cigarette.

"Listen, can we get back to business?" Clive sighed. "We can't stand here all day in the closet while you ogle my wife."

"I could think of worse fates," he said as he inhaled, giving Henrietta the tiniest of winks.

"Can't we go somewhere else?" Clive asked. "This really is unsuitable."

"No. What do you want, anyway?" Davis looked at him. "I'm kind of busy."

"I haven't been the one prevaricating," Clive said, annoyed. "Look—I need some sort of authority. If I'm acting for the police, I need some sort of badge. I'm getting nowhere saying I'm a private detective. Hired by who? I need some muscle."

Davis sighed and scratched his head as he studied the floor. "Well, what do you want me to do? I can't hire you. Can't you use your old badge?" he asked quietly. "No one's going to look that carefully."

"I turned it in," Clive said stiffly, "as was required."

"Of course, you did, didn't you?" Davis replied with a look of exasperation. "Well, what do you want *me* to do?"

"Make me your deputy. You have the authority."

"Do I? I don't think I do," he said, squinting one eye at him as he took another drag.

"You can in an extreme case."

"Which this is not," he said, folding his arms casually in front of him.

"Listen, Davis, stop fucking around. You either want me to help you or you don't."

"All right, all right," Davis said, holding up his hands. "There's a lady present, you know."

"Just do it."

"All right. Just a minute. Wait here," he said and left.

"Clive!" Henrietta said, looking at him with what seemed to be amusement. "I believe you're jealous."

"Jealous?" he scoffed. "Of him? Hardly."

Davis returned after a few moments and tossed him what looked like a thin, black wallet. "Here. Don't ask."

Clive opened up the wallet, which held a tarnished badge on the right and an identification on the left. "Joseph Smith?" he read aloud and gave Davis a skeptical look. It was barely a step above "John Doe." "Whose is this?"

"I said don't ask. You want it or not?"

Clive sighed. He was generally loath to break rules, knowing that once down that path, it was a slippery slope to all manner of sins. He had started his police career determined to uphold every letter of the law, but his own chief had ordered him on a number of occasions to look the other way. He had struggled over those cases, but in the end, his need to follow a direct order outweighed his better moral judgment. But doing so had plunged him into a gray sort of world from that moment on, no longer safe behind the black-and-white rules he had been upholding. The lines were blurred now, and each situation had to be read and interpreted on its own merit. For the most part he stuck to the law—never took bribes or sequestered confiscated material, never looked the other way on dirty cops. Politicians, though, he was ordered to ignore on various occasions. It burned him up to do so, but he felt he had no choice. It was for the greater good, the chief had said. They were out to win the war, and some battles would naturally be lost. It was just a part of it. Unfortunately, Clive was no stranger to speeches such as this; he had heard them all before in the actual war in Europe.

And as much as he didn't like the feel of using a fake badge, as this surely was, he saw it as a necessary means to an end. He felt he needed it as a backup, as a way to motivate certain suspects to speak. In the past, he could resort to brute force, but now, as a private citizen, he couldn't rely on throwing someone up against a wall. Nor did he wish to resort to such tactics in front of Henrietta, though that hesitation was also slipping further into the background as time went on. She had proved on more than one occasion that she was definitely not a fainting violet.

"I really must insist on speaking with Mrs. Tobin," Clive said now, his eyes darting toward what he was sure was the kitchen.

"Fine, fine, but she'll just repeat what I've already told you," Tobin said disgruntledly. "Louise!" he shouted. "Come in here!"

"Yes, Burt?" his wife answered immediately, as if she were indeed hovering somewhere nearby, and entered the room untying her apron. She was taller and more thickset than Clive thought she would be, but she had the rounded shoulders and the telltale diminutive air about her. She wore her dull, blonde hair short, in a bob, and her skin was porous and thick. A large brown splotch covered her right cheek, an obvious birthmark.

"Sit down," Mr. Tobin instructed her. "These two are working with the police, investigating that freak. They want to talk to you."

Louise Tobin looked up at them nervously and twisted her hands in her lap.

"Just a few questions, Mrs. Tobin," Henrietta said kindly.

The woman looked at her and curled one side of her mouth into a momentary smile, and then looked over at her husband, her smile instantly melting into a frown as she did so.

"Mrs. Tobin, why don't you tell us about your visit to Madame Pavlovsky," Clive said gently.

"What . . . what do you want me to tell you?" she asked.

"Let's start with when. When did you first go see her?"

Mrs. Tobin paused to think. "A few weeks ago. Maybe a month. Yes, it was a month ago, because I went on the anniversary of my mother's death."

"And when was that?"

"February seventeenth."

"And why did you decide to . . . well, to go see her? As I understand it, she's relatively new to this area. How did you know about her?"

"I . . . " she began and looked over at her husband. "I . . . some of the women at the Ladies Prayer Auxiliary at church were talking about her. Saying she could tell the future or the past . . . they . . . they had such amazing stories to tell." She glanced nervously at her husband again. "I . . . I could hardly believe it."

"You shouldn't have believed it, you dumb cow," Mr. Tobin spit out. "You should have asked me first."

Clive shot him a dirty look. "I'm not interested in hearing from you at the moment, Mr. Tobin. Go on, Mrs. Tobin," he said encouragingly. "What sort of stories?"

Mrs. Tobin again looked at her husband. "That she could . . . could talk to the dead," she said in a voice just above a whisper.

"Jesus Christ!" Mr. Tobin muttered, at which Mrs. Tobin winced, as if expecting a blow from him. When none was forthcoming, she opened her eyes and looked at Clive.

"And then what did you do?" he asked after glaring at Mr. Tobin again, but she didn't answer. She opened her mouth to speak, but no words came out.

My God, Clive thought, Tobin must really be a bastard. He

decided to switch his interview tactic to help Mrs. Tobin. "So you decided to see for yourself?" Clive asked, leading her.

Mrs. Tobin nodded gratefully.

"On the anniversary of your mother's death . . . perhaps hoping that Madame Pavlovsky might be able to speak with her? Is that right?"

Mrs. Tobin nodded eagerly. "Yes."

Clive debated asking her the details of the conversation, not wanting to further fuel Henrietta's imagination. And anyway, what did it matter what Madame Pavlovsky had told her? He could pretty much guess. "Did Madame Pavlovsky charge you for her . . . her services?" he asked instead.

"No, there was no fee involved," she said, looking hastily at her husband.

"Just told you to rob me blind," Mr. Tobin put in snidely.

"It wasn't like that, Burt! I told you that," she said, only glancing at him briefly before looking back at the ground.

"Why don't you tell us in your own words, Mrs. Tobin," Clive entreated.

"I wasn't bringing her all my jewelry like . . . like he says," she said eagerly, as if she were glad for the chance to explain herself. "Madame Pavlovsky said that I should bring a token, something that was my mother's. Something that would help her to communicate—"

"Oh, for Christ's sake!" Mr. Tobin burst out.

"One more interruption from you," Clive said, pointing his finger at him, "and I'm taking her in for private questioning. Understand?"

"Oh, all right. Don't get excited," Mr. Tobin said with an irritated wave of his hand, as he threw himself back into his chair and crossed his arms in front of him.

"Go on," Clive said to Mrs. Tobin, again.

"I . . . I admit I got overly excited," she began, tentatively. "I'm sure it's all my fault. But she . . . she told me things about my mother that she couldn't possibly have known, that I . . . " she paused here, twisting her hands again. "Well, anyway, I . . . I went home to find just the right thing. I got out all my jewelry and laid it out on our bed, trying to sort out which had been my mother's and trying to choose what I thought was the most special to bring back to Madame Pavlovsky's. That's when Burt walked in and he . . . well, you got the wrong idea," she said, looking at Mr. Tobin again. "I . . . I tried to tell him that."

Clive looked over at Mr. Tobin, sitting with his arms still stiffly folded across his chest, his lips pressed tightly together.

"You don't buy that, do you?" Mr. Tobin suddenly blurted out. "She was hypnotized by that . . . that witch!" he said, gesturing wildly. "We need to run her out of town! And by God, if the police won't do anything, we just might have to take the law into our own hands!" Mr. Tobin was almost shouting at this point.

"What a splendid idea, Mr. Tobin. I'd love a chance to lock you up."

"You don't have that authority!"

"Try me," Clive said, staring him down before he finally broke his gaze and looked back to Mrs. Tobin. "Mrs. Tobin," Clive continued calmly. "Do you feel you were hypnotized, coerced in any way?"

"No! I didn't. I don't. Nothing like that. I swear it."

"You felt . . . in your right mind the whole time you were with Madame Pavlovsky? And after as well?" Privately, given what he had seen of Madame Pavlovsky himself, he very much doubted her ability to do any such thing, but he felt he needed to ask.

"Yes! Of course, I was. I wasn't hypnotized or . . . or anything like that!"

"Don't get uppity, woman," Mr. Tobin instructed. "He's just asking a question. First good one he's asked yet."

Clive ground his teeth and sighed. He was getting nowhere with this ass in the room. Suddenly, an idea came to him. "Mrs. Tobin," he asked brightly, rubbing his chin. "I wonder if I might have some coffee. Could I trouble you for some?"

"Oh, my! Of course," Mrs. Tobin said. "I'm sorry I didn't offer you any before. How silly of me." She jumped up almost gladly, as if relieved to be back in the role of the servant and out of the spotlight. Clive looked at Henrietta with wide eyes and just slightly inclined his head toward Mrs. Tobin. He hoped she would understand . . . Delightedly, he saw her eyes light up in apparent recognition of what he wanted her to do and felt a flush of love for her.

"Would you like some help?" Henrietta asked Mrs. Tobin, looking from him to the woman in front of her.

"Oh, no! I've got it. I'll just be a minute."

"Well, perhaps I could just powder my nose, if that's all right," Henrietta asked smoothly, Clive thrilling at her prowess.

"Of course, you can. Burt put the bathroom in just last year," she said proudly. "I just put a fresh towel out, too. Just this morning. But I should've put out the nice guest one," she said as she led Henrietta out of the room. "Just down the hall, there," she pointed.

Henrietta went into the tiny bathroom, which held only a toilet and a sink and was so small, she could barely close the door with herself inside. Silently she waited several minutes, thinking about the situation before them. Clive obviously wanted her to get more information out of Mrs. Tobin, but she wasn't sure exactly what information. In truth, she was a little afraid to leave him alone with Mr. Tobin; she could tell he was almost at the end of his rope, and it would never do if Clive punched him or did something equally ridiculous.

She opened the bathroom door and paused to listen. She could hear Clive and Mr. Tobin discussing what sounded like politics, heatedly, on the part of Mr. Tobin, anyway. It was a subject she knew Clive despised, so he must be stalling for time, she speculated—time for her to hopefully get some information out of Mrs. Tobin. She took a deep breath and opened the bathroom door, walking softly back down the hall. She paused at the kitchen doorway, where she could see Mrs. Tobin hurriedly arranging cups on a tray.

"Need some help?" Henrietta asked again.

"No, won't be a minute," she said, smiling up at Henrietta.

Henrietta tried to think of something to say. "Sorry if we're making trouble for you," she said, nodding toward the front room.

"You mustn't mind Burt. He doesn't mean most of what he says. More bark than bite, really."

Henrietta wasn't so sure that his bark wasn't hurtful just the same, but she let it go. "I . . . we've been out to see Madame Pavlovsky ourselves," she said.

Mrs. Tobin looked up sharply. "You have?"

"Yes," Henrietta answered, encouraged by Mrs. Tobin's animated response. "I . . . I know what you mean about her saying things you can't explain," she added softly. "She told me things about . . . about my two siblings that died of the flu when they were little. And about my father . . . she couldn't have known . . . " Henrietta let her words hang there to see if they would be bait enough for Mrs. Tobin to take, and in the end she was rewarded.

"Yes, that's just it, isn't it?" Mrs. Tobin whispered excitedly. "Things she couldn't have known. Things that not another soul on this earth knows!"

"What . . . what did she tell you?" Henrietta asked, unable to contain her true curiosity.

"My mother died when I was young, just fourteen. I was an only child . . . and a lonely one. My mother worked in a factory, so I was alone a lot. One year for my birthday, an aunt gave me a little set of watercolor paints, and I loved them. I spent a lot of time painting and drawing. When my mother died, I was crushed with the grief of it. The night before her funeral, I stayed up painting a picture on an old piece of the Sears catalog because I didn't have anything else, for her. It was a tree that I painted, full of leaves and flowers and creatures, so that she would have some life, some green and some color where she was going in the ground. I put it in an envelope and wanted to put it in her casket, but Father wouldn't let me, so when he wasn't looking, I put it in the pocket of the dress they had laid her out in. No one noticed and no one else knew. But it gave me great comfort. And then, when I went to see Madame Pavlovsky," she said, bringing her hand shakily to her mouth, "she said that she could see my mother. That she was patting her pocket and saying 'thanks,'"

Mrs. Tobin said in a whisper. "Madame Pavlovsky just looked at me, not knowing what the message meant and waited for me to explain. It was clear as the nose on my face, she wasn't making it up. For God's sake, how could she?"

Henrietta felt her heart begin to race a little faster, and goose bumps shot up her arms again. Mrs. Tobin was right. How could Madame Pavlovsky have known that? She simply couldn't have. And if she really were some sort of fraud, why pick out such a loving, tiny detail to reveal? It made no difference in the grand scheme of things, and yet it was very meaningful to Mrs. Tobin.

"And then when I got home, would you believe I saw a cardinal? Right there on the windowsill, plain as day."

"A cardinal?" Henrietta asked, clearly not understanding the significance.

"Don't you know about cardinals?" she asked. "Cardinals are a sign from the dead. It means they're okay where they are; the deceased that is. That they're okay up in heaven."

"Oh!" Henrietta said, as she tried to remember if she had seen any cardinals following her father's death, or even now . . . but that was ridiculous, wasn't it? A baby couldn't send a cardinal to her.

"So that's even more proof isn't it?" Mrs. Tobin whispered excitedly. "I don't care what anyone says," she said, nodding toward the front room. "She's the real thing."

"But why did she want you to bring jewelry to her?" Henrietta decided to ask, determined to act like a detective, knowing that Clive would ask that when she told him later about this conversation.

"It doesn't have to be jewelry or anything valuable at all. Just something. A button, a pipe, a handkerchief. I don't have much left of my mother's; my father got rid of it all in his grief. There was just a bit of odd jewelry of hers he gave me. It's not worth anything, which Burt knows, or he would have wanted to sell it," she said, a trace of bitterness in her voice. "And, anyway, Madame Pavlovsky didn't necessarily say she was going to keep it. Just said to bring it."

"But why?" Henrietta asked.

Mrs. Tobin's eyes darted toward the front room. "She does séances," she whispered. "For those interested. In a séance, she can hear the deceased more clearly, she says, and she can actually speak to them, not just listen. If they choose to come forward, that is. And one way to get them to come forward, Madame Pavlovsky says, is to bring along something that belonged to the deceased. It draws them to the sacred circle."

Henrietta felt a chill run down her spine.

"She's having one this Friday. It's always on a Friday. Don't know why. But why don't you come? You can see for yourself. Maybe she could tell you more about your father or your brother and sister."

Henrietta wondered what Clive would say about attending a séance and was fairly certain she could guess. "Will . . . will you . . . how will you get away?" Henrietta asked her, nodding again toward the front room.

Mrs. Tobin let out a loud puff of air. "I'll just have to say that I'm going to visit a friend for the night. He won't know," she whispered.

"Why is he so upset by all of this?" Henrietta asked. "I mean, to go to the police? It seems extreme."

Mrs. Tobin shrugged. "That's just his way. He's awfully paranoid. Suspicious of everyone. That's why we're not close with any of the neighbors. Thinks they're after something of his all the time. He doesn't even like me going out to my church meetings at night or my sewing circle, but I have to have something, don't I?" she asked Henrietta, pitifully.

Henrietta was about to ask if he hit her, but she stopped herself. She didn't wish to humiliate the poor woman. And even if Mrs. Tobin told her the truth, there was nothing either of them could do to change it.

"Louise!" came a shout from the front room as if on cue, causing Mrs. Tobin to jump. "Get out here with that coffee, woman, so these two can get out of here. I've got to get to my Elks meeting!"

Louise Tobin hurriedly picked up the tray and shot Henrietta a nervous smile. "Ten o'clock this Friday," she whispered and bustled out under the load she carried.

Chapter 14

"What do you mean? I think it's smashing that you're going to Miami!" Melody exclaimed.

"Well, it's not for sure," Elsie said hesitantly from her little desk in the room she shared with Melody. "I'm still hoping I can get out of it."

"Why would you want to do that?" Melody asked, plopping down on the side of her bed as she wrapped a bit of her hair around her finger. "Miami's *the* place to be over spring break. That or Atlantic City. I think Douglas may be going there with his family, so you might run into him. Where'd you say you're staying?"

"The Flamingo, I think. But that's if I go. I'm not sure that—"

"It's positively beastly that Pops won't take us anywhere this year!" Melody interrupted with a pout. "Fred's graduating, so Pops is taking us to Paris over the summer to celebrate. That will be heavenly, of course, but it means I'm stuck in Wisconsin for break. Still, I'm being awfully wicked. I've been to Miami loads of times, and you haven't, so I'm done being envious and now I'm going to just be happy for you. You'll love it. It's terrifically fun. Plenty of swarthy Latin lover types to foxtrot with, though none of them were ever allowed even remotely close to me," she said with another charming pout. "But I did slip out one night and had champagne with a man named Rodrigo by the fountain in front of the Nautilus." She leaned forward conspiratorially. "He promised me all sorts of ridiculous things before Pops caught us! He would have thrashed him, if Mums hadn't held him back and stopped him. It was quite the scene, I'll tell you, and one which Pops didn't forgive me for for the longest time. Honestly, nothing happened. Unfortunately," she added with a laugh. "Anyway, you're sure to have the most exquisite adventures and at least one love affair, especially with only your old Aunt Agatha to keep an eye on you. I should imagine it would be terribly easy to outfox her—but be careful, those Latin types propose every two seconds, so . . . Oh! . . . Oh," she said, wincing. "Sorry. I forgot again—about the nun thing. Sorry," she added soberly.

"It's all right," Elsie said with a small smile. "But I do wish I were going with you instead. I'd love to see Merriweather someday."

"Why? It's terrifically dull. And, anyway, you don't want to come in spring."

"Why ever not? I would have thought it would be lovely that time of year."

"Some parts are, I guess, but spring in farmland isn't all that pretty. It's just mud and more mud."

"Surely you have a lot of flowers?"

"In a sea of mud? The effect is ruined. Unless you can train your eye to only see the yellow of the daffodil and not the vast brown that surrounds it."

"And here I took you for a romantic," Elsie teased, inclining her head at the book in front of her, where she just happened to be toiling over Wordsworth's "I Wandered Lonely as a Cloud."

"Speaking of romance," Melody said, obviously not catching Elsie's deeper meaning, "I know you're not keen to date, considering your . . . your condition . . . your intent . . . I mean your vocation . . . Jeepers! I'm getting this all wrong!" She paused to collect herself before starting again. "I was wondering, actually, if you . . . if you thought you might take pity on poor Clarence and go with him to the Delta Sig's Spring Formal?" she asked, her voice getting uncomfortably higher and higher. "I mean, just as pals. Nothing more."

Elsie sighed. Not yet another invitation to a dance! She despaired at the thought, and yet, she allowed herself to muse for just a moment, attending something as simple as a fraternity formal would be comparatively easy after having attended countless real balls at the most prestigious mansions on the North Shore. And without Aunt Agatha or Grandfather or any of the other Exleys, for that matter, sizing her up and watching her every move, it might actually be enjoyable for once.

But what was she thinking? she scolded herself, suddenly realizing the errant path her mind had wandered down. She didn't have time for this type of frivolity, nor did she want to, really. All of her free time was spent thinking about a certain other person and how she might help him. She had come up with an idea, actually, regarding Anna, but she was pretty sure Gunther would reject it—if she could ever find him to explain it, that is. He was never anywhere to be found these days.

"I didn't mean to offend you," Melody said, interrupting her thoughts and obviously misunderstanding her silence. "It's all right. Really. But don't you think you should have a little bit of fun while you still can, Els? I mean, there will be time for prayers and all that later, after you . . . after you take the veil. Is it true they make you shave your head?" Melody asked eagerly, drawing her legs up and wrapping her arms around them.

Elsie let out a deep breath. She couldn't keep up this farce any longer. It was weighing on her too much, and she truly liked Melody too much to continue lying to her.

"Listen, Melody, there's something I've been meaning to tell you about that. I . . . well, I haven't been exactly forthcoming . . . honest, actually, about becoming a nun." Carefully she set her pencil down, pressing it with her finger to keep it from rolling.

"Don't tell me you already are a nun!" Melody said, her eyes wide. "Please don't say that! You're not, are you?"

Elsie couldn't help but give a little laugh. "No, of course not! No, it's just that, I *did* at one point truly want to become a nun, but . . . "

"Yes?" Melody asked excitedly, seeming not the least bit offended so far by Elsie's confession.

"But now I . . . I've sort of changed my mind—"

"I knew it!" Melody exclaimed. "I knew you couldn't become a nun! How dreary would that be? I mean, if that's your calling, I guess, but, oh, Elsie, I'm so glad! You've no idea. I mean, who has a nun for a roommate? First Norma left after only one term, and then I get a nun. I was beginning to think it was me or something. But, oh, Elsie I'm ever so glad . . . even though it's wickedly selfish of me—God forgive me! You would have made a lovely nun, of course, and I'm sure God would be glad of it and everything, but, gee whiz," she gushed. "It's better this way, isn't it? Don't you think?"

Elsie could not help but laugh in earnest at Melody's joyous response despite the fact that Elsie basically lied to her. "But there's more to it than that," Elsie said soberly, knowing that it would do no good to leave Melody thinking that she was once again an open playing field for her romantic machinations. "More?" Melody crowed. "Oh, what a lucky day I'm having! Are you going to finally tell me your secret?" Melody whispered deliciously. "The one I knew you had! Oh, I wish Cynthia were here, too! But no matter . . . Let me guess! You're in love! I knew you were, you know!"

Elsie let out a deep breath, not a little disappointed that Melody had guessed so easily, but then again, she had been guessing that since nearly the first day they had met. Melody seemed under the impression that everyone was secretly in love with someone, so much so that if someone in her acquaintance actually *did* find themselves in such a state, it was, in and of itself, surprising.

"Well, yes, actually," Elsie said, blushing. "I . . . I do think I'm in love."

"I knew it!" Melody said, clapping her hands together excitedly. "But don't tell me it's with one of those stuffy North Shore stiffs your aunt is always trying to set you up with. From what you describe, they're positively elderly! Is it Clarence?" she asked after a moment's thought. "Do say it's Clarence! No—it's not Clarence, is it? That would be expected, so he can't be it. Is it Charlie? Is that it? Is that why you're telling me now, here, alone, without Cynthia?"

Elsie laughed out loud. Being with Melody was so light and amusing. Everything in her life was so marvelously carefree and trivial. Nothing bad or depressing or tragic ever seemed to happen in her world. It was delightful to be a part of; no wonder she had so many friends. "No, silly, it's not Douglas—or Bernie, in case that's the next question. Now, remember, this is a very big secret. No one can know. Especially Sister Bernard. The truth is that I'm in love with—"

But before Elsie could reveal any secrets, there was a rapid knock on the door just at that moment, which caused them both to jump. Before they could even react, another rapid knock was heard, and Elsie felt a dreadful sinking in her stomach. Somehow, she knew this wasn't good. She stood up and went to the door, opening it slowly. On the other side stood a panting Gunther, his face sweaty and pained. "Please," he said, his eyes momentarily darting toward where Melody still sat on her bed. "It's Anna." Frantically, he looked back at Elsie, then, his face crumpling. "They've taken her."

Chapter 15

"It can't be all that bad, Clive," Henrietta said, loosening his tie, as they stood together in their bedroom. Clive had spent the morning in his father's—his—study, trying to make sense of the latest stack of documents Bennett had delivered, which never ceased to bore him. Meanwhile, Henrietta, she had just related, had spent it closeted with poor Edna in an attempt to turn her into a private secretary rather than have her continue to toil as her maid. Personally, Clive did not see what Henrietta would exactly need a secretary for, but he hadn't said as much. After all, as she was so frequently reminding him, it was *her* maid, so he tried to stay out of it.

He was not surprised, however, by Henrietta's disappointed revelation just now that in fact, poor Edna seemed barely literate, and besides that, possessed the most atrocious handwriting she had ever seen. Clive had been tempted to say, "I told you so," but he wisely did not. He would have been happy, however, to continue to discuss Edna's considerable skills, or lack thereof, had he known that the alternative conversation was to *again* be about the events of the last couple of days, followed by Henrietta's recurrent attempt to convince him to attend the séance that night which Mrs. Tobin had told her about. A séance! The very idea of it was ridiculous, and yet, Clive wondered if it would be a chance to catch Madame Pavlovsky red-handed. And then there was the other topic—the Hennessey's party for their daughter and her new baby in a few days' time. Neither of them sounded the least bit appealing.

"This séance or the Hennessey's party?" he asked dryly, rubbing his forehead.

"Both, actually," she said, her fingers pulling at his tie.

"You can't really be serious, are you, darling?" he asked with a sigh. "And just why are you undressing me? Dinner isn't for a couple of hours yet, and Carter will be unbearably crabby if you do his job for him."

"He already doesn't like me, so what does it matter?" she asked, slowly pulling his tie free now.

He looked down at her, and she returned the look with one of mock innocence. She knew what she was doing all right, he thought, slightly amused, and unfortunately it was working. He found it powerless to resist her. Still, he had to try.

"The Hennessey's party I can halfway understand—but a séance?" he asked, clearing his throat.

"You have to admit you're curious, Inspector. I know you. Here's your chance to debunk it. Just think of how wonderful it would be to report back to Davis with the case solved," Henrietta suggested, unbuttoning his top button.

"That's hardly a draw," he said wryly.

"I know you're jealous of him, Clive, so here's your chance to one-up him."

Again, he observed that she knew perfectly well what she was doing, and he couldn't help but let a smile escape. "You've already stated this speculation once before, which I patently ignored at the time and so will do this time as well."

"I'm sure you've noticed the way he looks at me," she said, unbuttoning another button.

"Obviously I have, but I have utter trust in *you*, darling, so I have no need to be jealous, you see." As a matter of fact, he was a bit wary of Davis, who was forever ogling Henrietta beyond the point of annoyance. It was one of the reasons he stopped wanting to visit him at the hospital, but Henrietta had insisted, saying that she would go alone, then, if he didn't feel up to it. Minx! As a cop, a brother-in-arms, he trusted Davis implicitly for some reason—but where his wife was concerned, he decided, it wouldn't hurt to keep his eye on him.

"Don't you want to see Madame Pavlovsky's trickery, as you call it, in action? And Mrs. Tobin will be there as well. We can see what happens."

"I'm sure I can guess what will happen, and I know perfectly well that it's you who wants to witness another display of her so-called powers," he said, resting his finger under her chin and staring down into her deep-blue eyes. Why did he want to make love to her all the bloody time? "Oh, all right," he sighed. "If you really think we should go—professionally, as investigators—I'll agree. I suppose it can't do any harm," he added, hoping this was true. "But we're not calling up any spirits or dead relatives or any such nonsense, understand?" He attempted to make his voice stern, though in actuality he was more than a little unsettled. Already, he was beginning to have a bad feeling about this.

"And we'll go to the Hennessey's party, too?" she pressed.

He pushed a strand of her auburn hair behind her ear and cupped her cheek in his hand. "What am I going to do with you?" he asked softly.

"What do you mean by that?"

"I mean that you're trying to use your feminine charms on me to get your way," he said, running his finger along the side of her jaw. God he wanted her.

"How dare you, Clive Howard!" she said with an indignant tone that he was fairly convinced was put on. "Are you suggesting that I . . . that I'm prostituting myself?"

"Well, aren't you?" he said, leaning closer to her now so that there was only an inch between their lips.

"Beast!" she exclaimed and pulled his chest hair.

"Ow!" he said, and then pulled her to him, kissing her deeply. "Two can play at this game."

"I hope so," she said mischievously as she ran her finger down his chest and let it rest on his belt, tugging it just slightly.

"This isn't the way police business is supposed to work," he said in a thick voice.

"I wasn't aware there was a way." She kissed him as she pulled his shirt off so that it hung behind him, still tucked into his trousers. "Do illuminate me."

"That's it. I clearly have no choice," he said, taking her face in his hands and kissing her again deeply, his tongue meeting hers. His hands went around her and grasped her buttocks, pulling her sharply against him and holding her there. His lips left hers and traveled down her neck as she slipped out of her heels and began to unzip her skirt. Gently he lifted her silk blouse over her head, leaving her standing before him in her shimmering black slip and French silk stockings.

She was so lovely to behold that it still took his breath away. She stood before him now, completely unashamed though the afternoon sun shone in through the windows, illuminating them both and hiding nothing. She smiled at him so knowingly that he found his breath catching as she took his hand and led him to their bed. She lay down, gazing at him in a way that was different than any time before. It was a sensual and knowing sort of look, and he found it stirred his attraction for her in an altogether new way. He could see the desire in her eyes, the desire for him to make love to her and please her. She opened her legs slightly, lifting her slip just a little in such a provocative way that he thought he might go crazy.

He lunged for her, covering her mouth with his and melting as she wrapped her arms around him. Deeply he inhaled the scent of her, flowery and earthy at the same time, almost like honey, and he didn't think he could ever get enough of her. With one hand, he cupped her breast, the silkiness of her slip that tightly hugged it arousing him all the more. He bent to kiss the top of her breasts along the edge of her brassiere and slipped his fingers beneath. He felt her hands travel down his thighs, and breathing heavily, he paused to tug her slip over her head, catching her lips for a kiss as he did so, her hair splaying out wildly. He watched as she undid her brassiere, her breasts bouncing out from behind it.

Hungrily, he took her breasts in his hands and fondled them, slowly, gently, and bent to kiss her erect nipples, causing her to moan as she lay back down. He continued kissing her, moving down her body until he came to her underthings. He kissed her soft place through her knickers and then peeled them off as well, leaving her exposed and quivering.

"Oh, Clive," she said, her voice husky with desire and causing something to utterly snap within him. He wanted to plunge into her at that moment, take her and quell the angst that never ceased to burn within him—but he needed control, he knew, and forced himself to breathe deeply. He would never just take her. He wanted her to be ready. He moved back up and kissed her lips, and instead allowed his fingers to explore. He was surprised by how aroused she already was, and his urgency returned so violently that he felt in real danger of exploding too soon. He fought it, though, until she whispered, "Clive, Clive, please," and he knew it was time to act. He mounted her then, easing himself into her and began to thrust. When she whispered, "harder," he thought he might positively come undone. He indeed began to thrust harder now and faster, his passion rising until he thought he couldn't hold it any longer, breaking into a thin sweat.

Mercifully, just when he really thought he couldn't stand it any longer, he felt her begin to shudder under him, her fingers simultaneously digging into his back. With a couple of final thrusts, he exploded into her, groaning, not holding anything back, a blinding light piercing his senses as he did so.

He let the waves of his orgasm pass over him, fiercely kissing her, but as it ebbed, his kisses turned more tender, and he softly brushed her ear, her cheek, her shoulder with his lips. "Oh, Henrietta," he said as he continued covering her with soft kisses. "God in heaven, I love you," he said hoarsely.

"I love you, too, Clive. I love you, too," she said, rubbing her fingers along the taut muscles of his back. He collapsed beside her, holding her, and wished he could just lie there with her forever, to never have to leave the room ever again.

But duty called, he knew, as he rolled over onto his back with a sigh. It was only two in the afternoon, after all, and he smiled to himself at the scandal of making love to his wife midday, feeling fairly certain his father would never have engaged in such a thing. Even if it *might* have occurred to him, Clive guessed, his father more than likely would never have been allowed the opportunity, not with the irritating Carter constantly hovering around . . . But he didn't want to think of Carter right now! he scolded himself and instead turned back to Henrietta and brushed his finger down her pure white shoulder. Lazily, she opened her eyes to look up at him, so trusting, the love in them palpable. How could she be so innocent and trusting and naïve and yet so seductive and intoxicating all at the same time? "You're wonderful, you know," he said, propping his head up with his fist.

"So are you," she whispered and wrapped a finger in the hair of his chest.

"So now that you've had your wicked way and I'm utterly in your power, what would you have me do?" he said, brushing her cheek with the knuckles of his other hand.

"Clive! Don't say it like that!"

"Let me rephrase, then. Let's see. The last thing I remember is something about going to the Hennessey's party. But surely that can't be it," he said with a grin, though his brow was furrowed.

"Very well, Clive," she responded curtly. "If you insist on being a snob, I'll just go on my own. Fritz can drive me." He hoped it was only pretend hurt in her voice as she reached down to grab the sheet and pull it up around her.

"A snob? That's quite severe," he said, eyebrows raised. "Darling . . . don't be ridiculous. Of course, we'll go if you wish it. But, forgive me, I don't see the appeal. I predict it to be dreadfully dull, unless one is a novelist in search of new and only passably believable eccentric characters . . . "

"Clive!" I can't believe you! I've gone to more dinners and teas and luncheons and operas and theatre and balls than I can count. I've gone to every occasion that was ever presented by you—or your mother, for that matter. But not once, except Christmas Eve, have you attended something of my family's. Well, there was New Year's Eve, too, but that doesn't count because it was only Eugene. That's two things!" Clive could tell that what had begun as something playful was quickly descending into something more serious. He had been about to protest that there *weren't* ever any occasions to attend on the Von Harmon side of things and also that the Hennesseys hardly counted as her family, but he thought better of it, remembering that they sort of were, in a way.

"Darling, you're quite right," he said instead, kissing her forehead. "I've been remiss. Of course, we should go and celebrate with the Hennesseys. I just thought it might be difficult for you considering the reason for the celebration . . . " he offered, his voice trailing off

"Clive," she said, looking him in the eye. "I know you mean well in wanting to shield and protect me, but I can't avoid babies for the rest of my life until I . . . if I do ever . . . "

"Not *if*," he said, taking her hand and lacing her fingers with his. "It will happen when it's supposed to happen."

She lay silent for a moment and looked over at him with what seemed to be a forced smile. "So we'll go then?" she asked.

"Yes, of course," he said, raising her hand and kissing it. "You know I will deny you nothing."

"I know it might be hard to see their new baby," she said, thankfully breaking into his thoughts and delightfully mimicking his gesture and kissing *his* hand now. "But I feel I need to be there for them after all they've done for me. And I'm terribly curious to finally meet the sour Winifred after hearing about her all these years," she added with a small smile. "Aren't you?" She cleared her throat and shifted a bit. "But I must confess, darling, that there's another reason for me wanting to go."

"Oh?" he said, lying his head back on the pillow next to her.

"As a matter of fact, I'm hoping to speak to Mrs. Hennessey's niece."

"Mrs. Hennessey's niece?"

"You know, the one who used to work at Dunning?" she asked him eagerly.

Clive rolled onto his back and stared up at the ceiling. Not again. Henrietta had briefly told him about her conversation with Mrs. Hennessey and Rose, mostly in regard to what was happening with Rose and Stan, which was unfortunate, he had mused at the time, but also in regard to a niece of Mrs. Hennessey's and her former connection to Dunning, which Clive felt to be odd. What were the chances of that coming up in casual conversation? Well, however it had come about, Henrietta had taken whatever strands of gossip that Mrs. Hennessey had related (not to mention the ravings of Madame Pavlovsky) and had unfortunately twisted them together with the circumstances surrounding Liesel's death. Enough, anyway, to suggest to him over breakfast just this morning that there was perhaps still a reason to further investigate.

Again, he bemoaned the fact that what he had hoped would be simple distractions for Henrietta were possibly making her worse. She was even now more inclined to believe any old nonsense than she was before, if that were possible. He admitted that there were probably some shady things happening at Dunning, and had already said as much, actually, but nothing he wished to pursue. Why should they? It would solve nothing, and there was no real proof of wrongdoing in the case of Liesel Klinkhammer's death. But there was still another reason, he knew, if he were being honest, for adamantly declaring the Liesel Klinkhammer case closed, or better yet, not a case at all, a reason for which he was, frankly, more than a little ashamed. It was simply that he had no desire to return to Dunning. It had completely unnerved him once, and he didn't mean for that to ever happen again. He meant to give Dunning a wide berth from here on out. He knew he should simply tell Henrietta this, but it was a subject he did not wish to revisit, even with her, nor did he want her to do something rash like dash off there on her own under the guise of helping him. But unfortunately, she remained fixated on Dunning, and though he had already dismissed Liesel's death in his mind, he knew he would have to tread lightly if he did not wish to further upset his wife.

"Well," he said, turning to face Henrietta again, "we can certainly ask Mrs. Hennessey's niece—if she even actually attends the party— about her experiences there." He hesitated. "But dearest, remember, we can't read things into a case simply because we want to."

"Why do you always assume I'm doing that?" she asked, absently pulling a strand of her long auburn hair under her nose in a deliciously innocent way.

"Well, aren't you?"

"I don't know, Clive," she said, tossing her hair behind her. "I just have this funny feeling is all."

"Darling," he said, not being able to resist kissing her forehead. "It's tempting to read things into a case because it makes us feel better. We all want justice and for the case to be neatly closed. But sometimes it's not, and we have to live with it. Life isn't usually so cut and dried. You know that even from your own experiences, don't you?"

"Yes, I know," she sighed.

Clive, fearing he had said too much, put his arms around her then, and drew her to him, holding her until they both inadvertently fell asleep, only to be woken by Edna, timidly knocking at the door to inform them the dinner would soon be served.

Dinner proved to be somewhat strained, as Clive and Henrietta had not much been in attendance at Highbury these last few days, and Antonia had just this morning expressed to Clive that she was worried that perhaps Henrietta was overdoing it. Also, she noted, her brow furrowed, Sidney had mentioned to her that Clive had not been to the office in quite some time, the other day being the rare exception.

"Well, it happens I've been busy," Clive responded tartly as he helped himself to the stuffed trout which Albert now held before him, the fact that his mother had just referred to Bennett by his Christian name only registering for a few seconds. He was in no mood for any harassment from his mother. Having been woken from a blissful, naked slumber with his wife to hurriedly dress for dinner had irritated him. He had quickly donned his black tuxedo and white tie, but, in his haste, had in the end called for the blasted Carter to fix his cufflinks for him. He had tried on several occasions to argue with Antonia about doing away with "dressing for dinner" now that Alcott had passed. What did it matter if they did not don white tie night after night for just the three of them? It was ludicrous. But Antonia wouldn't hear of such a thing and accused him of insensitivity, not to mention low manners—the worse of the two, in her mind, anyway, probably being the latter.

"Doing what, might I ask?" Antonia sniffed, waving Albert away. She ate very little these days, Clive noticed and, assuming it was still due to grief, accordingly bit back his angry retort.

"We've been helping my sister, actually," Henrietta answered for him and briefly explained the sad tale of Gunther and Liesel and Anna. Clive watched Henrietta as she spoke, and as much as it was becoming an old-fashioned chore to dress for dinner each night, he did enjoy seeing Henrietta regaled in her various gowns and jewels. Tonight, she was wearing a long, shimmering blue dress that hugged her curves, the diamond necklace his parents had given her for their engagement glistening at her throat. And yet, he also loved the casualness they had together in their wing. The way she would kick off her shoes in the evening and tuck her legs up under her as they sat before the fire and talked or read. And as of late, she had even convinced him to listen to *Master of Mystery* on the radio some nights, and he was surprised by how much he actually enjoyed it. Listening to radio programs was not a form of entertainment he had ever indulged in before. They shared an intimacy he was nearly convinced his parents had never enjoyed. Not that his parents' marriage hadn't been happy; just that it was of a different era altogether.

"Well, I'm not sure what concern it is of Elsie's," Antonia said now, after Henrietta had finally told the whole story. "Isn't she supposed to be attending classes and studying at this nuns' school? How did she get mixed up in all of this?"

"Yes, it's unfortunate," Henrietta responded, taking a sip of her wine. "Elsie's the type, though, that wears her heart on her sleeve. She's always collected strays. Not that Ma . . . Mother . . . ever let her keep them, that is."

"Well, I don't see how she's going to keep these two, either," Antonia said wryly.

"No, I suppose not," Henrietta said, her mind wandering, oddly, to Rose.

"Seems to me this girl is in need of proper medical attention. That's the first thing that should be done."

"Yes, that's just what I said, Antonia," Henrietta said eagerly. "Perhaps we could get Dr. Ferrington to examine her—"

"Dr. Ferrington! Don't be absurd. Surely there are qualified medical men in the city. Why ever would we involve Ferrington?"

"Yes, I'm sure there are qualified doctors in the city, but how do we find a good one?" Henrietta asked, looking from Antonia to Clive. "If Dr. Ferrington examines her, then we know for sure she's in good hands. Who knows what kind of doctors they employ at that orphanage—if any, for that matter. Or who knows if the German doctor who diagnosed her knew what he was talking about. We could be looking at this all wrong!" Henrietta exclaimed.

"We?" Antonia said, looking down her nose at Henrietta.

"*We* are helping Elsie and Gunther with this," Clive put in stiffly, signaling Albert to bring over more wine.

"Well, you'd best hurry, then, because Agatha informs me that she and John are taking Elsie to Miami with them for spring break," Antonia said glibly.

"Miami?" Henrietta asked, confused.

"The Braithwaites will be there, staying at the same resort apparently," she added, looking at them as if they should be impressed by this tidbit of information.

"Poor Elsie," Henrietta murmured, wiping her mouth with her napkin.

"Why 'poor'?" Antonia interjected. "To be a young woman, going to such a fashionable scene for two weeks? Dancing? Champagne? And John and Agatha have a charming yacht moored there. Did you know?" she asked Clive. "Not as big as my father's in Newport, of course, but charming just the same. It'll be lovely for Elsie. Maybe she'll finally find a husband."

"I don't believe she wants a husband," Henrietta said sharply.

"Of course, she does. Every woman wants a husband, even if they say they don't. And when they will go on and on about not wanting one, it does become tiresome, doesn't it? I don't mind saying that I've never understood Oldrich Exley's methods or even been particularly fond of him, but I do think he's right in calling Elsie's attempts at education foolish."

Clive saw Henrietta's face flush and knew it was time to interject. Why was his mother so contrary tonight?

"I think we'll call it a night, Mother," he said, tossing his napkin on the table.

"Call it a night?" Antonia asked, looking bewildered. "Don't you want your glass of port? You poor thing, you remind me of your father, having to have his port alone. We should begin inviting people over again. It's too bad Sidney isn't here."

"I'll give it a miss tonight, Mother. Henrietta and I are going out, actually."

"Going out? Whatever for? I assumed we would have a game of rummy. We haven't played in ages, not since before Henrietta's . . . illness."

Clive took a deep breath. His mother's reference to the miscarriage at this moment was insensitive in the extreme, as if blaming Henrietta for their lack of socializing and thus, inadvertently, Antonia's apparent loneliness, though if anyone or anything were to be blamed, it would be his father's death. He felt sorry for his mother, of course, but she could be less than kind at times, but now was not the time to address it.

"Perhaps tomorrow, Mother. Tonight, Henrietta and I are helping Sergeant Davis with . . . well, with a case."

"Sergeant Davis? Who's that?"

"He's part of the Winnetka police. He was here the night of the Jack Fletcher affair, but you probably didn't meet him. And he was . . . instrumental in helping us to find Father's killer, remember?"

"I remember Chief Callahan . . . " Antonia ruminated. "But what are you doing, Clive?" She looked at him sternly. "You said you gave up detective work. And why would you involve poor Henrietta? It's admirable that you . . . that you discovered the true cause of Alcott's death, but it's over now. That's what you told me."

"Well, I've changed my mind."

"Changed your mind?" she repeated, looking at Henrietta as if she were to blame.

"Yes, I've been meaning to tell you this," he said with a sigh. "Now's as good as any, I suppose." He paused before continuing. "Henrietta and I have decided to go into private detective work. Just here and there, you know, as the need arises. So, if you hear of any cat burglars or art fraud, let us know," he said with a grin, not being able to mask his amusement at the look of horror his mother's face currently held. "We need to get our name out with the gilded set, you see," he went on mercilessly. "You can mention to the ladies at the club that we're very discreet. Illicit love affairs, that sort of thing." He shrugged as he swirled the wine in his glass and sent Henrietta a quick wink. He could see her trying to disguise her smile behind her napkin.

"Oh, Clive, you can't *really* be serious!" Antonia moaned. "What about the firm? What about your father?"

"My father would wish me to be happy," Clive said evenly.

"Your father would wish you to do your duty," Antonia retorted.

"As it turns out, I *am* doing my duty, Mother," he said, draining his glass. "Oh, don't worry; I haven't abandoned the firm. Bennett and I have it well in hand."

"Well, Sidney certainly does. I'll say that," she replied tersely, then moaned again. "Oh, Clive, must you? I've indulged you long enough in this sordid detective work. It's time you looked to the future now, to your place in society."

"Mother, might I remind you that it's 1936," he said, surprised by how similar it sounded to something his cousin Wallace might have said.

"What does that have to do with it?" Antonia snapped. "Are you so self-indulgent that you can't take up honest work? It's really rather childish on your part, Clive. I mean, running around the county looking for crimes when there simply aren't any? You heard Chief Callahan. Winnetka has no crime to speak of."

Clive felt himself bristle at the mention that his actions were self-indulgent and childish, but he forced himself to not respond. He had tangled often enough in the past with his mother to know that she usually threw out a personal jab when beginning to feel desperate. Clenching his jaw, he strove to keep his answer light. "No doubt you and Chief Callahan are right, of course. Except that Highbury itself has had several instances of theft in just this past year, hasn't it? And then there was my father's murder. That's two crimes, anyway," he said, looking at her with a tilt of his head and one eye squinted shut. "But who's counting?"

"You know very well that that was a different situation altogether."

"Well, I can see there's no use arguing with you on this score, Mother, so I'll just say you're right."

"This is hardly an argument, Clive!"

"Just put it down to a hobby," he said, standing now and Henrietta following suit. "It gives us something to do, you see."

"Something to do! I could suggest any number of things if that's the issue. You might take a more active role at the firm, for one thing, instead of leaving it all to poor Sidney to shoulder. And you," she said to Henrietta, "you could be helping Julia and me with the garden party."

"Perhaps the garden party isn't such a good idea this year, Mother," Clive said seriously. "Surely you'd be excused from it this year because of father's death. No one expects it."

"Nonsense!" she exclaimed. "Of course, they do! And Alcott would want it to go on."

"Well, we really must go, or we'll be late," Clive said, taking a final sip of wine. "Good-night, Mother," he said, coming around to kiss her on the cheek, wondering why the living always claimed to know the wishes of the dead.

Chapter 16

After their somewhat abrupt exit from the dinner table, Clive and Henrietta hurried upstairs to change into something more practical, though Henrietta wasn't sure what to wear to a séance and dared not ask Edna, lest she frighten her. In the end, she chose a simple tweed skirt and hat and her sturdy Oxfords. If they had to run, heels would never do, she reasoned. But why would they have to run? she nervously chided herself. She slipped them on anyway.

As anxious as she was to attend the séance, Henrietta could not help but feel a little guilty for abandoning Antonia, who so obviously wanted their company tonight, despite her ill humor. While it was true that Antonia could be sharp at times, especially of late, Henrietta was used to far worse from Ma over the years, and she was able to feel some little sympathy for the obviously still-grieving woman. She felt sure that Antonia would come through this sad chapter of her life eventually, unlike Ma, on the other hand, who had been stuck in her depression for years now with no hope, at least that Henrietta could see, of ever coming out of it. It struck Henrietta as odd, not for the first time, that Ma seemed the older of the two women, though in reality she was at least ten years Antonia's junior and still had small children at home. Henrietta could only put it down to the terrible conditions that her mother lived under all these

years, though perhaps it was also her sour mental state that had likewise contributed to prematurely aging her. With a sigh, Henrietta
put the final pin in her hat and resolved to try to be a better daughter
to Ma as well as more interested in Antonia's garden party, a project
which, at the very least, had as a happy consolation more frequent
conversations with Julia, if nothing else.

"You needn't wait up, Edna," Henrietta said as the young maid
handed over her gloves.

"Oh, but I don't mind at all, madame," Edna said.

"Well, it might be late."

"Oh, Miss," Edna implored, slipping back into the use of Henrietta's
old title. "Shouldn't you be resting more?"

"Nonsense! I'm perfectly fine," Henrietta responded, slightly irritated that even Edna should treat her as an invalid. "We're only going
for a drive," she fibbed.

"At this time of night? Whatever is Mr. Clive—I mean, Mr.
Howard—thinking? Anyway," she hurried on, "I don't mind. I'll sit
up with my darning. Several of your dresses have tears, and I daresay
I've hardly had time to mend them, what with you trying to learn me
these days."

Henrietta sighed and again contemplated whether or not her
grand scheme in regards to Edna's conversion was really going to
work. Well, she couldn't think about that now. She gave Edna a small
smile. "Yes, you've certainly earned your pay today, Edna. Sit up if
you wish, but please go to bed when you're tired. I'm quite sure I can
undress myself."

Rather than looking grateful for this emancipation, Edna's face
was one of hurt. "I'm sure you can, miss, but then you might not
need me at all before long."

Henrietta recognized the fear of unemployment in Edna's
voice. After all, hadn't she felt it often enough in her old life?
"I wouldn't worry about that," she said brightly, patting Edna's
arm. "I'll always need you. Now, I really must be going before
Clive scolds me." Henrietta knew she should refer to Clive as "Mr.

Howard" when addressing the staff, but Edna, she felt, should be an exception to this.

As expected, she found Clive waiting for her at the bottom of the steps, his hat and coat already on, and his pipe in hand.

"What took you?" he asked, his eyes bright as he looked her up and down. "Going for the Sherlock Holmes look again, are you?" he said with a grin.

"Clive!" she said, not being able to hold back her own smile. "You're the one with the pipe!"

Clive let out a deep laugh. "So I am. Come, then, the game's afoot. How's that?"

Together they stepped out into the darkness, Henrietta surprised by how warm the night air was. She took a long, deep breath and filled her lungs with the rich, earthy smell she could almost taste. It filled her with a delicious sort of hope; for what, she knew not, but it didn't matter. It was nearly spring! The only snow left was a few dirty, stubborn clumps here and there, lying in the shade of the garden wall. She removed her scarf as she slid into the Alfa and wished she would have worn a lighter coat.

As they sped down Willow toward Crow Island, Clive instructed her to play the role of the believer, which, he commented wryly, shouldn't require much acting, while he would look for evidence of foul play.

"Are you sure we can just turn up?" Clive asked seriously before she could respond to his direction. "That doesn't give her any time to research us ahead of time, the key to this malarkey, I'm sure. Surely one needs some sort of invitation, for obvious reasons."

"Since when are you the expert on séances?" Henrietta countered lightly, noting that his previous almost jovial mood was evaporating the closer they got to the abandoned schoolhouse.

"I'm an expert on recognizing a fraud when I see one," Clive said, shifting the car into a lower gear.

"Well," Henrietta reasoned, "I doubt Mrs. Tobin would have told me to come if it were invitation only. Anyway, what does it matter at this point? We're nearly there."

They had indeed arrived. From the outside, the schoolhouse looked dark and abandoned still, though several cars were haphazardly parked on the muddy ground surrounding it. Clive slowly drove the Alfa across the rutted field and parked it some distance away. Silently, he got out and went around to open the car door for Henrietta, and tightly held her arm as they picked their way across the dark, rough terrain. Despite her determination to be every bit Clive's partner, Henrietta was glad of Clive's arm as they went. There were no streetlamps out here in this remote locale, of course, and it was so dark, they could barely see in front of them, except for what light the stars and moon afforded. She continued to hold his arm, however, even as they mounted the few wooden steps and then stood on the little porch, as she suddenly felt a little wave of dizziness. No doubt it was nerves, she suspected, and tried to shake it off.

Above the doorway was an exposed lightbulb hanging from a short brown, fraying cord, but it was either burned out or simply not switched on—perhaps by design? Before Clive could actually knock, however, the door mysteriously opened to them, revealing not Madame Pavlovsky, as they had expected, but a small little man that Henrietta mistook at first glance for a child until she noticed his mustache and a faint shadow of whiskers on his cheeks. He was wearing a stained purple waistcoat with a dusty black suitcoat, several sizes too big, so that it hung from his shoulders, and baggy trousers.

"Enter," he said with an oddly squeaky voice, as if a child were indeed somehow trapped within him. After they had obediently stepped into the little antechamber, he stiffly held out his arms, which Henrietta realized, after a moment's confusion, meant that he wanted their coats. Quickly they shrugged out of them, and Henrietta placed both thick garments gently across his arms, fearing that they might be too heavy for his little limbs. He was apparently stronger than he appeared, however, for he promptly turned and disappeared with the load.

Henrietta smoothed down her blouse as she nervously looked around the room. The interior was dim as well, though the many candles of varying sizes on any available shelf, bookcase, or table gave off at least a glow of light compared to the inky blackness outside. Henrietta blinked several times, allowing her eyes to adjust, and was surprised that the whole room had changed since they had last been here. Gone were the sagging sofa and the ramshackle chairs. Even Madame Pavlovsky's throne seemed to have disappeared, until Henrietta spotted it at the head of the very large round table that had somehow made its way to the center of the room, around which sat several people. They were ten in number, Henrietta quickly counted, besides Madame Pavlovsky, who was the eleventh. The walls were now draped with what looked like thick velvet material, giving the guests, or Henrietta, at least, the feel of being on the inside of a soft toy or perhaps a cocoon. The only indication that an outside world existed at all was a circular hole cut into the ceiling. Henrietta wondered how she had not noticed the little opening the other day and, upon closer inspection, observed that there was a small, circular hinged door attached to it, laying open, flat against the roof to reveal the starry night sky beyond. She saw Clive looking at it, too.

"So, you have finally come," Madame Pavlovsky called from where she sat on her throne. "Come in, come in. We have been waiting for you before we begin," she said, waving a heavily beringed hand at two empty chairs at the far end of the table, directly across from herself. Henrietta felt her stomach roil a little. Had Madame Pavlovsky really been expecting them? How could she have known? She remembered Mrs. Tobin, then, and wondered if perhaps she might have told her. Her eyes darted around the table, and, sure enough, she saw Mrs. Tobin's nervous smile, and put Madame Pavlovsky's apparent foreknowledge down to her. But still, Henrietta countered with herself, she hadn't said for sure that they were coming . . .

"The spirits are anxious to speak to us," Madame Pavlovsky pronounced in a husky voice laden with mystery. "They are the travelers. And many of them are gathered around us tonight." She gestured dramatically at nothing in particular. Henrietta gave Clive a quick sideways glance, and when she saw him give her a barely perceptible nod, she approached the table and pulled out a chair. Clive followed. The massive table was covered with a thick, black cloth that had veins of what looked like gold thread woven through it in no particular pattern. Also covering it was what must have been hundreds of tiny candles, which gave this part of the room a warm glow and likewise cast eerie, distorted shadows on the faces of the people sitting around it.

As she looked around the table, she noted that their number was now thirteen and wondered, uncomfortably, if this had been on purpose. She wasn't sure who she had thought might attend such an event, but everyone, with the exception of one young woman who was oddly dressed in a black Victorian gown and whose long, stringy black hair was partially hidden behind an old-fashioned widow's cap, looked remarkably ordinary. A few returned her stare, but most of them had their eyes trained on Madame Pavlovsky, who had similarly dressed for the occasion. She was enshrined in long black robes and had a deep purple turban on her head, upon which was affixed a large silver brooch in the shape of a crescent moon. In front of her was the large crystal ball set on an ivory stand with clawed feet, the very same one Henrietta had noticed upon their last visit. She stared at it, but it was a murky, dull green and seemed only a lifeless ornament.

"The dead speak to us from other side!" Madame Pavlovsky repeated in the same deep voice. If she was ruffled by Clive and Henrietta's late entrance, it did not show. "The travelers' energy is very strong tonight. There is much power surging on this day. It is one of the high days of energy, the spring equinox, when veil between living and dead grows thin. In some places, gone!" she said, her voice thick and raspy, as she gave another wide gesture.

Clive cleared his throat, then, causing Henrietta to want to pinch him. Honestly!

"There are unbelievers among us," Madame Pavlovsky said, looking at Clive as she said it. "But this is not problem. We who know the truth . . . we will send our energy to those beyond and overpower this disbelief in our midst." She placed her fingertips on the crystal ball. "And now!" she said dramatically, "we can delay no longer. We threaten to anger travelers if we do. If you have brought loved one's treasure, place it on table in front of you now."

Henrietta watched as people began placing small trinkets on the table and tried to catalog them in her mind, though she was sure Clive was doing the same. Mostly, they all seemed to actually be just that—trinkets. A watch, a ring, a locket, a letter . . . Henrietta looked to the Victorian woman to see what she would place, and thought she saw what looked like a rabbit's foot. There was nothing she could see of any value, and Henrietta was surprised to feel a trickle of pleasant relief. So far so good, she thought. As much as it would be exciting to "crack the case," and reveal Madame Pavlovsky to be a fraud, there was a part of her that desperately wanted her to be real, no matter what Clive said.

"We must begin soon," Madame Pavlovsky was saying. "The zenith is nearly here, and I will not be able to hold them at bay much longer."

Henrietta's heart began to beat a little faster; she reminded herself to breathe.

"Take hands," Madame Pavlovsky instructed. "We must form unbroken circle. This is for our protection. Do not break circle," she warned.

Henrietta took Clive's warm strong hand, on her right, and held out her other hand to an older woman next to her. She looked to be about in her fifties and had a faux fox stole wrapped tightly around her neck. She gave Henrietta a quick, false smile and only loosely held Henrietta's hand.

"Close eyes," Madame Pavlovsky instructed. "We are beginning now!"

Henrietta looked at Clive, who gave her a wink and closed his eyes, so she did the same.

Nothing could be heard for several moments except the wind outside, which had oddly picked up, letting off a shrill moan as if encouraging them—or was it perhaps a warning? Henrietta was tempted to peek at what was happening in the room, when an actual moaning began. It was coming from Madame Pavlovsky. It grew louder, and Henrietta could not help but slightly open her eyes. She gasped when she saw Madame Pavlovsky's eyes rolling back and the crystal ball in front of her glowing! Clive squeezed her hand, and she returned his grip tightly.

Madame Pavlovsky began speaking in a deep, guttural voice that sent a chill up Henrietta's spine. "A traveler has come forward. We hear you. Speak!" she said, opening her eyes now and looking at the empty air above the table. Henrietta looked around the table and saw that almost everyone had opened their eyes, too. "He is brother, he says. Of woman here . . . I think he means you," Madame Pavlovsky said, looking directly at a woman two seats from Henrietta.

"You mean Randy?" the woman gurgled. "Is it really him?"

"Do not break circle!" Madame Pavlovsky said sternly when she saw the woman put her hand to her mouth. Quickly the woman obeyed and snatched back the hand of her neighbor.

"Oh! What does he say?" the woman asked anxiously.

Madame Pavlovsky closed her eyes for a moment and then spoke. "He says there is dark stranger that has come into your life. You should avoid this man."

"Oh!" The woman tittered. "A dark stranger?" she asked fearfully. "Who could that be?" she asked of the table in front of her, until a thought seemed to occur to her. "Does he mean the new mechanic at the garage where my Butch works? Randy, is that who you mean? The one Butch doesn't like?"

The crystal ball suddenly began to glow, causing the whole table to gasp in surprise.

"Did you see that?" the woman asked no one in particular, as she eagerly looked around the table. "It's him! Oh, thank you, Randy!" she said, looking up at the air above Madame Pavlovsky. "Thank you for telling me!"

As much as Henrietta wanted to believe this, even she could see, given Clive's previous example of debunking, that Madame Pavlovsky had offered very little and the woman herself had filled in the blanks. Still, she held out hope.

Madame Pavlovsky began groaning again, and when she opened her eyes, she was staring at a man not far from her throne. "You have wife that died?" Madame asked him.

The man looked at her incredulously, his eyes wide, and nodded barely an inch. It was hard to tell in the candlelight if his face was flushed or if it was merely the effect of the flickering candles. "Yes," he said hoarsely, his mouth open slightly as if astounded.

"She wishes you to know she is at peace and forgives you for cheating on her." A small gasp again went around the room. "She says you should marry this woman, that you will be happier with her."

The man simply stared at Madame Pavlovsky, shocked, and then suddenly moved to put his hand over his eyes.

"Do not break circle!" Madame Pavlovsky exclaimed, and the man hastily grabbed back the hand of the woman next to him. Henrietta continued to observe him, staring down at the table now, his shoulders hunched forward.

The crystal ball glowed again, and Madame Pavlovsky's attention perked up. She stared at something beyond the table. "Ah!" she said mysteriously. "You have come back, have you? I thought you would," she said, apparently speaking to some invisible presence. "It is man." She looked around the group until her gaze settled on Henrietta. "It is your father," she said simply, causing Henrietta to let out a tiny mewing sound. Her father?! Surely not . . . ! Her stomach was churning as she tried to force herself to remember Clive's words, that this woman was a charlatan and nothing more. Miraculously, she felt Clive's hand squeeze hers, and oddly, as he did so, Madame Pavlovsky continued. "The unbeliever cannot stop your father's speech tonight," she said, "as he did the other day." Henrietta wanted to look at Clive, but she didn't dare.

Madame Pavlovsky closed her eyes as if concentrating. "Your father says that he is sorry. Sorry for doing the . . . unforgivable," Madame Pavlovsky said haltingly, as she opened her eyes again.

"Oh, my!" Henrietta cried out, assuming that he (or was it she?) was referring to his suicide. How could she have known about that? Her heart was beating uncontrollably in her chest.

"He says that he was sent for long, long time to place of healing. But he sends his love to you. Yes, there is much love coming from him, like sun . . . radiate?" Madame Pavlovsky said, her eyes partially closed. "He has very strong presence." She paused before going on. "There is more," she said cryptically, still squinting, and Henrietta suddenly felt a warning bell go off in her mind, as if she somehow knew that what Madame Pavlovsky was about to say would be too much. She wanted to tell Madame Pavlovsky to stop, to implore her not to tell her any more, but no words would come out. Madame Pavlovsky spoke again, this time gently. "He holds child. Your lost baby, it is. A little boy."

No! screamed Henrietta inside her head and suddenly felt as if there wasn't enough air in the room.

"Your father holds your son and wishes you to know he is safe. That he will always be safe with him and that they will wait for you. Also, that they are never far from you."

Henrietta felt all the blood rush from her face, and the room began to spin. Everything went black before her eyes, blacker than the night air outside, and she felt herself falling, falling, falling, as if she had been on a high mountaintop, and it was taking a very long time to hit the bottom. She was aware that she would eventually feel pain, but miraculously, before she hit the ground, she felt someone catch her before she lost consciousness completely.

Chapter 17

"There's a telephone call for you, madame. In the study," Edna said in a low voice, after knocking softly and poking her head into Henrietta and Clive's bedroom. Having already delivered Henrietta a breakfast tray—still untouched—not an hour before and receiving an early morning set of instructions from Mr. Howard himself in the study, Edna had no fear of disturbing her master and mistress at their rest—or interrupting anything else, for that matter—and therefore crept in.

"Who is it?" Henrietta asked, sitting up sleepily.

"It's your sister, miss. I asked to take a message, but she said she would stay on the line and wait for you, if I wouldn't mind fetching you. I tried to tell her that you were indisposed," Edna said, wringing her hands, "but she was insistent, saying it was urgent, like. I didn't know what to do, as Mr. Howard said you weren't to be disturbed."

"My sister?" Henrietta asked and looked around, still confused. She saw the breakfast tray resting prettily in Clive's spot and had a vague recollection of Edna bringing it in earlier. Surely whatever it held was cold now, she thought regretfully, as she was suddenly aware that she was famished. "What time is it?" she asked.

"Almost eleven, miss," Edna said nervously.

"Eleven!" Henrietta exclaimed and tossed aside her covers. "Where *is* Clive?" she asked Edna, as she slipped her feet into the slippers by her bedside.

"I believe he's in the morning room with Mrs. Howard," Edna answered. "He's very worried about you, miss. He's in one of his moods, and Mrs. Howard isn't all that much better. I'm not supposed to let you get up," Edna fretted apologetically. "I think I should have told him about the call instead of you. It's only that your sister sounded so distraught; I didn't know what to do."

"Don't be silly, Edna. You were perfectly right to come tell me. I'm fine."

"But the doctor was called out and everything," Edna wavered.

"Dr. Ferrington was here?" she asked, as she picked up her pink silk robe that was laid out on the chaise lounge. Actually, she had no memory of going home, much less having been examined at all, but she remembered the séance now, as she leaned on the back of the chaise lounge. And then she remembered in a rush what Madame Pavlovsky had said about her father holding her baby, that it would have been a little boy . . .

Henrietta's stomach clenched, but she forced the image out of her mind. She would have to think about it all later. Right now, she needed to help Elsie. Elsie would never telephone her unless there was something really wrong. She prayed it wasn't Ma.

"He was, miss. He examined you and everything. Said you were to have only plain foods and no excitement."

"Well, be that as it may," she said, standing up, "I have to talk to Elsie. Something must have happened. I'll just slip out quickly and then come right back. Promise," she said determinedly as she moved past Edna.

"Well, if you're sure, miss, but—"

Henrietta walked down the long hallway, trying to concentrate on walking without wobbling, lest Edna, who was trailing behind her now, report it to Clive. She fumed at his overprotectiveness. All of it was so unnecessary! She paused for a moment at the top of the grand staircase, wondering if it would instead be better to slip down the servants' stairs in order to avoid being seen by Clive or Antonia. She decided against it, however, as she did not wish to appear this way—dressed only in her robe—in front of whatever staff members might be mingling in the kitchen at this hour.

Thus, she tightened the belt of her robe again—the silk was so maddeningly slippery!—and tried her best to tiptoe down the stairs. She was grateful for the thick carpet runner, and also for the fact that the morning room was on the other side of the house from the study.

Clive could be so unreasonable at times! As if fainting meant anything at all, she told herself. She thought about all the women she had known in her working days who had fainted on the job and had to get up and keep going or lose their job. But here in this world, which still had the flavor of a fairy tale to it at times, it was treated as a state of emergency. She knew it was only because he was worried because of her miscarriage (she forced herself to use the word, tired of people calling it a mishap, a misfortune, an illness, or any other euphemism), and was therefore attempting to exercise extra precaution. But, she countered with herself, working women lost babies all the time and had to carry on. Madame Pavlovsky's words from last night again attempted to resurrect in her mind, but she pushed them away.

She had reached the study and looked around, as if she were a criminal or a prisoner, and tried to quietly push open the pocket door. Edna appeared beside her.

"You stay and keep watch," Henrietta said to her quietly, "since you're here." Henrietta looked at her sternly, an eyebrow raised, and Edna nodded her acquiescence, wringing her hands worriedly as she did so.

Henrietta slipped inside and hurried over to the desk where the heavy receiver of the telephone lay waiting. Picking it up, she prayed that Elsie hadn't already rung off.

"Hello? Elsie?" she asked quietly.

"Oh, Hen! Thank God!" said Elsie in a quivering voice. "Are you all right? Your maid said you were ill. I wouldn't bother you except I didn't know what else to do . . . " she said frantically.

"Elsie, what is it? What's wrong? Is it Ma?"

"Oh, Hen! They've taken her to Dunning!" Elsie sobbed, apparently having kept herself together just long enough for Henrietta to get to the telephone before allowing herself to break down.

"Ma?" Henrietta asked in disbelief.

"No, not Ma! Anna!" Elsie said, sniffling. "They've taken Anna to Dunning!"

Henrietta felt as though she had been punched in the gut, and again found it difficult to breathe. She leaned one hand against the desk for support. "Oh my God, Elsie. Are you sure? Why would they have taken Anna to Dunning? And who is *they*, anyway?" Henrietta fired off.

"I . . . I don't know," Elsie cried. "We thought that maybe . . . Gunther is beside himself," she whined miserably. "The Lasiks said it wasn't their fault, but I . . . I don't know. There might be a bus, but then Sister said that—"

"Elsie!" Henrietta interrupted. Nothing she was saying was making sense. "Calm down. Start from the beginning. What happened?"

Henrietta could hear her sister attempt to take deep breaths, though it sounded more like panting.

"Yes, I'm sorry," Elsie said more calmly. "We don't know everything. Just that apparently Anna had a fit—a bad one—and the Lasiks—that's the couple that runs the home—had no choice but to take her to the hospital. They feared . . . feared she might die. The hospital kept her for a few days and then sent her on to Dunning. The Lasiks are terribly sorry. They said they had no idea."

"Dear Lord," Henrietta moaned and felt sick at the thought of that poor little girl in such a horrid place. "Where is Gunther in all of this?" she thought to ask.

"Gunther only just found out himself. He knew nothing about it. The Lasiks got word to him that they took her to the hospital, but by the time he got there, Anna was already gone. He demanded to know by what authority and why he had not been told, but apparently the Lasiks listed Anna's mother as deceased and the father as unknown. They say Gunther was listed as a friend of the family, but somehow he wasn't contacted, nor is he in the records at all, apparently. The Lasiks have been telling Gunther for a while now that the Bohemian Home isn't really a place for Anna, suggesting she be placed in some sort of institution—but they never intended for this to happen. They're as confused by what happened as we are."

"Oh, Elsie!" Henrietta moaned, twisting her silk belt. "What a mess!"

"Henrietta, please. I hate to ask, especially if you're ill, but we . . . we don't know what else to do," she said, her voice sounding dangerously close again to tears. "Do you think you and Clive could help us? Help us get her out?"

Henrietta bit her lip, knowing what Clive would say. She wasn't even supposed to be out of bed! "Yes, of course we'll help, dearest," she said, trying to muffle her voice. "I just . . . just have to arrange a few things. Where are you calling from so I can telephone you back?"

"From the desk at Philomena. Sister Bernard is letting me use the telephone. But we must hurry!"

"Yes, I understand. I'll—" she stopped midsentence, having suddenly heard what she feared was Clive's voice outside the room. Oh God, it was!

"Edna, why are you hovering here?" she heard him say. She did not hear a corresponding response from Edna and assumed perhaps she was offering what was surely an unconvincing shrug. "Is Mrs. Howard in there?" she could hear Clive ask incredulously. "What did I tell you!"

"Listen, Elsie, I must go," Henrietta said quietly into the receiver. "I'll ring you back," she said and hung up just as Clive pushed open the pocket door and stood there, his hands on his hips.

"What are you doing?" Clive demanded. "You should be in bed! I gave strict orders to Edna—and all the servants—that you weren't to be disturbed! Must I tie you to the bed to get you to rest?"

"That's already been done once before, remember?" Henrietta said, trying her best to keep her voice light, referring, of course, to their encounter with their nemesis, Neptune, at the Marlowe. "Am I a prisoner now in my own home? If it is my home?" she asked, her eyes narrowed.

"Henrietta, I refuse to be led into that old argument," he said with cxasperation.

"And you've no right to scold Edna," she went on. "She was acting under *my* orders, and she's *my* maid, so don't be cross with her. You can go, Edna," she said to the trembling girl still standing outside the door. "Set out my navy blue skirt," she added.

"Yes, madame," Edna said hurriedly and scurried away.

"Your navy skirt? You're not getting dressed today!" he said sternly. "You're to stay in bed all day. Doctor's orders, and mine, too," he said.

"Clive, listen to me. Something terrible has happened. I've just had a call from Elsie. We've got to go help her!"

"No, we don't," Clive said matter-of-factly. "You're very ill, and it's time you accepted that."

"No, I'm not, Clive. I'm perfectly fit!"

"Darling," he said, a sigh escaping, "you must be reasonable. Mother's right. You've been doing too much. I've just had to listen to it all again this past half hour, and as dreary as that was, for once I think she has a point. Please," he said earnestly. "You've not been well. Last night is proof of that. You're . . . you're overly excited, the doctor said."

"What does *that* mean?" Henrietta asked, crossing her arms in front of her.

"Just that, if you're . . . *we're* . . . not careful, you could, well, you could have some sort of breakdown. He said he's seen it often enough after such cases of miscarriage or even after a baby is born. A type of hysteria or even depression sets in. It's not uncommon. I blame myself, of course, for putting you in such trying situations. First exposing you to Dunning and then this charlatan, Madame Pavlovsky. It was so thoroughly irresponsible on my part.

Reprehensible, really. Let me make it up to you, darling. We'll go away. Just the two of us. Anywhere you wish," he said, attempting to put his arms around her.

Gently, she pushed him away, incredulous. Did he really think she was on the brink of hysteria or depression? Madness, even? How could he not understand and know her better than that? Suddenly she felt tears well up that he could so grossly misunderstand the situation. She blinked them back, determined not to cry in front of him. How *dare* he make such accusations! And how could he still call Madame Pavlovsky a charlatan? After all she had revealed last night about their dead baby! Had he not been moved by that at all?

"Henrietta, don't be angry," he said calmly.

"Don't tell me if I can be angry or not!" she said vehemently. She took a deep breath and steadied her voice. "I can assure you, Clive Howard, that I am perfectly fit. In every way." She emphasized each word. "And to treat me like a sick child is pretentious and patronizing. I am your *wife*—not to mention the future mistress of Highbury, and I'm made of stronger stuff than what you apparently imagine. You've been to war and seen horrible things, things that still haunt you," she said, looking into his surprised eyes. "Well, my life has been its own battlefield. Things I've seen or have lived through, some of which you are not even aware. What right have you, or your mother, for that matter, to dictate the state of my own emotions or my . . . my mind or to say what's best for me? That is surely not the role of one who claims to hold my heart." She paused. "How dare you!" she whispered then, her voice wavering, not being able to stop the angry tears from spilling forth.

Clive's previous stoic face crumpled then, and he gently gathered her to him. "Oh, Henrietta. What am I to do with you? Please don't go on. I can't bear it. You're right, of course. But I only want what's best for you. Surely you can see that?" he said, holding her against his chest so tightly that she could feel his heart beating.

She allowed him to hold her, wanting to say more, but she didn't know what to say—so many different emotions were flooding through her. How could she explain what she wanted from him when she didn't really even know herself? She felt guilty and morose and sad and angry, all at once.

"Well, I can tell you that locking me away isn't it," she said finally.

"Telling you to stay in bed for a day is hardly locking you up," Clive said softly as he pulled back to look into her eyes. "And you did actually faint, remember?"

Henrietta sighed. "Women faint all the time, Clive. I wouldn't think much of it."

"But I do," he said, kissing her forehead. "You're all I've got. I couldn't bear it if I lost you, Henrietta."

"Well, you'd still have your mother," she said wryly.

"That was unkind." He looked down at her remonstratively.

She sighed again. "You're not going to lose me, Clive," she said, wrapping her arms around him. "But you must trust me. I'm perfectly fine. And we can't stand here any longer discussing it. We've got to go help Elsie and Gunther. Please!" she urged.

"No, we don't. Whatever trouble Elsie has found herself in this time, she's going to have to figure her own way out."

"But, Clive—it's Anna! They've taken Anna to Dunning, and we've got to help get her out! You know Elsie and Gunther would be useless at that."

"Dunning?" he asked sharply, his face turning pale. "Why? Because of her fits?"

"Apparently. It's a long story. I'll tell you on the way. Obviously, there's been some kind of mistake. Clive, please. I can't stand the thought of that little girl there, alone and frightened and . . . and barely even able to speak the language! Elsie and Gunther are asking for our—your—help. Surely there's something you can do. Please, Clive," she said, putting her hand on his chest.

She could feel him inhale a deep breath and then let it out, closing his eyes as he did so. "Oh, all right," he said, his face looking decidedly paler. "I'll see what I can do. But, Henrietta, let me go alone. There's no need for you to come, too. Please, for your own good."

He was insufferable! Wasn't it he who had been mentally disturbed, unnerved, by Dunning?

"Clive, remember what happened last time?" she tried to ask gently.
"And you have no right to keep me here. And it's *my* sister."

Clive stared at her for several moments and brushed a lock of her
hair back behind her ear. "But the girl is not really Elsie's concern, is
she?" he asked. "And as your husband, I absolutely do have that right,
if I would claim it," he said softly.

They stood locked in each other's gaze, Henrietta feeling her own
heart beating wildly, before Clive dropped his hand from her cheek
and took her hand in his instead. "But I suppose we should hurry," he
said with a slow smile.

Henrietta let out a breath she didn't even realize she was holding
and quickly kissed him. In her mind she took back all of the unkind
things she had been thinking. He was wonderful after all, and she
chided herself to remember that in the future.

"But darling, we must be practical," he was cautioning now, as she
pulled him across the foyer. "Even if we succeed in extracting her
from the pit that is Dunning, what then? Where is she going to go
from there?"

"I don't know, Clive. We'll have to figure that out later." She toyed
with suggesting that they bring Anna back to Highbury and care for
her until a more appropriate place could be found, but she knew that
now was not the time to broach that particular subject. It needed
more thought, anyway. At the moment, they had to concentrate on
just getting her out.

Chapter 18

When Clive and Henrietta finally reached Dunning several hours later, Elsie and Gunther were already there waiting for them. Henrietta had related to Clive on the drive down all that she knew regarding Anna's admission to Dunning, which was admittedly sparse. He said little in reply, but he seemed, for lack of a better word, annoyed by the story and grew even more silent the closer they got to Dunning. Henrietta knew he must be fearing another attack in returning to the asylum and resolved that she would keep a close eye on him despite what she imagined would be the ensuing dramatics of finding and retrieving Anna. She wished she could have come alone—but she knew that was out of the question, knowing she had no authority to get a patient released.

As they approached the building, Clive adopted the stance of what Henrietta imagined a man going into battle might employ. Stiffly, he marched up the stairs, Henrietta hurrying to keep up. She was surprised that when they got to the top he did not hesitate, but instead gave the guard at the door a little salute with his finger.

"Think you're funny, do you?" the guard said, opening the door for them.

Upon stepping inside, the stench of urine and decay again assaulting their senses, Henrietta reached for her handkerchief and placed it over her nose. She was about to suggest that Clive do the same, when she was distracted from her attentiveness to him by Elsie rushing up and embracing her.

"Oh, Henrietta! I'm so glad you're here!"

Gunther, too, came up from where he had been standing, anxiously gripping his hat, and expressed his gratitude as he held out his hand to Clive, who shook it firmly. "I thank you very much," he said. "I am sorry to cause disturbance, but I—"

"How long has she been here?" Clive interrupted. Henrietta could see his jaw clenching.

"I am not sure. Few days maybe," Gunther replied.

Clive then strode toward the main reception desk, though no nurse seemed to be manning it at the moment. Joe the orderly could be seen, however, his feet propped on the desk at an angle from where he sat in a cane-back chair nearby. Casually, he slid his feet off the desk and stood up.

"Back again, are ya?" he asked, another toothpick (or maybe it was the same one?) dangling from his mouth. "I recognize yous two. Can't get enough of the place, eh?"

"We're looking for a little girl," Clive said deliberately. "Her name is Anna Klinkhammer. She would have been brought in from Swedish Covenant Hospital in the last couple of days."

"I think I know the one ya mean," Joe said. "Don't get too many kids in here. Only the ones that can't run fast enough," he said with a loud laugh and looked at them for a reaction. "That was a joke," he said with an exasperated gesture. "Jeez."

"Look, is there any way of checking?" Clive asked impatiently. "Who's in charge here?"

"That'd be Nurse McCormick."

"Well, can you go and fetch her?" Clive asked, irritated.

"No," Joe said simply.

Clive stared at him grimly until Joe reluctantly went on.

"She's tied up at the moment, you could say," Joe said with a grin and inclining his head toward one of the hallways behind him.

"Then maybe *you* could look it up," Clive suggested, pointing at the ledgers.

"Nope. Can't read, me. Well, not very good, anyway. School was never fer me."

Clive let out a deep breath of exasperation, turning his head away as he braced himself, his arms outstretched and leaning against the desk. Henrietta could tell he was nearing his limit already.

Joe must have observed this, too, and decided for whatever reason to have mercy. "Oh, all right," he said. "Hold yer pants on. I can take yous to her. I know where she is. She's on Ward 3C with the other spazzes. Cries all the time that one does."

Henrietta heard Elsie let out a little cry of her own behind her.

"Ward 3C?" Henrietta asked incredulously. "With the schizophrenics?"

"Well, most kids get taken to the mongoloids or the waterheads, but she ain't neither of those, so . . . Don't ask me," he said with a shrug.

"Well, hurry up, then, man. Be quick about it," Clive urged.

"All right, all right," Joe said, making a move toward the hallway that led back through the infirmary again. "Two minutes ain't gonna matter much. Not in a place like this, anyway."

The four of them followed Joe up the dingy back stairs and waited anxiously for him to unlock the door to Ward 3C. Henrietta looked at Clive several times as they went, trying to gauge his mental state. She linked her arm through his and took his hand, which she could feel was trembling, but he did not look at her. The sooner they could get out of here the better, she resolved, determined to find and extract Anna as quickly as they could.

As soon as they stepped onto the ward, however, Elsie surprised her by slipping in front of them all to call out, "Anna? Anna!" before any of them could say or do anything else.

"Anna?" Elsie called out again desperately as she moved toward one of the two hallways that radiated from the common area, Henrietta surprised by how different Elsie was than just the other day, when she had practically hidden behind her the whole time.

"Anna!" Gunther called as well, following Elsie. Elsie cupped her mouth as the two of them walked briskly down the hall to shout again, but before she could, a little gray ghost appeared from one of the rooms at the end, hovering there before she seemed to recognize the two people rushing toward her. Then, she broke into her own run towards Gunther, who was squatting now to receive her, and she flung herself into his arms.

"*Papa!*" she sobbed, burying her head in his neck as he stood up, her bare little legs wrapping around him.

"Why does she call him 'Papa?'" Clive whispered to Henrietta, and she returned his question with a quizzical look.

Their attention was diverted from the reunion, however, by the presence of Nurse Harding, who appeared out of nowhere and was charging toward them like a mad bull.

"What's all this?" she demanded. "Why are you here again?"

She looked down the hallway to where Gunther and Elsie stood, Gunther trying to soothe Anna. "Here for that one this time? A real brat, that one. All she does is cry, stirs up the rest of 'em."

"Are you aware that this child is Liesel Klinkhammer's daughter?" Henrietta asked, watching her carefully.

"Who?" the tank asked, and Henrietta could swear she was being evasive. Then, as if suddenly changing her mind, Nurse Harding responded, "Oh, the kraut? Well, whaddya know? Like mother, like daughter, I always say. Don't surprise me one bit."

"Don't you think it odd that she ended up on the very same ward?" Henrietta asked.

"Not if she's a schizo, too."

"Listen, nurse," Clive interrupted. "We're here to remove this child."

"Ha!" the tank burst out. "Fat chance of that. You ain't takin' her anywheres. Just who do you think you are, anyway?" She looked him over disdainfully. "You want to visit the brat, I can't stop yeh, but removing her's a whole different thing. And I've got work to do, so leave me to it."

Swiftly, Clive removed his fake badge from inside his jacket pocket. "As it happens, I'm an acting authority with the Winnetka police," he said sternly. "And I strongly suggest you cooperate."

"Where's Winnetka?" the tank asked, unruffled. "That up north somewhere? You'll have to do better than that, Mister . . . Smith," she said, squinting to read the name on the badge and laughed.

"One way or another, I'm taking this child," Clive growled. "And I could easily haul you in for obstructing justice. So you can decide now or later at the station if you want to believe I have the authority. Up to you. I'm done fooling around."

Henrietta thought she saw a slight glimmer of, if not fear, then certainly hesitation in Nurse Harding's eye. She was wavering.

"Look, I don't make the rules!" the tank huffed. "You need to talk to the administrator if you want someone checked out of here."

"Very well," Clive said calmly, tucking the badge back into his suit coat. "Where do we find this administrator?"

"Joe'll take you," she said sulkily, nodding at the orderly who had been watching the exchange with decided delight. Henrietta could swear she saw something in Nurse Harding's eyes, though, as she looked over at Joe. Was she trying to communicate something to him?

Elsie and Gunther silently approached as if they sensed they were safe. Gunther still held Anna, who was sobbing dry sobs now, Elsie following behind and petting Anna's little hands, which were still wrapped around Gunther's neck. Joe quickly unlocked the door and held it open, and Gunther, looking at Clive as if for direction, made a move to step through.

"Oh, no you don't!" the tank barked. "She don't go nowhere," she said, nodding at Anna.

"Oh, please," Elsie begged.

"I said no. You go get a release from the administrator and bring it back up for me to sign and then you're free to take the brat off my hands.

Good riddance, as far as I'm concerned. But I go by the book, I do. You'll not catch me in the act of doing something I shouldn't, though I can't speak for others," she said, giving Clive an accusatorily glare.

"You don't scare me," Clive said wryly. "I know your type."

"You do, do you?" the tank answered belligerently.

"Clive—you and Gunther go find this administrator," Henrietta interjected. "Elsie and I will stay here with Anna," she said, looking over at Elsie, who quickly nodded her agreement.

Pulling his gaze from Nurse Harding, Clive sighed and said, "That would probably be best. You don't mind?"

Henrietta shook her head. "Just try to be quick," she said.

"Here," Elsie said, holding out her arms to Gunther. "Give her to me."

As if she could sense what was about to happen, or maybe because she understood the language better than any had assumed, Anna began to wail. She clung to Gunther fiercely, refusing to let go of him despite Elsie's attempts to shush and soothe her.

"Anna, Anna," she tried to say over Anna's cries, but to no avail. Gunther tried to rock and soothe her, too, saying things in German into her ear. Still, her sobs and screams of "No!" continued until a few of the other patients began to shout as well, one of them screaming "Stop!" and another hitting the wall with her fist.

"Shut up!" another called.

"See what I mean?" Nurse Harding said loudly over the din. "If you're going, go."

Looking nervously at the tank, as if she might change her mind at any second, Gunther peeled the screeching girl off of him and handed her, kicking and screaming, snot and tears running down her face, to Elsie, who tried her best to hold onto her. Anna managed to squirm out of Elsie's arms, however, and ran toward the door which Clive and Gunther had just hurriedly stepped through.

"*Geh zurück, Anna! Bleib bei Elsie! Ich bin gleich wieder für dich da. Ich verspreche. Ich verspreche*—Go back, Anna! Stay with Elsie! I will be back for you in a minute. I promise. I promise!" he shouted.

As soon as the door shut behind them, the trembling little girl stood staring at it for a moment, as if in disbelief or wretched despair, and then crumpled into a heap on the ground, sobbing anew and burying her head in her hands as she rhythmically rocked. Elsie rushed forward and knelt on the ground beside her. Gingerly, she reached out and touched her back, tentative at first, as if it might set her off again, and when it didn't, she began to rub more.

"That's it. Best to calm 'er down before she has another one of those fits," Nurse Harding said calmly as she stepped over Anna's quivering body. "Had two already since she's been here. Three and you're done."

"What do you mean, three and you're done?" Henrietta asked, feeling nauseous after watching the scene that had just played out.

"Three fits and you get shocked. That usually calms 'em down for a while."

"You'd shock a child?" Henrietta cried. "How could you? That's cruel!"

"No, it ain't. Anyway, how would you know, Miss Hoity-Toity? After a few weeks some of 'ems are begging us for the shock. Calms 'em, they say. I wouldn't put it past some of 'em to fake their fits just so they can get the shock. Nurse Collins don't agree, though."

"Where *is* Nurse Collins?" Henrietta asked, looking around, puzzled. She had wondered that, actually, when they had first stepped onto the ward. Surely Nurse Collins would have taken better care of this child, wouldn't she? Henrietta reasoned. She was so kind and compassionate, and Henrietta remembered then how even the crazy woman—Mrs. Goodman, wasn't it?—had spoken of her as such, calling her "an angel." Henrietta wished she could speak to her more about Liesel, but what would she ask? Nurse Collins had already seemed to give her as much information as she knew.

"She's on nights," the tank answered. "Works every night but Sunday night, Collins does."

"Nights? Then why was she here the other day when we came?"

"Fillin' in. Worked a double that day. We all work doubles from time to time. Not enough staff."

Henrietta didn't wonder at why they were short-staffed. Who would want to work here? she thought. And yet, with the Depression, jobs were scarce. Beggars couldn't be choosers. She remembered Mrs. Hennessey's niece, Ida, then, who had quit this place and wondered what it was that had spooked her. Whatever it was, it must have been serious.

Nurse Harding was walking away now, apparently bent on finishing her duties. With a backward glance at Elsie, who was still kneeling on the filthy floor beside Anna, Henrietta followed Nurse Harding.

"Excuse me, Nurse Harding?" Henrietta called after her.

"Now what?" the tank asked, turning slightly. "Can't you see I'm busy?" In truth, Henrietta could not see what there was to occupy her time, given the floor's current deplorable state. Clearly not a large effort had been employed so far to meet any sort of standard, much less a high one.

"Do you know an Ida Lynde?" Henrietta asked and felt sure she saw a trickle of something in the tank's oily face. "She was a nurse who worked here a while back?"

"Yeah, I know her. Worked here a while, but she's a drunk. That's why she got fired. Liked her gin a little too much, if you know what I mean. Why do you ask? Actually," she went on before Henrietta could respond, "don't answer that. I don't really care. Now leave me in peace." She waddled off down the hallway.

A drunk? Henrietta thought, surprised. Wouldn't Mrs. Hennessey have mentioned that? Well, maybe not, Henrietta thought again. Alice Hennessey wasn't the type to air her own dirty laundry. But would Mrs. Hennessey have even brought up her niece at all if there was some scandal attached to her name? But maybe she had just blurted it out before thinking, which was the usual way of things with Mrs. Hennessey. That must be it, she decided, but she just couldn't shake the feeling that Nurse Harding was, if not lying, then certainly not telling the whole story. But what was it that Nurse Harding had said just a few moments ago? That she did everything by the book? Why the need to emphasize that? It did, however, put an idea in Henrietta's mind. She glanced down the hallway again and, not able to see Nurse Harding any longer, glanced over toward the desk where the ledgers were strewn. Perhaps she should just take a look? she wondered, her pulse quickening.

Without thinking about it further, Henrietta moved quickly behind the desk and picked up various ledgers, looking for what she knew not.

"Henrietta! What are you doing?" hissed Elsie, who had succeeded in getting Anna into her arms, though she was still tightly rolled up in a ball. "This is terrible! What are we going to do?"

"I just want to take a look," Henrietta said quietly. "I want to check something." She tried to say it with a calm voice, but her heart was quite literally pounding. Was she jeopardizing Anna's release if she got caught? Perhaps she could plead ignorance? she considered, though she doubted Nurse Harding would buy it. Still . . . it was too good of a chance. She picked up the only ledger that lay open, deciding that it more than likely contained the most recent events.

She studied the open page and tried to make sense of it. It seemed to be nothing more than a log of sorts with columned pages, not unlike an accounting book. There was a date at the top of each page and a list of patients, their room number, followed by what looked like a record of their medications or treatments each day. The far column was marked "activities," but only a few of those squares were filled in. Henrietta wondered if that was because there simply weren't any activities, or because the nurses didn't have the time or, more than likely, the inclination, to fill that lonely column in.

With a sudden burst of inspiration, Henrietta looked to see if "electric shock therapy" or something like it, was listed as a medication or a treatment anywhere. As her eyes quickly went down the medication column, she did not see electric shock listed, but did notice "EST" was written after several patients' names. Could that be it? she wondered excitedly. She quickly turned back the pages a couple of weeks to when Liesel would have still been alive, the pages repeatedly slipping as her fingers fumbled in her nervousness. When she finally saw "L. Klinkhammer" listed, her heart gave a little leap of triumph.

Nervously, Henrietta glanced up to make sure Nurse Harding was still nowhere in sight and then carefully continued flipping until she found the first page that listed Liesel and noted her admission, dated October 12, 1935. Henrietta then began quickly skimming the columns to see what this poor woman had been given. During the first week of her confinement, "salts of bromine" seemed to be the only thing listed next to her name, administered three times a day for what looked like ten days.

Henrietta kept turning pages, looking for the date when the dreaded "EST" began for poor Liesel. Finally, she saw it listed on October 25, and despite a quick flutter of triumph, she felt her heart sink a little. Slowly, her finger traveled down the rest of the medication column on the following pages, and each time she saw "EST" listed next to poor Liesel's name, she felt a little blow. If she was reading the ledger correctly, it looked as though she had been given EST twice a week for nearly four weeks. Wasn't that excessive? Henrietta wondered with a shudder. The last page that listed Liesel was dated December 1, 1935. Next to her name on that day was written "DECEASED," and after "CAUSE OF DEATH" was scrawled "heart failure."

Henrietta let out a tired sigh and stood up straight, glancing once again down the hallway. Something didn't seem right, but she couldn't figure out what. She gazed back at the ledger and reread the information again and again. Eventually, she saw the problem! According to this log, anyway, Liesel had been given her last electric shock treatment on November 15, but she hadn't died for another six days! which isn't what the staff had told them. If she remembered it right, they had said that Liesel died of heart failure as a result of an electric shock treatment, but a whole six days after the last treatment? Perhaps she had more treatments and the nurses didn't record it? Henrietta wondered.

Henrietta flipped back and confirmed that the last EST to be recorded for Liesel was November 25, after which, "salts of bromine" had been listed for each day up until her death. They had taken the time to record *that* medication, Henrietta reasoned, so more than likely, had Liesel had any more shock treatments, it would have been recorded, too, since it was merely a matter of writing a quick three letters. Laziness or a recording error due to haste or apathy did not seem likely. Henrietta went back again and counted. In total, if the log was correct, Liesel Klinkhammer had been given eight doses of electric shock. Surely, if she were to have had a "bad reaction," which is what Dr. Ingesson had told Clive, it would have occurred after the very first administration, wouldn't it? Not after the eighth one. And not six days later. It didn't make sense.

Henrietta jumped when she suddenly heard the booming voice of Nurse Harding, who was barreling down the hallway toward her.

"What are you doing back there?" she barked. "Don't you know that's confidential? You can't go reading the ledgers!"

Henrietta stepped back, her mind racing to try to think of something to say.

"I'm sorry . . . I . . . I just wanted to know more about what happened to Liesel Klinkhammer," she said nervously.

Nurse Harding had reached the desk now and took up the open ledger Henrietta had been perusing and shut it with a loud snap. "You already know everything there is to know," she huffed. "So get out from behind here!" She attempted to tidy a few of the ledgers, or perhaps she was trying to assess how many Henrietta may have read.

Henrietta slowly moved from behind the desk, trying to decide if she should confront the hulking nurse in front of her. She took a deep breath and decided to proceed, as this was probably her only chance. "You . . . you said that Liesel died after her shock treatment," Henrietta ventured, trying to keep her voice even. "But the log says she didn't die for six more days after that," Henrietta said, feeling more confident with each word spoken. "How . . . how do you explain that?"

Henrietta braced herself for what she was sure would be Nurse

Harding's angry response, so she was utterly surprised when it turned out to be a burst of laughter.

She looked at Henrietta dismissively. "Playing detective, are you? Trying to keep up with hubby? Well, guess away all ya want. Every so often we get do-gooders like you in here. Always the same, never what we're doin' is good enough. Why do you care, anyway?" she asked seriously. "She was an immigrant kraut, barely spoke English, mentally ill, poor as a church mouse. Seen hundreds like her. We tried to help her. Didn't work. She died. End of story. Why can't you leave well enough alone?" Nurse Harding's tone was bitter, all trace of amusement now gone from her demeanor.

"I care because she was that little girl's mother," Henrietta said, pointing to where Anna still lay curled up in Elsie's arms.

"Well, nothing can bring her back now, so I advise you to get over it. Some things shouldn't be looked at too closely, if you know what I mean. So stop yer snoopin'. Or else you might find yourself in your own kettle of hot water; understand me?"

"Yes, I understand you," Henrietta said slowly, thoroughly convinced that Nurse Harding really was hiding something.

"Go on," the tank said with a wave of her thick hand. "Go wait over there. You make me nervous, hanging about here. You're like a fly before the rain. Annoying as hell." She made a show of writing in one of the logs.

Henrietta walked back to where Elsie had scooted against a wall. Elsie looked up at her questioningly, and Henrietta gave her a half-hearted shrug. She looked around for a chair but there was none to be had except one in a far corner next to a woman in a crude, old-fashioned wheelchair. She had sores all over her face and was one of the patients who had a shaved head. Henrietta wondered if it was perhaps a requirement for the electric shock treatments, or maybe it was due to lice, remembering how her brothers had to have their heads shaved many times for just that reason. She tried not to stare, but she couldn't help looking at this woman, who sat looking at the floor in a sort of catatonic trance. Something seemed different about her, besides the shaved head, and after several sideways glances, Henrietta finally began to suspect that it wasn't a woman at all, but a man! But why would a man be on this floor? Henrietta wondered, dismayed. She had assumed this was a women's floor . . .

"Why is there a man on this floor?" Henrietta called to the tank, deciding to test her suspicion.

Nurse Harding looked up from what she was doing to where Henrietta was inclining her head and took a moment to understand the question.

"No room anywhere else," the tank said simply and looked back down at the log she was writing in.

"But isn't that against some sort of policy or something?" Henrietta asked.

"I don't make the decisions, Hoity-Toity. You just leave my patients alone. Lou ain't gonna hurt nobody," Nurse Harding replied, still scratching away at the ledger.

Henrietta's eyes went to "Lou" again, and she gave a little start when Lou's gaze suddenly left the ground and connected with her, giving a small, wicked sort of grin in the process. Henrietta quickly looked away. She looked back at Elsie, still cradling Anna. Her heart beating a little faster, she anxiously glanced at her wristwatch and wondered where Clive was. Why was it taking so long? She was getting tired of standing, but she did not want to sit on the filthy floor next to Elsie. She finally squeezed into a place nearby on the wall to lean and tried not to look at Lou.

Instead, she looked around at the other patients, milling about or sitting in chairs, either slumped over or visibly shaking and staring off into space. She tried to imagine their stories and how they found themselves in this wretched place. What horrors had they seen that were somehow worse than the horror of being here, if that were even possible? Mrs. Wojcik was there, sitting along the wall in a doze, her doll held so loosely in her arms that it threatened to drop to the floor any moment. One woman stood in a corner, talking in a low whisper to the wall. Another was pacing back and forth in precise steps, seven this way, seven back, and had no eyes for anything but the floor in front of her.

Henrietta looked around for Mrs. Goodman, but she was nowhere to be seen. Henrietta felt an unnatural desire to speak to her again, though her previous conversation with this woman had left her more than a little unnerved. She was tempted to walk down the hallway and look for her in one of the rooms, but she was pretty sure the tank would not allow this. She wished there was a window; it made her feel claustrophobic to not be able to see out, and she was feeling dizzy again. What was taking Clive and Gunther so long? she wondered again. She desperately needed some air . . .

"Can't we take Anna outside while we wait?" Henrietta asked Nurse Harding, who had meanwhile stood up, her charting apparently done for the moment. She was now in the process of dragging a small cart out of the stock room, which was laden with pill bottles and tonics. "It's not as if we can escape out in the yard," Henrietta pointed out. She had begun to feel desperately like a patient herself.

"Tuesdays and Thursdays is when we go outside," the tank said, pulling the cart behind her to the first patient in the row along the wall, closest to the nurses' desk. Roughly, she tilted the nonresponsive woman's head back and with a wet cloth, wiped the crust out of her left eye, which had the definite look of being infected. "Since this is Wednesday, then no," she concluded, not even looking over at Henrietta.

"But can't you make an exception, seeing as we're here now, as her visitors?" Henrietta urged.

"Nope. Rules is rules."

Henrietta wasn't sure how much longer she could endure standing there, locked up as it were, no better than an inmate herself. Where was Clive? Why did he not return?

"You don't have to stay here, you know. Go if you want; I can let you two out. Just leave the girl here until yer finished with your dillydallying."

"We can't leave her here alone!" Henrietta persisted.

"She was here three days by herself. Didn't kill her, as you can see. But suit yerself," the tank said and took the cloth she had used to wipe the woman's infected eye and used it now to roughly wipe the accompanying crust from the corners of the woman's mouth.

Feeling sick, Henrietta decided she had to move. She would walk up and down the hallways, if nothing else. "I need to walk a bit, Elsie," she said in a low voice so as not to wake the sleeping Anna.

"Are you okay?" Elsie whispered.

"Yes, I just need to walk," she answered.

Elsie gave her a nod and whispered, "Be careful."

Henrietta crept slowly toward the hallway, which contained the patients' rooms, hoping that the tank would be too distracted to notice. She was not in luck, however.

"Where you going, Hoity-Toity?" Nurse Harding called from where she was holding out a pill to another of her patients, though they more accurately seemed to Henrietta to be her victims.

"I . . . I need to stretch my legs," Henrietta fibbed, guessing that if she said she felt dizzy, the tank would make her sit down. "I'm getting a cramp in my leg," she said weakly.

"Oh, all right," the tank said. "No funny business, though," she called out after her.

No funny business? Henrietta wondered. Like what?

Carefully, Henrietta made her way down the hallway, occasionally poking her head into some of the bedchambers as she passed by. The patients left back here were mostly in bed, lying in the dark. No lights were turned on, and the few windows afforded each room were covered with thick wool curtains, which allowed only a muted amount of light to penetrate. The air here, too, was really quite thick, and Henrietta was obliged to again place her handkerchief over her nose. She was about to return to the common area, which seemed like heaven now compared to the dark, close bedchambers down here when she happened to catch sight of what appeared to be none other than Mrs. Goodman in the second-to-last room. Henrietta poked her head in farther and determined that it was indeed Mrs.

Goodman, lying, fully dressed, on top of a perfectly made bed. Henrietta knocked on the doorframe—there being no actual doors on the rooms—but Mrs. Goodman did not seem to hear her.

Gingerly, she stepped in. The room held five other metal-frame beds, a small chair beside each one, and a single sink at the far end. There were no bedside tables or lamps or mirrors, or ornamentation of any kind. Likewise, the room held no occupants at the moment except Mrs. Goodman, all of her roommates presumably up and out and sitting in the common area. Maybe the more ambulatory patients were given the rooms farthest from the sitting room, Henrietta surmised, but then wondered if that much thought had really been put into room assignments, given the little she already knew about Dunning.

"Hello," Henrietta called out softly. "Mrs. Goodman?" She tiptoed across the tiled floor. For a moment she wondered if the woman was dead, so still was she lying there, her hands folded on her abdomen as if indeed in death, her eyes peacefully shut. Henrietta stood over her, studying her chest to see if it was moving, alarm quickly stealing over her, when Mrs. Goodman's eyes suddenly sprang open. Startled, Henrietta gave a little gasp.

Mrs. Goodman, however, did not seem surprised or startled in the least by Henrietta's odd presence beside her bed.

"Where have you been?" she asked Henrietta without moving a muscle, her hands still perfectly folded across her abdomen. "I've been waiting for you. We found the door; it lies beneath the sphinx. From there we will travel beyond the Pillars of Hercules. Are you ready?" she asked Henrietta, looking at her closely. "Did you bring the bag of requirements?"

"I . . . I . . . " Henrietta began, not knowing whether to be amused or frightened. Actually, she felt a bit of both.

"No matter," Mrs. Goodman rushed on. "We will have to go without them. We leave tonight at midnight. Be ready. The angel of mercy will lead us."

Henrietta was utterly baffled. How could this woman utter such nonsense and yet sound perfectly rational? She certainly didn't seem "crazy"—raving and mad, that is— and yet she made no sense. Henrietta was vaguely aware that she probably shouldn't encourage her delusions by engaging with her, and yet she was irresistibly drawn to her . . .

"All right, you," Nurse Harding barked behind her, causing Henrietta to nearly scream with sudden fright. How had she not heard her approach? "Time for Mrs. Goodman's treatment, so you go on back up to the front."

"What . . . what treatment?" Henrietta managed to ask as she obediently took a few steps back from the bed.

"That ain't none of your business, Hoity-Toity," she said as she pulled a glass syringe out of her pocket.

Nervously, Henrietta looked back at Mrs. Goodman, who had still not moved an inch since Henrietta had come into her room. Henrietta was reluctant to leave her in the hands of the tank, and yet, Mrs. Goodman did not show any signs of distress at Nurse Harding's presence. Henrietta saw no choice but to obey the tank's direction.

"Can you at least tell me what's wrong with her?" Henrietta asked.

"What's wrong with her?" Nurse Harding barked out, not sparing the volume of her voice in any sort of respect for Mrs. Goodman. "Batty as a fruitcake, this one," Nurse Harding said. "Don't you mind what she says. Now, get going. Back to the dayroom where I can keep an eye on you. Ain't nothin' for you to see back here."

Henrietta made her way back to the dayroom, still feeling trapped and claustrophobic but not nearly as bad as she had before. At least she had Mrs. Goodman's odd story to keep her distracted, and she wondered, at one point, if that was all it was for that poor woman as well—a distraction from the reality of this horrible place and the sinking despair that covered it like a gray, polluted fog.

Henrietta leaned up against the wall for what felt like hours, though it was probably no more than thirty minutes. She was acutely aware of every irritating noise that had somehow gone unnoticed by her before: The tick of the clock on the wall, which was surprisingly loud and annoying, the repeated sniffling from a woman two seats over, and the unending muttered utterances, not to mention the occasional outburst of those poor souls around her. At one point, she even put her hands over her ears to block it all out, but to no avail. She supposed she could talk to Elsie, but neither of them seemed to have anything of note to say, at least not with the tank just a few yards away and Anna asleep in Elsie's arms. Neither seemed to want to risk waking her and so remained silent, merely looking at each other from time to time for comfort until—finally—the welcoming sound of a key scraping in the lock was heard.

Hurriedly, Henrietta quickly moved to the door and felt her heart clench with relief and joy at the sight of Clive (never had she been so happy to see him!) stepping quickly through with Gunther not far behind. He had a grim smile on his face, which told her they had been successful. She took his arm and tried to hide her distress and her dizziness.

"Darling, I'm sorry it took so long. It was quite a mess, as you can imagine. He was a bastard to weed out."

"Did you use the badge?" she asked in a low tone.

"In a roundabout way; I'll explain later." Clive looked around. "Was it too terrible?" he asked. "We should have all gone. I should have realized it would take an ungodly amount of time."

"It *was* terrible, actually, but I did find something interesting . . . "

"I can imagine," he said wryly.

"I was—"

"Back, are you?" the tank called loudly from farther down the hallway.

"I'll tell you later," Henrietta whispered, as Nurse Harding approached the little group.

Elsie had stood up when Clive and Gunther had come in, causing Anna to awaken, and upon seeing Gunther, she flung herself into his arms. Gunther stood holding Anna now, stroking her back and whispering to her in German, while she lay her head on his shoulder and wrapped her dirty legs around him. Elsie stood quietly beside the two of them, brushing Anna's fine, blonde hair with her fingers.

"Find him?" Nurse Harding asked Joe.

"If you're referring to the administrator, then, yes, we did," Clive said before Joe could answer. "In the end." He gave Joe an annoyed look.

Joe merely shrugged. "Not my fault he was in a meeting."

"A meeting? Is that what you call it?"

Joe gave him a sly smile and shrugged again.

Clive turned his attention back to Nurse Harding. "Here you are," he said crisply. "A signed release from Mr. Ainsworth himself."

Nurse Harding took the paper in her thick fingers and examined it, taking her time to read the whole thing, though from where Henrietta stood, there didn't seem to be all that much writing on it. Perhaps she was stalling? But why?

"All right. She can go," the tank said with a bit of a sigh. "Good riddance, if you ask me," she said dismissively.

Henrietta saw Elsie excitedly clutch Gunther's arm.

"You'll havta wait a few minutes, though," the tank said, moving behind the desk.

"Whatever for? We've been here far too long already," Clive said, giving his tie a little loosen, something Henrietta had never seen him do in public ever before. He must be feeling it, too, she surmised. The feeling of being trapped.

"Hold your pants on," the tank barked. "Can't do everything, you know. I'm the only one here at the moment, so you'll just have to wait while I sign this and then go get her things. Didn't come in with much, as I recall."

"You're the only staff member on this floor?" Clive asked, incredulously. "Surely that's against some sort of regulation?"

"Look, bub. Don't blame me," Nurse Harding said as she scrawled something across the release and handed it back to Clive. "Supposed to be two on, but can't keep the staff." She flipped through the log book. "Who's signing her out?" she asked the group.

Clive made a move toward the desk but paused when Gunther spoke up behind him. "It will be me," he said, then turned deferentially to Clive. "If you please."

"By all means," Clive said with a wave of his hand and stood back while Gunther shifted Anna to his hip and took the pen Nurse Harding handed him to dutifully sign his name.

The tank examined the paper one last time and pulled herself heavily back to her feet. "I'll go get her things," she said. "But first I've got to give Mrs. Dempsey her tonic. She'll be climbing the walls pretty soon if I don't get it in her right quick," she said, glancing at the dull black wall clock above the door.

"Oh, all right, but hurry up!" Clive snapped.

The release having been signed, Henrietta felt they were now just one small step away from getting out. She tapped her toe and looked around the room once again, and suddenly felt sorry for all these women that had no hope of *ever* being released, and she thought of poor Mrs. Goodman in particular. Henrietta looked from Elsie to Gunther and Clive, all of them standing silently, except Gunther, who continued to murmur to Anna. No one seemed to know what to say to each other, each of them deep in thought and periodically glancing at the door or the stock room or the patients' hallway every few seconds, all of them anxious for the reappearance of Nurse Harding.

"Elsie," Henrietta said briskly, deciding to break the silence. "Didn't you used to read us some myth or fable about a tribe of people living in the center of the earth?"

"What?" Elsie asked, confused.

"I seem to remember some story about different myths from around the world. It was a big book you once got from the library?"

Elsie shook her head slowly. For once she did not seem eager to discuss books. "I don't remember," she said absently. This has been terribly hard on her, as well, Henrietta noted, studying her carefully.

"You are referring to the myth of the Atlanteans, I am thinking,"

Gunther put in quietly. "Though there are some that do not believe it to be a myth."

Henrietta looked over at him, surprised that he had spoken.

"It refers to the *Unterirdisch*—what do you call it? Underground?—kingdom of Agharta," he said, turning himself, Anna still clutched tightly to him, so that he could see Henrietta better. "It is very old legend that has many versions. There was man, Edmund Halley, and also a man by name of John Symmes who spoke of these things."

All eyes were on Gunther now as he continued.

"They both wrote a theory of a hollow earth and its *Bewohner*." He paused to think of the word in English. "Inhabitants. Mystical thinkers describe a superior race there who are ruled by the 'King of the World' and that there are many tunnels that run under the earth with exits at each end . . . at the poles."

At his words, Henrietta felt goose bumps instantly appear down her neck. Is this what Mrs. Goodman was referring to? Surely, it was a delusion she had heard *after* she was put away here, wasn't it? Henrietta hoped, rather than it being the cause of her being locked up?

"It reminds me of the Jules Verne book," Elsie said. "Maybe that's what you were referring to, Henrietta."

"Yes," Gunther said eagerly to Elsie, "Verne had much influence from him."

Henrietta looked at Gunther as he spoke, amazed at this sudden revelation of knowledge, not to mention articulation. It was like he had been transformed into something else for just a moment, a remnant of perhaps his old self, which was trapped now by poverty and language and circumstance in the body of a poor custodian. By looking at him in his baggy, dirty clothes and his unruly hair, one would never guess that he had once been a respected teacher or a professor in Germany, Henrietta thought. But she could see, as she observed the way Elsie was looking at him at the moment, why her sister might be drawn to him.

"Here you go," Nurse Harding said, suddenly reappearing and tossing Anna's little clothes at Elsie.

"Come, Anna. Get down. It is time to go," Gunther said, attempting cheerfulness, as he tried to peel the girl off of him.

"No!" Anna wailed, clinging to his leg.

"Is there somewhere we can take her to change?" Elsie asked the nurse over the noise of Anna's shouts.

"Somewhere to change?" the tank exclaimed. "Where d'ya think you are? The Ritz? It's nothing anyone here ain't already seen," she said, gesturing around the room.

"But surely we can step into one of the bedchambers—" Elsie began, but was interrupted by a grunt from the tank as she swiftly approached Anna, who trembled at the sight of her. Despite her rolls of fat, Nurse Harding bent over Anna and grabbed the bottom of the striped gray gown the girl had been dressed in, which looked to be an adult gown that had been unevenly hacked off at the bottom, presumably with a scissor, and not a very sharp one.

"If you want somethin' done, best to just do it yourself," the tank said, irritated, and before Elsie, or any of them, could react, she yanked the gown roughly over Anna's head, leaving her standing there naked except for her underthings. "That'll get you to shut up," the tank said as she walked back to the desk.

Nurse Harding's cruel maneuver did have the effect of quieting Anna, who stood there looking forlornly at Gunther. Upon seeing her naked body, Clive immediately turned around out of politeness, even to a four-year-old, as Elsie rushed to put Anna's crumpled dress on her. Henrietta felt sick as she noticed the man in the corner with the sores greedily looking in Anna's direction, a sick grin on his face. Henrietta inadvertently gripped Clive's arm, feeling weak again. Clive studied her closely.

"Come," he said, putting his hand on hers. "It's almost over, darling," he said softly to her, though his voice was unsteady.

They turned around and saw that Anna was dressed now and back in Gunther's arms.

"Let's go," Clive commanded and nodded toward Joe to open the door. Henrietta was never so grateful to leave a place and eagerly made her way toward the door, only to be stopped again, this time by Anna herself.

"*Warte, Papa! Mein Buch! Wo ist mein Buch?*"

Gunther looked at her distractedly. It was clear that he was as eager as any of them to leave, but at Anna's pleading, he paused at the door's threshold.

"You brought your book here?" he asked her, his eyes looking horribly weary. "Are you sure?"

Anna nodded eagerly, her finger in her mouth.

"Nurse," Elsie said, approaching the desk. "Did she come in with a book? It was a book of poems by Robert Louis Stevenson. *A Child's Garden of Verses?*"

"Didn't see it back there," the tank barked, only briefly glancing up from the logbook she was writing in again. Henrietta wondered what she could possibly be writing, as the logbook contained only the briefest of notes on each patient. Perhaps she was slow? But how could she have become a nurse if she was actually mentally deficient? But then again, they seemed desperate for staff . . . Maybe she wasn't really a nurse, Henrietta mused. Oh! Nothing here made any sense!

"Are . . . are you sure?" Elsie ventured.

Henrietta, impressed by her sister's sudden courage, went to stand beside her.

"I . . . I could look if you want—" Elsie suggested.

"Oh, no you don't," the tank said, looking up at them fully. "Your snoopin' days is over. Nothin' back there for you to see. Now get out while you have the chance!" she barked.

Anna, apparently understanding this speech, began to cry. "*Mein Buch!*" she wailed.

"Anna, Anna," Elsie said soothingly, "I'll buy you another. I promise. I promise," she kept repeating. Miraculously, the girl stopped her crying and looked at Elsie with big, tear-filled eyes.

Elsie gave her a little smile, and Anna returned it with a small one of her own.

"Good girl," Elsie cooed, and Gunther took this as his cue to step through the door and begin their descent, Elsie following close behind.

"I'll be glad to see the back of this place," Clive muttered to Henrietta as they trudged down the stairs, bringing up the rear. "I hope this is the last time we'll ever need to be here."

"Yes, let's hope," Henrietta said, though she had the most unsettling feeling that she would indeed return. She earnestly prayed that it would not be as a patient.

Though the sky was dull when they emerged from Dunning, Joe having wordlessly deposited them outside, it seemed bright to Henrietta in contrast to the dark interior, and she blinked rapidly, holding her hand up to her eyes. She took a deep breath and welcomed the chilliness of the air, her coat unbuttoned. She hadn't realized she was perspiring. Gunther instructed Elsie to take his coat and drape it over Anna. As a result, he appeared to be a large, walking tent with a head sticking out.

As if one entity, they walked toward the Daimler that Clive had again driven in anticipation of having to drive them back to Mundelein. But what were they to do with Anna? Henrietta wondered. They obviously couldn't take her back to the orphanage . . .

"What now?" Clive asked Gunther, as if able to read Henrietta's mind.

"I do not know. I have not had much time to think," Gunther said, shifting Anna.

"Clive," Henrietta said quietly. "Perhaps we should take her back to Highbury with us. Remember that we talked about getting her a proper exam . . . ?"

"Yes, darling," Clive said, giving both Elsie and Gunther a nervous glance, "but I'm not sure if this is exactly the right time."

"But you said—"

"It doesn't matter," Elsie surprisingly interrupted. "I've already thought of a plan. We'll take her to Palmer Square."

Chapter 19

"Oh, you must try one of my cheese toasts!" Mrs. Hennessey exclaimed to Clive as he and Henrietta stood in the Hennessey's crowded apartment dining room above Poor Pete's.

"Thank you, Mrs. Hennessey," Clive said politely and transferred a small square from the platter she held in front of him and set it carefully on the little plate he held.

"Just one? A big man like you?" Mrs. Hennessey asked. "Here, have some deviled eggs," she urged, setting the cheese toast platter down and deftly picking up one which held the last of the slippery eggs. There were only three left, their filling unfortunately already crusted over.

"See? These is always popular. Lucky, I got more sittin' on the back porch to keep 'em cold. There you are." She slid them onto Clive's plate despite him raising a hand in protest. "You'd think now that you're married, you'd fatten up a little," she said. "But then again, Henrietta was never too good at cookin', was you?"

Henrietta's face flushed, and she wanted to point out to Mrs. Hennessey that she was never allowed even remotely close to the kitchen at Highbury, whether she wanted to or not, but she knew it would come out sounding "high and mighty" no matter which way she framed it. But could Mrs. Hennessey really have forgotten that she now lived in a mansion filled with servants? More than likely, Henrietta mused, she simply didn't think about it, much the same way Ma and most of her family seemed not to. Mrs. Hennessey no doubt still saw her as "little Henrietta," trying to make her way in the world.

Henrietta took a bite of a cheese toast and supposed she *was* still trying to make her way in the world, just a different one than before. Actually, it was comforting there was at least one person, besides her family, that is, who still saw her as she really was, or had once been. Even Clive tended to forget, she suspected, which is why he was perhaps at times confused about why she wanted to attend events such as this one.

"Here," Mrs. Hennessey was saying to Clive, "why don't you hold your napkin in your other hand? That way it'll be easier." She took hold of a corner of his napkin and tried to move it. The poor woman was not successful, however, nor did her efforts solicit any gratefulness on the part of Clive, but instead caused a severe eyebrow-raising. Unabashed, Mrs. Hennessey tried again.

"You might find it better to sit on the sofa," she suggested sweetly, gesturing toward the front room. "That way you can balance everything better on your lap. No? Fine as you are, eh? Well," she said, looking around a little uncomfortably. "You must try more of the food, like," she said, nodding toward the kitchen table where various dishes had been set out. "We've got pickled oysters, my famous veal loaf—Henrietta will tell you about that—deviled chicken, and then there's ham sandwiches. And the relish tray, of course. Rose has been so helpful; you'd never believe it! Don't know how I managed before. Winifred's not done a thing! But of course I don't expect it, not with caring for the baby, like, but still . . . ooh! There's Winifred now, come out of the bedroom, finally. I'll be back. Help yourselves; fill up your plates!" And with that, she squeezed her thick torso between several people to get to the other side of the room, where a frowning Winifred had appeared, carrying a similarly frowning little Prudence, who was bedecked in an enormous knitted pink bonnet.

Henrietta pulled her eyes from Winifred and the baby and looked over at Clive, who was staring disapprovingly at the fare piled onto his plate.

"Never had cheese toast before?" she asked, amused at the look on his face.

"Perhaps when I was seven," he said wryly. "It looks mildly similar to something Nanny would concoct if we were hungry and cook was having her afternoon rest. "*Deviled* eggs are a new delicacy for me, however. They look . . . interesting."

"Snob," Henrietta chided him with a small grin. "Actually, Ma's deviled eggs are quite good, when she used to cook, that is." Henrietta nodded toward the kitchen table. "This is actually quite a spread."

"Indeed," Clive said. Gingerly, he set his plate down on a nearby table and looked around the room. "Do you know all of these people?"

"I recognize some of them from the neighborhood," Henrietta said, arching her neck to try to observe people better. "Well, of course, you know Rose and Stan over there in the corner."

"Yes, I noticed them when we came in."

"And that big man over there by the food is probably Rose's brother, Billy, if I had to guess." She moved to the right a bit to try to see more. "Oh! I think that's Mr. Dubala, sitting in that armchair over there," she said, nodding. "The one with the striped tie? Elsie used to sew for him. I wonder why she didn't come? I thought Mrs. Hennessey had said she was going to invite her."

Clive gave a small shrug. "Maybe she didn't after all. Maybe to spare Stan and Rose?" he suggested.

"Yes, perhaps. But I was hoping to hear how Anna is doing."

"Hmmm. Yes, a pity," Clive said absently as he looked around the room.

Henrietta felt a heavy hand on her shoulder, then, and jumped. Quickly she turned to see none other than Mr. Hennessey himself! Henrietta gave a little cry and tightly embraced him, trying not to spill her drink as she did so. Mr. Hennessey held her for several moments before finally releasing her and grasping her free hand.

"Look at you, girl," he said, holding her at arm's length, his eyes bright with pride and pleasure. "You're a sight for sore eyes. Sorry I missed you the other day. But here you are, beautiful as ever!" he exclaimed. "Are you happy?" he asked with a smile, leaning close to her.

"Very," she said and could not believe how comforting it felt to see him. She could not stop smiling.

"Married life agrees with you, I can see that. But why wouldn't it? He treating you right?" he asked, nodding toward Clive, who was looking on with his own smile.

"Very much," Henrietta said.

"Clive," Mr. Hennessey said, releasing Henrietta and holding out his hand toward him. "How are you? Thank you for coming and bringing my girl back to see me."

Clive shook his hand thoroughly. "We're delighted to have been invited, Mr. Hennessey."

"That's all right," Mr. Hennessey beamed. "But what are you drinking?" he said, glancing down at the glass Clive held.

"Cherry cordial I think is what Mrs. Hennessey said it was," Clive said, holding it up uncertainly.

"Cherry cordial! Give me that," Mr. Hennessey said, taking it roughly from him. "You need a man's drink. So does young Stan. You come with me." Mr. Hennessey grasped him by the shoulder. "This way. A whiskey is what you need."

Clive managed to look back at Henrietta with another raised eyebrow, which made Henrietta want to laugh as Mr. Hennessey propelled him toward where Rose and Stan stood talking. The two of them stopped now, Henrietta could see, as Mr. Hennessey and Clive approached. Stan nervously slicked back his hair with one hand as he shook Clive's hand with the other. Clive leaned forward to say something to him, and Henrietta was glad when she saw Stan smile in response. Rose, meanwhile, caught Henrietta's eye and after whispering something to Stan began to make her way over.

Henrietta watched as Rose approached, drink in hand, pausing only once to avoid crashing into a child as he darted past her. Henrietta was glad to see her face was almost back to normal and that Rose actually wore a smile—a real smile—something she hadn't seen on Rose since their days at the Marlowe together.

"Hello," Rose said.

"Hello! I'm so happy you're here, Rose," Henrietta said excitedly. "All moved in?"

"How'd you know?"

"Mrs. Hennessey just mentioned it. She said you've been a big help."

Rose let out an unexpected sigh. "I didn't want to do it, you know, sweets," Rose said seriously. "I didn't want to take charity, but I had to. It was either this or move to Indiana, which I don't really want to do. I mean, Jesus, what would we do in Indiana?" She took a large drink from the highball glass she was holding. "In the end, Stan backed down with the other plan, of course. Said he just couldn't go through with the rushed wedding, that it would kill his mother if she ever found out, and, besides, he couldn't get the money for the apartment out of his savings account without his parents' signature for Christ's sake."

"Oh," Henrietta said, thinking that certainly sounded typical of Stan.

"That'll have to change, of course, when we're married," Rose said, looking over to where Stan stood with Clive and Mr. Hennessey.

"Still going to go through with it, then?" Henrietta asked, taking a sip of the cherry cordial. It wasn't bad, actually.

"Course I am. Can't stay here forever," she said, glancing around the apartment. "Stan's not a bad guy, really. He's crazy about me, and I'm obviously used to worse." She looked back at Henrietta now and gave a mischievous grin. "Says he wants to wait for our wedding night, if you know what I mean. Didn't know he was a virgin, though it doesn't surprise me."

It didn't surprise Henrietta, either, actually, especially since he had spent several years of his young life dogging her, but she didn't really want to discuss it. Instead she cleared her throat.

"Is that Billy?" she asked, nodding her head toward the large man she had spotted earlier. He was sitting on the floor now, in a corner, playing cards with several kids.

"Yeah," she answered, smiling as she looked over at him now, too. "Stan's real good with him. So's Mr. Hennessey. I can't believe how nice they've been to me, Hen. Finally caught a bit of luck, you know? Mrs. Hennessey has her quirks, and she's a bit annoying at times, but she has a real good heart. I can see why you always talked about them. She's taken a shine to Billy, too. Has him doin' stuff for her around the bar. I don't mind. We try to help as much as we can, which is all right, considering I still can't go back to the Melody Mill."

"Maybe that's not such a bad thing, Rose," Henrietta said, wondering if Rose's father would go looking for her there. "This way your dad won't know where to find you. How . . . how was it when you left?" she asked in a low voice.

"Not as hard as I thought it was going to be. I could have done it years ago if I'd have had somewhere to go. All I had to do was wait till he left for Lou's. I already had our things packed. It was different than those couple of times we ran for Lucy and Gwen's. I was calmer than I imagined I would be. I guess I'd fantasized about it so often over the years . . . that when it was finally time to get away, I wasn't frantic or anything. We just calmly took the bus here, and Mrs. Hennessey welcomed us like we were her kids or something."

Rose set her drink down and rummaged in her handbag for her cigarettes. She took one out and shakily lit it. "Things are good, but I'm kind of more of a wreck now," she said, turning her chin slightly to exhale a large cloud.

"What do you mean?" Henrietta asked, curious.

"I don't know. I . . . something kind of strange is happening. I'm afraid to go out. Ain't that queer? I'm afraid he'll find us somehow. I walk Billy to work at the electrics, make sure he gets there safe, then I walk straight back here. When I'm in here," she said, gesturing with her hand, "I feel okay, safe like. But when I go out, I can't help think he's going to pop out at me. You know? I come over all shaky. I know that doesn't make sense. He ain't got the brain power anymore to find me. I know that, but I'm still scared sometimes."

Henrietta reached out and rubbed Rose's arm sympathetically. "It'll be okay. It'll pass. I have a good feeling." She gave her a smile.

Rose merely nodded, her eyes squinting as she inhaled again.

"Why don't you introduce me?" Henrietta asked, not knowing what else to say in the moment.

"To who?"

"To Billy. I've never gotten to meet him, you know."

Rose paused in her response, peering at Henrietta through the cloud of smoke that surrounded her, as if trying to judge her sincerity, and then suddenly leaned over and swiftly kissed her cheek. "Come on, then," she said with the hint of a smile about her lips.

Henrietta followed Rose across the room, squeezing between people. Had the Hennesseys invited everyone they had ever known? she wondered. In a far corner of the dining room, Billy and three other children were sitting cross-legged and playing what appeared to be a game of war.

"Billy, this is my friend Henrietta," Rose said as they approached, gesturing at Henrietta with the hand that held her cigarette.

Billy looked up at Henrietta but didn't say anything.

"Say 'hi,'" Rose instructed.

"Hi," Billy said dully and flipped his top card. A couple of the kids looked up briefly at them, but then went back to scraping up the cards and flipping more.

"Nice to meet you, Bill," Henrietta said.

Billy did not respond, but continued to methodically turn cards, which the other kids collected.

"Billy. Not Bill," he said stubbornly.

"Sorry!" Henrietta offered. "Billy." She watched him as he silently flipped an ace, causing the kids to give a little shout and push the pile toward him.

"Billy!" Rose said impatiently. "What do you say?"

Billy looked up again and seemed to see Henrietta for the first time. "You're pretty," he said.

Henrietta smiled. "Why, thank you," she said.

"Billy!" Rose scolded.

"Oh, that's all right," Henrietta said. "Let him enjoy his game. War's always fun, 'specially with more than two. Let's let him be."

"He likes kids," Rose said, turning away from the little group. "I guess that makes sense given that he's really just a big kid himself."

"Say, Rose," Henrietta said, looking out over the room. "Which one is Mrs. Hennessey's niece? The nurse? Is she here?"

"Ida?"

"Yes, her."

"Yeah, she's over there by the front windows. See her?" Rose said, angling her head to see better. "She's got on the black-striped dress?"

"Yes, I see her," she said looking back at Rose. "I think I'll just go talk to her while Clive's preoccupied. Want to come?"

"Nah, I can take a hint. Besides," she said, grinding her cigarette into one of the many ashtrays sitting about, "I need to help Mrs. Hennessey."

"Thanks, Rose. We'll catch up in a bit, okay?"

As Rose made her way back to the kitchen, Henrietta looked across the room to where Ida stood talking to another woman. She was tall and nondescript in many ways. Her blonde hair was cut short and curled under, just like Loretta Young was wearing it these days. In fact, Henrietta thought, studying her, she looked a little bit like Loretta Young. She had a drink in one hand, and Henrietta recalled what Nurse Harding had told her about Ida Lynde being dismissed for being "a drunk." Henrietta watched her for a few moments, but the woman did not, to her eyes anyway, appear drunk or even tipsy. But Henrietta knew from experience that hardened drinkers could easily mask their condition. She had seen it hundreds of times just downstairs in Poor Pete's. There were always one or two regulars who would be waiting for them to open at ten in the morning, and whose hands would be shaking until

Mr. Hennessey laid down their first few shots for them. After that, they were able to speak like any other sober person, and no one would guess that their first drink of the day had not been coffee or tea.

Henrietta took a deep breath and began to walk toward Ida, wondering just how she was going to bring up Dunning. As if for moral support, she looked back over her shoulder to where Clive stood and was surprised to see him laughing with Mr. Hennessey, his pipe out and what looked like some sort of whiskey in hand. Clive rarely laughed, so the sight of him doing so, especially in public, momentarily warmed her. Encouraged, she turned back toward Ida and the woman she was chatting with. Henrietta felt sure she recognized the woman from her days as a 26 girl down below in Poor Pete's but couldn't remember her name.

"Hello, forgive my intrusion, ladies, but I thought I would introduce myself. I'm Henrietta Howard," she said confidently, holding out her hand first to the familiar woman and then to Ida.

The woman shook her hand limply, looking her up and down as if trying to place her. "Mrs. Brzezicki," she said, looking at Henrietta curiously. She was an older woman with gray hair and black glasses that were pinched up at the ends to give her the appearance of a cat. All of her features were small except for her stomach, which seemed disproportionately large, almost as if she were pregnant, which was obviously impossible given her advanced years.

Ida, however, shook her hand firmly. She was older than Henrietta had first observed from across the room. There were several wrinkles radiating from the sides of her eyes, which were big and brown and looked as though they might be permanently apprehensive.

"Ida Lynde," she said.

"Are you Mrs. Hennessey's niece by any chance?" Henrietta asked.

"Yes, I am," she said, seeming surprised that Henrietta knew this. "Are you a friend of the Hennesseys?"

"I used to work here. For years, actually," Henrietta said. "First as a cleaner, then a waitress, then as a 26 girl—"

"That's it!" Mrs. Brzezicki exclaimed. "That's how I know you!

You're from down below. The bar. You're the 26 girl! Or you used to be, anyway. Me and Mack always used to come in on a Sunday. You look different, though," she said, looking her up and down again.

Henrietta smiled. "I got married."

"I'll say! Must be doin' well!" the woman sniffed.

Henrietta had tried to dress in something plain and with little jewelry to better fit in tonight, but with her manicured nails and styled hair, the sheen of Highbury was nevertheless apparent.

"It's nice of Winifred to come back, isn't it?" Henrietta asked in an attempt to change the subject.

"Yes!" Ida chimed in. "I haven't seen her in years! Not since we were kids. Aunt Alice is so pleased, isn't she?" Ida looked over to where Mrs. Hennessey sat holding little Prudence with Winifred looking on, an annoyed expression on her face.

"Yes, she's wanted a grandchild for so long; it's a shame they live so far away."

"Yeah, but that daughter of hers don't look so happy. She's a real sourpuss that one. Look at her. Been watching her all this time. Hasn't smiled once!" said Mrs. Brzezicki, joining the conversation now.

"Well, maybe she's nervous. New mother, you know," Ida suggested kindly.

"Do you have children?" Henrietta asked.

"Me? No. I'm not married," Ida answered. "I live with my mom. Take care of her."

Henrietta nodded. She had once upon a time thought that was going to be Elsie's fate, caring for Ma as she aged and having to forgo getting married. But things had changed for them in a way she could never have imagined.

"I was in the very same boat." Mrs. Brzezicki gave a knowing nod. "Though that was years and years ago now. But havin' to take care of Ma didn't stop *me* from getting hitched. Simply brought Ma along with me. Worked out fine," she said with a little sniff at Ida.

Henrietta sighed. How was she going to get rid of this woman so that she could talk privately to Ida?

"Have you tried Mrs. Hennessey's veal loaf?" she suggested as a possible lure. "It's her specialty, you know. It won second place one year at the St. Sylvester carnival."

"Oh, believe you me, I've had Alice's veal loaf before! She talks about it constantly. But I suppose we all have our downfalls, don't we? Truthfully, though, I couldn't eat another bite," Mrs. Brzezicki said, indelicately patting her rounded middle. "Not if you paid me! I don't really eat all that much these days," she said with a bit of a proud flourish. "Always laid up with indigestion, I am. Doctor calls it heartburn," Mrs. Brzezicki sniffed. "So I have to watch myself. I really do. But I will confess that I did have just a tiny slice of Alice's veal loaf. I couldn't resist, but now I can feel already I'm going to pay the price." She patted her stomach again. "In fact," she said with a wince, "I'd better be going now. Excuse me, won't you? Better go find Mack and say my good-byes to Alice. Don't s'pose I'll get a hold of that baby yet today; Alice ain't about to give it up for one second, is she?"

Mrs. Brzezicki began to try to budge her way through the crowd when she suddenly stopped and turned back around.

"Nice seein' you again, girlie," she said, addressing Henrietta. "You were the best 26 girl they ever had. Miss seein' ya about. Got a new girl in now. She's okay, but a little rough 'round the edges, if you know what I mean. I'm Mrs. Brzezicki, if you don't remember. More than likely you don't."

"I remember," Henrietta said with a smile. "It was nice seeing you again, too, Mrs. Brzezicki." Henrietta watched as the woman made her way over to where Mrs. Hennessey still sat with baby Prudence.

Henrietta turned back to Ida and smiled unsteadily, wondering how to begin. She should probably ply her with more small talk, but she worried that if she prevaricated too long, someone else would come along and join the conversation and she would lose her chance. "I . . . I hope you don't find me impertinent, Miss Lynde—"

"Ida."

"Ida. But Mrs. Hennessey happened to mention that you once worked at Dunning."

Henrietta observed a slight shift in Ida's stance, though her face remained a blank.

"Yes, I did," Ida answered shortly, draining her glass.

"How long ago was that?" Henrietta tried to ask casually.

"About a year ago, I suppose. I work at Jefferson Park Hospital now. I didn't much like it, as you can imagine," she said with a thin smile. "At Dunning, I mean. Why do you ask?"

"A friend of my sister's, well . . . actually, a friend of *her* friend, was recently sent there, but she died as it turns out. Unexpectedly."

"I'm sorry to hear that," Ida said matter-of-factly. "Well, it was nice meeting you, Mrs. Howard," Ida added after only a moment's pause.

"Oh, please call me Henrietta."

"Henrietta, then," she said with a hurried smile.

"Ida, please," Henrietta said, "I don't mean to pry, but Mrs. Hennessey mentioned that you quit because of something that happened there? Something that scared you?"

Henrietta saw Ida's face blanch as she nervously looked in Mrs. Hennessey's direction and let out a deep breath. "You know, I love my aunt; I really do. But sometimes she says more than she should. It was nothing," Ida said, pulling her gaze from Mrs. Hennessey back to Henrietta. "Aunt Alice exaggerates things, as I'm sure you must already be well aware of since you worked here for so long. I have to be going now, though. I should get back and check on my mother." She tried to move past her.

"Ida, please," Henrietta said, laying her hand on the woman's arm. "It's important. My husband and I are trying to get to the bottom of this."

"Of what?" Ida asked her suspiciously.

"Well, it's just that we—well, *I*—think there might be more to this woman's death. There are . . . there are several odd things about it all, and I was hoping you could help me."

"Why? Who are you?" Ida asked, her eyes narrowing.

"We . . . well, we're trying to be private detectives, but we're not really acting in that capacity right now. We're just trying to help my sister's friend."

"Forget it," Ida said worriedly. "I don't want to get involved in a police case. I have enough troubles of my own."

"But it's not a police case," Henrietta said as Ida moved past her, not looking back. "Please," Henrietta said in a slightly raised voice, "there's a child involved."

Ida paused and stood still, her tall, stiff back to Henrietta for several moments before she turned around, gazing about the room as she did so. She took a step toward Henrietta and leaned close to her. "All right, then, but not here," she whispered.

A tingle of excitement ran up Henrietta's spine. So there *was* something this woman could tell her! Henrietta hurriedly looked around the room for a quiet corner, but every nook was filled with people.

"Come on," Ida said with a slight incline of her head.

Henrietta followed her through the crowd, pausing with her at the little window that had been cut out in the wall between the kitchen and the dining room, presumably to make it easier to hand food through, but which currently held various bottles of booze. Henrietta watched as Ida filled her glass with gin and, without looking to see if Henrietta followed, slipped around the corner and down a short hallway where the bedrooms presumably were. Ida paused outside one of the doors and knocked. When no one answered, she let herself in.

The sun was just setting, so the room was dark except for the rosy glow that shone through the one window. Henrietta looked past the twin bed piled with guests' coats to the extra mattress on the floor and guessed it must be the room where Rose and Billy were staying. Ida soundlessly closed the door.

"What's all this about?" Ida asked quietly, taking a sip of her drink.

"We were looking for a woman, the friend of my sister's friend," Henrietta explained quickly, sensing she did not have much time. "A woman named Liesel. We found out that she had been taken to Dunning, which we believed was somehow a mistake in the first place. She suffered from fits, epilepsy, we think. But when we finally traced her to Dunning and went to get her out, we were shocked to find she was dead! We asked for a report, a cause of death, and all they would tell us, reluctantly at that, was that she had a bad reaction to the electric shock treatment they tried on her and that she died. They were very quick to dismiss us."

Ida nodded as if this made sense. "Which ward?"

"Ward 3C," Henrietta answered and watched as Ida took another drink.

"Go on," she said quietly.

"So I found myself there again, recently, this time to retrieve this woman's child, if you can believe it, who had also been sent there, again, we believe wrongly. When the nurse wasn't looking, I . . . I snuck a look at the log and saw that the woman, Liesel, had no less than eight treatments in the short time she was there and, what's more, that she hadn't died for nearly a week after the last one . . . " Henrietta's voice trailed off, waiting for Ida to say something, but she just continued to stare at Henrietta.

"So don't you think that's odd?" Henrietta urged. "If it was really a result of the electric shock treatments, wouldn't she have died immediately? Or very soon after? Not six days!"

Again, Ida's face remained a blank.

"So when Mrs. Hennessey mentioned that you saw something there, too . . . I just wondered if perhaps you could shed any light on it. I just get this funny feeling that maybe they're hiding something?" Henrietta's voice trailed off.

"Like what?" Ida asked.

"Like maybe something else happened to Liesel? Something not quite accidental? But I can't understand why. Why would someone want to kill a poor immigrant woman?" Henrietta sighed, repeating Clive's words. "I guess I was hoping you might be able to add something to this. Can you?" she looked at her pleadingly.

"Why should I?" Ida asked bitterly. "Why should I risk my neck? Already did once, and look where it got me."

Henrietta considered this. She didn't really have a good answer. "Because of the child?" she finally said. "So that someone else doesn't lose their mother?"

Ida sighed deeply and took several moments to answer. "Yes, I . . . I do think something odd is going on there," she said hesitantly. "I don't have any proof exactly, but I'm . . . I'm almost sure of it." She looked up at Henrietta nervously.

"Yes?" Henrietta asked, trying to hide her excitement.

"I was assigned to Ward 3C for a while," she said in a very low voice, so low that Henrietta had to strain to hear her. "I usually worked the day shift, but I would sometimes fill in on nights, too. A lot of times, we worked double shifts. I was always asked to stay because I don't have a husband or a family. It was harder for some of the other nurses. So, one night, one of my patients had somehow untied herself from the bed—"

"Untied herself?" Henrietta interrupted, shocked.

"Yes, the patients are often tied into bed at night to keep them from wandering—"

"You can't be serious!"

"I know it sounds bad, but it's sometimes necessary for their own safety. Or the safety of the other residents," she said grimly. "There are a lot of terrible things that go on in that place."

At those words, an image of the man with the sores on his face looking lecherously at Anna suddenly came into Henrietta's mind, and she had to actually shake her head to dispel it.

"I'm sure you're right. I'm sorry. Please, go on."

"As I was saying, one of my patients had gotten out of bed and smeared feces all over the wall."

Henrietta swallowed hard, trying to block out the repulsive image that came to mind.

"It took some time to restrain her," Ida went on. "I called for help, but no one came, so I finally managed to do it myself. After I got her back in bed, I hurried to the stock room to get something to clean up the mess with. As I grabbed some towels, I noticed a brown bottle sitting there on the counter. It struck me as odd at the time because it was brown, and most of our bottles are clear. Or sometimes green. And it didn't have a label. Curious, I decided to open it and smell it, wondering if it was alcohol—hootch, you know—of some kind. Either one of the nurse's or maybe something they had confiscated from a patient. But it wasn't alcohol," Ida said, pausing to take a long drink herself. "It had a smell of almonds to it . . . "

Here Ida looked at Henrietta as if that detail should mean something to her, but when Henrietta did not react, she went on. "It wasn't until the end of my shift that I remembered it and went back to the stock room to investigate further, but the bottle was gone. I couldn't find it anywhere. It's as if it disappeared into thin air. Not long after that, Nurse Collins arrived to relieve me, and I left."

"Did you mention it to Nurse Collins?"

"No," Ida said, shifting uncomfortably. "It didn't seem like something important enough to mention, and, anyway, I was in a hurry to get home. My mother was quite ill at the time, and I needed to care for her. All thoughts of work went out of my head."

Henrietta took a drink of her cherry cordial and felt sorry for this poor woman who had to work all night as a nurse and then again at home. Before she could ask anything more, however, Ida hurried on, apparently eager to finish the story.

"Imagine my surprise the next day when I went in only to discover there had been a death in the night! It took a little while, but it finally occurred to me that the stuff in the bottle . . . it must have been cyanide!"

"Cyanide!" Henrietta exclaimed. "You mean poison?"

"Yes, exactly."

"But . . . but how do you know?" Henrietta asked, thinking that this was sounding a little farfetched despite her eagerness for proof of some sort of wrongdoing.

"Don't you see? Cyanide gives off a smell of almonds," Ida said anxiously. "It must have been it."

Henrietta felt a thrill run down her spine. This is just the sort of thing she had been hoping for! But as excited as she was, she made herself play devil's advocate, Clive's voice in her mind, telling her to be cautious. "But . . . couldn't the death have just been a coincidence?" she asked hesitantly.

"It could have been," Ida said with an annoyed shrug. "But no one was even close to death. We sort of know when it's going to happen. The other patients do, too, somehow. They start shunning that person. Call it a sixth sense, if you will. But I hadn't felt anything like that. None of us had. It was an older woman, Mrs. Leary, I think it was. A sudden heart attack, they said. The morning nurses had already taken her body down to the morgue, stripped her bed, and given it to a new patient by the time I got in. Of course, it's not unusual for someone to die, but I just couldn't shake the feeling that something was odd about the whole thing. That's when I remembered seeing the funny bottle, but I could hardly believe what my mind was suggesting. The first chance I got, I went to the stock room to look more closely for it, but there was no trace of it. I looked everywhere, but I didn't see any brown bottle. I wondered, then, if in my exhausted state I had possibly imagined it."

"Who was on duty with you that night? That seems like the obvious person to question."

"No one."

"No one? What do you mean?"

"It was a floater. If we were ever short, Harding would assign someone to float between wards and help as needed," Ida said, taking a drink.

"So Nurse Harding was there that night?"

"I think so, yes."

"Who was the floater?"

"That's just it. I don't remember," Ida said with a sigh. "I've tried and tried to recall, but I don't think I ever saw her. That's why when I called out for help with my patient, no one responded."

"Hmmm. I see," Henrietta mused. "Then what happened?"

"I guess I forgot about it for a while," Ida said with a shrug. "But then I started noticing over the next few months that there were more sudden deaths which no one, it seemed, was paying attention to or cared about really. That may seem unusual or harsh, but every death at Dunning is the end of suffering for someone and at the same time, one less person to clothe and feed, and an open bed for someone assigned to a mattress on the floor. But *I* was trying to pay attention, trying to make some sort of connection. I'm not sure why, really, just that it felt odd. The only thing I was able to discover was that the sudden deaths always occurred on either Ward 3B or 3C. I kept looking for a brown bottle but could never find one. I even checked the stock rooms on both wards, but I found nothing there, either. But the deaths kept happening. Not all at once or with any pattern, so that I eventually began to question my own sanity. Working in a place like that does something to you."

"I can only imagine," Henrietta agreed with a shudder. "Were you *ever* able to make any connections?" Henrietta asked. "Something that linked them?"

"Not really. Just that they oddly never occurred while I was on duty. Only on days or nights when I was off."

"Men? Women?"

"Both."

"Old?"

"Didn't matter."

"Any connection in their diagnosis?"

Ida thought about that question. "I'm not sure," she said, thinking. "Not that I can remember."

"Didn't any of their families ever question their loved one's death?" Henrietta probed.

Ida again paused to think. "Well, there's something," she said slowly. "None of them seemed to have any family, come to think of it. No one ever came to collect their remains or their possessions. We keep their things for sixty days and then give them out to other patients if no one comes forward to claim them."

"Sixty days? That's not long."

Ida shrugged. "Like I said, none of them had any family. No one missed them."

"So, none of them had a family," Henrietta mused, thinking it wasn't much of a connection. "So then what?"

Ida took another drink. "I . . . I started losing sleep over these deaths. Wondering if I was seeing too much into them. Finally, I couldn't take it anymore. I worked up my courage and confronted Nurse Harding with it. I told her about the brown bottle I had seen on the night Mrs. Leary died."

"You did?" Henrietta whispered excitedly. "What did she say?"

"You can imagine," Ida said bitterly. "She didn't believe me, of course. Said I was imagining things. I admit that what I was proposing—that someone there was . . . well, was poisoning patients—was ludicrous. I had told myself this countless times, but it was the only thing that seemed to explain what was happening. The only thing that this all added up to. I asked Nurse Harding who the floater was the night Mrs. Leary died—the night I saw the bottle—but she said she couldn't remember and to mind my own business. Said I should keep my mouth shut and get on with my work."

"And then you got fired."

"Yes," she said looking up at Henrietta in surprise. "How did you—?

"I asked Nurse Harding if she knew you. She said you had been dismissed for drinking," Henrietta said, observing her closely. "A fondness for gin, I think is what she said." Henrietta could not help her eyes from glancing at Ida's current glass, which was nearly empty at this point.

"Yes, I was fired not long after I confronted Nurse Harding. That's peculiar, isn't it? Especially as they're so short-staffed. There's not much you can get fired from Dunning for. Drinking is one of them, for some reason, as if there aren't worse things that happen there," she said with a little shudder. "But I'm no drunk." Then she knocked back the last of her drink, which took some courage, Henrietta conceded, given the current conversation.

Ida let out a deep sigh. "As much as I was tempted to beg for my job, I was afraid as well, and given what I suspected of happening,

I just wanted to get out of there. And since I had clearly made an enemy of Nurse Harding, I knew my life would have been hell there anyway after that."

"Did she at least give you a reason? Did she mention drinking?"

"No, she didn't," Ida said wryly. "Just said my services were no longer needed. As I was packing up my things, she found me and reminded me that confidentiality and trust were two of the hallmarks of the nursing profession and that a nurse with a loose tongue quickly lost her professional reputation. I'll admit—it scared me. I needed a reference, and I knew what she was implying. That I needed to keep my mouth shut if I ever hoped to find another place."

"She said that?" Henrietta asked, surprised that Nurse Harding was capable of such eloquence.

"Not in those exact words," Ida said, comprehending Henrietta's meaning, "but I understood her message, which was to keep my mouth shut if I ever hoped to get another nursing job. Like I said, I was desperate to care for my mother. I *needed* a job. Thankfully I was able to get a place at Jefferson Park and all seemed fine; I tried to forget about my suspicions and put it behind me. Imagine my surprise, then, when I heard through a colleague the rumor going around that I was dismissed for drinking! The evil witch made sure to cover her tracks. First get rid of me, threaten and scare me into silence, and then put it about that I was let go for drinking, thereby discounting my suspicions should I ever decide to voice them," she said bitterly. "Oh, she was clever, all right."

Henrietta was stunned by this information. How could someone be that calculating? That evil? She shuddered and a brief image of Neptune came to mind. She pushed it away as another thought occurred to her. "But . . . but what about Nurse Collins—" Henrietta began to ask, suddenly wondering what her role in all of this was. Had she, too, noticed something out of the ordinary? Surely, she would have been sympathetic if Ida had thought to confide in *her* instead of Nurse Harding. But before Henrietta could finish asking about her, there was a brisk knock at the bedroom door, and Clive poked in his head. He seemed surprised to see the two of them standing there in the dark.

"I beg your pardon," he said hurriedly. Though his face was partially in shadow, Henrietta could see his concern. "I just wondered where you were. Forgive me," he said with a bow.

Before he could retreat, however, Ida said, "I have to go. I've told you everything I know. Now, please let me be," she begged, pushing past Clive, stumbling a bit as she did. Clive reached out and steadied her, but she did not look at him and merely mumbled a thank you.

Henrietta tried to perceive if her speech was slurred, but she could not tell.

"Everything all right, darling?" Clive pulled his gaze back to Henrietta.

"I'm not sure," she said, coming up and linking her arm through his. "Let's go home."

Chapter 20

Henrietta remained seated in the back of the Daimler for several moments, even after it had rolled to a stop a block away from the main gates of Dunning. She checked her wristwatch and confirmed there was still at least an hour left of visiting hours. She took a deep breath, steeling herself against the prospect of going in. She had hoped after the last time that she would never return to this awful place, but she felt she had no choice now and prayed it would be quick.

She had related to Clive all that Ida Lynde told her at the Hennessey's party, but he seemed unconvinced, saying that it was farfetched and that, according to Mr. Hennessey, anyway, she was a boozer. Her story had the typical flavor of alcohol-induced paranoia to it, he said, which he had witnessed too many times to count. And even if they did take seriously for one moment the suspicion that several deaths at Dunning were not the result of natural causes, Liesel Klinkhammer's in particular, what would the motive be? The theory fell apart there, Clive reasoned. Add to that Ida Lynde's reputed alcoholism, and it was pretty much a hill of beans.

Henrietta argued that she didn't believe Ida to be an alcoholic; she had seen plenty of those in her lifetime. Irritatingly, Clive then pointed out how Ida had stumbled from the bedroom at the Hennessey's.

"Honestly, Clive, anyone can stumble!" Henrietta admonished, but they had dropped the conversation when Antonia happened to enter the room where they were sitting.

But Henrietta could not stop thinking about it. She had come up with several more questions she wished she could ask Ida, but she had no idea where she lived or how to contact her. She supposed she could ask Mrs. Hennessey about how to reach her, but she was hesitant to involve the older woman in this, given Mrs. Hennessey's fondness for gossip—especially if it turned out to be nothing. And anyway, even if she could talk with Ida again somehow, she wasn't sure how much more she could share. She seemed to have already told her all she knew. Except, Henrietta had wanted to ask her more about Nurse Collins; she had been about to before Clive walked in on them. Surely Nurse Collins, working in such close quarters with Ida, had noticed something, too? Had Ida ever whispered her suspicions to her colleague? Henrietta wondered, or was she fired before she could do so?

It occurred to Henrietta, then, that perhaps she should return to Dunning herself and attempt to find a record of exactly who was working the night Mrs. Leary died, and to possibly question Nurse Collins if she could find her. Perhaps she knew who the mysterious floater was that night, or saw something after Ida had gone home? Perhaps she shared Ida's wild theories of a murderer, more than likely a murderess, on the loose. Or, on the other hand, maybe Nurse Collins could corroborate that Ida was indeed a paranoid alcoholic. Yes, Henrietta reasoned more and more as each day passed: speaking directly to Nurse Collins seemed to be the thing to do . . . if she could work up the courage, that is, to return to Dunning and interview her.

But even if she could muster the courage needed, convincing Clive would likewise be difficult, she knew. As far as he was concerned, this was a closed case, and one she sensed he additionally did not like talking about—not only because it reminded him of his breakdown, or "mental weakness," as he referred to it, when they had been there, but because it invariably led to a discussion about what to do with Anna, which he also seemed keen to avoid.

Henrietta was beginning to understand him more now as the first year of their marriage slipped past. There were certain subjects he did not wish to speak of unless she really prodded and insisted, sometimes having to resort to that tender time right after they made love, but even then, he was occasionally more reticent than she would have wished. One such subject, she had discovered early on, was his experience in the war and another was closely related to this—the subject of his first wife, Catherine, who had passed away in childbirth while he was off fighting. Also, he did not like to linger on the subject of his father's blackmail or any of the grisly crimes he had been involved in investigating as an inspector with the Chicago police. And recently, he was likewise reticent about the case of Madame Pavlovsky. Ever since she had fainted at the séance, he refused to talk about it, even becoming harsh with her at times when she persisted.

"But, Clive," she had said softly one night. "Don't you wish to talk about our baby? Do you . . . do you not feel some sort of comfort from knowing that he is safe and cared for?" she asked in a wavering voice.

Clive had put his hand over his eyes and sighed and seemed to be considering his words carefully. "Henrietta, my dearest darling," he said gently, looking up at her now, "please put this from your mind. I was . . . I was quite remiss in involving you with that . . . that . . . *woman*," he said archly.

"Why are you so afraid of what she tells us, darling?" she asked. "Does it pain you to . . . to talk about our son?"

Henrietta saw his right jaw clench, a sure sign that he was feeling emotion. But was it sadness or anger?

"Henrietta, we do not know if it was a boy or a girl," he said firmly.

"Is it that you don't believe he is in heaven because he wasn't baptized?" she asked in a low voice. "I asked Father Michaels about that when he came to see me as I recovered."

Clive did not say anything but just looked at her.

"He said that God has a special place for those children who die before they are born," she went on eagerly. "That we needn't worry and he himself would say a special mass with that intention," she said, putting her hand on his. "So you see? What Madame Pavlovsky says could very well be true!"

She looked into his eyes, and he returned her look with such sadness, or was it pity?

"Henrietta," he said, "let us not, for both our sakes, discuss Madame Pavlovsky any further. It cannot be good. For either of us. Do you understand?"

Reluctantly, she promised him then that she would no longer speak of Madame Pavlovsky or ever return to her on her own, but she could not stop herself from thinking about it every so often. Clive could not control that, and neither could she, it seemed.

It was only recently, actually, in the last couple of days that an altogether new idea—a quite daring one—came to her, which was that perhaps, knowing Clive as she did, she should make a quick trip to Dunning on her own and save him the mental anguish! It could be under the guise of visiting Mrs. Goodman, for example, nearly convincing herself for one brief moment that this was indeed the real purpose of her proposed venture. Yes, she thought, growing more excited at the prospect. Perhaps it would be good to go alone, especially as Clive seemed preoccupied of late with some goings-on at the firm which were requiring him to be more frequently downtown, and for Bennett to likewise be more present at Highbury. She needn't bother him with this . . . well, this nonsense, as he would call it.

It would be easy enough to sign in as a visitor, speak to Nurse Collins, perhaps have a few words with Mrs. Goodman while she was there, and then leave again, hopefully with the needed information. Perhaps she would discover that Liesel really had died naturally and that would be the end of the story, she reasoned. But maybe she would find something else . . . something more sinister.

While it was exciting to think about uncovering some sort of foul play and being able to return to Clive with real evidence in hand, there was a part of her, in truth, that hoped it was all just a fantasy and that she could put the case to rest. She was tired of thinking about it and tired of it being a sore subject between her and Clive. Well, she resolved, she would be ruled by whatever Nurse Collins had to say on the matter. And that would be that.

Having decided upon a plan of action, finally, it was harder to decide what to tell Clive. She knew he would never approve of her going to a place like Dunning on her own, even if she framed it as merely an innocent visit to Mrs. Goodman. She did not wish to deceive him, but then again, he could be so maddeningly old-fashioned, so worried and overly protective of her, despite his attempts lately to disguise it. If she told him, he would only worry—so in the end, she decided that she would say she was going to visit Elsie or Julia, or that she was going shopping downtown, thereby requiring a car in the morning.

Surprisingly, Clive had agreed to her plan without question, barely looking up from the documents he read as they sat together in his study. Bennett had been announced, then, and she had risen from the sofa to let them discuss business matters. She politely greeted Bennett and said her good-nights and gone upstairs to bed. However, as she lay waiting for Clive to come up, she regretted her fib. After all, they had made a promise to each other that there would be no secrets between them, and she knew, even in this, that she had to be honest. She would tell him the truth when he came up and hoped that, instead of forbidding her to go, he might still be persuaded to come along. Or maybe he would send someone to escort her? But who? And would he really expect one of the servants to escort her to an insane asylum; surely that was above and beyond their call of duty. She almost laughed at the idea of Billings in such a place and wondered what Joe the orderly would make of him. She could see Clive assigning the role to Carter, just to punish him, but Carter, in his advanced years, didn't seem able to fight off a flea. Oh, why was she worrying about this?

The rococo clock on the mantel struck midnight, and still Clive did not return. Henrietta could feel herself getting sleepier. Perhaps she should rise and write him a note? She was so dreadfully tired, however, and as she lay there trying to convince herself to get up and do it, she fell asleep. At one point in the night, she discovered that he had slipped into bed beside her. It was too late, she knew, to discuss such a thing and curled up beside him instead. She would speak to him in the morning.

But when she awoke, to her dismay she found that he was already gone. She sat up groggily and looked around the room. Almost as if on cue, she heard a quiet rap at the door followed by Edna coming in, again carrying a large breakfast tray.

"What's this, Edna?" Henrietta said, sitting up. "I'm not ill."

"Mr. Howard's orders, miss . . . I mean, madame," she said, setting the tray down now on the end of the bed.

"Where *is* Mr. Howard?" Henrietta asked. "Is he downstairs already?"

"Already gone, madame," Edna said, attempting to reach behind Henrietta to fluff her pillows.

"Gone?"

"Yes, gone into the city. Some sort of business, he said. Didn't wish to wake you, so he had Mary prepare this for you." Edna reached for the tray and carefully balanced it over Henrietta's lap. "There's a note there from him, too," she said, nodding at the missive wedged between a teacup and a vase, which held a single white rose.

Henrietta picked up the note and smelled it, enjoying the scent of Clive that still lingered there. He did not often write to her. Eagerly, she slipped her finger along the edge of the envelope and opened it.

"Thank you, Edna." She glanced at the waiting maid, who apparently, by her remaining position beside the bed, was likewise eager to know the contents.

At this dismissal, Edna gave a sad little curtsey, and then occupied herself with arranging Henrietta's robe on the chaise lounge. From there, she moved to the vanity and began studiously rearranging Henrietta's hairbrushes.

Giving Edna a last look, Henrietta pulled out the note and began reading.

My dearest,

You were sleeping so peacefully that I had not the heart to disturb you. Unfortunately, I must attend several meetings in the city today in regard to the firm. Forgive my not telling you before, but it was decided late last night. I know you were planning on visiting Elsie or Julia today, so I have left the car and Fritz at your disposal. I look forward to seeing you tonight, darling, when I hope to make it up to you. I miss you already.

Your own, Clive

With a sigh, she set the missive aside. Now what was she to do? she thought with a small groan. She supposed she would have to put off the visit until another day, but it was terribly disappointing. She had been so sure that today would be the end of it all. She wondered then if *intending* to tell him might count just as much as actually telling him. She knew this to be a gross stretch of their promise to each other, but it was so tempting. They wouldn't be able to go tomorrow, Saturday, Henrietta mused, thinking it through, as they were expected at dinner with the Exleys, and Sunday, Henrietta remembered Nurse Harding telling her, was Nurse Collins's only night off. They couldn't possibly wait until Monday! Oh, what was she to do?

She reached for a piece of toast and took a small bite.

"Any instructions, miss?" Edna said, coming back over to her now.

"No, thank you," Henrietta said absently. "You didn't have to bring me a tray, though," she said. "I could have come downstairs on my own."

"Oh, it's my pleasure, miss," Edna said, moving to lift the silver dome covering Henrietta's main plate for her. "Don't usually get to fuss over you as much as I used to, except when you were ill, of course—"

"Oh my!" Henrietta exclaimed, interrupting her. "What is that?" she said, pointing to a grayish piece of what looked to be meat on the plate.

"Oh, that's liver, madame," Edna said, looking at her in a puzzled way. "Ain't you never had liver?"

"Well, yes, but not like that!" Henrietta said, making a face. "Please take it away, Edna," she said with a gesture. "Mary's never served that for breakfast before! What's gotten into her?"

Edna's face looked as though she was personally slighted by Henrietta's rejection of the special breakfast. "It was Mr. Clive's—I mean, Mr. Howard's—orders, actually," she said as she removed the offending plate from the tray.

"What do you mean?" Henrietta asked.

"Well, I don't know exactly, but I overheard him talking on the telephone not but a few days ago with Dr. Ferrington, I believe."

"Go on," Henrietta said stiffly, setting down her cup. Clive hadn't mentioned a telephone call from the doctor.

Edna began to look uncomfortable. "I think it had something to do with you fainting the other night, remember?" she asked, shifting her weight.

"What did he say?"

"Well, I'm not for certain, but from what Mary told me, he thinks you are an-mean-ick...ana-me-ick . . . oh! I don't know! An- something—"

"Anemic?"

"Yes, I think that was it! Mr. Howard told Mary all sorts of food she's to make for you from now on."

"Like liver?" Henrietta asked incredulously. How could Clive have not included her in this discussion? As if she were no more than a child! Would he ever learn? she wondered, pressing her fingertips to her forehead.

"Yes, miss," Edna said, seeming relieved that her mistress understood now.

"What else was on this list?" Henrietta asked irritably, which significantly diminished Edna's momentary enthusiasm.

Edna gave a sad little shrug. "Don't know all of it, madame. But let me see," she said in response to Henrietta's disappointed face. "Liver," she said, ticking off one of her fingers, "dark beer, bloody beef—I remember that one because Mary had a proper harrumph and said 'whoever heard of serving bloody beef?'—something called black pudding, dock root tea, juice of beet root. . . " She had switched to ticking on the other hand now and cocked her head toward the ceiling, thinking. Finally, she let her hands drop. "I don't remember any more," she said with another shrug, then picked up the plate again. "Are you sure you don't want to try a bite of this? Mr. Howard is sure to be angry . . . "

"No, Edna, take it away," she said, plugging her nose and almost gagging at the sight of it, lying in a pool of blood. "Or better yet, do you want it?"

"Oh, no, miss! I couldn't do that!"

"Well, I certainly don't want it!" she fumed.

How dare Clive interfere this way? He had probably discussed it with his mother. In fact, she was sure of it. When would he stop treating her like a child, or worse, an invalid! Well, that decided it, she said, moving the tray and throwing off the covers, much to Edna's dismay. She would proceed with her plan to visit Dunning today. She would show him that she didn't need protecting and would not be confined to this house or to their bed!

As it turned out, only a modicum of stealth was required to slip out of the house unnoticed. It being Friday, it was Antonia's afternoon for bridge, and the usuals, namely Agatha Exley, Victoria Brathwaite, and Hortensia Amour, had already arrived. Hortensia was not always faithful in her attendance of the Bridge Club, however, and therefore on some occasions of her absence, poor Henrietta was required to make up the fourth.

Luckily, Hortensia had indeed turned up today, and Henrietta's reluctant participation was therefore not needed. Quickly she donned the little disguise she had concocted and hurried down the servants' staircase in order to avoid a second potential obstacle in the form of Agatha Exley. If Agatha caught sight of her slipping down the main staircase, Henrietta knew she would detain her in a not very subtle attempt at collusion against Elsie. With a continued bizarre lack of perception as to anyone else's state of mind or opinion, Agatha was ever attempting to persuade Henrietta to be a co-conspirator in her endeavors to bring Elsie more deeply into the inner bosom of the Chicago aristocracy, not realizing, apparently—or perhaps simply choosing to overlook the fact—that it was Henrietta herself who was not only responsible for introducing the idea of higher education to Elsie, but who was the one actually funding it, or rather Clive was. It was maddening!

"Surely now that you are ensconced at Highbury," Agatha had more than once twittered to Henrietta, "you can perceive the advantages. You must dissuade her from these ridiculous notions she stubbornly, I might add, insists on pursuing. I'm convinced this is nothing more than a silly phase," she would whisper nervously. "We must persuade her of this, you and I."

Aunt Agatha was absolutely relentless in her pursuit of Elsie, just as Clive was, Henrietta considered, in his bothersome protectiveness of her. Well, she determined, she could be relentless, too.

Having now arrived in the kitchen, it was easy to slip out the back door, where she had arranged for Fritz to wait with the car, the long black skirt of her disguise billowing around her. It wasn't really a disguise, per se, but was rather an old black dress procured, with Edna's help, from one of the junior maids along with some old black oxfords. The finishing touch was a vintage black hat she had persuaded Andrews, Antonia's maid, to dig out of the back of her mistress's closest. It was a Victorian affair, one which Antonia's grandmother, according to Andrews, had apparently worn to the funeral of her husband, the esteemed Theodore J. Hewitt, Sr. It was fitted with a black veil that completely covered her face, and when pinned in place on Henrietta's head, gave her the look of a perfect specter, clad all in black.

Perhaps such lengths at disguise were not really necessary, but she didn't want to take any chances of her plan failing. She had decided it might not be wise to appear again at Dunning as Mrs. Howard, fearing that their probing questions and troublesome removal of Anna might have resulted in some sort of ban on her reentry—though a part of her doubted such instructions would have been written down, much less observed, in the disarray that she witnessed at the front desk during their previous two visits. Even if no formal steps *had* been taken at barring them entrance, she would still have to get past Joe the orderly and wondered, irritably, if he didn't ever take a day off! If he were indeed on duty, she knew he was sure to recognize her. She had first tried on a plain, black scarf and tucked her auburn hair up under it, thinking that if she bent her head, it might be enough of a disguise. In the end, however, she had determined that it was too risky and instead chosen the hat with the veil.

Also, in keeping with the ruse, she had likewise instructed Fritz to drop her off a block south of Dunning, concluding that walking up the long drive would be preferable to being ostentatiously dropped off in front in a Daimler. Before she left, Edna had nervously offered to accompany her, but Henrietta declined her company. Edna begged her then to at least reveal her intended destination, as it was obvious that she couldn't possibly be going shopping downtown with Julia, seeing as she was practically dressed for a funeral! *Was* she going to a funeral? Edna had asked anxiously.

"Of course, I'm not going to a funeral," Henrietta had responded, but did not offer any other information as she pulled on her black gloves. Briefly, she considered telling Edna the plan but decided against it lest Edna, in a moment of weakness (the chances of which were very high), inform Mrs. Howard, or worse, Clive, of her true whereabouts. No, best to go it alone, she resolved, though Edna had whined about what she should tell Mr. Howard should he ask.

Henrietta crisply instructed her to simply tell him the truth, that she didn't know—and then assured poor Edna that she would more than likely be home before Clive and that no one, therefore, would be the wiser.

Now, however, as she gingerly stepped out of the car onto Oak Park Avenue, she reconsidered her decision, thinking that having a companion along might not have been such a bad idea. Well, it was too late now, she sighed. She said a quick good-bye to Fritz, telling him she should only be an hour at most, and pulled the veil down over her face. She walked quickly down the street toward the big iron gates but paused just outside, steeling herself and looking uneasily at the guard booth. From this vantage point, she could see that there was a pedestrian gate just to the left of the main gates, which she hadn't noticed the other day.

She took several deep breaths and then began her approach, her body involuntarily bending slightly forward out of anxiety as she walked. She quickly realized, however, that this position had the advantage of probably making her look more like an old woman. She endeavored to further adopt this role by concentrating on slowing her pace to match. Again, not much skill seemed required, that or she was brilliant in her performance, as the guard at the gate merely jerked his thumb in the direction of the pedestrian gate without so much as a second glance, the newspaper in front of him claiming the better part of his attention.

Keeping her head down, Henrietta walked slowly toward it, where she spied another guard whose back was to her. He appeared to be throwing what looked to be breadcrumbs at a squirrel who hovered nearby. At Henrietta's approach, the squirrel scampered away, and the guard turned back toward the gate, looking rather disappointed.

"Just visitin'?" he asked, pulling the gate open.

Henrietta merely nodded and shuffled through, sweat trickling down her back now, and could not help but jump a little when the gate clanged shut behind her.

The driveway up to the main building was rather long, and she used the time to try to slow her breathing and rapid pulse. She wasn't sure why she was so nervous. Surely talking to Nurse Collins, despite what she might or might not reveal, wouldn't be unpleasant in and of itself, she reasoned, remembering how kind she had been previously. And Henrietta was pretty sure that in coming at this hour, she would avoid Nurse Harding, so she shouldn't be worried about that. Upon closer reflection, she supposed her anxiety must have something to do with her previous temporary incarceration with Elsie and poor Anna. She tried to remind herself that she had not, in fact, been locked in, that she was free to go at any time and that she had *chosen* to stay on the ward with Anna. When she thought of it this way, she became calm, but it was a fleeting calm, only lasting a few seconds before she was back to taking deep breaths, feeling like she couldn't get enough air.

Stop it! she scolded herself, envisioning what Clive would say if he were here. But that was no good, either, as she knew that he would certainly have some choice things to say at this moment, namely that this was unnecessary and foolhardy to boot. Perhaps he was right, she considered, pausing just outside the main doors. Perhaps this really *was* a bad idea . . . she could still turn back . . .

No, she resolved. She had come this far. She would quickly talk to Nurse Collins, who would hopefully dispel her doubts, maybe say hello to poor Mrs. Goodman, and then go. Doubtless she would be back home before Clive even arrived, as she had told Edna, at which point she would confess all, she decided. Yes, that's what she would do, she determined in an attempt to shake her nagging guilt and unease. And so, with this penitential compromise with herself, she entered the asylum.

The interior was unusually quiet and dim, which unnerved Henrietta more than the chaos had on her previous visits. None of the big wooden double doors that led to the various wards were propped open today, so that no sound—no mutterings or bangs or groans—could be heard from within. The stench was still there, though, as was the thick feeling of despair that seemed to emanate from every surface, even from the dull, peeling walls themselves. It was a sort of sad heaviness that hung over everything and which was nearly impossible to shrug off.

Henrietta approached the desk, behind which sat an unfamiliar nurse. After the pains she had gone through to disguise herself, Joe, almost disappointingly, was likewise not present. She let out a deep sigh as she looked down at her gown; she had apparently gone through all this effort for nothing!

In a low voice, she asked to see Mrs. Goodman, on Ward 3C, she believed, and though the nurse raised an eyebrow, probably because no one had ever come asking to see poor Mrs. Goodman, she signaled for the orderly on duty to take her up. "Sign in first, though," the nurse instructed her. Henrietta didn't recall having to sign in before. She assumed, though, that some staff were perhaps more lax than others in their enforcement of the protocols, so she did as instructed.

Henrietta silently followed the orderly up the stairs, keeping her black veil over her face in case she did happen to run into Nurse Harding, and tried to concentrate on what her first action would be. With every step they took, however, she found it increasingly more difficult to think clearly. Indeed, by the time they reached the top and the orderly was bending to unlock the door, she was almost panicking. She grabbed hold of the railing, fearing that she might fall backward, but it was loose and her hand slipped. Instinctively, she grabbed the orderly's arm instead to keep steady.

"Hey!" he said, looking at her curiously. "You all right, lady?"

"Yes, I'm . . . I'm fine. Just a little winded, I suppose," she said, trying to catch her breath. The door stood open now, but she didn't move from where she stood, her hand still on the orderly's arm. "You goin' in, or not?" he asked impatiently.

"Yes, of course," Henrietta said weakly and made her legs move her forward. She stood just inside the door, forcing herself to breathe in through her nose and exhale slowly. She held her hands to stop them from trembling as the orderly closed and locked the door, the key scraping in the lock. "Just calm down," Henrietta muttered, determined to find Nurse Collins as quickly as possible.

Oddly, however, there was no nurse present behind the desk. The usual assortment of patients were sitting or mingling in the common area, though Henrietta thought that there seemed fewer of them—or was she just imagining it? Where was everyone? She glanced down one of the hallways and wondered if maybe some of the patients had been removed to their rooms and put to bed for a nap; after all, it was midafternoon and what else did they have to do, poor things? She turned her attention back to the dayroom, assessing the ones left behind, and was unexplainably relieved to see Mrs. Goodman among them. She was seated at the end of the row of chairs against the far wall, and by the way she was leaning dangerously close to her neighbor, she appeared to be sound asleep as well.

Henrietta fought her desperate desire to simply call out for Nurse Collins. For one thing, she didn't want to wake the dozing residents, especially Mrs. Goodman, as she didn't want to stop to listen to her crazy ramblings just at the moment. She would perhaps do that later when she had gotten the information she had come for. Besides that, what if Nurse Harding was still on duty? She didn't want to risk calling attention to herself just yet. In fact, it occurred to her as she walked softly toward the nurse's desk, that this might be the perfect chance to have another look around. Maybe even in the stock room? she thought temptingly. Maybe *she* could find the mysterious brown bottle of cyanide, she hoped, though she admitted this was unlikely given the number of times Ida herself had supposedly searched for it. Still, she thought excitedly, it was worth a look . . .

Hastily, she removed her veil and made her way around the desk, glancing at the open ledger. She considered stopping to take another look through it, but to what end? And besides, she considered, she might never get such a perfect chance to search the stock room. She paused just outside the door, listening, but no sound was heard from

within, and no light shone out from underneath. Quietly, she turned
the handle and was surprised that it was unlocked. If it indeed held
medications, surely it should be locked more than any other door?
Perhaps it was kept unlocked because a nurse normally sat at the
desk?

Whatever the case, she gently opened the door. It was dark inside
and smelled faintly musty and medicinal. A bit of light shone in from
the dayroom, however, enough for her to be able to perceive a single
lightbulb hanging in the center of the room from a fraying brown
fabric cord. She reached for the thin string hanging alongside it and
pulled. The room now lit by the dim glow of the bulb, she quickly
closed the door behind her and looked around, trying to decide
where to start. She knew she had little time and wished she had a
way to keep a lookout. With the door closed, she felt more nervous
and jumpy, imagining Nurse Harding flinging it open at any moment
and catching her in the act. She considered leaving it open just a
crack, but then decided against it, thinking that the light might catch
someone's attention sooner.

She would just have to act fast. Along one wall ran a counter of
sorts, below which were many drawers of all sizes. Above the counter
was a sort of hutch with beveled glass doors, which appeared to be
the main storage unit for the medications. It held various bottles and
jars of liquids or powders and small boxes of different sizes as well.
Along the opposite wall ran several wooden shelves that went almost
to the ceiling and which appeared to house a whole assortment of
items that did not seem arranged in any particular order. Henrietta
looked from one wall to the other and sighed. How was she to find a
small bottle of cyanide among all of this? If Ida had already searched
this room multiple times, what more did she hope to find?

Still, she decided to give it a try and moved toward the hutch filled
with medications, deciding to rule out the obvious place first. The
glass doors were equipped with small locks, Henrietta saw, but a small
brass key sat at the ready in one of them. Henrietta turned it easily
and opened one of the doors. She started at the top and went across,

. reading each taped-on paper label as best she could: Mercurochrome, Chloroform, Ergoapiol, Nembutal, Laudanum, Salts of Bromine, Castor Oil, Sulfa, Norodin/Methamphetamine . . . nothing. Her heart gave a little leap, though, when her eyes rested on a brown bottle at the back, but she was disappointed when she pulled it down only to see that it had a label: Tincture of Iodine. She was about to put it back when she thought to smell it. Carefully, she unscrewed the cap and gingerly put it up to her nose. Her head jerked back at the familiarly abrasive odor of iodine. She screwed the cap back on and replaced it on the shelf. She opened the other door and after a quick perusal, saw nothing unusual there, either. With a deep breath and a glance at the door, she decided to move on to the drawers.

She put her hand on the thick brass drawer pull of the top drawer and pulled, but it barely moved, stuck in place in the cabinet. She yanked, then, and it opened, distressingly accompanied by a loud screech as the wood rubbed against wood. Henrietta froze in place, her heart racing as she listened carefully for approaching footsteps, but she heard nothing. Carefully, she pulled it out just a little farther and peered inside at its contents. Why was the lighting in here so bad? Shouldn't it be brighter for the nurses having to dispense medication? she wondered. Her big hat, she realized, was also contributing to the dimness by blocking out whatever little light there was. Hurriedly, she unpinned the hat and placed it on the counter, glad to be rid of the heavy thing.

At first glance, the drawer seemed to only be filled with rubber stoppers and corks of various sizes. Henrietta rummaged through them, beads of sweat forming on her neck, but she found nothing. Slowly she opened the drawer beside it, which mercifully did not stick or make a noise, and found rolls of bandages. She pulled it all the way out and searched the back, again finding nothing. She went on this way, as quickly as she could, pulling out all the drawers and rifling through them to no avail. She was surprised, actually, as she went along, to see how random and unorganized they were. Elsie would have a hay day in here, Henrietta mused.

Determining that there was nothing to be found on the cabinet side of the room, Henrietta turned toward the shelves with a heavy sigh. These would be a much more daunting endeavor, as they reached almost to the ceiling and were packed to overflowing with random items. She stood in the middle of the room, her hands on her hips, staring up. From where she stood, the upper shelves seemed to house what looked like extra bedding. Hiding a bottle of cyanide up there would be perfect, Henrietta guessed, but not exactly practical. Wouldn't the murderer have chosen a hiding spot with easier access? Still, she should probably have a look, but how did anyone get up there, anyway? she wondered, looking around. She spotted an old step stool in the corner and determined that must be the means, though it didn't look tall enough for a person to be able to reach the top, even with its help. She didn't relish dragging it over to the shelves and climbing it, particularly as she was still feeling a bit dizzy, so she decided it would be her last resort and started to search the other shelves first.

They contained a whole assortment of supplies and implements. Besides the bedding at the top, there were a few blankets at the far end, closest to the wall and stacks of haphazardly folded towels, stuffed hurriedly on the shelves by the look of it, and various pieces of equipment whose purpose Henrietta could only guess at. One large gray box looked particularly ominous with wires and cords coming out of it and a whole array of dials and switches. She shuddered to think what it was used for. She moved past it and rifled through enamel bedpans, basins, rubber tubing, glass trays, suction bulbs, wooden crutches of differing sizes, and other medical oddities; still she found nothing. She moved toward the towels and other linens, then, gingerly sticking her hand behind them and brushing it blindly along the back wall, hoping she wouldn't discover anything else besides what she was looking for, such as a spider or, worse, a rat.

Fortunately—or unfortunately—she found nothing and took a step back. There was nothing left to search except the very top shelf and the space beneath the bottom shelf, under which various open, wooden crates had been shoved. Henrietta hated the thought of pulling all of them out and rummaging through them, but it was better than having to climb the stepstool.

She pulled on the first crate. It was lighter than she had expected, though, and she was thrown off balance and stumbled backwards. She caught herself before she fell, though, righting herself, and then bent over the crate to look closer. It appeared to be full of rumpled clothing. She lifted the top item, which turned out to be a man's suit coat, dirty. Gingerly, she pulled out the next item, which was a waistcoat, and under that was a crumpled lady's hat. Setting these items aside, she was able to unearth more, most of which were smaller and therefore had fallen toward the bottom. There was a scuffed pocket watch, a comb, even a small bible. These must be the personal effects of the patients, Henrietta realized, either those of the current patients or the ones who already died. Nurse Collins had said that Liesel had few personal effects, but Henrietta wondered if perhaps they missed something or maybe she lied? But to what end?

Henrietta began to paw through the items looking for something that might have belonged to Liesel, but what? Besides perhaps something written in German, she would hardly recognize anything of the poor woman's, she realized, having never known her. She fought the temptation to pick up and carefully examine each item, reminding herself that the minutes were ticking by. She felt sad, as she had when she cleaned out old Helen's cottage last summer, of the transitory nature of life. How all of one's treasures simply ended up in a box at the end of the day, considered to be just junk by everyone else who beheld it. Her hands continued to listlessly pick through the items, nearly forgetting her mission, when they inadvertently came upon a set of teeth, causing her to recoil. What was she doing? she scolded herself. She had to keep moving!

Quickly she stuffed all of the contents from the first crate back into it, and, kneeling on the floor, pulled out the other crate. This one was heavier, which, in and of itself, suggested that it be discounted as a likely place for the murderer to hide the poison. Too heavy and awkward to pull in and out, but she decided to search it anyway. Like the other crate, this one, too, held various items of clothing and personal effects, which Henrietta pulled out rapidly without perusing them and tossed them on the ground. As she searched through, Henrietta was again surprised, or not surprised, really, that there was not a better system of organization in such a big institution. How could the staff possibly remember which things belonged to whom? But then again, she remembered, that once here, most never left.

She lifted a large brown handbag and was in the process of setting it to the side when her eyes fell upon the item lying beneath it, which was a book—*A Child's Garden of Verses*. Henrietta paused, thinking. Could this be the book Anna claimed to have lost here? Gingerly, Henrietta pulled it out, excited to have potentially found something, even if it was only this. She opened the front cover and read the inscription—in Elsie's handwriting!

> *To Anna ~*
> *Something for the times when you find*
> *yourself alone and in want of a friend.*
> *~With fondness, Elsie Von Harmon*

Ah-ha! she thought and clasped the book to her chest. Obviously, Nurse Harding had not looked very hard for it the other day, Henrietta thought. Typical. Setting the book on the floor next to her, she was about to stuff everything back in the crate when her eye suddenly fell upon a small brown bottle sitting innocently among the junk of the dead or dispossessed. Henrietta stared at it as if it were the spider or the rat she had minutes before been afraid of finding. Her heart racing, she reached out finally and picked it up carefully, several small items sliding into the hole created by its removal. Holding it away from her at first, as if it were dangerous just by proximity, she examined it. No label, no markings of any kind to describe the liquid she could see inside through the thick brown glass. Slowly, she unscrewed the top and gingerly held her nose over it, her stomach roiling when she caught a whiff of almond.

My God! she thought wildly. This must be it!

It took a moment for Henrietta to fully grasp the magnitude of this. Though she had come here today with the purpose of proving Ida's—and her own—suspicions, she realized now that a part of her hadn't really believed it, or hadn't wanted to believe it. It seemed like a puzzle before, trying to piece it all together, but now it didn't seem such a game. It was chillingly real, and she was suddenly very much afraid. Somewhere in this place, a murderer walked. Oh, what should she do? she thought desperately. How could she get out?

Before she could figure out the answers to her own frantic questions, however, she heard footsteps approaching, fast and clipped. Without thinking, she quickly stood and hastily set the bottle on the counter behind her hat, just as Nurse Collins appeared in the doorway, looking surprised.

Henrietta breathed a sigh of relief. "Oh, thank God it's you," she said.

Nurse Collins's face was one of concern as her eyes darted around the room, resting momentarily on the hat before coming back to Henrietta. "Mrs. . . . Howard, isn't it?" she asked. "Are you all right? You look like you've seen a ghost. What are you doing back here?"

"I . . . I was looking for you, actually," Henrietta said, leaning a hand against the counter to support herself. Standing up so quickly had made her feel light-headed again.

"Back here?"

"I . . . I'm pretty sure something terrible is going on."

"What do you mean?" Nurse Collins asked, her voice laced with concern as she noiselessly shut the door behind her.

"I hardly know where to begin," Henrietta faltered, trying to steady herself. "I've been doing a little investigating, you might say, and it seems there have been several mysterious deaths around here."

"Mysterious deaths?" Nurse Collins asked, her face contorting slightly. Henrietta could see she had upset her.

"It's just that . . . well, take Liesel Klinkhammer, for example. You remember her, don't you? The German woman we came here to visit?"

Nurse Collins nodded slowly. "Yes. What about her?"

"Well, don't you think there was something odd about her death?" Henrietta continued, disappointed that so far nothing she was saying seemed to register with the woman she had hoped would be her ally. Was she really not aware of what was going on just under her nose? "You must have noticed . . . ?" Henrietta asked, looking at her hopefully. She thought she saw something respondent in Nurse Collins's face, but she couldn't read what it was exactly.

"Let me explain," Henrietta hurried on. "Dr. Ingesson told my husband that Liesel died from complications due to electric shock. But she didn't! I snuck a look in the ledger when I was here the other day and found that Miss Klinkhammer didn't die for almost a week after her last treatment. So it couldn't have been from the electric shock!" she said triumphantly.

"Ah. Yes, well, sometimes things aren't recorded as well as they should be, I must confess," she said plainly, though she looked upset as she said it.

"Be that as it may, there's more," Henrietta said hastily. "You see, I happened to speak with a former employee of this place, Ida Lynde? Do you remember her?"

Nurse Collins's face remained very still, again unreadable. "Yes, I remember her," she said coldly. "She was dismissed. How do you know her?"

"She's the niece of a very good friend of mine. It was quite by accident that I was able to talk with her. She . . . she told me some terrible things," Henrietta said in an urgent whisper.

"She has a record of drinking," Nurse Collins interrupted. "You mustn't believe anything she told you. Please, for your own good," she said, her eyes briefly traveling to the hat again.

Why was she so distracted by the hat? Henrietta wondered. Or had she seen her place the bottle there when she first came in? Something prickled on the edge of her mind, but she tried to ignore it.

"But she's not a drunk!" Henrietta instead plunged on, further upset by the fact that her conspiratorial conversation with Nurse Collins was not going as planned. "Those rumors about her were false! It was Nurse Harding that had it in for her. She was the one who made that up!"

"Now, why would Nurse Harding do a thing like that?" Nurse Collins said, her eyes narrowed.

"She saw the bottle!" Henrietta raced on, while a small part of her brain wondered how she could be so blind as to Nurse Harding's true character. "The bottle of cyanide!" she exclaimed. "And look, here it is! I found it!" she said, reaching for it now. "Someone's been murdering patients. That's what Ida discovered. She found the bottle of cyanide and then the very next day, she discovered that a patient, a Mrs. Leary, had died unexplainably in the night. Ida began to notice more and more odd deaths over time and finally went to Nurse Harding with her concerns. A lot of good that did, as she was dismissed for her troubles. But there was a floater on that night. Do you happen to remember who it was? And it's obvious that Nurse Harding is somehow in on it, isn't it? Though I suppose it really could have been anyone . . . " she said, her voice trailing off in anticipation of what Nurse Collins might say.

Nurse Collins put her hand on her forehead and looked worried, finally, for the first time. She was finally understanding!

"This is terribly unfortunate," she muttered, holding her hand out now for the bottle. Henrietta gladly gave it to her and wiped her hands on her dress as if they were contaminated.

"Yes, it is! But have you really not noticed anything unusual?" Henrietta asked. "I had hoped you would be able to shed some light on this."

"And so you came here tonight? Alone?" Nurse Collins asked. "I barely recognized you." She looked her up and down.

"I . . . I dressed like this on purpose," Henrietta answered, wondering why something this trivial mattered at a moment like this. Something wasn't sitting well. "I didn't want anyone below to recognize me, you see."

"What about at the front desk? Did you sign in? As Mrs. Howard?"

"No! I used a different name!" Henrietta said proudly. "Mrs. Jones."

"I see. Well, that makes things a lot easier, then," she said, slipping the bottle into the front pocket of her pure-white uniform, Henrietta's eyes following it as it disappeared. Something about Nurse Collins's tone alarmed her, and a warning signal went off in her mind. Surely . . .

"What do you mean, easier?" she asked nervously.

Nurse Collins did not respond but instead walked slowly to the shelves and calmly selected a piece of faded red rubber tubing.

"Mrs. Howard, or Mrs. Jones, I should say, I fear you really are quite ill. You're obviously suffering from some sort of delusion."

Henrietta's skin prickled, and she felt a sudden rush of fear as Nurse Collins stepped toward her, the tubing held taut.

"I really must insist you lie down until I can take care of you."

"What are you talking about?" Henrietta asked, panic ripping through her as she stepped backward. "What are you doing?"

"You couldn't just let well enough alone, could you?" Nurse Collins asked bitterly, her face twisting strangely. Before Henrietta could even think what to do next, Nurse Collins lunged toward her and swiftly wrapped the tubing around her wrists, pulling it so tightly that Henrietta cried out from not only the shock of what was happening but from the searing pain of the rubber against her skin.

"It was *you*? Why? Why are you doing this?" Henrietta murmured, cold realization flooding over her, though she was flushed and perspiring.

"Yes, of course it was me," Nurse Collins hissed.

"But . . . but, why? Why murder these people?" she asked, her heart beating wildly

"Murder? Murder is a harsh word," Nurse Collins said sweetly, which unsettled Henrietta all the more. "It's not murder. I'm doing them a favor. Look around you. So much suffering; no one gets better, no family comes to visit them. Rotting away in this hellhole. Surely, you can see it as the mercy that it is?" she asked calmly. "I merely set them free. And as soon as one is removed, another slides into their place. It's endless!" she said, her voice rising a bit now. "They don't want to live! I am an angel of mercy for them," she said, sickeningly reminding Henrietta of Mrs. Goodman's very same words. "What I do is a mercy," she repeated.

"It's still murder!" Henrietta sputtered. "You can't just take life and death into your own hands! How do you know these people don't want to live?" Henrietta fumed, even as she saw a kernel of sense in what Nurse Collins was saying. "You murdered a little girl's mother. You took an oath!"

"An oath to ease people's sufferings," she said calmly, pulling on the tubing that held Henrietta tight. "Which I am doing. But other people don't see it that way, I know, like your friend Ida. I thought I had dealt sufficiently with her, but I see I was wrong. Well, I won't make the same mistake twice," she said, her brow furrowed now as she looked Henrietta over. "It will be fast. You won't even feel anything."

"No! Please," Henrietta begged, her heart exploding in her chest as she tried to twist away. "I won't tell anyone—"

"Too late for that. You're altogether too nosy for your own good. Come," she said, pulling the bottle of cyanide back out from her pocket. "Obviously I can't force you to drink this, so I'll have to make up an injection." Her voice trailed off as she rummaged in one of the drawers with one hand, presumably to find a syringe. "You can't just kill me!" Henrietta cried. "I'll scream!" she threatened. Without waiting for a response, Henrietta let out an ear-piercing scream. "Help!" she screamed. "Help!"

"You can scream all you want," Nurse Collins said unmoved and not even looking up from the syringe she was filling. "No one will hear. Or care. After all, this is an insane asylum. It's full of screams of the already dead." She pulled Henrietta toward her, who continued to struggle to push away.

"You can't get away with this! They'll find my dead body!" Henrietta said in a shrill voice. "Clive will find me," she said, hot tears forming.

She felt dizzy, and the light on the edge of the room was beginning to dim.

"No he won't. There's plenty of places to hide a body here. The whole place is one big tomb," she said, which were the last words Henrietta heard before she sank to the ground.

Chapter 21

"So as I was saying," Bennett said from the far end of the boardroom table where he stood with various charts arranged on easels behind him, "we really should consider divesting ourselves of Kalamazoo. We'll be digging our graves in Detroit if we don't. It's too much of a financial drain. We've been carrying them for too long without a profit."

"Agreed," said another man halfway down the table, as he tapped the various papers splayed out in front of him into a neat stack. "I think we should vote. Any objections to putting it up for a vote, Mr. Howard?"

Clive's face was taut. "Before we vote, I'd like to hear more about the economic implications for the families that would be affected. If we shut down Kalamazoo, where will those—two thousand, did you say?—men find jobs?"

"Mr. Howard, with all due respect," said another man, "that is none of our concern. We have to think of our shareholders. We can't keep the Kalamazoo plant afloat much longer without seeing some sort of profit."

Clive glanced over at Bennett.

"I think what Mr. Howard is saying," Bennett said, clearing his throat, "is that we might consider an alternate employment opportunity to—"

Bennett was then interrupted by a loud buzzing from the large black telephone sitting on the table in front of Clive. Clive frowned at it. Mrs. Novotny, the secretary he had inherited from his father, knew she was not to interrupt board meetings.

"Excuse me, gentlemen," he said, irritated, and picked up the receiver. "Yes?"

"I'm sorry to bother you, Mr. Howard," the high-pitched voice of Mrs. Novotny came through. "But there's a telephone call for you."

"Mrs. Novotny, I told you to hold my calls."

"This one says it's urgent," Mrs. Novotny responded dully.

Clive bit the side of his cheek and tried to push down his sense of dread. He had been distracted all day, feeling that something wasn't quite right. Unfortunately, Madame Pavlovsky's parting words to him the night he had carried Henrietta out of the schoolhouse in a faint still haunted him. "She is in grave danger," Madame Pavlovsky had said in a voice laden with theatrical effect. He had snarled some response to her at the time, thinking that it was an easy, cheap prediction on her part, considering the situation. Since then, however, he had frustratingly not been able to completely shake her words from his mind, a fact that annoyed him to no end. He had of course not related any of this to Henrietta, and he chastised himself for so weakly falling prey to Madame Pavlovsky's quackery. On this particular morning, though, his sense of unease lay heavily on him for some reason, a feeling which had increased as the day went on, so much so that he was even tempted at one point to telephone home just to make sure everything was okay. Before he could, however, Bennett had wanted to review some figures with him before the afternoon meeting, and he let it go.

He looked briefly around the room at the men assembled there, hating the idea of having to stop the meeting for a personal reason, but knowing that he was going to have to.

"Who is it?" he asked brusquely into the receiver, trying to mask his nerves.

"Says it's Adolph Fritz. Claims to be your chauffer," Mrs. Novotny relayed, as if she hadn't a care.

At her words, however, Clive felt as though someone had just punched him in the gut, and he hastily stood up. Henrietta. It must be Henrietta. He leaned a hand on the table and tried to slow his racing heart by telling himself that it could be something as simple as a flat tire, though another part of his brain told him that Fritz would never telephone him for something that trivial. No, something was definitely amiss.

Since his marriage to Henrietta he had instructed Fritz to be a bodyguard of sorts for her, going beyond the role of simple chauffer as a set of eyes for Clive. Frequently, Clive had called him into his study for a private chat to this effect. Fritz was an older, wiser servant who was perfectly suited for this role, at least in Clive's mind. Fritz knew when to remain silent, allowing Henrietta to dictate where she went and when, believing herself to be wholly independent and unobserved, and when to report back to Clive. For example, unbeknown to Henrietta, even to this day, Fritz had reported her trip to the Melody Mill in the city where she had borrowed a gun from Rose. Fritz, of course, had not witnessed the actual handoff of the gun, but had judged that the brevity of Henrietta's visit to such an establishment, not to mention the neighborhood, was worrisome enough to warrant a report to Clive later that night in the study.

Clive therefore was used to the occasional evening report, but Fritz had never actually *telephoned* him, the fact of which nearly crippled Clive now. Something must be seriously wrong.

"I'll take it in my office," Clive snapped and hung up. "Excuse me, gentlemen," he said hurriedly without looking at anyone but Bennett, who held his gaze until Clive pulled it away and strode quickly out of the room. He almost ran to his office, passing by Mrs. Novotny's desk and barking out, "Which line?"

"Two," she said, slowly filing her nails.

Clive burst into his office and picked up the receiver without even taking the time to turn on the lights.

"Hello? Fritz?" he said.

"Sorry to disturb you, Mr. Howard, but I thought you should know."

"Where is she?"

"She went into Dunning over an hour ago, and she hasn't come out, sir. Don't like the feel of it."

"Jesus Christ. I'm on my way," Clive said and banged down the receiver.

Without Fritz or a car at his disposal, Clive was forced to take a cab, which painfully inched north in the late afternoon traffic. "Hurry up, man!" Clive said, slamming his hand on the leather seat. "I could run there faster than this!" he grumbled, throwing himself against the back seat.

At one point, he considered flagging down a patrol car, but he knew from experience that he would not be taken seriously. After all, it wasn't a crime for someone to walk into an institution such as Dunning for a visit, nor was it cause for concern, especially as only an hour had passed. Likewise, he did not have the power to commandeer a squad car. *Damn it!* he thought, as he fretfully ran his hand through his hair and looked out the window at the buildings on Irving Park Road slowly passing by. He attempted to calm himself by running various scenarios through his mind, formulating a plan for each. Why had she gone to Dunning? he thought miserably. It obviously had something to do with this woman, this former nurse she had met at the Hennessey's party . . . Ida was her name? Based on what Mr. Hennessey had told him, Clive had dismissed her ramblings about finding cyanide and patients being murdered as fantastical. He had thought Henrietta understood that when he explained it, but obviously she had not. Oh, why was she forever going off on wild-goose chases? he thought irritably, though a small part of his brain reminded him that she was right more often than not. *Damn it!* he fumed again. Why had she gone alone? And why was he so worried? So what if she had gone into Dunning? If he really didn't think there was anything to these wild theories, then why did he feel so uneasy?

The farther north they went, the blessedly faster they were able to go. The sky was aglow with smears of pink and orange, like a child's painting, as if nothing at all were wrong in the world. Once they turned onto Oak Park Avenue, Clive spotted the Daimler parked on the side of the road, just down from the entrance.

"This will do," he said to the cab driver, leaning forward and quickly tossing some money onto the front seat. He opened the door before the car had even fully stopped and jumped out.

As if on cue, Fritz stepped crisply out of the Daimler. "I'm very sorry, sir," he said.

"It's not your fault, Fritz," Clive said, clapping him hard on the shoulder. "You did as you were instructed. Any sign of her?" he asked wildly, his adrenaline pumping, as he looked up at Dunning. He needed to be calm, he told himself. He needed to think logically and tried to keep the sketchy plan he had come up with on the way over in the forefront of his mind.

"No, sir, unfortunately not."

"I'm going in."

"Shall I come with you, sir?"

"No, you stay here in case she comes out. Keep a sharp eye."

"Yes, sir," Fritz said with a nod.

Clive began walking briskly toward the main gate. "If I'm not out in an hour, call the cops," he called out over his shoulder.

"Very good, sir. Good luck, sir," Fritz called from where he stood beside the big maroon car.

As Clive approached the gate, he began to try to assess the situation in front of him. The big gate was closed, as usual, and there was a lone guard sitting in the little booth, again reading the newspaper by the look of it. As he got closer, Clive observed that it wasn't the same guard as he had encountered the other day. This might be in his favor, he decided. He was close enough now to see steam coming from what looked like a thermos cup perched somewhere inside.

The guard looked up as Clive approached and slid open the little pane of glass beside him. "Visiting hours is over," he called out, leaning his head out of the booth.

"Yes, I know," Clive tried to say casually. "But I'm quite certain my wife is still in there," he said, nodding toward the hulking edifice. "Visiting, you see. She must have lost track of time. You know women," he said, trying to chuckle, but the man did not join in.

"They gives 'em plenty of warning. Bells going off every fifteen minutes the last hour. Nuisance is what it is."

"Well, mind if I just go in and look for her? You could accompany me if you wish."

"Can't do that. Can't leave my post and can't let anyone in past five."

Clive let out a deep breath, trying to remain calm. "Can you at least telephone someone?" he asked impatiently, eyeing the tall fence and wondering if he could scale it. The metal spikes at the top probably meant no.

"I s'pose," the guard said, after a pause. "Don't think it will do any good, though," he said reluctantly. He picked up the receiver of the telephone inside his booth and looked back out at Clive, both of them staring at each other in the ensuing silence. Clive tapped his foot impatiently as they waited for someone to answer.

"Look—" Clive began.

"Yeah, Ralph?" the guard said finally. "All the visitors signed out?" He paused, listening to whatever Ralph was saying. "What's her name?" he asked Clive now.

"Henrietta Howard," Clive said impatiently.

"Henrietta Howard," the guard said into the receiver. "Okay, thanks, Ralph," he said and hung up. "No one by that name," the guard said with a shrug. "Sure she came here?" He wagged his thumb over his shoulder. "Probably went shopping," he said and inched himself back onto his stool, apparently assuming that his exchange with Clive to now be over.

"Look," Clive said desperately as he pulled his fake badge out of his jacket. "I'm with the police, actually. I have reason to believe that there's a woman in danger inside. You must let me in, or I'll be forced to call for backup."

"Well, why didn't you say that in the first place?" the guard said irritably as he again slid off his stool and emerged from the booth. "You don't look like no cop," he said skeptically as he adjusted his cap. He led Clive over to the pedestrian gate and then reached for the heavy ring of keys hung on his belt loop. Easily, he selected the key to the small side gate, opening it only a crack, before he paused. "Let me see that badge," he said with a furrowed brow as he held out his hand for it.

Clive did not hand it over but merely held it up, hoping a quick flash of it would suffice. Unfortunately, however, the guard was somehow able to read it.

"Hey! That's Winnetka police!" he said. "Tryin' to pull a fast one? You ain't got no jurisdiction down here!"

"Oh, yes I do," Clive said, thinking quickly and hunching forward with his good shoulder to take a running pass at the slightly open gate. The guard, taken completely by surprise, stumbled backward as Clive plowed into him and burst through the gate. In a sprint, Clive took off running toward the main building.

"Hey!" the guard shouted after him, righting himself. "Come back! You can't go in there!" he shouted again. "I'm calling for backup!" But Clive could barely hear him by this time; he was almost to the main doors. He ran up the front stairs, skipping steps as he went. Furiously, he tugged on both doors. Locked. He banged on them and shouted, "Open up! Police!" He banged on the doors again. "Open up!" he shouted again.

Out of breath and distraught, he gave one of the doors a kick, but to no avail. He stepped back, his foot throbbing now, and looked back toward the gate to see if the guard was following. He could see no one, however, which probably meant that the guard had instead stayed in the booth to call for backup, as he had threatened. Clive hoped that the "backup" was the Chicago police and not the man's fellow guards alerted from wherever they were stashed on the property. Though it didn't look good—a man breaking into Dunning with a fake Winnetka police badge—it might be easier to explain himself to the city cops, who might know him from his days on the force, rather than the lunkheads employed here.

"Henrietta!" he shouted, stepping back onto the grass so that he could see the upper floors. "Henrietta!" he screamed, but no one and nothing responded.

Chapter 22

When Henrietta awoke, she found she was on a strangely uncomfortable bed in a room she did not recognize. It took her a moment to realize where she was. *Dunning.* Oh, God, she was in Dunning! She moved to sit up and found that her wrists were tied to the bed. Panic rushed through her, and she twisted and turned, trying to free herself. A cry for help was on her lips, but she miraculously thought better of it before she did so and instead clamped her lips shut.

It was all coming back to her now.

Nurse Collins, the stock room, the cyanide. She must have fainted, she guessed, and looked around the room as best she could from where she lay. She appeared to be in one of the bedchambers, a patient in a long row of beds, all of them seemingly occupied with sleeping lumps. By the light coming in from the hallway, she observed that her clothes had been removed and she was wearing a hospital gown only, with no shoes or stockings.

Why was she here? she tried to work out, painfully attempting to think back to the last thing she remembered. In her mind she saw Nurse Collins filling the syringe with cyanide. Had she injected her? But why wasn't she already dead, then? she worried, frantically pulling at her bonds at the thought. Perhaps it wasn't instantaneous?

"Help!" she said to one of the lumps in a low voice. "Can someone please help me?" she asked with quiet desperation, not wanting to attract Nurse Collins's attention, wherever she was.

"Shut up!" one of the lumps shouted.

Henrietta tried peering into the darkness. "Can someone untie me?" she asked in a strained voice.

"Shut up, or you'll get what's comin' to ya," snarled the same lump.

"Yeah, shut up," several others mumbled.

"Shhh!" Henrietta hushed.

"Don't shush me!" cried out a woman near her.

Henrietta bit her lip and remained silent. She was afraid now that they were on the brink of working themselves up into some sort of shouting match, which would surely attract Nurse Collins's attention. Her heart racing, Henrietta lay as still as a mouse, praying they would follow suit and quiet down.

She closed her eyes, trying desperately to think of what to do and, more importantly, to assess if she could feel the poison coursing through her. She was sweating and having difficulty breathing, but she didn't think this was the effect of cyanide. She knew little of poisons, but she was pretty sure that had she been injected she would indeed be already dead. With these thoughts swirling around in her mind, she nearly screamed, then, when she felt a bony hand on her shoulder. Quickly she opened her eyes and saw what appeared to be a large black vulture standing by her bed. Her heart nearly bursting out of her chest, she eventually realized that it was not a vulture, but only Mrs. Goodman, peering at her with her large, hollow eyes, and somehow wearing what looked very much like Antonia's hat.

"You're ready now for the angel to come to you, aren't you?" she asked.

"Mrs. Goodman!" Henrietta whispered, relief flooding through her, so much so that she almost went numb. "I'm so glad you're here! Can you . . . can you help me? Untie me?"

"Untie you? Why?" the old woman asked, and Henrietta could see even in the shadowy light that she looked puzzled.

"Because . . . because I've got to get out of here!" Henrietta tried to say without becoming hysterical.

"But the angel is coming . . . " Mrs. Goodman said, glancing at the hallway. "She will be angry if I interfere again. I heard you scream before and interrupted the angel in her work. She was not happy with me, so she brought you here until she can minister to you. She does not like anyone to watch her as she frees souls. This must be done in secret, she says. But I'm to watch you until she can come. So I'm watching you," she said, opening her eyes wide like an owl.

So that was it! Henrietta realized. Mrs. Goodman must have come into the stock room just before Nurse Collins had been able to administer the cyanide. Henrietta offered up a silent prayer of thanks—but now how was she ever going to get out of this? she wondered wildly. Surely Nurse Collins would reappear any moment . . . !

"But there's been a mistake," Henrietta said, madly pulling at her cords again but to no avail. She stopped straining and lay back on the bed, trying to calm herself. She decided to take a gamble. "Mrs. Goodman, you must untie me. I'm to go to the golden city," she said, trying to remember Mrs. Goodman's fantastical story. She glanced over at Mrs. Goodman, who was staring at her as if in disbelief. "I was instructed," Henrietta tried to say convincingly. "You are to show me, they said. You are to be my guide."

Mrs. Goodman's face, half of which was illuminated by the light from the hallway and half of which remained in darkness, remained oddly rigid, as if she were frozen, much like when Henrietta inadvertently came upon her lying in her bedroom the other day. It momentarily struck her as wholly bizarre that they seemed to have now switched places.

Finally, she spoke. "Who told you that?" Mrs. Goodman hissed, causing Henrietta to fear she had said the wrong thing. "Was it the cat?"

Henrietta hesitated, trying to decide how to answer. "No, it was . . . it was the rats," she ventured.

"The rats? No!" Mrs. Goodman whispered, looking confused. Her eyes darted toward the hallway.

"They are waiting for me," Henrietta continued. She felt a twinge of guilt in playing on this woman's insanity, but what else could she do?

"I see," Mrs. Goodman said almost absently and then went silent, apparently thinking something over in her mind.

Valuable seconds ticked by, and Henrietta was tempted to speak again, wanting to urge the woman on. She sensed she should wait, however, and forced herself to remain silent.

"But what about the angel?" Mrs. Goodman finally asked slowly. "She will be very angry . . . "

Henrietta's mind raced for something to say, trying to remember what Gunther had told her about this myth, if it even was the same myth at all. Well, what did it matter? she concluded hurriedly.

"The king commands it," she tried to say sternly and hoped Mrs. Goodman did not hear the accompanying catch in her throat.

Blessedly, something seemed to shift then in Mrs. Goodman's face. "Yes . . . yes, this is true," she said hesitantly. "I see. Yes, you must come." She pulled back the flimsy sheet covering Henrietta's lower half. Henrietta's heart leapt for joy, amazed that it had been that easy to fool the woman.

Mrs. Goodman mercifully bent to untie the cloth holding one of her wrists. It came undone with surprising ease, which made Henrietta suspect they were simple knots tied very quickly and that Nurse Collins had probably not anticipated Henrietta waking up before she returned, which only increased Henrietta's sense of panic. Quickly, she turned onto her side to try to help Mrs. Goodman with the second knot, but she stopped cold at the sound of clipped footsteps coming down the hall.

"The angel must not find us," Mrs. Goodman whispered apprehensively. "She will be very angry."

Henrietta hurriedly flung herself flat onto the bed and put her free arm back by her side. "Hide!" she whispered to Mrs. Goodman, who obediently backed into the shadows in one corner of the room. Henrietta's heart was beating so hard in her chest that she was sure Nurse Collins would hear it in the hallway. A layer of sweat broke out on her body, and she could feel it actually dripping down her back. Silently she lay there, listening, barely daring to breathe, her lungs burning. The steps came closer and closer, and just as Henrietta thought she was going to scream, the steps went past the chamber where she lay and sounded like they entered a different room farther down. Henrietta let out a long, deep breath, trying to calm herself again and stop the tears that had gathered in the corners of her eyes.

"Mrs. Goodman," she whispered after a few moments. "We have to hurry!"

Mrs. Goodman emerged from the shadows, nervously rubbing her hands. She hurried over to the side of the bed where Henrietta was still tied. Swiftly she bent to undo the knot, but then abruptly stopped and slowly straightened. "No, this isn't right," she said, throwing Henrietta into a panic again.

"Please," she begged . . .

"It is not the right time for the journey. The moon is not aligned," Mrs. Goodman said cryptically.

"It . . . it doesn't matter," Henrietta said, rolling onto her side again and trying to untie the knot herself. "We . . . we have to listen to the rats," she whispered fiercely. "Remember?"

"Yes," Mrs. Goodman nodded. "Yes, you're right. But the oracle did not foretell this," she said, as the bond fell to the floor.

Henrietta quickly stood up, rubbing her wrists and trying to steady herself. She looked around for her clothes, but they were nowhere in sight. Neither was there any wardrobe or table. She couldn't take the time to search for them, she decided agitatedly. She would have to go as she was. She tiptoed toward the doorway and peeked out into the hallway, Mrs. Goodman following close behind. Now what was she to do? Getting free of the bed was just the first of her problems, she realized, breathing heavily. How was she to get off the ward without a key?

"Come," Mrs. Goodman said, taking one of Henrietta's hands in her own. Mrs. Goodman's hand was so cold and bony against her own fevered skin that she felt as if she were being led by a skeleton. Antonia's black hat was still absurdly perched on Mrs. Goodman's head, and Henrietta found herself staring at the intricate threadwork that wound around the brim, wondering distractedly how a living person could still be this cold.

"Where are we going?" she finally whispered, giving her head a shake to clear these thoughts as they crept along.

Mrs. Goodman did not answer but pulled Henrietta behind her. They paused at the first chamber doorway they came to, hesitating to cross lest Nurse Collins see them. Like Henrietta, Mrs. Goodman must have deduced by listening to Nurse Collins's footsteps earlier that she had stopped somewhere nearby. Tentatively, Mrs. Goodman inched her head ever so carefully past the doorframe to peer into the dark room. Determining that the coast was clear, they slunk past. They continued to do this before each doorway until they finally reached the common area.

"Do you have the keys?" Henrietta whispered frantically as they stood huddled alone together. No patients remained in the dayroom at this hour. "Do you know where they are?"

"Keys?" Mrs. Goodman asked, as if that was a ridiculous question. "This way," she said, leading her toward the storage room. "This is the way out . . . "

"No!" Henrietta hissed and groaned internally, quickly realizing how stupid she was to think that Mrs. Goodman could lead her to safety. She didn't have any more of an idea of how to get out than she did! It was the blind leading the blind! Henrietta chided herself and looked desperately around the room now for something . . . anything!

"Come, this way," Mrs. Goodman repeated, attempting to pull her. Henrietta pulled back, managing to free herself from what turned out to be Mrs. Goodman's amazingly strong grip.

"No! I don't want to go in there," Henrietta whispered, though it did occur to her that her clothes might be in there. But was going in to look for them worth the risk of being trapped in there? Well, she countered with herself, wasn't she trapped anyway?

"But you must!" Mrs. Goodman insisted, looking puzzled. "The tunnel is there!"

"The tunnel?" Henrietta asked in a low voice, trying to remember Mrs. Goodman's ramblings. Yes, the tunnel . . . the tunnel to the golden underground city, wasn't it? But what could she possibly be referring to? Henrietta wondered, knowing as she did, having just been in there and searching every corner of it, that there was no other way out and certainly no tunnel. Clearly, this was part of Mrs. Goodman's delusion . . .

All thoughts were ceased, however, when she heard fast footsteps from farther down the hallway. Terror instantly returned to her heart as she looked around for somewhere to hide! Behind the desk?

"Quickly!" Mrs. Goodman hissed from where she stood just in front of the stock room door, waving furiously at Henrietta. Without thinking, Henrietta rushed toward her and ran into the stock room after her. Perhaps they could hide in here, she thought wildly, thinking of the bedding on the top shelf. For a moment, though, they remained motionless, huddled together, listening. The light had been left on, probably in Nurse Collins's haste to drag her out before, but Henrietta did not dare to even move her arm to turn it off.

"Mrs. Goodman?" they heard Nurse Collins call out loudly. "Damn it!" they heard her say then.

Henrietta guessed that she was just discovering Henrietta was no longer in her bed. "Where are you?" Nurse Collins called loudly, her footsteps coming closer, pausing every few feet to presumably look into each bedchamber.

Mrs. Goodman dropped her embrace of Henrietta and put a finger to her lips. Silently, she moved toward the corner where the step stool rested. Carefully she lifted it up and set it to the side, revealing, to Henrietta's astonishment, a small hatch cut into the floor. How had she not seen that before?

Mrs. Goodman clasped the thick ring at the edge of it and pulled on the heavy door. Thankfully, the hatch did not make any noise as it opened, which suggested that perhaps it was opened frequently. "Here!" Mrs. Goodman whispered, beckoning her with her hand. "Down you go!"

Henrietta gasped. So this was "the tunnel" Mrs. Goodman had been referring to?

"Hurry!" she hissed.

Henrietta stepped closer and stood at the edge of the hole cut into the floor. As she bent over it to peer inside, a cold dampness hit her face. She could not see anything down there but utter blackness. "Where does it lead?" she asked, taking a step back.

"To the golden city, of course!" Mrs. Goodman said. "Why do you hesitate?" she urged.

Henrietta's stomach churned. Anything could be down there. And who knew how far it went? She could kill herself! Was it a waste chute? Or a coal chute? she wondered, imagining how horrible— probably fatal—it would be if she landed on a pile of coal. Though a coal chute in a stock room didn't really make sense. Maybe it was where Nurse Collins stuffed bodies? she wondered, her heart racing. She fought down an urge to retch.

"Hurry!" Mrs. Goodman said in a frenzied voice.

"I know you're in there! Mrs. Goodman! Are you hiding that woman?" Nurse Collins called out from the other side of the door.

Henrietta hurriedly sat down on the edge of the hole and gingerly dangled her legs into the dark cavity. The air coming from it smelled musty and dank. "What's down there?" Henrietta asked worriedly. "Have you gone down? Will I hurt myself?"

"No, it's soft—" Mrs. Goodman began before Nurse Collins banged open the door.

"There you are! What are you doing?" she demanded, her eyes wide at the sight of Henrietta already half in the hole.

"Go!" Mrs. Goodman shouted, and with one last look, Henrietta jumped.

Chapter 23

Henrietta could not help but scream as she dropped through the darkness, her hands and feet kicking wildly, her heart in her throat. It seemed like she was falling a long, long way, and she tried to brace her body for the impact. The bottom came sooner than she expected, however, and she landed with a thud on a pile of something surprisingly soft, just as Mrs. Goodman had said she would.

She lay there for a few seconds, dazed, staring up at the hole through which she had come. She couldn't make out Mrs. Goodman or Nurse Collins; all she could see was a small square of light, which was, by the look of it, the only thing illuminating the dark, dank room she now found herself in. Taking a few moments to determine that she wasn't hurt, Henrietta began to grope around, trying to ascertain where she was and what she was lying on. She managed to stand up on the uneven mountain and peered into the darkness, her eyes trying to adjust.

It seemed she had jumped down some sort of laundry chute and was haphazardly balancing on a pile of sheets and towels and gowns. The stench was horrible—the smell of feces and vomit and blood hitting her all at once. Quickly, she half walked, half slid down the pile, trying to keep her footing. Once at the bottom, she became aware of some type of bilious liquid smeared down one of her arms, and as she tried to wipe it off with the edge of her gown, she uncontrollably vomited herself. She stood bent over until it was finished and then stood up unsteadily, wiping her mouth with the back of her hand.

Her eyes were becoming adjusted to the light now, and she was able to make out giant baskets of laundry very near her. Along the far wall stood huge washing tubs, and drying lines crisscrossed the room. She tried to ascertain if she was at ground level or below, but it was impossible to tell without the presence of windows.

Reaching her hands out in front of her, she made her way gingerly around the room, desperately looking for a door or a way out. She shuffled around two long tables, her fingertips brushing against stacks of folded linen of varying heights, and then around a large vat. By the caustic odor that reached her nose, she guessed it to be lye. The washing tubs were the only things that lay before her now, and as she squinted in the darkness, she thought she saw a small door set between the last two tubs in the row. She hurried to it, but in her haste, she tripped over a bucket full of powdery material and banged her shin. Small tears came to her eyes at the resultant pain in her leg, but she righted herself after only a moment and hobbled on. Upon reaching the door, she pulled at its small black knob, which in and of itself told her it was not an outside door, but, still, she almost broke into tears of despair when she saw that it was just a storage closet with brooms and rags and more buckets. Oh, what was she to do?

She leaned against one of the massive washing tubs, forcing down her tears, a massive ache welling up in her throat instead. Despite the hysteria she was beginning to feel, she swallowed hard and tried to remain calm. Wiping her eyes of any stray tears, she listened for some sign of life around her. Surely, she did not have much time until she was discovered, she thought. Either Nurse Collins was probably on the way, or she had sent someone down here to find her before she could escape. Or maybe Nurse Collins knew there was no means of escape and was therefore allowing her to scurry around in a tortured frenzy before leisurely coming to collect her when she was good and ready.

Either way, Henrietta knew she couldn't just stand there. She had to at least *try* to find an escape. She looked back across the room she had just picked her way across, and then thought she saw—oh, please!—what looked like a set of double doors just beyond the mound of laundry upon which she had landed.

As much as she wanted to run to them—a flicker of hope erupting in her heart—she made herself walk carefully across the floor, which was untidily littered with laundry and other odd objects. Even so, she nearly tripped again, this time ironically on what looked to be some sort of trap. She gave it only a momentary glance when her foot banged into it, but as she carefully sidestepped it, she thought she saw . . . yes! A rat, of all things! . . . lying dead within. She covered her mouth with her hand, fighting a scream, and hurried past, giving it as wide a berth as she dared lest she run into something else. At the last few yards, however, she couldn't help but break into an actual run.

Upon reaching the doors, she stopped herself from just barging through, considering that she didn't know what lay on the other side. What if someone was in there? Another nurse, or even some orderlies? Even if they had not yet been alerted by Nurse Collins or some other authority, surely it didn't look good for a woman to be wandering in the bowels of an asylum dressed like a patient in a dirty gown with vomit on it? Would anyone believe that a nurse was trying to kill her? Or that she wasn't a patient at all, but Mrs. Clive Howard? She severely doubted it. If she *was* detained, would she be allowed one phone call as people were in jail? Well, there was nothing for it, she reasoned, her pulse racing. She would have to risk it.

Gently she pushed on one of the doors, wincing at the low screech it made as she did so, and poked her head into the room. It was completely dark, which precluded her running into any staff, she assumed, and exhaled a quick breath of relief. So far, so good. Silently, she stepped inside and again allowed her eyes to adjust.

Just as the laundry room was slightly illuminated by the small square of light from the chute, she realized that this room, too, must have light coming from somewhere, as she was able to make out certain objects the longer she stood—the most surprising being an old-fashioned truck that somehow materialized right in front of her! This was an odd place for a garage—right next to the laundry, Henrietta mused, but her heart simultaneously filled with hope that she might at least be at ground level.

The room held a faint scent of diesel and oil but seemed abandoned but for the truck. Perhaps it had once been a maintenance room, Henrietta guessed, as she walked the length of the truck. Or maybe it had been a sort of loading dock for the laundry, once upon a time. Thoughts of the room's original purpose flew out of her mind, however, when she reached the back of the truck and saw that it sat in front of two large, dark green (or were they black?) garage doors! *Of course, they will be locked*, she tried to school herself, but still she rushed to them anyway.

They were the type, she observed, that opened outward instead of the ones that rolled to the side. Eagerly, she grasped the big iron handles and attempted to open them with a push. Though the handle clicked under her hand, the door was held fast and did not budge. Perhaps it was stuck? she thought, pushing again, this time harder. The doors swelled slightly at the pressure, enough for Henrietta to agonizingly feel cool night air on her skin and catch the smell of the earthy wet grass just beyond the doors—but they would not budge any further. Henrietta stopped her pushing and allowed the doors to thud back into place. She took a deep breath, then, and pushed again, straining, her muscles quivering, but to no avail. Each time she pushed, she could see a tantalizing crack of the outside world before the doors closed again, like a baby's head crowning before being pulled back into the womb. Eventually through her efforts, Henrietta was able to make out that there was a chain and a padlock wrapped through the outside handles, permanently binding them shut. At the sight of this, she finally stopped, accepting that she was not going to get out this way, and sunk to the floor, tempted to give in to despair. She had been so close!

Hot tears filled her eyes, but after a few moments, her despair turned to anger. She was determined to get out of here! She roused herself and stood, trying to find some inner strength, and looked around again.

In the back corner, she could see an ancient set of stone steps left over from perhaps the original estate. She guessed that they led to either the main floor or maybe the second floor. Either way, she felt instinctively that she would indeed run into some staff members if she chose to ascend that way. Looking around again, her eyes then miraculously fell upon a small side door to the left of the main garage doors, a pedestrian entrance perhaps! It was behind the truck in the corner, which was why she probably hadn't seen it at first. It was oddly placed in that it butted right up to the wall, with barely any left-hand frame at all, which suggested the wall had been added later or that the door had perhaps been a haphazard addition.

Henrietta ran toward it and tried the handle, which, of course, was also disappointingly locked. The door held a small window, however, which glowed slightly with moonlight, a little bit of which made its way through the thick grime. This must be the room's mysterious source of illumination, Henrietta realized. It was so dirty, however, that it could barely be recognized as glass at all. She tried rubbing the window with a corner of her gown, but the dirt seemed permanently etched into the glass. Still, she could make out the lawn beyond, glistening wet with dew in the moonlight, and she was filled with renewed agony to escape. She was tempted to bang on the window for help, but she instantly knew it to be useless, as surely no one was out there anyway—no passersby whose attention she could attempt to grab. Only the surrounding woods were visible beyond the lawn. No, she would have to try something else . . . but what?

Apprehensively, she looked around for anything that could help her. There was a workbench along one wall, but upon approaching it, she saw that it held nothing but mouse droppings and a rusting tin of Prince Albert tobacco. There was a wooden shelf hanging above it, which she tentatively reached up and tapped her hand along and found that it, too, held nothing but a small oilcan and more mouse droppings. Disgusted, she quickly wiped her hands on her gown, and as she did so, her eyes fell upon the truck itself. Could it possibly help her? she wondered. She doubted it even ran anymore. It looked like an old Model A. Even if it did run, she concluded quickly, she didn't have the keys, and the garage doors were chained shut. Maybe she could hide in it? she thought desperately, but quickly dismissed this idea as being too obvious. Surely it's the first place they would look.

Nonetheless, Henrietta opened up one of the doors and peered in. It was hard to see anything, the moonlight not reaching all the way in here. It appeared to be empty, though. Hesitantly, she reached inside, her hand passing through a cobweb as she tried to feel for any keys. Predictably, the ignition was empty, and she quickly pulled her hand back and rubbed it against her gown, trying to rid herself of the sticky strands. She shut the door quietly and moved toward the truck bed. Upon first glance, it, too, appeared to be empty, except for . . . except for what looked like a box sitting up against the cab. She assumed it was empty, but decided, with the barest flicker of hope now, to look anyway.

Henrietta put her bare foot on the tire and, holding onto the sides of the truck, tried to hoist herself up. Her foot slipped, however, and she found herself back on the ground, her big toe scraping painfully against the tire in the process. With renewed effort, she put her foot on the tire again and strained her weak muscles to lift herself over the edge, but still she fell back. She tried a third and a fourth time until she finally flipped herself onto the truck bed and allowed herself a small moment of pride before eagerly crawling toward the box.

Henrietta pulled at it—it was heavy!—and found that it was a toolbox of sorts. She began to rummage through it, looking for what exactly, she knew not. There were no keys that she could see, but—

What was that? Henrietta froze, her hands still in the box. There was movement above her . . . Footsteps? And now she heard shouting . . . Was it the staff or a patient? she wondered, panic filling her heart, and she suddenly remembered what Joe had told them about dangerous patients being held on the basement level. Oh, God! she thought. But this wasn't the basement, was it? It didn't matter; she had to hurry!

Henrietta gave the contents of the box one more quick look through, and her hand closed around a hammer. She held it up and wondered if she could use it to defend herself, but then just as quickly wondered if perhaps she could use it to open the doors? Maybe hit the handle hard enough to smash it? But what about the chains on the other side? she fretted. Besides, smashing the handle would take a long time and it would be extraordinarily loud. What about the window? Yes! She could use it to try to smash the little window!

Quickly Henrietta sat on the edge of the truck, her legs hanging down, and jumped the few feet to the ground. She dropped the hammer in the process but quickly picked it up and ran to the little side door. Wouldn't it be horribly loud as well, though? she wondered, as she stood hesitating in front of the window. Well, she didn't have a choice. She would have to be quick and hit it hard enough to shatter it in one blow. Still she hesitated.

But when she again heard movement above her, Henrietta clutched the hammer and swung it with all her might. The sound of the shattering glass pierced the air, and shards fell everywhere. She paused, terrified, listening; she could hear nothing now. All had gone silent, which filled her with a new sort of dread. She poked her head through the jagged hole, hoping she would be able to reach down and unlock the door from the outside, but it was padlocked, too! The feel of the cool night air billowing about her and caressing her hot and sweaty face made her almost delirious. If only she could crawl through this jagged hole! Well, she decided, she would try it . . .

Frantically Henrietta attempted to smash the remaining stubborn pieces of glass with the hammer and with the other hand, gingerly pick out the smaller pieces. She heard shouts again and jumped. In her fright, her fingers momentarily slipped in their delicate task, and a particularly ragged piece of glass sliced the skin between her thumb and forefinger. She winced at the resulting pain and put her hand to her mouth to keep from crying out. She pulled it back, half afraid to look at the damage, and gasped to see the open gash, blood pouring from it. She put her hand to her mouth to try to stem the bleeding, and then lowered it, attempting to wrap it with the corner of her gown, though it was hard to find any part of that rag that was still clean. She held it there for a few moments before she realized she would have to deal with it later . . . She needed to keep going.

Carefully, Henrietta put her hands on two spots of the frame that were relatively clear of glass and tried weakly to hoist herself up. She barely got herself up, however, before dropping miserably back to the ground. She was going to need something to stand on, she realized wildly, and looked around desperately. At the sound of footsteps running now, she moved to the truck and looked in the back again, hoping that she had perhaps overlooked something or that something had since magically appeared. There was nothing, though, except the already discovered toolbox . . . The toolbox! she thought in a sudden rush. Perhaps she could use the toolbox! Her adrenaline racing, she hoisted herself into the truck bed on the first try, even with her injured hand—she could barely feel the pain at this point—and crawled toward the box.

Quickly, Henrietta tossed out the heavy tools until it was light enough for her to lift the whole box and tip it upside down to dump the remainder of the items, the sound of which was deafening (it couldn't be helped!), and then threw it over the side of the truck. She heard the door above the stone steps open and saw the beams of several flashlights begin their search of the room. She jumped off the truck, carried the box toward the door, and quickly stepped up on it. She put her hands again on the frame, and with this extra bit of leverage, she was able to at least lift herself up toward the window, but before she could pitch herself forward and through, she lost her balance and fell back into the room.

"There she is!" came a shout from the top of the stairs. Utter, true panic seized her, then, and, allowing herself one horrible look over her shoulder at her captors, Henrietta heaved herself up again. Her heart was pounding, and with some newfound strength born of complete desperation, she managed to not only lift herself up this time, but to pitch her upper body into the opening. She balanced there precariously, wedged in with her hands unfortunately trapped at her side. She wiggled her body as best she could, resembling a sort of mermaid, as she struggled to get free. She realized as she squirmed, that with her hands trapped and unable to break her fall, she was destined to land on her head should she really manage to push herself out. She could hear her captors approaching now—they must only be mere feet behind her!—and with one last supreme effort, she burst through the opening, landing on the wet ground on her face.

Luckily, she only fell a few feet, and felt, at least initially, to be relatively unharmed. She stood up, shaking, and backed away from the window, nearly screaming when she saw Joe's face in the window, grinning at her.

"She got out!" he called back toward someone inside the room.

"Open that door!" Henrietta heard someone shout, sure it was the voice of Nurse Collins. "She can't get far."

Henrietta stood, anchored to the spot, her mind a blank. She knew she should run, but she couldn't make her legs move. Run! she commanded herself, but it was as if her legs were paralyzed! Her pulse was racing and her body wet from sweat, but the cold night air was quickly drying it and turning her flesh to goose bumps. The sound of someone jangling a set of keys and scraping it against a lock, however, somehow broke the spell she was under. She took several deep breaths, as if she had been under water, and then turned and ran. She had no idea where to run but headed for what she hoped was the front of the building. Maybe she could get through the gate? Or maybe she should run for the surrounding woods? She glanced over her shoulder to check the progress of her pursuers and nearly slipped on the wet grass in the process. She somehow righted herself, though, and as she swung her head back around, she felt herself plow into something—someone! She screamed and tried to fight as she felt strong arms encircle her, clutching her tightly.

"Help!" she screamed again, trying wildly to pull from her captor's grip.

"Henrietta! Henrietta!" shouted an oddly familiar voice. "It's me! I've got you now. It's me! You're safe. I've got you."

Henrietta looked up briefly into Clive's face, her eyes frantic, and then collapsed into his arms.

Chapter 24

"Elsie, there is much we need to discuss," Gunther said agitatedly.

"Yes, there is," Elsie agreed, sitting across from him in the front room of the Palmer Square house.

"Elsie, we both know this is not real solution," he said gently.

It had been over a week since they had shown up on Ma's doorstep, Gunther carrying a sleeping Anna in his arms, having come directly from Dunning with her. Ma had been surprisingly agreeable to Elsie's sketchy plan, which was to house Anna in the nursery with Doris and Donny until something further could be arranged. Ma had even held the sleeping girl for a time while Elsie had gone upstairs and explained the situation to Nanny Kuntz, who was not enthralled with the idea of taking on another charge, especially one that was given to fits, she had said, making the sign of the cross repeatedly. Elsie reminded her, respectfully, of course, that she was originally hired to care for *five* children, and, seeing as three of them were off at boarding school now, it didn't seem all that unfair to be adding one to her already lightened load. Still, Elsie hurriedly added, she promised to see about hiring some sort of additional nurse to tend to Anna's peculiar needs.

"Well, that's just what we need, another person in this house,"

Nanny grumbled, referring to the proposed additional staff person. "She ain't sharin' my room, that's for sure. An' she wouldn't be over me, just cause she's a nurse. *I'm* in charge of the nursery," she said, folding her arms across her midline.

"Well, perhaps we can cross that bridge when we come to it," Elsie said patiently.

"Yer grandfather ain't gonna like it, either," she said, her face already trying on an "I-told-you-so" expression.

"Let me worry about that," Elsie dismissed, though she *was* in fact worried about Oldrich Exley's reaction when he heard the news, which was sure to happen before too long, probably from one of the servants themselves. "Listen, Nanny, she's a little German girl. You speak some German, don't you? It would be wonderful for her. Surely you will help, won't you?" Elsie pleaded softly. "And it won't be forever, just . . . just for a short time."

Gretchen Kuntz managed to keep her face stern and emotionless for a few moments before it finally crumpled, and she threw her hands up in the air. "Oh, all right," she said, "as long as it ain't permanent. And you get someone to deal with those fits. Best get a priest, I'm thinking. Was she baptized?" Nanny asked apprehensively.

"I'm sure she was, Nanny," Elsie said, though she of course had no idea. Had she been baptized? Elsie worried.

"And what if Doris and Donny catch it?" Nanny asked.

"It's not something you can catch, Nanny," Elsie sighed.

Ma, on the other hand, was surprisingly easier to win over. The sad truth was that Ma had not bothered much with Doris and Donny since they moved to Palmer Square. Actually, even back in the apartment on Armitage, she had never seemed to really bond with them, born in the wake of Les's suicide. Any warmth that Ma possessed before Les's death, which was little enough, had left her after his death, as she began to spiral into her own deep place of despair and depression. It was Henrietta and Elsie who had tended to the twins the most, Elsie more than Henrietta, who was usually instead out working.

Then when they had been forced by Oldrich Exley to move to this grand house in Palmer Square, little Doris and Donny had been swept up into the nursery and were now cared for by the servants. Privately, Elsie was of the opinion that the change had been good for them. She could see that over time, Nanny Kuntz really came to care for them, and they her. In fact, Elsie observed, the twins were not only growing bigger and stronger, but they were coming out of their shell, finally. Indeed, they almost seemed more comfortable now in Nanny's presence than in Ma's, and they frequently gave Nanny hugs and kisses up in the nursery, something which Ma could never abide.

And Ma, Elsie had likewise noticed, did not seem to mind that her children were essentially gone from her, despite her fussing and fuming to the contrary at the beginning of it all. It was very peculiar, and Elsie had, more than once, wondered how Ma whiled away her days with apparently nothing to do and no one to care for.

So it seemed more than a little curious when Ma took to Anna so quickly. It was as if she were a stray dog or a cat that needed attention, which was odd, considering that all of the Von Harmon children could have been seen as strays themselves at one point in time and certainly in want of attention. Maybe it had something to do with the fact that Ma was not obligated to care for Anna, as she was her own children; she could *choose* Anna. Or maybe it was because Anna was not connected to Les . . . or maybe it was just some sort of fluke born of boredom or fickleness. At any rate, Ma had taken to visiting the nursery on occasion these last couple of weeks, which she had almost never done before and which was reportedly making Nanny nervous and upset as a result.

"Yes, I know it's not permanent," Elsie said to Gunther now, the two of them having arrived at the Palmer Square house for a visit. "But isn't it good enough for the time being? Ma doesn't mind, and I . . . I've made inquiries about a nurse. And Anna seems happy enough, doesn't she? Except for the nightmares," she added quietly. "But she hasn't had any fits," she went on hopefully. "Surely that's a good thing?"

"Yes, it is good," Gunther agreed sadly. "But it will happen. I have been fooled before into thinking they were somehow gone, but they will return. It is like circle . . . cycle . . . in some way."

"All the better that she is here, then, safe," Elsie pointed out. "And Henrietta said she would have a doctor—a good doctor—examine her. Maybe there's something different we can do, some new treatment that we don't know about—"

"Elsie, she is not your child," Gunther interrupted quietly.

Elsie looked at him blankly for a moment. "She's not yours either."

Gunther looked away and let out a deep breath. "I have made decision. We are going back."

"Gunther, you know you can't go back to Germany with her! Remember what you told me? What will most likely happen to her there?" Elsie exclaimed. "It's foolish. And cruel."

"We will not go to Germany, but instead to Austria. I have cousin there outside of Graz in the south, a small town in countryside. We can live there, maybe, unnoticed. I will find a woman to come and take care for her. I could be teaching again."

"But . . . but what if Austria becomes like Germany?" Elsie argued nervously. "You . . . you could live quietly here, as you're doing now."

"Elsie, I cannot just leave her here for your mother and your grandfather's servants to care for. And I am thinking that he will not be allowing this anyway when he discovers what is happening in his house. I cannot blame him. I have already very much taken advantage where I should not," he said sternly. "If we stay here, I will always be having worry that Anna will be put in institution, as she already has been. I cannot stand to think of her in that awful place where poor Liesel died. I would rather die myself than little Anna be there again," he said bitterly. "And I cannot keep her with me at Mundelein, so . . . " He shrugged.

"But—"

"Even if Sister Bernard somehow would be allowing it, which she will not, I know, she is right," Gunther insisted. "It is dangerous and not appropriate, and not good life for a child. She would not be able to be going to school . . . No, we are going back. Though it causes very much pain to say it." His blue eyes held her gaze for several long moments before he finally pulled them away. "And I cannot burden you any more with this," he said mournfully, bracing his head on his hands.

Elsie felt herself beginning to panic. "Gunther," she said quietly and dared to reach for one of his hands, causing him to lift his head in surprise and look at her again. The corners of his eyes tightened, and he took a deep breath.

"There is another way," she said quietly. "We . . . we could get married. I'd like to marry you," she said softly, barely above a whisper, "if you'll have me." Never in a thousand years could Elsie ever have imagined herself uttering words such as these—so bold and well . . . unladylike! But she had thought it over a corresponding thousand times, and she knew that given her circumstances and Gunther knowing them as well, that he would never dare to ask her. He was too honorable and if it was true what she suspected—that he loved her, too—then he would have all the more reason to walk away from her. Her guess was that he did not believe himself a suitable suitor, which was absurd to the point of amusement. It was *she* that was the unsuitable one! Or so she had felt until he began to convince her otherwise. No, he was more than suitable to her; he was indeed a kindred spirit. She couldn't imagine living without him, and if she had to follow him to Germany, she determined, she would.

Gunther's face twisted up as if in pain, and he remained silent for several moments. "No, Elsie," he said finally, giving her hand a small squeeze. "We . . . we cannot get married, you and I. But I know how much it took for you to say those words, and I want you to know I feel it deeply. I will remember this moment all the days of my life."

Elsie's face blushed red. "Gunther, I . . . I love you," she said haltingly. "I think I've always loved you. And I . . . I thought—I imagined, anyway . . . that you loved me, too," she said, barely above a whisper.

"I saw what you wrote in your diary; I saw all of those poems. So many about love . . . "

Gunther's eyes closed and he pulled his hand away from hers and stood up, causing Elsie's stomach to clench painfully. No, don't go away! she wanted to scream.

"Elsie," he said, turning from her, "there are many things you do not understand. It is impossible that I marry you." He began to pace. "The whole thing is impossible. Out of the question."

Impossible? Elsie wondered. Nothing was *impossible* about this, unless . . . she paused, a new thought suddenly coming into her mind, one she had just barely considered . . . one that was always floating on the periphery . . .

"Gunther," she began slowly, "is there something you're not telling me? Some reason you cannot marry me?" He continued to pace. "Does . . . *did* someone else have a claim on your heart?" she asked softly. "Liesel, perhaps? Was this the reason for your desperate quest to find her?" She looked up at him fearfully, but his back was still to her. "Gunther, please. Be honest. I will not judge you. Did you love Liesel? Are you Anna's father?"

He turned slowly around and looked at her steadily, his eyes awash with an emotion she couldn't read. At first, she feared it was anger, but then she thought perhaps it was fear. Regret? Silently he walked toward her and gently took hold of her upper arms. "Elsie," he said hoarsely, "I have never lied to you, and I will not ever. I know you have been . . . treated very much badly . . . in the past, and so I will not be offended by your questions. But I have told you truth. There is only one person who holds my heart," he said, looking at her with such longing she felt she would burst. She wanted nothing more than to melt into him, to hold him, to belong to him, and she felt ashamed that she had doubted him, even for a moment.

"Then why?" she asked, looking up into his face. "Why can't you marry me?"

"It is not that I cannot," he said gently, releasing his grip and sliding his hands down her arms to take her hands in his. "It is that I *will not* do such thing."

"Is it because of my grandfather?"

"That is part of it, yes." He gave her a sad smile.

"But that doesn't matter! Not if we . . . not if we love each other, Gunther!"

"It is *because* I love you that I cannot marry you," he said softly.

Elsie felt a wave of warmth steal over her at his words, his declaration, finally, of love.

"Elsie, you must be able to see all of the difficulties, all the obstacles," he said, cupping her cheek in his hand and causing her to tremble. "Yes, it is true that I love you. With my whole heart." His eyes searched hers, and Elsie felt an ache well up inside her that was so big it threatened to cut off her air. "There was a time, a time before we discovered Liesel's death and Anna's true state of being an orphan," he went on, "before I knew everything about your . . . your life, that I did allow myself to have hope. But I . . . things have changed now. I cannot . . . cannot do this to you, cannot allow you to give yourself to me. You have everything in front of you, and pledging your life to me would be very much a grave mistake. You know this in your heart," he said gently. "Listen to it."

"I am listening to it!"

"No, you are not."

"So, you, too, would not have me choose for myself?"

"Elsie, this would be *Selbstmord* . . . suicide . . . for you."

"Suicide to be with the one I love? How can you say that?"

Gunther sighed. "You will find another love, Elsie. A cleaner, brighter, better love. A love that does not have so much complication. Let me go."

"No!" she said, surprising herself with her own forcefulness. "I don't want to let you go! I . . . I want to care for you," she said then more softly, taking hold of his hand at her cheek. "You are not so unkind that you would make me beg, are you?"

He closed his eyes and lowered their hands. "Ach, Elsie. I have nothing to give you. I have no money, no way to provide for you—"

Elsie opened her mouth to counter this, but he stopped her. "And I cannot take your money—your grandfather's money."

"He will more than likely cut me off, just like he did with my mother. So I will come to you with nothing as well," she said with a small smile. "If you don't mind, that is."

"I cannot let you throw that away, Elsie."

"Do you not know me better than that by now, Gunther? What I wouldn't give to be done with being paraded about by Aunt Agatha and Grandfather, using me as bait for the highest bidder."

"Think how you could be helping the poor with that money, if nothing else."

"So now you would have me sacrifice myself for the poor, but not for you?" Elsie said hotly, the hurt of it cutting her to the quick and causing small tears to form in the corners of her eyes. "Again, I'm not to have a choice, apparently! There are more ways than one to serve the poor, Gunther; this you should know."

"I beg your pardon, Elsie," Gunther said sincerely. "I was wrong to say that." He paused for a moment before going on. "But what of your dreams of helping the poor? Of studying . . . becoming a teacher?" he asked gently. "You would give that up so easily? And I would never forgive myself for stopping you."

"You can teach me," she suggested.

"No," he said shaking his head. "No, it cannot be like that."

"Didn't you once ask me if I thought I could be a wife *and* a teacher?" she said, triumphantly remembering his words. "Are you going back on that?"

"So I did," he said, smiling at her. "But with a child underfoot?" he went on, his smile disappearing as suddenly as it had appeared. "A child who is not yours, and one who is ill and will not ever get better? A child who will probably never go to school and who will always be a burden?" His voice caught a little.

"I can teach her," she said softly after a few moments.

"No," he said, looking down at her hand that he still held.

Elsie was near despair now, fearing that she might never be able to convince him of what was so obvious to her. Her mind was racing as to what to say next when it suddenly came to her, an inspiration that she could only describe as divine.

"Light, so low upon earth," she began unsteadily, quoting Tennyson's poem she had once read in his journal and subsequently memorized, for what reason at the time she did not know, perhaps just as a way to feel closer to him, but which in this moment seemed miraculously clear . . .

> *You send a flash to the sun.*
> *Here is the golden close of love,*
> *All my wooing is done.*
> *Oh, all the woods and the meadows,*
> *Woods, where we hid from the wet,*
> *Stiles where we stayed to be kind,*
> *Meadows in which we met!*
> *Light, so low in the vale*
> *You flash and lighten afar,*
> *For this is the golden morning of love,*
> *And you are his morning star.*
> *Flash, I am coming, I come,*
> *By meadow and stile and wood,*
> *Oh, lighten into my eyes and my heart,*
> *Into my heart and my blood!*

She paused and took a deep breath before continuing on, slowly and clearly . . .

> *Heart, are you great enough*
> *For a love that never tires?*
> *O heart, are you great enough for love?*

She could see the tears in his eyes, which caused fresh ones to fill hers, too. Huskily, her throat aching, she said the last words . . .

I have heard of thorns and briers.
Over the thorns and briers,
Over the meadows and stiles . . .

"Over the world to the end of it, flash for a million miles," he said in unison with her, and paused for only a second before he encircled her with his arms. He did not take her roughly or swiftly but looked deeply into her eyes as if to confirm her feelings, and as if to somehow mark this moment, to perhaps commit it to memory. Just when she felt she could endure it no longer, he slowly leaned toward her and brushed his lips against her trembling ones. Elsie returned his kiss in full, giving herself to him completely. He was so lovely, so good, and she felt she might die, right this moment, the ache of a million miles inside of both of them.

"Elsie," he said hoarsely, pulling his lips away but resting his forehead against hers. "Are you sure?"

Her answer was to nod, a small smile on her face.

"Then I must ask you and not have you beg, as you put it," he said, clearing his throat slightly. He paused for several moments. "Elsie Von Harmon," he said solemnly, looking lovingly into her eyes, "will you marry me? Will you be my wife?"

"Yes," Elsie said, her heart full to breaking. "Yes," she said, crying now for joy in the very room in which she had cried so many lonely tears over Stanley and Harrison, she leaned her head on Gunther's chest. "Yes, I will be your wife. Over the world to the end of it, flash for a million miles."

Chapter 25

"There's nothing really there," Clive said, tossing his fake badge onto the table in front of Davis. "She hasn't broken any laws, so there's nothing to charge her with." He took a large swig of the whiskey he held. They were back at the Trophy Room.

"Nothing?" Frank Davis asked skeptically. "That's hard to believe. Sure she didn't hypnotize you with her voodoo?" he asked with a laugh, wiggling the air with his fingers.

"Fuck off, Davis," Clive said irritably.

Earlier in the week, Davis had telephoned him at Highbury, asking if he'd gotten anywhere with the Madame Pavlovsky case, as he himself received yet another annoying call from Mr. Tobin demanding some sort of justice. Clive had relayed to Davis that they were making progress, just that there were one or two things he still wished to clear up and he would get on it right away. But there hadn't been a chance to go back to Madame Pavlovsky's since the fateful séance, nor had he much time to think about it, really, not with the concern at the firm over the Kalamazoo plant and Henrietta's obsession—nearly fatal, as it turned out—with Dunning. How had what started as a simple case of a missing person ended up as a case involving nothing less than a deranged killer? he thought for the hundredth time. Just thinking about the sight of Henrietta running from Dunning, her hospital gown billowing about her, streaked with blood and grime, her hair wild, still caused a wave of sweaty angst to course through him. It was like something out of *Jane Eyre* or *Wuthering Heights*—one of those silly books, anyway, that he had been forced to read at school—and it had nearly unhinged him.

He had been nearly frantic by the time he found her that night, scooping her up in his arms as she collapsed. Joe the orderly was not far behind her, as well as one or two others—but they all turned and ran in the other direction when they caught sight of Clive. As much as Clive had wanted to go after the bastards—clearly something terrible had happened—his first concern was to tend to Henrietta. Quickly, he ascertained that she was not fatally injured despite her bleeding hand and then swiftly carried her back to where Fritz waited with the car. All the while, various guards could be seen scurrying around the grounds in confused alarm.

Amateurs, Clive thought distractedly, despite the adrenaline coursing through him, as he deposited Henrietta as gently as possible in the back seat of the Daimler. He barked for Fritz to stand watch while he ran to the now-empty guard booth and commandeered the telephone to call the police, demanding to speak to the precinct captain. Rapidly he explained who he was, and when he had sufficiently related the need for several patrol cars, he left the booth. He was sorely tempted to go after at least Joe, who was clearly guilty of something, and furiously tried to prevent his mind from supposing the worst.

Fighting his panic, he instead dashed back to the car and slid in beside Henrietta, taking her in his arms while they waited for the police. At one point, he came very close to instructing Fritz to drive them post haste to Highbury instead of waiting around any longer—but then Henrietta had come to a little bit and was able to tell him briefly what happened and that Nurse Collins was the guilty party. At this surprising revelation, Clive felt it imperative to wait for the police, and when they did show up, not a few minutes later, he got out of the car to inform them of what he knew.

Only when he was satisfied that the detective inspector on the scene was thoroughly apprised of the situation did he finally give Fritz the command to drive them home. For only a brief moment did Clive consider having Fritz drive them instead to a hospital. He decided, however, that taking Henrietta to yet another institution, given the situation, might not be for the best. It was hard to judge just how deep the cut on her hand was, but he knew he had to get her home first.

It was late when he carried her into the house, asleep in his arms. He had put his coat around her while in the car, but even so, her bloody gown poked out from under it as he carried her up the main stone steps, the sight of which threw the servants into a frantic uproar as they dashed around, trying to help. As he carried Henrietta up the stairs, Clive instructed Billings to telephone Dr. Ferrington and for Edna to run ahead and get a bath ready and to stoke the fire. Without being told, Mrs. Caldwell herself went and prepared a tray of warm cocoa and some biscuits, as Mary had already gone to bed hours ago.

Gently, Clive sat down on the bed, still holding Henrietta as if she were a child, while he waited for her bath to be ready. At one point she awoke. Her eyes were large and fearful as she looked around quickly as if to assess where they were. "We're at Highbury? When did we get here?" she asked blearily.

"You've had a terrible shock, darling. But you're going to be okay. I'm here now."

She looked down at her blood-stained gown and started. "Oh my," she cried out, and then seemed to remember her injured hand, which Clive had since wrapped with his handkerchief. "I cut myself on the glass," she said, looking up at him. "Oh, Clive, I'm so sorry." Tears filled her eyes, which caused him to crush her to him tightly as he kissed her filthy hair.

"My brave, foolish girl," he said thickly. "What am I to do with you? Don't leave me, Henrietta. You mustn't ever leave me. Promise," he said through his own tears.

"Promise," she whispered back.

Edna had knocked softly, then, saying that the bath was ready. Gently, she took her mistress and led her to the bathroom. Afterward, she dressed Henrietta in a warm cotton nightgown and bed socks and entreated her to take a few sips of Mrs. Caldwell's cocoa before helping her into bed.

Dr. Ferrington arrived not long after and was quickly shown to the patient's room by Billings. After his subsequent examination and bandaging of Henrietta's hand and several other small cuts on her arms and legs, presumably procured as well from the jagged opening she had passed through, Clive invited him into his study for a quick drink. He nearly broke down in front of him when the doctor related that, in his opinion, anyway, Henrietta would certainly recover. "She needs rest, though, Mr. Howard. No excitement of any kind. Maybe a quiet walk in the garden in a day or two, nothing more. Understand?"

"Yes, of course, Doctor. I'll see to it."

"She's sleeping now, but when she wakes up, have the servants make her toast and a beef tea. I've given her maid some sleeping powders to mix up for her tomorrow if needed. Your wife hasn't fully recovered, physically that is, from the miscarriage, and I suspect she is still anemic. If you don't take my advice, I can't be responsible," he said grimly, knocking his whiskey back and taking his leave.

Dr. Ferrington's words struck terror in Clive's heart, and as soon as he showed him out, Clive dashed back up the stairs, two at a time, to their bedroom. Edna was standing outside where he had stationed her, and she confirmed what Dr. Ferrington already said, that Madame was sleeping. Without knocking, Clive poked his head in to gaze at her. She looked like an angel asleep in their bed except for her bandaged hand and bruised face, both of which filled him with fury and fierce helplessness, so much so that he found it difficult to breathe. He went to the bed and lay down beside her, not even bothering to undress, so desperately did he want to be near her. He took her in his arms and held her, Dr. Ferrington's words still in his mind, as well as a myriad of other thoughts. Eventually he dozed off, but he slept fitfully.

Finally, in the wee hours of the morning, he slipped out and bathed and dressed, for once allowing Carter to assist him, and went downstairs. The morning *Tribune* lay on his desk; "Angel of Death Apprehended" was the headline. Somehow the press had already gotten ahold of the story. Clive skimmed through it, thankful that at least Henrietta's name was not mentioned, and telephoned Captain Densmore, whom he had spoken to last night and who now apparently held not only Caroline Collins, but one Joe Ferrari, in custody. Captain Densmore related that Caroline Collins had been rather easy to apprehend, as it turned out, and that she had indeed confessed, under questioning, to no less than twenty-six murders, including that of one Liesel Klinkhammer. It looked to be a pretty open-and-shut case, Captain Densmore had gone on, especially as they already had a confession. That notwithstanding, however, Mrs. Howard would still be required to give an official statement when she was recovered, he added, and promised to keep Clive abreast of any new developments. "She's loony, this one is," Captain Densmore said wryly, referring now to Caroline Collins. "Heart of ice. No remorse. Not gonna go well with a jury." With a weary sigh, Clive decided that he would go back upstairs to check on the patient. At that moment he was interrupted by yet another telephone call, this one from Davis, who, without preamble or niceties, informed him that Mr. Tobin was threatening to get Chief Callahan involved if something wasn't resolved quickly in the Madame Pavlovsky case—which, Davis reminded Clive, would not be beneficial for either of them.

Certainly, it would threaten the rather tenuous relationship he and Davis had so far forged, Clive knew, and likewise, he knew he risked losing the little jurisdiction he held, which was shaky at best, propped up as it were with a fake badge. Clive crisply informed Davis that he had the case well in hand, thanks very much; that he and Henrietta had indeed done some investigating, and it revealed much. He only needed to ask this Madame Pavlovsky a few more questions, and then he felt sure he could haul her in. Davis's response was to inform him that he could have one more day, but that was it.

Clive hung up the telephone with another heavy sigh and rubbed his brow. He couldn't possibly leave Henrietta right now, he worried, and yet, what else was he to do? Perhaps he really should just let Chief Callahan get involved in the case and extricate both himself and Henrietta. After all, what did he care? He hadn't wanted to pursue this case in the first place. He had just done it to distract Henrietta, who, it turned out, had not needed distracting. And yet, his sense of justice niggled at him. He found it hard to contemplate just walking away from the case, without coming to some sort of conviction or resolution. Plus, he felt he owed Davis somehow. If Mr. Tobin filed a complaint, Davis was the one who would get the brunt of Callahan's anger when he found out that Davis had partnered with someone outside the force. In light of what they had been through together, Clive just couldn't do that to him.

Quickly Clive downed the last of his coffee, thinking. He glanced at his wristwatch and saw that it was only 9:00 a.m. No doubt Henrietta was still asleep and would remain asleep for a good while longer, he reasoned, if the servants had indeed given her a sleeping powder. If he left now, he could probably get to Crow Island and back before she even awoke. Accordingly, he rang for Billings and left strict instructions that no one was to disturb Henrietta and that she was not allowed to leave her room under any circumstances—at the risk of their jobs. He then took the extra precaution of popping his head into the morning room to warn his mother to likewise not disturb Henrietta, and not to say anything controversial to her should Henrietta happen to wake up while he was out . . . running an errand, he had explained.

"You hardly need to instruct me in deportment, Clive," Antonia lightly scolded him, though he knew that she was very worried about

Henrietta as well, having been up to check on her at least four or five times since he carried her in last night.

His last instruction was to Billings, as the staid servant handed him his hat and coat, which was to order several dozen bouquets of roses to be delivered to the house.

"Very good, sir," Billings had mumbled with a slight bow.

Clive sped down Willow probably faster than he should have, his mind a mess with worry over Henrietta, mixed with disturbing thoughts about the cold, calculating murders of Nurse Collins. Again, Henrietta had been right, and he marveled at the fact that she really did seem to have some detective sense to her, despite her persistent naiveté and innocence. And what about these "murders?" Clive asked himself, the wind whipping his hair through the window he had rapidly cranked open, feeling overwhelmingly overheated and anxious. It was wrong, of course, for this woman to end these poor souls' lives, especially as she was a nurse and entrusted with their care—but there was a small part of him that could understand her logic, however warped. Was living in such a place really living? Was it not already a tomb? he thought, turning down the unmarked Crow Island lane. Were some of her "victims" perhaps glad to be released from their misery, as she claimed they were?

It was too much to think about right now, he concluded, knowing that dwelling on these thoughts for too long would be straying into dangerous territory. He rolled the Alfa to a stop just in front of the schoolhouse and tried instead to concentrate on the task at hand: the slippery Madame Pavlovsky. Quietly, he walked up the steps, steeling his resolve and pushing all thoughts of Henrietta and Dunning to the back of his mind. As he raised his hand to knock, the door was mysteriously opened by the lackey who had answered it the other night. He did not seem surprised at all to see Clive and waved him in as if he were expecting him.

Clive stepped inside and quickly looked around, disappointed that the room had already been turned back to its original state—the large table which they all sat around during the séance now gone (but where?)—replaced by chairs, the old sofa, and pillows scattered around the floor. He had wanted to have another look at that table . . . Well, no matter, he thought to himself as he walked toward Madame Pavlovsky, who was seated on her throne-like chair at the other end of the room. He was pretty sure of his theory without needing further proof.

"Ah, Mr. Howard," Madame Pavlovsky called out to Clive now. "Or would you rather I call you *Detective* Howard?"

"Either will do," he said, striding calmly toward her, his hands in his pockets. Did she just sit there all day waiting for some poor sap to pull up? More than likely, he guessed, the lackey kept watch and called to her to take her seat once he heard the gravel crunch or the sight of easy prey approaching.

"Your wife does not come with you today?" Madame Pavlovsky asked, her thin bony fingers pressed together as if in prayer against her lips. "It is too bad she is ill."

For only a moment Clive wondered how she could have known that, but then realized that it was a good guess considering he had carried Henrietta out of here not a few days ago in a faint. He almost admired her craftiness. "I have some questions for you," he said bluntly. "So you can cut the bullshit."

"Yes, I can see that you do. So much anger in you. So much sadness. And fear," she said, her eyes brightening a bit as she said it.

Clive resisted the urge to look away.

"I saw the wires," he said. "Under the table. It's how you make your 'crystal ball' glow, isn't it?" he asked with an arched eyebrow and a condescending tilt of his head.

Madame Pavlovsky merely peered at him.

"And the trinkets? That's a nice racket, too. They bring you mostly rubbish, but every once in a while, something decent shows up, doesn't it?"

Madame Pavlovsky's lips curled up, and she let out a little laugh.

"This isn't a laughing matter," Clive said sternly.

"No, it is not," she replied. "It is you that amuses me. You will not see the obvious in front of your eyes."

"Are you aware of the fact that I could take you in for questioning?" Clive asked severely.

"You could," she said with a shrug. "But it would do no good. I have no laws broken."

"Oh, I'm sure we could think of something. Theft. Impersonation."

"Impersonation?" she said with a loud bark of a laugh. "I am not impersonating anyone; I am exactly who I say."

"Assuming a false identity with the intent to defraud another," Clive said matter-of-factly, rubbing his chin. "That's the law's definition of impersonation. And I think there's enough evidence of that here to charge you."

"All right!" she said, throwing her hands up dramatically. "Yes, it is true I use wires and cheap tricks for this illumination during séance. That is more work of Sergei's, though," she said without any trace of worry in her voice. "And I am not 'defrauding' anyone, as you say. I do not want these rubbish things; I keep them not. Look around if you so like," she said, gesturing widely. "You will find nothing."

"Most likely because you've sold it all by now."

"Is this still what you think, Detective? You saw yourself what they bring in. I tell them to bring something like personal, not of value. I will tell you truth. I do not need any of these rubbish to see the spirits."

"Then why tell them to bring anything at all?"

"Because they need to. They want to. Everyone likes show. Candles . . . crystal ball. It is more real for them, more . . . how you say? Exciting? Convincing?"

"Aha! My point exactly."

"But this does not make my gifts any less real, Detective. I am here to help people, believe it or no. *And* souls on other side. Sometimes they cannot go to eternal rest until they make peace with those left behind."

"So you're a charity now," Clive said. "You don't charge for the séance, you don't keep and resell their trinkets," he said, ticking off his fingers. "How *do* you make your money? Pull it out of a magic hat?"

"I charge for readings, if you must know," she said, giving him a faint scowl, the first sign of real emotion she had yet revealed. "People come for private communication with loved one. It is good, very healing. For both."

"Now we're getting somewhere," Clive said. "I knew there had to be a catch."

"There is no 'catch,' Detective. As you say, I need to live somehow. I merely use my gifts—same as you use detective skills. Often you have—how you say? Hunch? That something is not right as should be? That is same for me. I give service like any other. Like doctor."

"A witch doctor, maybe," Clive said wryly.

"I am not doing anything wrong. Nothing against law."

Clive had to admit that she was unfortunately correct. He had no proof that she was stealing items, and he knew that the charge of impersonation was loose at best. He said it to scare her, but it obviously hadn't worked. That or she was skilled in masking her fear. Well, that would make sense, wouldn't it? Still, if people chose to pay her money to talk to their dead relatives, he, or any law enforcement body, couldn't really do anything about it. But why did he feel so uneasy? He didn't like being in her presence, he decided, but simultaneously chastised himself for it. What was he so afraid of?

"Would you like me to do reading for you, Detective?" she asked in a throaty voice, completely taking him off guard as he stood contemplating what to do next. She was looking at him in a strange way, and though he tried to look away, he found he couldn't. "No charge, of course. There is much I could tell you."

A small part of him was absurdly tempted . . .

"No!" he exclaimed, instantly annoyed that he had said it so emphatically. "You've already told me that you saw my father and he loves me and all of that. Nice guess," he managed to say aloofly.

"That's pretty vague and applicable to anyone, really." He folded his arms across his chest.

Madame Pavlovsky closed her eyes and remained silent for several seconds. "There is woman near you," she began. "A young woman," she continued, "holding baby—"

"Yes, yes," Clive interrupted dismissively, breathing a secret sigh of relief that it was again predictable, that it was nothing worse. "You've already told us all of this . . . the baby, it was a boy, Henrietta's father is holding it . . . Nice touch, you know. I'll give you that."

"Is not Henrietta. No. Another woman . . . "

No, Clive worried. *Not this*, he silently pleaded. Not Catherine. How could she possibly know about Catherine? He supposed she could have looked it up, he reasoned quickly. After all, it was public record.

Madame Pavlovsky opened her eyes then and smiled. "She says to tell you that she does not blame you for her death and that you must not blame yourself anymore, too."

Clive's breath caught in his throat. He wanted her to stop, and yet . . .

"I am seeing strange scene now," Madame Pavlovsky said, her eyes closed again. "It is same woman, only is when she is just young girl. There is bird, in snare."

Clive's heart was beginning to beat unnaturally fast. "No—"

"This girl says that when you freed this bird for her, this is when she first began to love you. She says thank you for returning her love for short time. She says she is happy, content. She wants you to be happy, too . . . "

Madame Pavlovsky abruptly stopped speaking, again opening her eyes wide in time to see Clive quickly wipe his own eyes with his thumb.

"There is much light shining from her," she went on. "She is very bright. Full of love. But she could stay no longer. The baby was yours, yes?"

"Yes, they both died in childbirth," Clive said absently and then became incredulous. "How do you know this? How could you possibly have known about the bird we found that day? We were only about twelve."

In short, he was stunned. There was no rational explanation, no way she could have known that. It was something only the two of them had known about. They had found a partridge trapped in a snare set by the groundskeeper on the Highbury estate. They thought at first that it was dead, but when Clive nudged it with his boot, it flapped its wings distressingly, trying to fly away. Catherine, startled, had let out a little scream and begged Clive to do something. Clive felt torn, as he knew that he would be in grave trouble if he released the trapped game, but, in truth, he felt pity for the creature just as much as Catherine did. He had not known what to do. Finally, at Catherine's continued begging, he knelt and pried open the trap, the bird immediately flying free. Catherine had kissed him, then, on the cheek in thanks. He made her promise not to tell anyone, and she swore she would not. And he knew, beyond the shadow of a doubt that, even with the evidence before him in the form of Madame Pavlovsky's story, Catherine could not possibly have told anyone. It was completely against her nature. And even if she had, he argued with himself—that was over twenty years ago. An incident surely forgotten, even by him, he had to admit, until this very moment. He had not thought of it once since the day it happened. How could Madame Pavlovsky have known this? It sent chills up his spine.

"I told you," Madame Pavlovsky said in response to his questions. "I can speak with the dead."

Utterly shaken, Clive walked out and drove directly to the Trophy Room to meet Davis, as he had previously arranged, resolving as he drove that he would say nothing of all of this; he would simply recommend they officially close the case. He wished to have nothing more to do with Madame Pavlovsky. Mr. Tobin would just have to be told that Madame Pavlovsky was not a danger to society, and that he should keep a better eye on his wife. After all, Mrs. Tobin had already explained what she was doing with all of her jewelry out and admitted that Madame Pavlovsky had not asked her to specifically bring jewelry, especially not the whole lot, but that a piece of jewelry was the only sentimental item of her mother's she could think to bring.

Upon hearing Clive's report, Davis blessedly agreed with him, though he admitted he had been hoping for an excuse to run Madame Pavlovsky out of town. He didn't like loose ends, and he felt for sure Madame Pavlovsky's operation was as loose as they came.

"Listen," Clive said to him, his throat still dry no matter how much whiskey he knocked back. "You want to arrest her, you go out and get her. She's a charlatan all right, but there's nothing to charge her with," he said uneasily, not meeting Davis's eye. "At least not yet."

"You're not afraid, are you?" Davis asked with a grin, taking a long drag of his cigarette. "Kind of seems like you are. She got you believin' in ghosts now?"

"Piss off, Davis."

All the way back to Highbury, Clive tried to stop himself from thinking anymore about Madame Pavlovsky or the supposed communication with Catherine—but it was useless. He couldn't stop turning it over in his mind. He tried to find a hole in Madame Pavlovsky's story, some rational explanation, but he could find none. Was it so hard to believe that ghosts were real? he finally asked himself. He had heard dozens of stories while on the beat of strange happenings and eerie sightings, but he always put them down to fanciful stories. But he believed in God, he confessed—an afterlife—so perhaps there *were* souls that still somehow roamed the earth. Who could really say for sure?

Eventually these thoughts gave way to thoughts of Catherine herself. He had loved her, of course, but not exactly in the way a man should love his wife. He married her for duty before he shipped off to France, and when she and their baby died in childbirth, while he lay injured at the front, he could not stop thinking once he returned home that his misguided sense of duty to produce an heir for Highbury had been the ultimate cause of not only Catherine's death, but that of a child—an innocent child. A little girl, it had been. Antonia had insisted that she be given a name, and when he had refused to, she named her Margaret Cornelia after her mother and informed Fr. Michaels so that it could be recorded, at least in the parish record, to mark her life, however short.

Clive had never told another living soul about his terrible feelings of guilt, about his dark thoughts of reproach in the wee hours of the night that it was somehow all his fault. The nightmares had gone on for months, maybe years. And now here was Catherine, telling him she didn't blame him—that she was happy and wanted him to be so, too. Emotion welled up in him as he eased the car toward Highbury. Well, damn it, he meant to be! he thought, suddenly pounding his fist against the steering wheel. He had been given another chance at happiness, and he wasn't going to bungle it this time, he decided, as he gazed up at the massive structure in front of him. He was so lost in thought that he didn't notice Albert approaching the car.

"Good afternoon, sir," he said, opening the door for him.

Clive peered up at the servant in front of him and then listlessly got out of the car. "Park it, will you, Albert?"

"Very good, sir."

As much as Clive was eager to go up and check on Henrietta, he felt unsteady and undone. He needed to collect his thoughts before going to her and found himself walking around to the back of the house. Lake Michigan was greenish and choppy today, the cold spring wind stirring it up. He stood there, his hands in his coat pockets, staring at the lake. Catherine had implored him to be happy, but, he thought, turning this over and over, his happiness depended wholly on Henrietta's. And now she was worn down, anemic, and possibly depressed. She needed rest, the doctor had said . . .

Gradually, then, an idea came to him as he stood gazing out at the lake—an idea he had actually proposed to Henrietta not but a couple of weeks ago. The more he thought about it now, the more it took hold, intriguing and even exciting him a little in its terrible rashness.

Yes, he thought wildly . . . why not do it? What good was having all of
this wealth if he couldn't make his wife happy? She had been through
some terrible shocks these past months, and he was determined to
amend that. Yes, by God, he meant to make her happy! He knew his
idea would not be popular with his mother or Bennett, most likely,
but he didn't care.

He turned and walked swiftly back toward the front of the house
and hurried up the stone stairs. Billings was there, as usual, to take
his hat and coat. "How is Mrs. Howard?" he asked, adjusting his tie.

"By that I assume you mean the younger Mrs. Howard?" Billings
asked nasally.

"Don't be impudent, Billings."

"She is resting, I believe, sir."

"Did the flowers come?"

"They did indeed, sir."

An unusual buoyancy overcame Clive, then, and he bounded up
the stairs, two at a time, though he cautioned himself that Henrietta
might still be sleeping, especially if Edna had given her one of the
sleeping powders.

When he reached their wing, he was surprised that Edna, or
any servant, actually, was nowhere to be seen. He had given strict
orders! With a fresh wave of irritation, he poked his head into the
room, and his heart skipped a beat when he observed their bed to be
empty! He opened the door wider, beginning to panic, when he saw
Henrietta seated prettily at her little desk, writing. He was utterly
relieved that she was at least still in the room, but what was she
doing out of bed?

He stepped inside, Edna giving a little gasp at the sight of him and
halting her arrangement of a vase of roses. Guiltily she looked over
at her mistress.

"What are you doing out of bed?" Clive exclaimed to Henrietta,
incredulous. "That will be all for now, Edna." He inclined his head
toward the door.

"Yes, sir," she said with a slight curtsey, which she was no longer required to do but forgot in times of extreme stress. Hurriedly, she scooted out of the room.

"Please don't intimidate my maid," Henrietta said, not looking up from what she was writing. "Edna's very sensitive, you know. And she's terrified of you."

"Well, I'm glad to see someone is," he said, striding toward her, still not knowing what to think. "Henrietta, why are you not in bed? Darling, please. This is madness. The doctor gave me quite serious instructions."

"Don't be silly, Clive," she said, looking up at him, the sight of dark circles under her eyes nearly crippling him with secret anguish.

"Henrietta, I really must insist," he said sternly. "Please, darling," he begged. "Humor me."

"Honestly, Clive," she said, her voice sounding unusually normal, "there's absolutely no need to treat me this way."

"What way?" he asked, puzzled.

"As if I were an invalid or a child . . . or unbalanced," she said, setting down her pen.

"Of course, you're not unbalanced," he said, though he did wonder about how the horrific recent events might have affected her. She seemed to have come through it remarkably strong, as always, but Clive knew from unfortunate experience that wounds of the mind were not always obvious from the outside. "But you *are* ill, darling. You've been through a terrible ordeal. You promised me you would stay in bed."

"I did no such thing," she said, casually folding her arms. "I may have promised to rest at some point last night. And there was something else, I think," she mused, putting a finger to her chin. "Ah, yes. Not to leave you, but I thought that was meant in a broader sense. You made arrangements, I discovered, to prevent me from leaving the room. So much for trust," she quipped.

"Darling, I know how you are. As it turns out, my precautions were apparently needed," he said, gesturing at where she sat.

"And so now I'm your prisoner?" she asked, shooting him an

accusatory glance. "And you're my jailer? Funny, you don't look like Nurse Collins." Her brow furrowed.

Clive couldn't help but let out a short burst of laughter, despite the situation. She was amazing, and if anything, he was *her* prisoner, his heart utterly hers. "Why are you so dammed difficult?"

"I did try to warn you, you know. Several times, as I recall."

"Henrietta," Clive sighed, "we've got to be serious. You really must stay in bed for a time, darling. Dr. Ferrington suspects that you're anemic—"

"Yes, so Edna informs me. Thanks for confiding that to me."

"Of course, I meant to, darling, it's just that, well, we haven't had time. And . . . and he suspects you're not completely recovered from . . . from the miscarriage," he said softly. "Henrietta, you must go easy."

"Clive, please stop fussing," she said, standing up. "I'm fine. Honestly. You worry too much. You're becoming an old mother hen," she said, briskly patting his cheek.

"Tell you what," he said, ignoring her comment and instead taking her hand and raising it to his lips. "You be the damsel in distress, locked in the tower, and I will come rescue you." He kissed her on the cheek.

"I rather think I rescued myself this time," she said with a wonderfully mischievous look in her eye, as she wrapped her arms around him and laced her fingers behind his neck. "Except at the end, of course." She arched her neck and kissed him, tugging at his bottom lip and running her tongue along it. His response was instantaneous, and he pressed her to him, shocked by his swift arousal. He took a deep breath, then, remembering Dr. Ferrington's advice against any excitement. Only a brute would make love to her right now, he chided himself, though she did seem to deliciously be suggesting it . . .

"What was so urgent?" he asked, detaching her arms with great deliberation from around his neck, "that you had to leave your bed?" He held her hands and forced himself to breathe deeply.

She shot him a sly smile as if perfectly aware of his current state of torture. Mercifully, however, she answered him. "It's a letter to Herbie, if you must know," she said crisply. "He's very ill again. I think he might not be cut out for boarding school. We might have to implore Grandfather to bring him home. And then there's Elsie. I telephoned her, but she wasn't in. I'm terribly worried—"

"Shhh!" Clive hushed her. "This is just what I mean. You're much too worried about others. You've had enough of worry. We *both* have," he said, putting his arms back around her. "As it is, I've had an idea. One that I came up here to expressly tell you, in fact—"

"Yes, I'm sure it's a good one, darling, whatever it is, but we can't ignore the situation."

"What situation?" he asked, puzzled.

"The situation with Anna of course. Elsie tells me that—"

"Darling," he sighed, "we've been through all of this before. Anna is not my concern right now. *You* are my concern."

Henrietta stared up at him with her big blue eyes. "I think she's in love with him, you know," she said absently, totally throwing him off.

"What? Who?"

"Elsie. I think she's in love with Gunther."

Clive let out a little groan, allowing himself a moment to actually consider what she just said. A kraut as a brother-in-law is not what he needed just now, though he had to admit Gunther seemed a decent enough fellow. He dreaded the uproar it would cause with the Exleys. But all that could wait! "Darling, I'm trying very hard to tell you something."

"I'm sorry, dearest. Yes, go ahead," she said penitently.

"I want us to go away."

"Go away? Where?"

"Back to England for a bit and then maybe on to Europe," he said carefully. "We need to finish our honeymoon. You made me promise that I would bring you back to the fairy bower. And so I will. I mean to keep my promise."

"Clive! That was just a tease!" she said with a little laugh. "You can't really be serious! We can't leave now. We've only just got home!"

"I'm perfectly in earnest," he said, searching her eyes for . . . for something. "Why shouldn't we go? What's holding us here?"

She looked at him incredulously, as if he were the unbalanced one. "Darling," she said, placing a hand on his chest, "there are many things here that require our attention. Besides Anna and Elsie!" she said quickly before he could interrupt her. "There's Highbury itself, your mother, of course—we can't just leave her! And what about Julia and the boys? You yourself have suggested many times that we should try to involve ourselves more with her and Randolph, if only to get her away from him. And what about the firm? What will poor Bennett say?"

"He can handle it. And my mother can handle Highbury, I dare say. Or Billings can, anyway."

She was still staring at him, unconvinced.

"Darling, this may be our only chance in a long time," he went on eagerly. "If God should bless us with children, it will be a long time before we will be able to go. And anyway, I feel we need to get away from here. Away from all these trappings and the sad things that have happened of late."

"So we're just going to run away?"

"Yes. Let's," he said, cupping her face in his hands. "Henrietta, you mean the world to me, and I mean to make you happy, all the days of my life." He kissed her forehead. "If you really wish to remain, then so be it. I will be ruled by you. I only want to please you, to make you happy," he whispered, Catherine's words doggedly coming to his mind again. He bent and kissed her tenderly and long and could not help allowing his hands to roam down her back to her buttocks, where they rested, pulling her into him. She correspondingly wrapped her arms around his neck again, not breaking their kiss, and delicately ran her fingers through his hair, which caused him to stiffen.

He released her, then, before things got out of hand, and he was surprised that she was breathing heavily, too. Did nothing stop her?

"All right. You win," she said, looking up at him with a smile that oddly reminded him of how she looked the night they had met at the Promenade. "When do we leave?"

Chapter 26

Mrs. Goodman sat in her chair in Ward 3C, peering only occasionally up at Nurse Harding, who blustered about as usual. Mrs. Goodman wore a large black hat on her head and held a book in her hand. She had found it the night that woman had descended to Agharta in the tunnel of the Atlanteans. The woman had not returned, so she must have made it, and Mrs. Goodman felt a burst of happiness and not a little pride that the woman had escaped, though she herself had never been successful. She was, as it happened, losing her desire to leave, to find her way to the center of the earth and to the race of kinder beings. She didn't think she was up for the journey any longer, nor did she think she would again survive the punishment should she fail. No—it was better to make the best of it here, she sadly decided.

Mrs. Goodman had taken the book back to her room and hid it under her dirty pillow. Occasionally, when the nurse changed her sheets, which luckily only occurred if she wet them, which wasn't often, she carried it about with her or hid it in her dress. Initially, she had just liked to look at the pictures, but as time went on, she found she was able to read some of the words as well. She had forgotten that she knew how to read. Some of it made sense to her, and some of it didn't. There was one passage she liked more than the others, and this one she read over and over. It reminded her of something, but she couldn't think what. It had become her favorite:

> *To Any Reader*
> *As from the house your mother sees*
> *You playing round the garden trees,*
> *So you may see, if you will look*
> *Through the windows of this book,*
> *Another child, far, far away,*
> *And in another garden, play.*
> *But do not think you can at all,*
> *By knocking on the window, call*
> *That child to hear you. He intent*
> *Is all on his play-business bent.*
> *He does not hear; he will not look,*
> *Nor yet be lured out of this book.*
> *For, long ago, the truth to say,*
> *He has grown up and gone away,*
> *And it is but a child of air*
> *That lingers in the garden there.*

She closed the book, then, and went to the room that held her bed so that she could lie down and close her eyes and try to remember . . . exactly what, she did not know.

Epilogue

Sergei slithered into the room where Madame Pavlovsky sat, gently caressing her crystal ball, freed for the moment from its elaborate stand.

"So Howard's gone?" he asked in a raspy voice. "Why did you let him go?"

"Do not have worry," Madame Pavlovsky said absently, a smile curling her lips as she gazed at the ball. "He will be back."

Notes and Acknowledgements

As I have written before in various other places, the character of Henrietta Von Harmon is based upon a real woman and her adventures in the 1930s and '40s Chicago. Though most of the other characters and places in the early books of the series are fictional, some of them, such as The Green Mill, The Aragon, St. Sylvester Church, Palmer Square, and Humboldt Park are, like Henrietta, very real. In the fourth book of the series, *A Veil Removed*, I added my alma mater, Mundelein College, to the list, but instead of merely mentioning it in passing or assigning it a paltry scene or two, as I had done with the others, I decided to boldly use it as a setting for almost half of the book.

Likewise, in this most recent addition to the series, *A Child Lost*, I again used Mundelein as a backdrop for some of the chapters, but I decided to add even more actual locales to the story, namely, Mundelein Seminary, The Bohemian Home for Orphans and the Aged, and, sadly, Dunning Asylum. The problem with using real, historic places in a novel, however, is that whilst researching, the author very often unearths a treasure trove of stories and facts attached to them, and the desire to share all of those interesting tidbits is overwhelming in the extreme. I suspect it might be easier to simply continue to use fictional settings, as one can then avoid the temptation to dump all of these extra morsels of fact into an otherwise sufficiently lean and agile plot. The danger of bloat is very real once you go digging.

My response to this situation was to cleverly take this seemingly unwanted space at the end of the book to share just *a few* of the extraneous bits that didn't make it into the story proper. Only the most ardent readers will have made it all the way back here, and if you are one, then you will undoubtedly welcome the added information, as you've apparently come looking for something in the first place.

As already stated, Dunning Asylum, or the Chicago State Hospital, as it was officially named, was unfortunately a very real place and was commonly referred to as "a tomb for the living." Generations of Chicago parents really did threaten naughty children that they would be "sent to Dunning" if they didn't behave. Dunning began as a poor farm in 1851 and was located some twelve miles northwest of what was then the Chicago city limits. As many of the poor, even in those days, were suffering from some sort of mental affliction, it soon became populated with the city's mentally ill. Very quickly, what was supposed to be an idyllic refuge in the country for honest work and peace became an overcrowded, chaotic asylum rife with abuse in the face of little or no oversight. More and more people were brought to the asylum, so much so that in 1882, the Chicago, Milwaukee and St. Paul Railroad extended its track by three extra miles so that a train could run almost right up to the facility itself. The "crazy train," as it came to be called, loaded with supplies and stuffed with the "insane," would run from downtown Chicago directly to the asylum, where the new patients were easily herded inside. The fact that the remains of over 38,000 bodies have so far been unearthed from the cemeteries or mass graves surrounding the now demolished facility points to what was the ultimate fate for most of those poor people boarding the train.

While it is true that by 1936, when *A Child Lost* opens, Dunning had already gone through several serious reforms, it was still not a very pleasant place in which to end up. Forced electric shock and hosing, as well as severe overcrowding, were but a few of the abuses that still existed. In writing *A Child Lost*, I struggled with how much of the depravity I had uncovered should really be included in a Henrietta and Clive novel. I wanted to depict Dunning as bleak as possible without getting *too* dark, which would constitute a step outside the scope of the series. I hope I succeeded in walking that fine line.

The University of St. Mary of the Lake, otherwise known as Mundelein Seminary, is also a very real place and is now the largest Catholic seminary in the United States. What is more interesting, however, at least to me, is that somewhere on what is now the seminary's grounds once stood a business school, which was started by an eccentric salesman by the name of Arthur Sheldon. Sheldon called his school AREA, which stood for "Ability, Reliability, Endurance, and Action." He was so charismatic that he persuaded the town to change its name to AREA to match, which the town elders seemed to have no problem doing, as they had already gone through a whole list of names for their town over the years, beginning with Mechanics Grove, and then Holcomb, and finally Rockefeller. When Sheldon's school eventually folded after only about ten years, the Catholic Church, under the direction of Cardinal Mundelein, bought the school and the 600 acres upon which it sat and began construction of a seminary. Later, the town voted to again change its name, this time to Mundelein, which pleased the cardinal so much that he donated a fire truck to the town, their first.

Again, it was tempting to somehow throw all of this into a conversation between Henrietta and Clive on their drive to the seminary in search of a missing woman, but I refrained. If you are yourself perchance an author, you will read the final version of that chapter, which has only the briefest reference to all of the above, and feel my pain.

Lastly, The Bohemian Home for Orphans and the Aged was also a real place and one which I had the fortune to work at before it, too, closed down. It began as a 43-acre farm in Bensenville, Illinois, but was later transferred to Crawford Ave (now Pulaski) on the city's northwest side in 1901. It was common around the turn of the century for independent ethnic groups, private charities and religious groups to found their own hospitals, schools, asylums, orphanages, or shelters in an effort to firstly take care of their own, and, as time went on, other unfortunates as well. The Czech's were no different, and one of their many contributions to the city of Chicago was the construction of the Bohemian National Cemetery and the nearby Bohemian Home for Orphans and the Aged. Like all orphanages in the city at that time, some of the children living there were true orphans, having lost their parents, but many of them had living parents, usually just a single parent, who could no longer afford to care for them. These children were placed in orphanages until the parent's financial situation improved, but in some cases, they were adopted by other families.

By the time I was an employee of the Bohemian Home in the early 1990's, there were of course no orphans running about the place. In fact, that part of the facility had since been converted into apartments for the staff, which mostly consisted of Czech, Polish and Filipino immigrants. There were many stories still floating around, however, of days long gone, many of which I managed to hastily jot down. Most of these stories came from the residents themselves, many of whom were of Czech origin and could remember coming to the Bohemian Home every year as children and playing on the grounds with the orphans during the Home's annual picnic, which was open to the general public. These stories now form the basis for my blog, "Novel Notes of Local Lore," which features a different "forgotten Chicago resident's" story each week. You can check them out here: http://michellecoxauthor.com/blog/ if you'd like more reading material. Also, watch for some of these stories to appear in future novels! Likewise, I have often thought that the Bohemian Home would be an excellent setting for a spin-off series. It might be just the place, for example, for Elsie and Gunther to set up shop...

And now I suppose I should get on with the acknowledgements, as I really am now in danger of running out of space.

Firstly, it is my great pleasure and privilege to again thank my publisher at She Writes Press, Brooke Warner, for not only taking a chance on me, but for providing a women's-only space within the publishing industry. Brooke is a force to be reckoned with, and she is absolutely changing the world around her. I consider myself lucky to be in her orbit. Thank you, Brooke, for continuing to champion women's voices.

I'd also like to thank Lauren Wise for not only being my project manager but for being my trusted editor once again. I cannot thank you enough, Lauren, for everything you do to keep the series running smoothly. Every single day, you go above and beyond. Your enthusiasm is contagious!

Thanks as well to the many other industry professionals who always have time to answer my questions and offer advice, namely Liane Paonessa, Tabitha Bailey, Yolanda Facio, and Michelle Fisher, among many others. Your support and guidance over the years has meant, and continues to mean, so much to me. Thanks, too, to all of the libraries across the country, and the world, actually, who continue to carry and suggest my books to new readers, and to all the indie booksellers that champion my books, especially Janet Elliot of This Old Book in Grayslake, Il. and Suzy Takacs of The Book Cellar, in Chicago. In am particularly indebted to both of you!

And this time around, I'd really like to thank ALL OF YOU! I'm so very grateful to each of you for reading or listening to the book, writing reviews, following me on social media, and/or for dropping me a line to let me know how much you are enjoying the series. This has given me immense joy, and it is why I continue to write, actually. You cannot know what your support and encouraging words have meant to me. It makes the months and months and months of writing and editing all worth it in the end. So thank you! Please keep reading!

Lastly, of course, I thank my family, who continue to either help or go without, without complaining. Apparently frozen pizza is an acceptable, even welcome, dinner substitute. Who knew? Thanks to each of you for helping to hold down the fort when I need to spend my evenings working or my days traveling. I especially want to thank my husband, Phil, for your unwavering support, and more importantly, your love. You are still my sweetest song, and I am truly blessed.

About the Author

© Cliento Photography

Michelle Cox is the author of the multiple award-winning Henrietta and Inspector Howard series as well as "Novel Notes of Local Lore," a weekly blog dedicated to Chicago's forgotten residents. She suspects she may have once lived in the 1930s and, having yet to discover a handy time machine lying around, has resorted to writing about the era as a way of getting herself back there. Coincidentally, her books have been praised by Kirkus, Library Journal, Publishers Weekly, Booklist and many others, so she might be on to something. Unbeknownst to most, Michelle hoards board games she doesn't have time to play and is, not surprisingly, addicted to period dramas and big band music. Also marmalade.

Sign up for Michelle's free newsletter for a chance to win big prizes and to be part of her latest happenings and events.

And make sure to follow her on Bookbub, too!

SELECTED TITLES FROM SHE WRITES PRESS

She Writes Press is an independent publishing company founded to serve women writers everywhere. Visit us at www.shewritespress.com.

A Girl Like You: A Henrietta and Inspector Howard Novel by Michelle Cox
$16.95, 978-1-63152-016-7
When the floor matron at the dance hall where Henrietta works as a taxi dancer turns up dead, aloof Inspector Clive Howard appears on the scene—and convinces Henrietta to go undercover for him, plunging her into Chicago's gritty underworld.

A Promise Given: A Henrietta and Inspector Howard Novel by Michelle Cox
$16.95, 978-1-63152-373-1
Just after Clive and Henrietta begin their honeymoon at Castle Linley, the Howards' ancestral estate in England, a man is murdered in the nearby village on the night of a house party at the Castle. When Clive's mysterious cousin Wallace comes under suspicion, Clive and Henrietta are reluctantly drawn into the case.

A Ring of Truth: A Henrietta and Inspector Howard Novel by Michelle Cox
$16.95, 978-1-63152-196-6
The next exciting installment of the Henrietta and Inspector Clive series, in which Clive reveals that he is actually the heir of the Howard estate and fortune, Henrietta discovers she may not be who she thought she was—and both must decide if they are really meant for each other.

The Great Bravura by Jill Dearman $16.95, 978-1-63152-989-4
Who killed Susie—or did she actually disappear? The Great Bravura, a dashing lesbian magician living in a fantastical and noirish 1947 New York City, must solve this mystery—before she goes to the electric chair.

After Midnight by Diane Shute-Sepahpour $16.95, 978-1-63152-913-9
When horse breeder Alix is forced to temporarily swap places with her estranged twin sister—the wife of an English lord—her forgotten past begins to resurface.

In the Shadow of Lies: A Mystery Novel by M. A. Adler
$16.95, 978-1-938314-82-7
As World War II comes to a close, homicide detective Oliver Wright returns home—only to find himself caught up in the investigation of a complicated murder case rife with racial tensions.